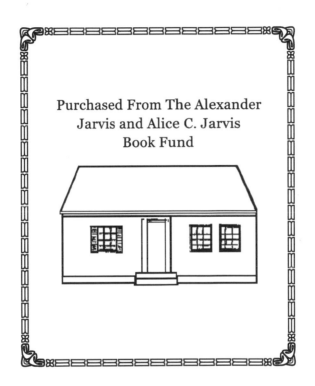

Purchased From The Alexander
Jarvis and Alice C. Jarvis
Book Fund

A
ROYAL
AFFAIR

Also by Allison Montclair

The Right Sort of Man

A Greece truly independent is an absurdity. Greece is Russian
or she is English; and since she must not be Russian,
it is necessary that she be English.

—EDMUND LYONS, BRITISH AMBASSADOR
TO GREECE, 1841

The most important tool for a King of Greece is a suitcase.

—ATTRIBUTED TO GEORGE II, KING OF GREECE, 1922–1924;
DEPOSED KING IN EXILE, 1924–1935; KING OF GREECE,
1935–1947 (INCLUDING SECOND EXILE, 1941–1946)

A
ROYAL
AFFAIR

ALLISON MONTCLAIR

MINOTAUR BOOKS
NEW YORK

First published in the United States by Minotaur Books, an imprint of St. Martin's Publishing Group

www.minotaurbooks.com

Designed by Devan Norman

The Library of Congress Cataloging-in-Publication Data is available upon request.

ISBN 978-1-250-17839-8 (hardcover)
ISBN 978-1-250-17840-4 (ebook)

Our books may be purchased in bulk for promotional, educational, or business use. Please contact your local bookseller or the Macmillan Corporate and Premium Sales Department at 1-800-221-7945, extension 5442, or by email at MacmillanSpecialMarkets@macmillan.com.

First Edition: 2020

10 9 8 7 6 5 4 3 2 1

TO MY NEPHEW, BENNET,

WHO ILLUSTRATES HIS STORIES SO BEAUTIFULLY,

AND LIVES HIS LIFE EVEN MORE SO.

ACKNOWLEDGMENTS

In addition to sources cited in her previous work, the author gratefully acknowledges books and articles written by Philip Eade, Fiammetta Rocco, Hugo Vickers, Anne de Courcy, André Gerolymatos, Sir Compton Mackenzie, John Sakas, Paul Halpern, and Father Simon Thomas. Questions on smaller points were more than adequately answered by Paul Negus, Stewart Gilles, and Peter Gilbert.

The author takes full responsibility for any errors made. Indeed, she cheerfully embraces them as evidence of her own humanity.

No plinths were harmed in the making of this book.

A
ROYAL
AFFAIR

CHAPTER 1

M en find me intimidating," boomed Miss Hardiman. "That's the problem."

"Surely not," Sparks protested.

"Oh, it's been like that ever since I was little," Miss Hardiman continued, at a volume that made Sparks fear for her eardrums. And the windowpanes. "Not that I was little for long. I was the tallest early on. You have no idea what that's like."

"I never have," Sparks agreed, shrinking back at the onslaught. "But they must have caught up with you eventually."

"By that time, they had grown up terrified of me," said Miss Hardiman. "And I had got used to being the Terror of Tiny Town. I liked it, to tell the truth."

"The truth is what we require here at The Right Sort," said Sparks.

From our clients, at least, she thought.

"So, you came to London in thirty-nine?" Sparks asked, holding her steno pad in front of her, painfully aware of its inadequacy as a shield.

"Right. Perfect timing. Things went potty right after I showed up."

"Not cause and effect, of course."

"Oh, dear! You are a caution, and that's no lie! No, I showed up in July, two months of dashing about, looking for work, then came the war. I joined up right away, of course."

"Well done," acknowledged Sparks. "Where did they assign you?"

"Office jobs at first," said Miss Hardiman. "But I presented too much of a distraction, or so they told me, and not for my bombshell looks, which was disappointing. Yes, I'm joking, I know what I look like. No, I was too much of a tiger in a cage. I switched over to the motor pool, which was boring. Finally, I found my true calling."

"Which was?"

"I was an Ack-Ack Girl," declared Miss Hardiman proudly. "Started as part of a team, worked my way up to commanding my little squad."

"Really?" exclaimed Sparks, perking up. "You got to fire the big guns?"

"Oh, yes, and it was glorious! Perched up on the hilltop with the twin 525s, watching the searchlights scour the sky, trying to spot the Messerschmitts coming out of the clouds, calculating trajectories on the fly, bellowing commands at the tops of my lungs! Then BOOM!"

Sparks involuntarily snapped her pencil in two.

Gwen, where the blazes are you? she thought. I need reinforcements.

They were sitting on opposite sides of her decrepit desk in the small office which constituted the entire premises of The Right Sort Marriage Bureau. It was a humid Tuesday morning in early July, and the standing fan that Gwen had managed to sneak out of her in-laws' home pushed the thick London air only a few inches forwards before it gave up, leaving the rest of the office, particularly the space around Sparks herself, unrefreshed.

Miss Hardiman had, since only one of the two proprietors was present, plunked herself down in the single guest chair directly across from Sparks. She was tall enough, even seated, to bring the top of her head in line with the dartboard that hung on the wall behind the door. This gave her the appearance of having a gaudily striped halo, the bull's-eye perched over the top of her energetically bobbing bun.

Sparks found her eyes drifting towards the bun, her hand itching for a dart.

"One moment," she said, taking the surviving portion of her pencil and sharpening it. She licked the point when she was done, a habit left from childhood.

"Right," she said. "Ack-Ack Girl. Any success?"

"Two confirmed, shared a third," said Miss Hardiman. "Do you know that we were the only women in the services who actually killed the enemy?"

Not the only ones, thought Sparks, maintaining her bland expression.

"How about you?" asked Miss Hardiman. "How did you spend your war?"

Who do you work for? shouted Carlos, his hands around her throat, her own scrabbling for the knife under the pillow . . .

"Clerical work," said Sparks. "Nothing as exciting as what you did."

"But essential, I'm sure," said Miss Hardiman with more than a touch of condescension.

"Every cog in the machine matters," said Sparks.

"Is it odd to say I miss it?" asked Miss Hardiman. "It was terrifying, but I felt I had purpose like I never had before. And now, of course—honestly, I envy you."

"Me? Why me?"

"You still have purpose," said Miss Hardiman. "You're in charge here."

"I am only in charge of myself," said Sparks. "Mrs. Bainbridge and I are equal partners and have no other employees. I'm hardly a mover and a shaker."

"But you run your own show, with no ridiculous men to boss you about," said Miss Hardiman. "That seems like paradise, in a way."

"It is different," said Sparks. "We're making a go of it, I'm glad to report."

"After all the publicity about solving the La Salle murder, I should think so."

"That's not our normal line of work," said Sparks. "It fell into our laps, much the same way a grand piano does in those American cartoons. Now, let's get back to finding you a good candidate. Would you say, given your . . . enthusiastic personality, that you would be happier with a man who stands up to it, or one who would give in to it?"

"Ohh, that's the nub, isn't it? I'd think the first, except the arguing could get exhausting over the long run. But if the lad folds the moment I challenge him, there's no fun. Could I ask for a bit of both?"

"You could," said Sparks, jotting down the answer. "Finding him is the trick."

"Which do you prefer?" asked Miss Hardiman.

"I've had fun. I've been exhausted. I'm back to fun at the moment."

"You're not married yourself, I notice."

"Correct."

"How do I know you're any good at setting people up?"

"Because we had enough faith in our abilities to do so to start a business doing it, and we've had enough success for others to share that faith. Yes, I haven't followed a flower girl down the daisy-strewn aisle myself, but I bring a particular perspective to the search, and Mrs. Bainbridge brings a different but equally useful one. We are now on the hunt, Miss Hardiman. We shall put our minds to it, and contact you with a suitable candidate shortly."

Maybe one who's hard of hearing, she thought as she rose to shake Miss Hardiman's hand.

She quashed the thought immediately.

Iris was in the middle of typing up her notes when Gwen returned, waving a pair of keys dangling from a metal tag.

"Got them," said Gwen. "Sorry I took so long. Mr. MacPherson was particularly difficult to find today."

"Where did he turn up?"

"Napping in a vacant office on the second storey, broom in hand. How did things go with the ten thirty?"

"Letitia Hardiman is now our latest client, I am happy to report. Tall, almost your height, in fact. Assertive, extremely loud. She led an antiaircraft battery during the war, which is impressive."

"When you say 'extremely loud' . . ."

"She brought down two bombers by yelling at them."

"Hmm," mused Gwen. "We have Mr. Temple amongst our eligibles. Didn't he lose most of his hearing to an explosion?"

"I thought of him, but it shouldn't be that superficial. And with all the shouting that would come from that match, I would fear for the equanimity of their neighbors. Maybe we should match her with someone who lives in a detached house. At the end of a street. In a cul-de-sac."

"Right. Well, I'll take a look once you've typed it up. Who's next on the schedule?"

"We have a Miss Oona Travis at eleven thirty, then a Miss Catherine Prescott at noon. Nothing after that, so I suggest lunch."

"Suits me. Shall we take a look at the office next door since we have a free slot?"

"Let's."

Iris pushed herself up from her desk, which creaked ominously in protest. She glared at it.

"It's been doing that more and more," she said as she walked between the desks to the door. "One of the legs has gotten rickety, but I can't figure out where the problem is. I'd get Mr. MacPherson to fix it, but he's been even more rickety lately."

"It's what we get for taking what came with the office," sighed Gwen. "At least your desk has four working legs. Mine has three and *The Forsyte Saga* supporting the fourth corner."

"A sturdy choice," commented Iris as she followed her down the hall. "Have you read it?"

"I keep meaning to," said Gwen. "It's very long. That's what drew me to it for its present purpose. Here we are. 'Cooper and Lyons, Chartered Public Accountants.' I wonder what ever happened to them."

"Any idea of when they last occupied the space?"

"Mr. MacPherson was uncertain on that point," said Gwen, turning one of the keys in the lock. "As he is on most points."

She opened the door, peered inside, and gasped.

"Iris," she said in awe. "There are desks!"

"Let me see," said Iris, pushing past her. "Oh! How lovely!"

The office itself was wider than their own by some four or five feet, which gave it room for a second window compared to their single one. There were no signs that it had been inhabited by anything human in years. There were signs of inhabitation by smaller species, and the place might have been swept and dusted within living memory, but that was not certain.

What had drawn their immediate attention was a pair of massive matched mahogany desks, one in front of each window. They were broad, sturdy behemoths, resting on thick square columned pedestals, each of which in turn contained a drawer and a cabinet facing the two women.

"Tell me it's true," whispered Gwen.

She walked between them, her arms spread, trailing her fingers across the faded burgundy leather inserts, gently wiping the coating of dust from the gold-tooled ornamentations along the borders. She knelt reverentially in front of one of the desks to examine the logos on the drawers.

"Harrods," she breathed. "Partners' desks from Harrods, Iris. I could positively swoon!"

There were no keys apparent, but the center drawer had been left unlocked. Gwen slid it open. It was empty.

Iris did the same at the other desk, and grimaced. "Something was living in mine," she said.

"So you've already taken possession of that one," said Gwen, smiling.

"Well, if we do expand, we should try to get the office furniture thrown into the deal."

Iris tried the other drawers. Some were empty. The rest were locked. "I left my lock picks in my handbag," she said with chagrin.

"You carry those with you all the time?" asked Gwen. "What on earth for?"

"For occasions like these," said Iris, feeling about the underside of the center drawer. "No, no secret compartment here. Maybe in the bottom drawers."

"Listen!" urged Gwen, sliding one open, then closing it. "So silent, so smooth. The craftsmanship—my God, I could sit behind this all day and spend my idle minutes opening the drawers."

"Easy for you with your height," said Iris. "I would require a chair. And so would you, if only for appearances' sake."

"There aren't any," observed Gwen, looking around.

"So we'd need two for the desks and two for our clients."

"Only one, surely," said Gwen. "We're matching up individuals."

"Two, because I've noticed that having one centered between us smacks of an official interrogation after a while. And because sometimes they come with a friend or a relative for moral support, and we've made them wait in the hallway, or I end up sitting on my unstable desk, which is like roller skating during an earthquake."

"And your legs distract the gentlemen," added Gwen.

"Precisely," said Iris. "So, four chairs, and a new filing cabinet. Desk lamps. Another fan. A second telephone line, with some form of intercom system connecting it with the first. We'd need to paint."

"A rug would be nice," said Gwen. "I wonder if there are any I could filch from the attic at home. Yes, I'm beginning to see that we'd have to come up with the funding for all of that, not to mention the security deposit on the additional office. And you've forgotten the key element."

"A secretary," said Iris. "Secretary slash receptionist slash clerk. Our very first employee. We may become employers, Gwen. How very capitalist of us! Do we have enough to make this expansion?"

"We do not," said Gwen. "We may have it in a few months if things keep going at the present rate. Six more wedding bounties would give us enough. If only . . ."

She paused and sighed.

"What?" asked Iris.

"If only I could pry control of my estate away from that irritating guardian of mine," said Gwen. "I could invest in our business."

"Have you approached him about it?" asked Iris.

"I still need the final approval from Dr. Milford declaring me capable of managing my life without a straitjacket."

"How's that working out?"

"He wants me to get through two more months of therapy to make certain that I'm stable."

"Then don't sit on my desk," advised Iris. "Shall we get back to work?"

"I suppose," Gwen said. "Iris, is it wrong that I am experiencing lustful feelings towards this desk?"

"I am not one to judge," said Iris. "I've had a few interesting encounters involving desks. Not with the actual desks themselves, mind you, but they make my short list of favourite pieces of furniture."

"How would you rank them?"

"Hmm. Third. No, fourth. I forgot about the ottoman. That was a precarious but ultimately very rewarding experience."

"You short girls are so versatile."

"There have to be some compensating factors. Gwen, stop playing with that drawer or I will call Dr. Milford myself."

Gwen guiltily slid it closed and stood.

"Goodbye, Cecil," she whispered, giving it a pat.

"You've already named the desk?"

"I've already named all the drawers."

"Dear God."

They left the office of Cooper and Lyons and locked it behind them, then stood side by side on the stairwell, peering out the grimy window.

"Mr. MacPherson says they have two new tenants coming into the second storey," said Gwen.

"The third is still completely vacant," said Iris. "We're the only tenants up here, but I sense that things may be picking up. And I hear they're breaking ground on the new building next door. I feel we should grab that office while the grabbing's good."

"We could go back to the bank for another loan," said Gwen.

"We had to go to, what, fifteen different banks the first time? None of them took the idea of a marriage bureau seriously."

"Until we saw Mr. Lastings. He liked us. And we've been prompt with our payments."

"We've only been in business for five months," Iris pointed out.

"Precisely. And it's taking off. Well, rumbling down the runway. Picking up speed. Gaining lift, or whatever the term is."

"No airplane metaphors, please," shuddered Iris.

"Sorry. So, assume we're paying double to the bank, double to the building, and a secretary—"

"We can't manage it yet. Let's hope for Cupid's arrows to work their wonders soon. Back to work, partner."

Their present desks had once provided a sense of ambition and optimism. Now they seemed shabby and resentful, as if they knew that the women they had faithfully served had found something better and they would soon become a distant memory.

Iris slid into her chair and rested her chin on her elbows for a moment. Her desk creaked, and she pulled back immediately and glared at it.

"Someone's coming up the stairs," said Gwen.

"Miss Oona Travis, I assume," said Iris, checking her watch. "She's early. Always a good sign. You take the lead on this one. I'm still getting my hearing back from the last one."

They both busied themselves with paperwork to avoid the appearance of idly waiting for their next customer. Gwen glanced up with her best smile. Then it became real as she saw a woman standing in the doorway.

"Patience!" she exclaimed. "What a lovely surprise!"

"Hallo, darling," said the woman, coming in to receive a kiss on the cheek.

"Iris, meet my cousin Patience Matheson," said Gwen. "Lady Matheson, I should say."

"How do you do?" said Iris, coming around the desk to shake her hand.

Lady Matheson appeared to be in her late thirties, which meant that she was probably ten years older than that, guessed Iris, basing her assessment on the expertise and expense invested in the makeup and coiffure. She was dressed in a light blue linen suit with three ropes of perfectly white, perfectly matched pearls around her neck; the strands joined at a lovely ruby pendant surrounded by white diamonds.

"What on earth brought you here?" asked Gwen.

"I came to see you in your new enterprise," said Lady Matheson, looking around. "Well. Remarkable, I must say. I never thought I would see you doing this sort of thing."

"No one did," said Gwen. "Not even me. It goes to show you how unpredictable life can be."

"We've all had more than our share of unpredictability," agreed Lady Matheson. "In fact, my being here must fall into that category."

"We weren't expecting you, certainly," said Gwen. "Not that I'm not delighted to see you. It's been some time. Iris, Patience is— Well, I'm not quite sure how to describe it. She's not exactly a lady-in-waiting—"

"Oh, heaven forbid!" said Lady Matheson, giving an exaggerated shudder.

"But she works for the Queen in some capacity."

"Do you?" said Iris. "I've always found the phrase 'in some capacity' both wonderfully vague and intentionally concealing."

"How so?" asked Lady Matheson with a smile as she sat down in the guest chair.

"It's boring enough to fend off further questions while hinting at areas of occupation too mundane to warrant any interest. People, as a result, have the idea that you do something without knowing what it is, or even thinking it's something that it isn't."

"You're the one who went to Cambridge, aren't you?" observed Lady Matheson.

"Yes."

"So you think you're smarter than most people."

"Just the ones who went to Oxford."

"Lovely!" Lady Matheson laughed. "I must repeat that one to— Well, I have an Oxford friend or two, of course."

"Patience, it is wonderful to see you," said Gwen. "But we do have a client coming in."

"I could handle the interview if you want to have a cousins' reunion," offered Iris.

"That won't be necessary," said Lady Matheson. "I am Miss Oona Travis, your eleven thirty."

"What?" exclaimed Gwen.

"I am also Miss Catherine Prescott, your twelve o'clock," said Lady Matheson. "That gives us a full hour together. I know that you have the only occupied office on this level, and that the one below us is entirely vacant, but I would like to ask you to close and lock your door, if you don't mind."

They stared at her, then at each other. Iris shrugged and got up.

"That's ten pounds down the drain," she muttered as she walked to the door.

She stepped out into the hall and peered down the stairwell. There was a man in a brown three-piece suit on the third-storey landing, nonchalantly smoking a cigarette. He looked up at her, gave a quick two-fingered salute, then resumed his pose, watching the stairs below him.

Iris returned to The Right Sort and closed and locked the door behind her.

"Brown three-piece suit, brown shoes, five ten, black hair, clean-shaven, well-built, mid-thirties," she said as she retook her seat. "Yours?"

"Mine," said Lady Matheson.

"Armed?"

"Possibly. I've never asked."

"Does he have a name?"

"Possibly. I've never asked."

"Patience, what on earth is going on?" asked Gwen.

"Ten pounds, you said?" Lady Matheson asked, ignoring her and looking at Iris. "What does that get one?"

"In the cases of our now mythical female customers, our efforts to find them a suitable husband," said Iris, sitting behind her desk.

"How does that fee work out per hour?"

"It varies," said Iris. "We're up to nine weddings now."

"And several promising relationships," added Gwen.

"I see," said Lady Matheson.

She reached into her bag and pulled out her purse.

"For your lost time," she said, placing two five-pound notes on Iris's desk.

"Oh, Patience," protested Gwen. "We can't possibly—"

"Yes, we can," said Iris firmly, taking the notes and stuffing them into her top drawer.

"But Iris—"

"Think of Cecil and all the other little mouths to feed," said Iris.

"Fair point," conceded Gwen.

"I thought your son's name was Ronnie," said Lady Matheson.

"It's a private joke," said Gwen.

"All right, you have our time and attention," said Iris. "Let's talk. I take it you're not here to find a husband."

"No, I've got one already," said Lady Matheson. "He's out in the country somewhere, I'm not sure which place. Probably in Scotland, blasting birdshot into unarmed pheasants."

"While you get to suffer through the London summer with us," said Gwen.

"I will be joining the royal family when they go to Balmoral," said Lady Matheson. "Might even bump into Lord Matheson if he's not too careful, but I have an errand or two to run before I do. I was having tea with Emily Bascombe on Monday and your names came up."

"Oh, how is Em?" asked Gwen. "We heard she's in the family way."

"Glowing and voracious," said Lady Matheson. "She mentioned that the two of you met at her wedding."

"Essentially," said Iris. "That was when we became friends."

"She takes indirect credit for your decision to start up this odd little business. She told me that you, dear cousin, were responsible for bringing her and George together."

"I planted some seeds that took root and bloomed quite nicely," said Gwen.

"And that you, Iris—may I call you Iris?"

"Certainly."

"That you did some digging into George's background at Emily's request."

"There were some rumours that needed debunking," said Iris. "I was able to make some satisfactory enquiries."

"And you both put your talents to use in solving the La Salle murder. We were all quite abuzz about that."

"Have you brought us another murder to solve?" asked Iris.

"Oh, dear," Gwen sighed. "I'm still not over the first one."

"No, no." Lady Matheson laughed. "This is more in your line. But before I go any further, I need to ask for your assurances that everything we discuss from this point on will be absolutely confidential."

"Of course," said Gwen immediately.

"Hold on a tick," said Iris. "You do understand that we are not legally entitled to make those assurances."

"But Iris—" began Gwen.

"Gwen, you remember how well our protests of client confidentiality went over with Detective Superintendent Parham when he came barging in here with his bully boys. Lady Matheson, if you are here to discuss any criminal matters—"

"I am not," said Lady Matheson. "At least, not yet."

"Ominously put," said Iris. "Do you expect them to become criminal?"

"I would doubt it highly, but I cannot say to a degree of absolute certainty that they won't. But if that does turn out to be the case, you have my word that you may then bring that information to the proper authorities."

"Meaning the CID," said Iris.

"Meaning the proper authorities," said Lady Matheson.

"So it may involve matters not involving the CID," said Iris. "Are we talking about international affairs?"

"At the moment, we aren't talking about anything, and I won't subject myself to further interrogation until I have Miss Sparks's agreement," said Lady Matheson, a huffy tone creeping into her voice.

Gwen was looking at her carefully.

"This involves the Queen in some way, doesn't it?" she asked quietly.

"Miss Sparks, do I have your word?" asked Lady Matheson. "I am asking on behalf of Queen and country."

"I served the King during the war," said Iris. "I suppose I ought to extend the courtesy to his missus. You have my word, under the condition that the moment things turn sour, it is no longer binding upon me."

"Done," said Lady Matheson. "And I anticipate that all of this legal-ish verbiage will turn out be quite unnecessary. Now, to the matter. We would like the two of you to vet someone, much as you did with George Bascombe."

"That sounds easy enough," said Gwen.

"Why us?" asked Iris. "Surely you have people at the Palace who can do that sort of thing."

"This is a matter of particular delicacy," said Lady Matheson. "We'd rather not have it known internally, given how gossip flies about, nor do we want the subject of the vetting to get wind of it. We don't want a word of it anywhere near the press. It's probably nothing, but we need to make sure that it's nothing and that it stays nothing."

"The 'we' in that sentence?" asked Iris. "Is it the same 'we' as in, 'We were all quite abuzz,' or a different 'we'?"

"Myself, one other person working directly under me—and the Queen," said Lady Matheson.

"Oh, my," breathed Iris.

"Patience," said Gwen. "Are you asking us to vet Prince Philip?"

CHAPTER 2

What do you know about him?" asked Lady Matheson.

"Mostly what's in the newspapers," said Gwen. "There was quite a stir after that photo of the two of them gazing adoringly at each other at Lord Brabourne's wedding."

"Wasn't Brabourne in the running for the princess's hand?" asked Iris.

"I cannot comment on that," said Lady Matheson. "But yes, things recently seem to have taken a certain momentum towards Philip. Lilibet's had a crush on him since she was thirteen—"

"Thirteen?" exclaimed Gwen.

"Oh yes, when he was a pretty boy of eighteen," continued Lady Matheson. "She kept his picture on her mantelpiece throughout the war."

"Adolescence versus a Royal Naval uniform," said Gwen. "The poor girl never stood a chance."

"There is still the matter of parental approval."

"Yes, and no ordinary parental approval," said Iris. "It's not exactly, 'Dad! Mum! Meet the boyfriend! We're in love! We're getting married!' I imagine that a great deal of negotiating must take place."

"You have no idea," said Lady Matheson. "It would be difficult enough if she were merely the princess, but she is also the heir apparent. The entire course of British history runs through her bloodlines. What else do you know?"

"He's a Greek prince," said Iris. "Which is to say, not really Greek at all, and they don't have a monarch at the moment, so it's not much of a title. He must be a cousin to her somehow—they all are, what's left of them, aren't they?"

"The princess and he are cousins on both sides," said Lady Matheson. "He's descended from Queen Victoria through his mother."

"Princess Alice," remembered Gwen.

"Exactly. Princess Alice even lived with Queen Victoria towards the end of her reign."

"Imagine that," said Gwen. "One keeps forgetting that there are people alive who knew her. It's like meeting people from fairy tales."

"How far down the line is he from the nonexistent Greek crown?" asked Iris.

"Fourth or fifth, I think," said Lady Matheson. "Not close enough to unite the thrones, should the Greeks choose to retain the monarchy."

"Right," said Iris. "What exactly is it that concerns you about him? He's royal, he's educated, he's tall and dashing, and he serves in the King's navy. Is he a fortune-hunter? A womaniser? What's the flaw? Citizenship?"

"Is it his family?" asked Gwen.

"The family is not all what we'd want for in-laws," admitted Lady Matheson. "His father's dead. His mother was in various sanatoria for years—"

"If that's a problem, then it is one that I share with her," said Gwen quietly. "You should know that before we embark upon this expedition."

"Your sojourn was a completely understandable reaction to the loss of your husband," said Lady Matheson, softening for a moment for the first time since she had come in. "We knew about it, of course. We don't hold it against you."

"So the Queen knows I was away," said Gwen. "It wasn't meant to be common knowledge."

"We are not common people," said Lady Matheson. "The Queen is quite cognisant of the sacrifices made by the families of our fallen men. You are held in a place of honour."

"Thank you," said Gwen.

"Fallen men—and women," said Iris.

"Excuse me?"

"You said fallen men," said Iris. "Women died for the country as well."

"Yes, of course. I didn't mean to—"

"Although the phrase 'fallen women' has come to mean something else entirely," said Iris. "We should fix that."

"I'll leave that campaign to you," said Lady Matheson. "In any case, getting back to Philip, throw in the fact that his sisters all married Germans, a couple of whom were quite active with the Nazis, and there are any number of reasons why his candidacy is on thin ice."

"So we may be treated to the spectacle of the future Queen of England sobbing in her royal four-poster because the boy she loves is not good enough for the country she's going to rule," said Iris.

"Hopefully, love will find a way," said Lady Matheson. "But there is also this." She reached into her bag and pulled out a manila folder.

"We screen her mail, of course," she said, placing it on Iris's desk. "Oh, gloves on, if you don't mind."

"It's summer," said Iris. "We don't wear them at the office."

"I have some," said Gwen, opening her bag and retrieving a pair. She slid them on, picked up the folder, and opened it carefully.

There was a single piece of stationery inside, its top edge torn off. There were traces of black powder on it.

"You had it dusted for fingerprints," observed Iris.

"Of course."

The letter was handwritten in a crude, barely legible scrawl. Gwen held it up to the window for a moment.

"The stationery is from Smythson's," she said. "I recognise the watermark. Bespoke, no doubt, which is why the top was torn off."

"Naturally," said Lady Matheson.

"What does it say?" asked Iris.

"'Princess,'" Gwen read aloud. "'I have what Talbot found in Corfu. I know what he knew. Ask Alice if she wants them back. There will be a price.'"

"What was in Corfu?" asked Iris.

"Philip's family, once upon a time," said Lady Matheson. "They still have a villa there. Mon Repos, they call it."

"Continuing the theme of 'not Greek at all,'" commented Iris. "Lady Matheson, this sounds like a police matter already."

"Not yet," said Lady Matheson. "If the information is real and troubling, and if the terms are not unreasonable, we may prefer to handle it privately."

"You've done that before, haven't you?" asked Iris.

"If I had, would I be talking about it?"

"Not at all. What about Talbot? Who was he, where does he come into the story, what could he have had in his possession?"

"The problem with my asking these questions internally is that they lead to other people asking why I'm asking questions," said Lady Matheson. "I have given you what I have given you, and that is all I can give you."

"You want this done, but you don't want to help us do it?" asked Gwen.

"Correct."

"Because you want deniability at your end," said Iris.

"Exactly."

"You are going to compensate us for our efforts, aren't you?" said Iris.

"What do you charge for this sort of thing?" asked Lady Matheson.

"It depends on expenses. What if we have to travel to Corfu?"

"Oh dear," said Gwen. "I don't know if I have the right wardrobe for Corfu in July."

"The envelope was postmarked at the London Central Post Office," said Lady Matheson. "I doubt that plane tickets will be needed."

"We get forty pounds when a marriage results from our efforts," said Iris. "But that's the price for common people, isn't it?"

"And you are not common people, are you?" added Gwen.

"No, we are not," said Lady Matheson, smiling. "What surcharge will you be imposing for God's representatives in England?"

"How soon do you need results?" asked Iris.

"The sooner, the better. We anticipate that the prince may propose at Balmoral."

"Shall we say—" Iris began, then glanced at Gwen, who nodded slightly. "Eighty pounds? Plus expenses?"

"Reasonable expenses," said Lady Matheson, reaching for her purse again. "No investigating Greek island beaches."

"Will you be needing an invoice?" asked Gwen.

"I don't know what that is," said Lady Matheson, counting out the notes. "Nor do I know what a 'receipt' or a 'contract' are."

"In fact, you were never here," said Iris.

"No, I wasn't."

"How do we contact you?"

"At this number," said Lady Matheson, handing over a card with the money. "Use the names under which I made this appointment.

The woman who answers the telephone will connect you to me. She won't know who you really are."

"What happens when you receive the follow-up note demanding payment?"

"We will address that when it happens," said Lady Matheson, rising from her chair. "Good luck, ladies."

She shook hands with Gwen and Iris, then stood by the door for Iris to let her out. The two women watched as she walked briskly down the stairs past her bodyguard, not even acknowledging his existence as she went by. He looked up at Iris and Gwen, winked, then followed.

"We just made ninety pounds, and I'm still not quite sure how it happened," said Gwen as they returned to their desks.

"It puts us well on the way to reuniting you with Cecil," said Iris.

"Start up a new type of business, and you scrimp and scrounge," commented Gwen. "Solve one measly little murder, and the world beats a path. Don't we need to be licensed to be detectives?"

"This is not being detectives," said Iris.

"What is it, then?"

"Advanced gossip. Well within our capabilities. Oh, do you want to be Oona Travis or Catherine Prescott for our contact calls?"

"Does it matter?"

"We should be consistent, just so the secretary won't be surprised by different voices for the same names."

"It makes no difference to me. Which one do you want?"

"I shall be Oona, then," declared Iris. "I'm the exotic one, aren't I?"

"If you say so. This is all so strange. I feel as if we're doing something unseemly, charging the Crown for this."

"They have more money than we do. And this is business, not noblesse oblige."

"Still, it seems inappropriate."

"Think of it as helping out family."

"Family?"

"You're related in some fashion, aren't you?"

"Oh, I suppose I am," Gwen laughed. "I can't remember how many degrees of consanguinity lie between me and the throne. I think Mummy once told me that I was one hundred seventy-third in line when I was born, but what with some dying and others producing heirs, I have no idea where I stand now. Oddly enough, my son is closer than I am, thanks to the in-laws."

"There was a pair of aristocratic lads at Cambridge who were in the mid-two-digit range," remembered Iris. "They used to keep a massive chart on the wall, crossing out and adding names as events dictated. They had a running bet as to who would be closer when they graduated. It was all rather tasteless and obnoxious."

"Who won the bet?"

"No idea. One of them bought it later, commanding a tank division at El-Alamein, so the other has moved up a notch by now. Now, to the matter at hand. The princess loves a prince."

"Thirteen years old," Gwen sighed. "Can you imagine marrying someone you fell for at thirteen?"

"Who was your crush when you were thirteen?" asked Iris.

"I don't want to say," said Gwen, blushing.

"Come on, you tell me yours, and I'll tell you mine," urged Iris, grinning at the other's discomfort.

"A stable boy at my grandfather's estate," said Gwen. "Actually, my immediate love was my horse, Sir Prancealot—"

"Did you name him that?"

"I did. His real name was something boring and lineal."

"I never thought that I could feel embarrassed for a horse until now. So, off to the stables you'd go, in your jodhpurs and boots, a pocket full of sugar cubes—"

"Yes. And I would pat his muzzle while Derek—"

"Ah, Derek. Now, there's a proper name for this story."

"While Derek would saddle him and lead him out. Then he'd give me a leg up."

"I'll bet he did. How old was this strapping young lad?"

"Fifteen, and don't try to make this into a D. H. Lawrence novel."

"Sorry. Pray, continue."

"Derek was handsome, and kind, and courteous," said Gwen dreamily. "Of course, my attentions were quickly transferred from Sir Prancealot to him. He smelled of horses and straw, and wore suspenders over his undershirt in the summer so that his arms and shoulders were bare. And magnificent."

"Mmm," said Iris, closing her eyes for a moment. "Right. Go on."

"There's not much more to tell," said Gwen.

"There isn't?" exclaimed Iris. "Why not?"

"It was a crush, no more," said Gwen. "The physical contact we had was limited to his hands making a step for my foot when I climbed into the saddle, and his hands on my waist to steady me as I dismounted."

"Did you at least accidentally stumble on the dismount so that your body pressed against his? It's a standard move."

"I did once," confessed Gwen. "And I couldn't sleep at all that night. I fantasised that he was a noble in disguise, fleeing some evil plot, and that he would reveal himself and carry me away to his Bavarian castle. I wasn't even certain where Bavaria was at the time, but it sounded like the right place to end up."

"And after that?"

"Tragedy!" cried Gwen with a sob, pounding her fist into her chest. "I learned that he loved another!"

"Oh, my sweet wronged Gwendolyn! Who dared come between you?"

"A girl of fifteen from the village who actually knew what to do with a fifteen-year-old stable boy, which I certainly did not. They were caught aloft in the loft. Or was it in the croft? I always mix those up."

"Acroft in the croft?"

"Perhaps. In any case, he was discharged from my grandfather's service. I heard he married the lass, and they had seven children in seven years."

"No Bavarian castle for her, then. Just as well, given how things went in Bavaria after that."

"Who was your crush at thirteen?"

"Oh, I was a good girl at thirteen."

"No, you were not."

"No, I was not," agreed Iris. "And curse you for seeing through me so easily. His name was Trevor. He was also thirteen—none of your older-stable-boy ambitions for me. We were in school together. He had a keen interest in the sciences, and we often went after school to the Natural History Museum."

"Ah, I know it well. I've chased after my son there on many occasions. Did you hold hands under Dippy? Kiss amidst the creepy crawlies?"

"No, but we discussed beetles at length."

"A solid basis for romance."

"We were the smart ones in the class. He was the only boy who treated me as an equal, so naturally I responded. I was frequently left on my own at that stage of my life. Mummy was off pamphleting and organising clinics, Daddy was doing whatever Daddy did, which was unclear after the Crash—I suspect it involved drinking at whatever club was still willing to extend him credit—so I was frequently on my own. No nanny at that point—the household staff was down to the cook and one overworked maid, so when Trevor and I came home from the museum one day, there was no one else around."

"Aha!"

"It was purely for scientific research," said Iris blandly. "We wanted to see what the human body looked like. We were very solemn and serious about it, and sat across from each other on the rug in my room without touching. Then we put our clothes back on and played backgammon in the drawing room. So, it was a much more prosaic experience than yours."

"Prosaic!" exclaimed Gwen. "You saw a naked man at thirteen!"

"A naked boy."

"I didn't see a live naked man until after I was married!"

"Did your husband know about him?"

"I shall throttle you. I was referring to my husband, of course."

"Didn't you tell me you took some art class with life models when you were younger?"

"They were draped, you ninny. Whatever happened to Trevor?"

"I ran into him earlier this year. He talked about beetles. He continues to study them."

"Not as interesting when you're an adult, I suppose."

"Well, he was off to the Amazon to find some new ones, so not quite as dull as all that. I felt the old stirrings, to tell you the truth. There was a moment where we looked at each other and I knew that he remembered that afternoon without saying anything about it. He smiled, and I blushed, can you believe it? I actually blushed. But I was otherwise involved at the time, so that was the end of it. I didn't become a naturalist, and I don't think I would have been happy tramping through the heart of darkness unless there was at least one good club within walking distance."

"The Amazonian jungles are noted for their lack of decent night-life," agreed Gwen. "Well, let's get back to our new client."

"Have you ever met them? The royals? You were presented at court, weren't you?"

"Before the old King, unfortunately. All of those fittings for the perfect gown, hours of curtsy lessons with Miss Betty at Vacani, hours of waiting on the actual day because I was in the latter half of the group. I made it as far as the entrance, clutching my Card of Command to be passed by the nine footmen to the Lord Chamberlain, and then His Majesty looked at his watch and announced, 'Consider the rest of yourselves presented,' and hurried off to what we later learned was a date with Mrs. Simpson. We were all shuffled downstairs for a perfunctory champagne toast, and that was that. It was all rather shabby, looking back at it."

"How dreadful! I'm so glad Mummy's politics and divorce kept me from having to go through all of that. Where did you have your ball?"

"My mother's parents' house by Courtfield Gardens. Grandmother had been presented to Queen Victoria, of course, and talked about it incessantly. I danced with several boys, only three of whom were tall enough to look me in the eyes, and those three couldn't dance for toffee."

"So that's not when you met Ronnie."

"No, that was a year later. Someone else's season, someone else's ball. He could look me in the eye, and my God, he could dance!"

"And that was all you needed in a husband," teased Iris.

"No, but that was all I needed at a ball. It turned out that he had everything else as well."

"How long did it take you to find that out?"

"The second dance, I think. I didn't want to rush into things."

"You fall hard when you fall."

"I only fell once," said Gwen. "I don't know if I'll ever fall like that again. One only falls that hard when one is young and dewy-eyed. In any case, getting back to your question—I've never met our current king and queen, much less Princess Elizabeth. I wouldn't have, given the difference in our ages. Have you met her?"

"No," said Iris. "I saw the prince a few times back in the beginnings of the war. He was squiring Osla Benning around back then. Do you know her?"

"I know of her. I didn't know about her and Philip. What happened?"

"He wanted her, according to rumour, but she ended up marrying someone else. Smart girl—I ran into her once towards the end of the recent festivities. She was doing something hush-hush, I gathered."

"As were you."

"Yes, but she wasn't with my group. She never talked about what she did. I never talked about what I did. It wasn't an enlightening conversation."

"And her husband survived the war?"

"Yes, so presumably she's happy and not some ex-lover trying to botch things for someone courting in the court."

"I was wondering if there could be others in that category," mused Gwen. "Frustrated wartime affairs and the like. He's in the navy. We would have to check every port."

"I think our best bet is to take the letter at face value for now," said Iris. "The threat stems from something in his mother's past. I thought the handwriting was quite coarse in nature."

"But the stationery was from Smythson's, and they sell to quality," said Gwen. "So whoever wrote this was faking the coarseness. There were no misspellings."

"No, there weren't," agreed Iris. "But that doesn't necessarily mean that it was written by someone of quality. It could have been someone with access to someone else's stationery, which opens the doors to servants, staff, friends. I wonder if Lady Matheson brought in a handwriting expert."

"Might be worth the suggestion, although she may not want to bring any more outsiders into this affair. What did you make of her?"

"Condescending as hell in an outwardly courteous way, which suits her for her present environment. It never occurred to me that the Queen would have someone like her, but it makes sense. They all need someone to clean up their messes behind the scenes, even if they're wearing white gloves while they're doing it."

"What about this Talbot fellow? We don't have anything other than his name and that he must have some connection to the prince's family."

"Especially to his mother. Some scandal in her past, perhaps? That could scotch the engagement before it even happens. The odd thing—"

She stopped, putting her fingers to her brow, staring into her palms. Gwen waited for the lightning to strike.

"I'm not certain," said Iris finally, "but the name rings a soft, muted chime somewhere in the distant recesses of my memory."

"Something you can talk about, or something stored in the secret archives?" asked Gwen

"The latter. I should ask Sally. Which reminds me, we have his play reading tonight."

"Yes. I'm trying not to think about it."

"Why?"

"I'll be performing in front of people. I'm not a professional actress."

"It's just a small gathering of writer and actor friends in his living room. No critical reviews after, at least not for us. It should be fun."

"You know very well that I don't like fun," said Gwen in a se-pulchral tone.

"Come on. It's for Sally."

"Yes, for dear Sally," said Gwen. "I shall set aside my fears. Well, General, what's our next step until then?"

"We need to know the basics about the prince and his past. I think that I shall toddle off to the library and do some research."

"I'll go with you," offered Gwen.

"No, no need," said Iris. "Division of labour. You man the office, I'll dive into the stacks."

"We don't have any appointments this afternoon," said Gwen. "We can split the research."

"Have you ever done research of this nature?"

"No, but you could show me where—"

"Look, I've been trained in this, and it would be much quicker if I did it on my own."

"Yes, but I would like to learn how to do it," said Gwen.

"Gwen, I would be happy to teach you sometime when the clock isn't ticking," said Iris. "But we have a deadline, and not to put too fine a point on it, I can get it done in half the time if I'm on my own."

"That's not a fine point," said Gwen hotly. "It's a sledgehammer."

"We have a business to run," said Iris. "Two businesses, at the moment."

"This is why we need a secretary," fumed Gwen.

"Yes, it is," agreed Iris. "But until that happy day, it makes sense to do it this way."

"You like me being the Watson to your Holmes, don't you?" said Gwen.

"What? Where did you get that silly idea?"

"Our first adventure. You flouting your education and your secret training while I trailed along, taking all my cues from you and blundering about."

"I had the education and I had the training," said Iris. "You roped me into that mess because I had them and you needed them. So who was following whom?"

"You enjoyed every moment of it, playing your characters, getting into rows, putting your life on the line . . ."

"Saving yours," Iris reminded her.

"Yes, and don't think I'm not forever in your debt for that," said

Gwen. "But we were equal partners in that investigation, and we should be equal partners in this one."

"Fine, you're not Watson," said Iris. "If I'm Holmes, who are you?"

"I'll be Bulldog Drummond," declared Gwen, smacking her fist into her palm, then wincing slightly.

"I fight better than you do," Iris pointed out.

"You had to say that," said Gwen. "Fine. You can teach me how to fight after you teach me how to do research."

"I will, I promise," said Iris. "But right now, give me this afternoon. I'll meet you at Sally's, and we'll ask him a few questions after the reading. Please, darling? May we do it this way today?"

"Very well, go," grumbled Gwen. "I hope the dust makes you sneeze uncontrollably."

"No doubt it will, pouty girl," said Iris, rising and putting on her hat. "I'll see you at Sally's."

She left, fluttering her fingers in farewell. Gwen watched her in chagrin.

"When did it become Let's All Be Condescending to Gwen Day?" she said to herself.

She stared moodily at the keys to Cooper and Lyons, Chartered Public Accountants, and fought back the urge to go back into their former office and play with the desk drawers some more. She looked at her watch. Their normal lunch hour had passed, and she was feeling peckish. She picked up the keys, hung their "Out to Lunch" sign on the outer doorknob and adjusted the little hands on the clock indicating her return time, then went downstairs.

Mr. MacPherson was in front of the building, eating a sandwich and drinking from a thermos, the contents of which she did not wish to know.

"Here are the keys, thank you," she said, returning them to him.

"Think you might take the place?" he asked, his mouth full.

"We are seriously considering it," she said. "Would the desks inside be part of the price?"

"Desks?" he replied in puzzlement.

"There were a pair of desks still there," she said nonchalantly, not wanting him to investigate it any further. "We thought we could take them over with the office. It would save us some bother."

"Oh, those bloody things," he said, remembering. "Makes no difference to me. They were more trouble to move than to leave, so we left them. They're not moveables if you can't move them."

"Did you know the previous tenants?" asked Gwen.

"I've been in this building thirty-five years," said Mr. MacPherson, taking a sip from his thermos and exhaling in satisfaction. "I knew them."

"How long have they been gone?"

"Ah, that would be end of thirty-two, wouldn't it? Or maybe thirty-three. Or thirty-one."

"And no one has occupied it since?"

Mr. MacPherson shrugged.

"Well, then I would think that Mr. Maxwell would be glad to have us in there," said Gwen.

"Mr. Maxwell will barely even notice as long as the rent gets paid on time," said Mr. MacPherson. "Let me know if you're moving in, and I'll have some more keys made up."

"Will do," said Gwen.

She walked up to Oxford Street and purchased a sandwich and a plum from a tea shop. It was abysmally hot, and she could feel the sun burning into her fair skin. She walked quickly back to the office, put her lunch on her desk, and heated up the tea kettle on the hot plate on top of the old filing cabinet.

It was churlish of her to whine about her lack of education when she had so much of everything else, she realised. She had been so accustomed to the aristocratic life that it never occurred to her that she was missing anything of importance. The whirlwind of the seasons, the thrill of romance—and then the bloody war had to come and destroy everything.

Could she go back to school now? Did people do that?

Did women do that?

Could Gwen herself do that, tied up as she was with running a struggling business while fighting to regain full custody of her son?

No, she thought. There isn't enough time. She'd have to settle for holding Iris to her offer of informal tutelage.

Library skills and martial arts, the beginnings to a proper education for every postwar widowed mum in her late twenties.

She would start a movement once she had Little Ronnie's status secured, she decided. She'd round up all the girls who had found new purpose during the war and then were kicked out once the men got demobbed and came back to their old jobs.

Yes, and she was exactly what they would not be looking for in a leader, having spent her war either in her titled in-laws' country estate or the sanatorium.

She finished her sandwich, then bit slowly into the plum, tilting her head back to let the juices flow across her tongue. It was her first of the summer, and between rationing and her time in treatment, there hadn't been many over the previous six years. She ate it slowly, concentrating her entire being on each bite, making them small so that the simple experience of eating a plum would last as long as it could.

When it was down to the pit, she wiped her mouth and fingers carefully, then wrapped the remains in the napkin.

Like a corpse in a shroud, she thought, looking at it mournfully.

Stop it, Gwennie. Those thoughts will take you down a dark corridor.

She quickly tossed it into the wastepaper basket, then stared at her desk. She spent the next hour comparing notes from her two boxes of index cards, coming up with matches that she wanted to run by Iris before sending letters on to the bachelors. Always the bachelors, so they could make the first contact, as gentlemen should. Whether they were gentlemen or not.

Gentlemen, she thought suddenly.

She picked up the receiver from the telephone and rang home.

"Bainbridge residence," answered Percival, their butler.

"It's Mrs. Bainbridge, Percival," she said. "I would like to speak to Ronnie, if he's not busy. And Agnes when he's done."

"Master Ronald is in the playroom," he said. "I will summon him for you."

"Thank you, Percival."

She waited, then smiled as she heard a clattering of rapid footsteps coming towards the telephone. She held the receiver away from her ear.

"Mummy!" shouted Little Ronnie.

"Indoor voice, please," she admonished him. "Hello, my lovely boy. How are you?"

"Agnes is teaching me how to make large numbers," he said. "We got all the way up to five hundred!"

"What fun! Do you have a favourite number?"

"Seventeen."

"Really? Why seventeen?"

"I don't know, I just like it the best."

"Then seventeen it shall be. I was thinking—would you like to go to the Natural History Museum on Saturday?"

"It's Tommy's birthday party. Grandmother is taking me."

"Ah yes," said Gwen, her heart sinking slightly. "Well, we'll go together some other time. Anyhow, I wanted to remind you that Mummy will be going out later, so I won't be able to kiss you good night tonight."

"Where are you going?"

"To a play reading."

"What's that?"

"Well, our friend Sally has written a play, and we're going to read all the parts out loud so he can hear what it sounds like and decide what he needs to change."

"Is it a panto?"

"Not exactly."

"Are you going to wear costumes and sing? You could dress up like Puss in Boots!"

"Oh, that would be fun," laughed Gwen. "But I'm afraid it's a play for grown-ups, so we won't be doing any of those things."

"It doesn't sound like much fun without songs and costumes," said Ronnie.

"You have different kinds of fun when you're a grown-up."

"Then I don't want to grow up," he declared.

"Well, that's fine with me," said Gwen. "You're absolutely wonderful the way you are right now."

"But I want to be taller!"

"You will be, my darling. Now, blow me a kiss, and I shall blow you a kiss."

She heard a loud smack, and matched it in volume.

"Good night, my lovely boy, and let me talk to Agnes for a moment."

"Good night, Mummy!"

There was a rustling, then a woman's voice came on the line.

"Hello, Mrs. Bainbridge," said Agnes. "Little Ronnie has been very good today."

"I am glad to hear it," said Mrs. Bainbridge. "Agnes, would you do me a favour?"

"Certainly, Mrs. Bainbridge."

"Could you go downstairs to the library? I'd like you to look something up for me."

CHAPTER 3

Sally lived in a bachelor flat in Soho, on a block largely occupied by actors and musicians because of its low rents and its tolerance for odd noises at odd times of the day and night. Before the war, Gwen would have been appalled at the idea of going to such a place unaccompanied, when even a hint of scandal might get one struck from the invitation lists to all the better parties. But the war happened, she was now a working widow, and invitations to parties were few and far between.

She looked at her directions and verified the flat number for the fifth time, then walked up the stairs to the third storey. She needn't have checked—a group of rowdy but well-trained voices could clearly be heard through one of the closed doors. She walked to it, summoned up her courage, and knocked.

It opened a second later, and Sally filled the doorway.

Sally was a large man. Large to the point that other large men looked at him with respect and awe. Large enough that, were one possessed of a classical education and versed in the tales of the Greek gods defeating the Titans, then encountered Sally, one might think, Oh, they missed one.

Sally was possessed of a classical education. When his classmates at Cambridge nicknamed him Titan, he'd immediately say,

"Clever. Which one?" And before they could wonder why they could never remember those names, he would quickly rattle them off, complete with citations to Hesiod, and be sure to mention that one of them was mother to the Muses, from whom all art derived. By that point, his nicknamers would realise they were not quite as clever as they initially thought. Nevertheless, the nickname stuck.

Gwen knew this from Iris, who had been at Cambridge with Sally. Gwen suspected some other details about Sally, stemming from his months behind enemy lines in Italy. In her imagination, these alternated between detonating explosives that brought down bridges and silently dispatching Nazis and Fascists with his bare hands or a knife. Sally acknowledged the explosions, not the dispatchings. He had a knack for appearing suddenly in places without any prefatory footsteps. Sally was whom The Right Sort called upon when they needed to collect a debt from a pair of recalcitrant newlyweds. There was no violence involved. There was no need for it. People would take one look at Sally and feel compelled to adopt a peaceful resolution to their disputes.

But that was not the Sally who loomed over Gwen in happy welcome. This was Sally, the aspiring playwright, his smile beaming down from on high. He took Gwen's hand in his massive one.

"Mrs. Bainbridge," he said, raising it to his lips.

"Mr. Danielli," she returned.

"So good of you to come," he said, leading her inside. "Be careful, it's somewhat crowded tonight."

"Somewhat?" she said as he parted a path for her through the mingled assembly.

The parlour was filled with folding chairs, and what furniture had originally been there had been shoved against the walls or, in the case of some low tables, stacked to make more room.

The guests were mostly men in their twenties or thirties, some still in uniform. A dozen conversations were already in progress, as was the smoking, evenly divided between cigarettes and pipes.

The windows were fully open, which did nothing to cool down the room.

There was a long, threadbare, overstuffed green sofa at the far end of the room, and it was towards this that Sally guided her.

"Make way," he proclaimed. "Make way, good people. Our leading lady has arrived."

"I thought I was your leading lady," said Iris, who was already on the sofa, her legs curled up under her.

"In your universe, always," said Sally. "But tonight, you are in mine, and I determine who is who."

"I don't believe in a deterministic universe," declared Iris. "I believe in chaos."

Then she sneezed abruptly, clutching her handkerchief to her face.

"Oh dear," said Gwen sympathetically as she sat gracefully next to Iris. "Ran into some dust somewhere, I gather."

"When you put a curse on someone, you mean business," muttered Iris, wiping her nose.

"Right," called Sally. "Places, please."

A man sat in the space remaining on the sofa next to Gwen and offered his hand.

"George Weatherby," he said. "Looks like we're in for it now."

"Terrifying, isn't it?" said Gwen as she shook it. "Gwendolyn Bainbridge. This is—"

"Oh, I know her, don't I, Sparks?" he said, grinning. "We climbed the wall after curfew more than once."

"Behave, George," Iris admonished him.

Sally stood in front of them, as a man and a woman pulled chairs up on either side.

"Good evening, and thank you for coming tonight," he said. "This is the first reading of my play, *The Margate Affair*. That's a working title, by the way."

"What works about it?" called a man sitting in the back.

"Save the comments for after," said Sally. "Let me introduce the cast. That's George on the sofa, playing Bill. Next to him is Gwen, playing Lydia, and rounding out the central cast, which is why I, in a brilliant directorial touch put them in the center, is the one and only Iris Sparks as Muriel. Loretta, in the chair on the right, will be playing all the secondary female roles, and Alec, on the left, will be playing all the male ones."

"I wanted to play the women, but you are so damned conventional," said Alec dolefully.

"Alec's a ringer, by the way," said Sally. "He's going to be in the new Priestley play this autumn, so keep on the lookout for that."

The assembly applauded politely.

"The cast, with the exception of Sparks, hasn't read the play," continued Sally as he handed them their scripts. "I let them know the basics of each character, but I didn't send them copies in advance."

"That's because you were afraid we'd lose them," said George.

"In your case, a definite concern," said Sally. "But more because I wanted to give one tiny hint of direction: speak the speech, I pray you, as I pronounced it to you—"

"Trippingly on the tongue!" chorused the room.

"Yes, like that," said Sally. "I'm joking. No, I'm not. We're in a living room. Speak like we're all here, talking to each other in a living room, not projecting to the top of the balcony. I didn't give anyone a script because I want you to discover what you're saying as you say it, not as if you're expecting to say it. Does that make sense? Let yourselves invent the words as they happen, as if they were emerging naturally from your thoughts. I'll call out stage directions at the beginning of each scene just for clarity, but don't worry about any bits of business with imaginary props. And don't bother with the kissing, of course."

"Damn the luck," said George.

"Let's begin," said Sally, taking a seat in the corner. "Act One,

Scene One. A bar in a middle-class seaside hotel in Margate. Bill is seated at a table, nursing a scotch and soda. The bartender comes over to him."

"Will you be having another, sir?" said Alec.

"I'll wait, if it's all right with you," said George.

"Expecting someone?"

"My wife's coming by the later train. She should be here shortly."

"What does the lady drink?"

"Ah," said George, hesitating. "Gin and tonic, I should think."

"Does she?" said Alec, smirking. "Gin and tonic? You're certain about that?"

"Of course I'm certain."

"Very good, sir. I'll be sure to have one ready."

Gwen uttered a silent prayer as George read her cue.

"Ah, there you are, darling," he said brightly. "Good trip?"

"Awful," she said, her voice quavering slightly. "The train was beastly crowded."

"I've got us a table by the window. Come sit and have a drink."

"Here you are, ma'am," said Alec. "Gin and tonic for the lady, scotch and soda for the gent."

"But I don't—Oh, yes. Gin and tonic," said Gwen. "Lovely, thank you."

She paused, pretending that the bartender was walking away.

"Why on earth did you order me this?" she hissed. "I detest gin."

"Sorry, I panicked," said George. "He asked me what you drank. I had no idea. I had to come up with something or he'd be suspicious."

"He's suspicious anyway."

"Any trouble getting away?"

"None. I told Arthur that I was visiting my friend Carol for the weekend. He was going out to his club. I don't think he even absorbed the information."

"What if he calls Carol?"

"She'll cover for me. She owes me a few."

"Nice friend."

"How's the room?"

"Adequate. Couldn't get one with a view of the beach, unfortunately. We overlook Dreamland."

"How poetic."

"We could ride the Scenic Railway tomorrow, if you like. Or go for a swim—I've brought my trunks."

Gwen turned to look at him steadily.

"Did you actually think I would come all this way to this wretched place to waste my time swimming?" she asked.

This brought a laugh from the room, and the knots inside her began to loosen.

Iris's Muriel entered halfway through the third scene, and things became complicated. Things always get complicated when Iris enters the scene, thought Gwen. The interplay between her Muriel and George's Bill were laced with genuine vitriol, the snappish rhythms coming from somewhere deep inside. Rooted in the past, guessed Gwen.

Another ex? She wouldn't put it past Sally to cast them according to their histories. All those young Cambridge pals grown up, clinging to those memories, with an overlay of war distorting them now.

There were some lags in the latter portion of the first act, but the second, which they continued after a brief break, raced along, eliciting some surprised gasps from the audience.

The final scene was between Muriel and Lydia, Bill having met an unfortunate end at the hands of Arthur, who proved to be not so oblivious after all, and powerful enough to avoid any legal consequences. The two women read their lines glancing at each other while still playing to the audience.

"It's horrible to say, but I miss the war," said Gwen. "I miss working in the factory."

"Don't be ridiculous," said Iris.

"I'm not. I had a sense of direction for perhaps the only time in my life. Then the men came home and took it away from me. They had seen battle; I hadn't. I couldn't begrudge them that, but it's all so empty now."

"What will you do?" asked Iris.

"My choices are limited," said Gwen. "Maybe I never really had any. I could jump off a cliff, or I could go back to Arthur. Both are suicide. One takes longer."

"We could run away," offered Iris.

"No," said Gwen. "Not with the way things are. He'll find us. There are no more hiding places. They've lit up Dreamland with carbon arc searchlights and surrounded it with barbed wire, and no dreams can escape it anymore."

"What will you do?"

"I don't know, Muriel. I don't know."

"And curtain!" called Sally.

There was applause. Gwen tried to gauge whether it veered more towards politeness or genuine enthusiasm.

"Damned good, Titan," said one of the pipe-smokers. "A shade Shavian, not at all Cowardly. The moment I heard 'affair' in the title, I was worried that we would be down for 'Lengthy Encounter' or some such, but this was much grittier."

"I've noticed that you've toned down Muriel's bisexuality considerably," observed Iris.

"That would have made things awkward at work in the morning," said Gwen.

"Oh, I don't know," said Iris, batting her eyes at her. "It might have livened them up for a change. But did you do that for fear of censorship?"

"Not at all," said Sally. "I thought that I didn't need to push that angle so blatantly for it to play. I threw in the reference to the club at Shepherd Market. I thought that would be enough."

"I didn't get that reference," Gwen whispered to Iris.

"That's the club where all the best lesbians go," Iris whispered back.

"Really? I had no idea."

"Of course you hadn't."

"Do you think it's commercial enough?" asked a man. "All we have going on the West End are high-brow classics and low-brow sex farces, minus any real sex. Here you are pushing the collapse of British morality, and you don't even have a decent drawing room scene."

"I am sick to death of drawing room scenes," said Sally heatedly. "Every high-minded attempt to depict so-called real life has a bloody drawing room and servants rushing about serving comic relief with the tea. That's not the way things are anymore."

"New forms are what we need!" shouted Alec in a thick Russian accent. "New forms!"

"Thank you, Mr. Chekhov," said Sally. "My point is, the affair here happens because the war destroyed the old ways of class structure like nothing has before, and those who obstinately cling to them will be unceremoniously dumped into the dustbins of history."

"If you're going to quote Trotsky, you should at least use a Russian accent like Alec did," said Iris.

"I wasn't quoting Trotsky, I was quoting Petrarch," said Sally.

"Petrarch said 'rubbish heap.' Trotsky said 'dustbin.'"

"It all depends on the translation. If you had read it in the original—"

"I have," said Iris. "Both of them."

"Where's the wine?" Gwen whispered to George. "Once they get going like this, they'll be on for the duration."

"Capital idea," George whispered back. "Follow me. We'll make a break for the sideboard."

The room split into small knots of discussion and debate. George and Gwen threaded their way through to where a half dozen bottles of cheap red stood amongst stacks of paper cups purloined from a commissary somewhere. George filled two, handed one to Gwen, and held his up.

"To our 'Affair,'" he said, and tapped his cup against hers.

"We'll keep that in quotes," she replied.

"Of course," he said, his eyebrows raising in mock surprise. "All of that was acting. I don't find you attractive at all."

"Thanks very much," she said, laughing.

"Especially when my wife is seated right over there, looking daggers," he added in a lower tone.

"Tell her I find you repulsive as well. I was only acting, too."

"And may I say, from one amateur to another, you were very good."

"You're too kind."

"No, I mean it. You had that cool exterior down pat, but when the shell cracked, the inner turmoil came through quite authentically."

"That may not be acting," she confessed. "That may be how I am."

"Then Sally knows you well," he said.

He glanced over to where Sally, Iris, and several others were in full debate.

"Look at the two of them," he observed. "Just like it was ten years ago, with no war in between. That's why they've stayed friends."

"You were at Cambridge with them, I take it."

"Indeed I was. She was a whirlwind back then. He was her rock. One of those giant stones you see off the shore, standing tall and solid while the waves crash around it."

"Mr. Weatherby, you are a poet."

"I scribbled some pretentious lines when I was young and foolish," he admitted. "That was then. Well, better carry a peace offering over to the wife if I'm to avoid sleeping on the sofa tonight. Until the next draft, Mrs. Bainbridge."

He poured another cup of wine and wandered into the scrum. One of the men in uniform immediately took his place.

"You were jolly good up there," he said.

"Thank you," she said.

"So you and Sparks work in the same office, do you?"

"We do."

"Lucky boss to have a pair of lookers like the two of you coming in every day," he said. "Wouldn't mind being in his shoes, I must say."

"I'm afraid I don't understand," said Gwen sweetly. "Which boss would that be?"

"Why, your boss. You know, the fellow you two work for."

"There is no fellow we work for."

"Now I'm the one who doesn't understand," he said.

"The two of us own the business," said Gwen. "The two of us run the business. You are now addressing a boss."

"How very novel," he said. "I have gone and put my foot in it, haven't I?"

"Both, I would say."

"I'll just slink away and lick my wounds, then," he said. "Cheers."

"We have an opening for a secretary if you're interested in applying," she called after him. "Do you type?"

He moved as far from her as the crowd and the size of the room would permit.

She heard a low, appreciative laugh, and turned to see another man standing a few feet away. Also in uniform—a captain, she observed.

"Grenadiers?" she asked, noting his insignia.

"Got it in one," he said. "Captain Timothy Palfrey, Second Armoured, at your service."

"Mrs. Gwendolyn Bainbridge," she replied. "How do you do?"

"I enjoyed your performance. Both of them, in fact."

"Both?"

"Your brush-off of that military assault just now. Superbly done."

"How poor a soldier he must be to undertake such an action without assessing the defenses first."

"Ah. You must be a soldier's daughter."

"And a soldier's widow," she said.

"My condolences," he said, holding up his cup in salute.

She grimaced for a moment.

"Was that the wrong thing to say?" he asked.

"I'm sorry," said Gwen. "You were being polite. Condolences are always polite. And politeness is always correct. But it's tiresome."

"You did bring it up," he pointed out.

"Because I saw you glance at my wedding ring," she said. "And you were wondering how to play the game."

"The game?"

"The game where two men size up a woman and decide who will go after her. One goes first and deliberately fumbles badly, then the second swoops in to look dashing by comparison. I've known that dodge since I was sixteen. I saw the two of you together when I came in, a pair of matched Grenadiers. He's batted out, and you're the new striker. Am I correct?"

"Madam, your defenses are indeed formidable," he said, bowing slightly. "My bails have been toppled. I admit defeat. Rather than retreat to the sidelines, would you permit me to continue the conversation sans romantic objectives?"

"On that condition, yes," said Gwen. "How did you like Sally's script?"

"Condolences again," he said, raising his cup. "To the death of the 'well-made play.'"

"Really? I thought it was very well-made."

"That's a term of art, kicking around since the last century. Some fellow declared that the 'well-made play' must contain certain required elements."

"Like a drawing room?"

"That, the sudden third-act revelation through discovered documents or letters, and secret identities revealed. It's the sort of thing Wilde parodied so brilliantly. You know *Earnest*?"

"My name is Gwendolyn. People have been shoving that one at me since early childhood."

"Naturally. Well, I'm no critic, but that sort of thing is old hat, and what Sally is attempting to do is something new. I don't think he took it far enough, to tell you the truth. He's trying to rip the covers off the world, but he's still stopping short. He has to let the anger out if he really wants to make a mark."

"An angry Sally would be truly terrifying."

"Yet it's in him," he said. "Ever since he came back. He hides it under this persona, but if he can ever tap the source, he'll write something great, instead of merely good."

He sipped his wine thoughtfully.

"Or he'll kill someone," he added. "But my money's on the play."

"I hope so," said Gwen, shuddering.

"One thing, at least," said Palfrey. "He's no longer writing about his not-so-concealed desire for Sparks. That was almost embarrassingly obvious back in Cambridge days."

"He told me about that. Do you think it's over and done with?"

"Maybe," he said. "If I were to analyse the script for unconscious desires based upon the creation of characters and how he cast it, I would guess that his attentions have shifted elsewhere."

"Oh? Where?"

He smiled at her.

"Sometimes, one's defenses can be too good," he said. "The walls can become so thick that you never hear anyone approaching. Mrs. Bainbridge, it was a pleasure to meet you. Perhaps you will permit me to call upon you in the future?"

"You have regrouped, I see, Captain."

"The sappers have been at work," he said. "The walls may yet crumble in time. What say I take you to the opening of Alec's play? That's in October. You have three months to think about your answer."

"My life is complicated at the moment," she said.

"Every life is complicated at every moment," he replied, handing her his card. "I'll look for you when autumn comes. Until then, Mrs. Bainbridge."

He crumpled his cup and tossed it into the waste basket, then fetched his cap, and left, the first Grenadier joining him as he went, to her absolute lack of surprise.

Others took this as a signal to follow. Alec came over to Sally and reached up to clasp his shoulders.

"It's a good start, Sally," he said. "I'll send you my notes when I'm sober."

"You're not sober now?" asked Sally.

"I am, but I am in need of getting drunk and don't want to wait. Call Kenny, won't you?"

"You know how I feel about that."

"But it's time for you to resume treading the boards."

"I trod the boards, and the boards cried out in anguish. I can show you the clippings."

"Call Kenny," urged Alec, patting him on the cheek. "For me."

"All right," said Sally.

As the stragglers filed out, still chatting away, Sally began to fold up the chairs and lean them against the pile of tables.

"We'll help," said Iris. "Won't we, Gwen?"

"Of course."

"Thanks," said Sally. "I should be going out to the York Minster and getting hammered. I might still."

"Who is Kenny?" asked Iris.

"Kenny is a director," said Sally. "He wants to cast me in a new production."

"That's wonderful!" exclaimed Gwen. Then she saw his expression. "It's not wonderful?"

"Caliban," said Sally. "He wants me to play Caliban. Another stupid, ugly giant. I could make a decent living playing nothing but Caliban, Frankenstein's monster, or that mental deficient in that American play we saw."

"*Of Mice and Men*," said Iris.

"I don't want to play monsters," said Sally. "That's why I'm hiding behind my scripts. Let the masses rise cheering at the end, 'Author! Author!' and I'll leap out and yell, 'Boo!' and watch them run screaming from the theatre. Ideally, they'll run screaming from the words, if I can ever get them right."

"You got them right in this one," said Gwen.

"Most of them," said Iris.

"Well, I don't feel like throwing the scripts into the fire, so that's an improvement," said Sally as he collapsed onto the center of the sofa. "Is there any wine left? Pour the dregs into a cup for me, if you would be so kind. Spare the hemlock. I choose to live another day."

"On it," said Iris, locating an unused cup and filling it from two bottles.

She brought it over to him, and he gulped it down.

"Thanks," he said. "Pontificating leaves me parched. Come, ladies! Come cuddle with the playwright."

He threw his arms out over the back of the sofa. Iris slid under one and curled into him. Gwen hesitated.

"You should try it, Gwen," said Iris. "He's very comfy."

"And there are no appearances to be kept up," added Sally. "It shall be our illicit secret."

"First you have me committing adultery. Now cuddling. I shall never be able to look anyone in the eye again," said Gwen as she sat down and leaned into him.

He enveloped her gently, and she felt herself drift into a memory of her grandfather reading poetry to her as she nestled into the crook of his arm, letting the gentle rumble of his voice carry her wherever Tennyson was taking them.

"He is comfy, isn't he?" said Gwen.

"Told you so," said Iris. "Now, tell me about all those men who swarmed you."

"The Grenadiers attempted to try me on," said Gwen. "The first seemed MTF. The second was definitely NST."

"What on earth are you on about?" asked Sally.

"Deb code," explained Iris, snickering. "MTF means Must Touch Flesh, and NST means Not Safe in Taxis."

"Good God," said Sally. "Have you reduced them to their essences so quickly?"

"Friends of yours?" asked Gwen.

"Bresnahan's an ass," said Sally. "Palfrey's not a bad fellow when you get to know him."

"He wants to take me to that play Alec's in when it opens."

"Blast," said Sally. "I was hoping the three of us could attend together."

"I'd much rather go with the two of you," said Gwen. "Tell me honestly—how much of this was a setup?"

"Excuse me?"

"I've been lured into a room containing wine and eligible men," said Gwen. "I feel the unseen presence of benevolent ulterior motives."

"That was not my intent," said Sally.

"Nor mine," said Iris. "I'd be direct about it. Declare your availability, and I will have the best men in London queued up at your doorstep in a trice, flowers in hand."

"Then forgive me," said Gwen, unconvinced.

"I'm glad we've got that settled. Sally, I want to pick your brain about something," said Iris.

"My brain? There's nothing remaining of it after tonight. I've left it all in those pages."

"Let me draw upon your memories, then. Do you recall a fellow named Talbot? Showed up during training?"

"Talbot," mused Sally. "The name's familiar. Anything more to go on?"

"Possibly Sir Gerald Francis Talbot," said Gwen, pulling her notebook out of her handbag. "KCVO, CMG, OBE. Got himself knighted on the fourteenth of December 1922."

"Where did you get that?" asked Iris in surprise.

"*Burke's Peerage*," answered Gwen in a lofty tone. "Where does anyone get anything about anyone if not there? He was naval attaché in Athens at the end of the Great War."

"Was he?" exclaimed Iris, sitting up and peering over Sally at her. "That's interesting."

"How so?" asked Gwen.

"Naval attachés are usually British Intelligence. It's one of the standard posts."

"And what's a CMG? I know the KCVO is Knight Commander of the Victorian Order."

"You ask me a question, then you ignore me," complained Sally. "I am not accustomed to being ignored on my own sofa."

"Do you know what a CMG is?" asked Gwen.

"Companion of the Order of St. Michael and St. George," said Sally promptly. "An honour given to someone who did something for the Crown while overseas somewhere."

"Like Athens," said Iris.

"Like Athens," agreed Sally. "And I remember the chap now. He was—Wait. Are we allowed to talk about this in front of Mrs. Bainbridge?"

"Why can't you?" Gwen asked indignantly.

"Because it involves topics that we're not supposed to talk about," said Iris.

"Exactly," said Sally. "On pain of prosecution by the Crown."

"Damn you both," said Gwen. "Shall I leave the room?"

"Absolutely not," said Iris. "Sally, there are exactly two people in the world whom I trust, and they are both sitting on this sofa. We can talk about this with Gwen. I'd trust her with my life. So would you."

"You're not including yourself in that total?" asked Sally.

"I don't trust myself," said Iris. "Sally, darling, we are not asking for state secrets. We are vetting a marriage prospect for a client, and this Talbot fellow came up as a possible reference. I remembered you mentioning him to me back in training. You thought he was amusing."

"Amusing and useless," said Sally. "Fine, to hell with the Official Secrets Act, you Mata Hari. But if I end up swinging for it, I will take you with me."

"Agreed," said Iris. "We can have our last meal together, only I'm choosing the wine. Tell us about Talbot."

"This was back before they knew where they were going to send me," said Sally, lying back with his eyes fixed on a point on the ceiling. "I was being trained for either Italy or Greece. It turned out that my Greek was more classical than colloquial, but that's another anecdote entirely.

"They brought in some of the old Greek hands from the Great War. One was this fellow with an absolutely enormous dome of a head, like someone had stuffed five human brains inside a mushroom and stuck the whole assembly on top of a three-piece suit. He was charming enough, but not all that helpful for our missions. He was a spy from an earlier era. He believed that the best way to gather intelligence was to find the best café in town, order a pot of coffee, and sit and pretend to read the newspaper. Eventually, anybody worth spying on would show up, and if they didn't, at least you'd have a decent pot of coffee before you went off to the office."

"He makes spying sound like a pleasant, genteel occupation," said Gwen.

"Oh, no doubt he saw his share of horrors," said Sally. "He downplayed them—no one wanted to scare us away in training."

"How long was he posted there?"

"I'm not exactly sure. End of the war, then through the Greek-Turkish hostilities after, maybe three or four years in all. I'm not certain what he did then, being but a wee small lad at the time, if you can imagine me as a wee small lad at any time."

"I can," said Iris, resting her head on his chest. "I wish we had known each other when we were children. Any idea where he is now?"

"Probably in a café somewhere, drinking coffee and reading a newspaper," said Sally.

"In England, at least?"

"I had the impression he was no longer in the Service," said Sally. "I remember he had this funny little tie pin shaped like a train locomotive. Now, are you going to tell me what this is really about?"

"It's exactly what I said," replied Iris. "We're vetting a prospective groom for a client."

"Who is tied to a former English spy," said Sally.

"If this is the right Talbot," said Iris. "And I have a feeling it is. What was the date of that knighthood, again?"

"Fourteenth of December 1922," said Gwen.

"Odd time of year to be knighted," said Iris. "It didn't come with the Birthday Honours nor the New Year Honours. He must have done something unusually significant."

"But he wasn't the naval attaché anymore," Gwen pointed out.

"Once a spy, always a spy," said Sally. "He may have had some particular talent or connection."

"It does narrow down the time frame," agreed Iris. "That's helpful."

"What does 1922 have to do with a current engagement?" asked Sally.

"We don't know yet," said Iris. "We're excavating old skeletons."

"Well, don't go digging in Greece, if you can avoid it," said Sally. "Things are dicey there. I just had a thought—one fellow who might know where to find Commander Talbot."

"Who's that?"

"Your old boss," said Sally. "He was working that neck of the Mediterranean back then."

"Only if I'm desperate," said Iris.

"Very well," said Sally. "Will that be all the interrogating? I have people waiting to buy me drinks."

"You wouldn't rather keep cuddling us?" purred Iris, dragging her nails across his chest.

"I would, except you and I know it won't go anywhere," said Sally. "Not even Noël Coward lives in a Noël Coward play. Come to the pub with me?"

"I have to work tomorrow," Iris said regretfully, getting to her feet and retrieving her hat, Gwen following suit.

"So responsible now," said Sally. "Not at all like the girl I once knew. We have heard the chimes at midnight, Sparks."

"That we have, that we have," said Iris. "Now, there's a role you should play. You'd be a marvelous Falstaff."

"I'm not old enough to do it justice," said Sally. "But when I am, will you be my Mistress Quickly?"

"No, darling," said Iris, coming over to kiss him lightly on the cheek. "I'll take my time with it. Good night, Sally."

"Good night, sweet ladies," he said, rising and walking them to the door. "Beware of Greeks bearing gifts, won't you?"

"But those are my favourite Greeks," protested Iris.

"We will," promised Gwen, dragging Iris out of the flat. "Good night, Sally. Smashing play. Good cuddle. Thank you for letting me be part of it."

CHAPTER 4

Iris's party smile faded as they descended from Sally's flat, and her pace, normally quick and frenetic, became slow and contemplative. Gwen, whose height advantage over her partner was a frequent cause of Iris's frenetic pace, slowed down to match her. She maintained a companionable silence, waiting.

"I owe you an apology," Iris said finally.

"Yes, I believe you do," replied Gwen.

"I should have taken you along to the library, shown you some research techniques, and split up the work. Instead, I lorded my education over you and made you feel small and resentful."

"Not small," said Gwen.

"Still, it was not a nice thing to do," said Iris. "Not a nice thing to do to anyone, but even worse to do to a friend. I'm not used to having a close female friend. I never have been. My problem, one of my problems, and this is by no means an attempt to justify any of my behaviour, is that I have a great deal of lingering resentment for women like you."

"Women like me? In what category are you placing me?"

"The aristocracy. The rich girls who get presented at court and drink champagne while wearing exorbitantly expensive frocks and have their entire lives of luxury laid out for them before they're even born. The ones who know to go to *Burke's Peerage* to look people up. Which was a very good idea, by the way."

"Darling, *I* didn't look it up," drawled Gwen. "I had someone do it for me. That's how one does that sort of thing. There are advantages to being in the aristocracy."

"Yes, there are, and I have envied and despised them. My mother divorced my father when I was fifteen, so we were anathema to that world. Forget any chance of my coming out at court, or being invited to the best parties. I never got to vent my spleen with a shotgun at some blameless grouse or fox. But I got into Cambridge on merit, and became that gorgeous brainy girl who was always up for a bit of fun with the upper-class boys, and that got me entry into a lot of places that money didn't."

"I thought you enjoyed being that girl," said Gwen.

"I did. Well, I thought I did. Looking back, the reputation I so eagerly earned probably shot down my first engagement, although I have no regrets over not being stuck with that dolt for life. But I'm not a Good-Time Charlie anymore, and I don't want the old school boys treating me like one."

"You are dating a gangster," Gwen pointed out.

"I've gone out with Archie twice. He's a marvelous dancer, and he's taken me to out-of-the-way places where nobody knows either of us and we can lower our defenses and talk like human beings. It's not at all the same thing."

"That sounds rather pleasant," admitted Gwen.

"He has a friend—"

"Absolutely not."

"Had enough male attention for one evening?"

"More than enough, thank you. Is the apology over?"

"Have I covered everything? I may not have actually said 'I'm sorry.'"

"Consider it said. And consider it accepted. Do we have a date for the library tomorrow afternoon?"

"We do."

"What have you learned so far?"

"I was concentrating on the prince and his parents, looking through the *Times* index. I wasted a good half hour before I realised that they were mostly listed under 'Greece' rather than their names."

"Well, of course they would be," said Gwen. "How else would you index royalty?"

"I really hate you right now," said Iris, glaring at her. "In any case, I've been working backwards in the chronology. It turns out that their departure from Greece was rather dramatic."

"How so?"

"Prince Andrew, or Andrea, was a commander of an army during the Greco-Turkish war after the Great War. His older brother was the king."

"The one who died from the monkey bite?"

"What?"

"One of the Greek kings died after being bitten by someone's pet monkey, or something like that. I remember hearing about it when I was a child, and it always stayed with me. It was such a ridiculous way to die, yet he died nevertheless. I've never quite trusted monkeys after that."

"Maybe the monkey is still plotting against the family," speculated Iris. "How long do they live?"

"I suppose it depends on the breed. I could ask Ronnie. It's the sort of thing he would know."

"Well, let's rule out the monkey. For now. In any case, a battle was lost, so when the Greek government is overturned and the king flees, which is an annual occurrence there, from what I can determine, a bunch of former prime ministers, cabinet officials, and generals are arrested and given very quick trials and even quicker sentences. Prince Andrea is one of them."

"Really? What did he do?"

"It's what he didn't do. They said that he refused an order to have his army advance, so he became one more scapegoat in a vast herd."

"What were the consequences?"

"Firing squad for the first lot. But, as you said, there are advantages to being in the aristocracy. Andrea was a cousin to our King George the Fifth, and Alice is Victoria's great-granddaughter. I suppose that King George was still feeling guilt over not saving the tsar and family, so when he's confronted with another cousin facing death by revolution, he intervenes somehow. Prince Andrea is convicted, but instead of inhaling a hail of bullets, he's banished. There's a British cruiser, the HMS *Calypso*, conveniently waiting at the dock. Andrea and his wife are escorted to the boat personally by someone in power, and off they go to Brindisi, making one stop along the way to pick up the children and servants."

"Corfu."

"Exactly. There are several dispatches detailing their journey from that point. They meet the pope, they arrive in Paris, they come to London."

"And Talbot?"

"Not mentioned in a single article about the prince in the *Times*. But this all happened in the last few months of 1922. Andrea is freed by the Greeks in early December, which is why the timing of Talbot's knighthood ten days later is intriguing. I wonder what role he played in this affair."

"Assuming he played any. So, back to the British Museum to read some more newspapers?"

"Not the museum," said Iris. "Have you never done research like this before?"

"Not a lick."

"Then you're in for a treat. We shall be spending a lovely afternoon at the British Library facility for newspapers in Colindale. Ever been there?"

"I never even knew it existed. What fun!"

"You say that now," said Iris.

"What about this former boss of yours? The one Sally mentioned?"

Iris didn't answer.

"I see," said Gwen. "We're back into the war years, aren't we? Someone you worked for in Special Operations, I take it?"

"Someone I'd rather not owe any more favours to," said Iris.

"How many do you owe him now?"

"More than I can repay."

"Will he call in that debt?"

"He tried to," said Iris. "About a month ago."

"What did he want?"

"Me. Working for him again."

"As a—as a what, exactly? Would you be a spy? Do they even use that term?"

"An operative. A vague word for an undefinable business."

"Is that something you want to do?"

"No," said Iris firmly. "And I told him as much."

"Hmm," said Gwen, looking at her closely.

"What? And stop with the voodoo perusal. Do you think I want to work there again?"

"Maybe."

"Why?"

"Because I thought that last little speech in Sally's play about missing the war years might have been based on you."

"Me? I was the other woman."

"You were cast as the other woman," said Gwen. "But Sally knows you better than anyone, and it wouldn't surprise me a whit if he excised a sample of you to insert into Lydia. Not to mention her having an affair with a married man."

"Yes, let's bring that up, shall we? May I also point out that

Lydia was also married in the play, which I never have been, despite the best efforts of several suitors."

"Has Sally ever proposed to you?" asked Gwen.

"Good Lord, no," said Iris. "He's too good a friend to spoil a relationship with marriage."

"You do lead him on an awful lot," said Gwen.

"That's just teasing," said Iris. "We both know it. It's been our way forever."

"Your way, perhaps."

"Why must you take a perfectly lovely evening and spoil it like this?" asked Iris. "If I wanted to be analysed—oh wait. I agreed to that already, didn't I? When is my appointment, again?"

"This Thursday afternoon," said Gwen. "Right after mine. Then drinks to celebrate."

"Unless your doctor discovers that drinking is the root of my problems," said Iris.

"In which case, cake should be an adequate substitute."

"I think I'm going to like psychotherapy," said Iris.

"Getting back to your old boss . . ."

"I don't want to contact him if I can avoid it," said Iris. "To put it in Freudian terms, I want to figure this out myself before I go running off to Daddy for help. Let's see what we can find out on our own."

"'We,'" said Gwen. "You're saying 'we' again. Better."

"It is, isn't it? And here's the cab stand. See you bright and early, partner. Matchmaking in the morning, library in the afternoon."

"So exciting," said Gwen, getting into a waiting cab. "Remember: The world must be peopled!"

"The world must be peopled," echoed Iris, waving as the cab drove off.

The next driver in the queue looked at her expectantly. She opened her bag, assessed her available funds, then exchanged rueful shrugs with him and started walking towards Marylebone.

* * *

Gwen let herself into the Bainbridge house in Kensington as quietly as she could. It was after eleven, and she doubted that anyone would still be awake to greet her. She was mistaken. Agnes, Little Ronnie's governess, came to the top of the main staircase, her dressing gown wrapped tightly over her nightgown.

Gwen's heart gave a quick leap of concern when she saw Agnes waiting up, but Agnes quickly smiled and put a finger to her lips, allaying Gwen's fears.

"It's nothing," she whispered. "He's fine. He's been asleep, but he made me promise I'd wait up for you."

"Why?" Gwen whispered back as she climbed the stairs.

"Come," said Agnes, beckoning.

She led Gwen to her room, which was next to Ronnie's. She went in to retrieve a piece of paper.

"He was very excited that Mummy was going to be in a panto," said Agnes, handing the paper to her.

Gwen held it up to the light. It was a drawing of a woman dressed up as a cat on a stage with red curtains all around her. Triangular black ears jutted out of a yellow mane of hair.

"Is that me?" asked Gwen in delight.

"Yes, Mrs. Bainbridge," said Agnes. "You as Puss in Boots."

"And there's Sir Oswald the Narwhal in the audience," said Gwen, laughing. Sir Oswald was Little Ronnie's creation, a heroic narwhal who battled Nazis on and under the seas. "He's wearing a little top hat!"

"What else would a narwhal wear to the theatre?" replied Agnes.

"Oh, this is wonderful!" said Gwen. "Thank you for waiting up for me."

"You're more than welcome, Mrs. Bainbridge," said Agnes. "He is a treasure. I hope he stays in London for his schooling."

"Ah, so you've heard about that battle," said Gwen.

"Lord Bainbridge wants him to hew to the family tradition and go off to St. Frideswide's. I know its reputation. It's an antiquated institution that propagates antiquated thinking. We need our Ronnie to save the world from his ancestors, not run it aground on their behalf."

"I agree, but don't spout off like that where anyone else can hear you," said Gwen.

"I know better than that," said Agnes. "Good night, Mrs. Bainbridge."

"Good night, Agnes."

The governess glided through her door and closed it silently behind her.

Gwen tiptoed into her son's room and sat by his bed, gazing down at him fondly as he slept. He was so much a copy of his father. She sometimes wondered what of her was in him. She couldn't see any features that echoed any from her reflection, but he was still six. She didn't need to re-create herself; she had herself. Or used to—she was still working on getting that woman back.

And then getting her son back. Lord and Lady Bainbridge had seized legal custody after the news of Gwen's husband's death had sent her to the sanatorium. Her current regimen with the psychiatrist was not merely a medical necessity, but a legal one to complete before she could even begin the process of regaining custody of him. Lady Carolyne and she had reached an uneasy rapprochement recently, but Lord Bainbridge was the rigid one. The anticipated eruption over Little Ronnie's schooling, which Gwen naturally wanted to take place in London, was a daily source of consternation.

Well, that battle would not be fought until His Lordship returned from inspecting the family holdings in East Africa. The autumn term was still a month or so away, Little Ronnie and she were still together, and Sir Oswald would be there to protect her. Even in the theatre.

She yawned, the stimulation of the evening's activities finally draining away. She smoothed the curls away from her son's fore-head and kissed him softly. He murmured something in his sleep that she could not catch, then began breathing deeply again.

She crept out of the room and closed the door.

How do narwhals applaud? she thought drowsily. Such a wonderful picture. Agnes was a darling for staying up to give it to her. Governesses are our national treasures. Our national nannies.

Nannies.

She thought about Philip, fleeing Corfu with his family at the point of a gun. How old would he have been? He was five years older than the princess. In 1922, he would have been one or two.

There must have been a nanny, she thought. No doubt an English one, given Princess Alice's background. And a lady's maid. Probably two, given all those girls to handle.

I wonder what they knew?

Iris was first to the office the next morning. She held up an opened letter with a triumphant grin when her partner came through the door.

"Good news," she announced. "Miss Pelletier has received a proposal from Mr. Carson!"

"Bravo!" said Gwen, hanging up her hat. "That was one of yours, I recall."

"You supported it fully," said Iris. "Do you know what that means? We are only one marriage away from reuniting you with Cecil!"

"Oh, Cecil!" cried Gwen. "How I long to see you again! To slide my legs—Well, there is no way to complete that sentence without committing an impropriety."

"I wonder who will be next. Mr. Trower did not hit it off with Miss Sedgewick."

"No surprise. She wanted him for the frisson of dating an exonerated man. Does he wish to continue through the list?"

"He does, and I would hate to disappoint the rest of the thrill seekers. There may be one or two amongst them who will work out."

"Do you think so?"

"Miss Conyers might be a good fit for him."

"Hmm."

"You don't like Miss Conyers?"

"Not for our Mr. Trower. Miss Donnelly, on the other hand—"

"Care to make a small wager on who gets him?"

"We promised that we wouldn't bet on a client's success or lack thereof," said Gwen.

"We did," remembered Iris. "A sound policy, now that I consider it. Best get back to work."

"Yes," said Gwen. "Oh, before we do, I must show you this."

She carefully unrolled Little Ronnie's picture and handed it to Iris, who held it to the window and examined it critically.

"That is you in a cat costume being watched by a narwhal in a top hat," she said. "This is quite nice. Your son is going through a surrealist phase. I like it much better than his early cubist work which, frankly, I found derivative. Talented boy."

"Thank you," said Gwen.

"When do I get to meet him?" asked Iris.

"Oh," said Gwen in surprise. "You haven't, have you?"

"Haven't met your son, haven't been to your house, haven't met your in-laws."

"I haven't exactly been in a position to have people over," said Gwen. "I still live there at the sufferance of the Bainbridges."

"And they wouldn't want me sullying their doorstep," said Iris.

"You wouldn't like them, anyway."

"Probably not. You don't like them, and you're an astute judge of character. But I would love to meet your son. I adore children. In theory. We could talk about art and aquatic mammals and other things beginning with 'A.'"

"I'll see if I can pry him away for a visit to Mummy's office," said Gwen. "Would that be acceptable?"

"Entirely."

She grabbed her half of the daily correspondence and opened the top letter. The two worked in silence for a few minutes.

"What sort of wager did you have in mind?" asked Gwen.

"Tuppence on Conyers," said Iris.

"Same on Donnelly," said Gwen.

"Done," said Iris.

They broke for a light lunch, then closed the office for the afternoon.

"If we had a secretary, we could do this without guilt," said Gwen as she hung up the "Closed" sign. "We could waltz out the door, calling over our shoulders to the prim and efficient Miss Betsy—"

"Miss Betsy?"

"For the want of a real name. 'Mind the store, Betsy,' we'd call out. 'We're off to investigate a prince.'"

"And she would say, 'Again?' and then resume her typing," said Iris. "Betsy sounds ideal. We should hire her immediately."

"Maybe we could find out from Sally who typed his script," said Gwen. "It was neat and error-free, I noticed, and I was using the third or fourth carbon."

"Good thought," said Iris as they reached the street. "Now, on to Colindale! You can read my notes on the train."

An hour later, they walked towards the entrance to the British Library's newspaper repository.

"It's enormous!" exclaimed Gwen.

"Newspapers take up a lot of space over the years," said Iris. "And there are an awful lot of them. Every town has one."

Gwen stopped suddenly, looking off to one side. The burnt ruins of a large building lay beyond a temporary fence.

"They bombed a library?" she asked in shock.

"Errant hit," said Iris. "There are factories nearby. Or someone jettisoned their bombs while fleeing. It doesn't matter much the reason. The records and times of hundreds of places over hundreds of years were destroyed, mostly small-town and Irish papers. It's not exactly the burning of the Library of Alexandria, but a terrible loss nevertheless."

"Birth announcements, weddings, ribbon-cutting ceremonies, all gone," said Gwen sadly. "All of those people existed once."

"Well, the London papers survived, so let's go find our Mr. Talbot," said Iris.

"Assuming he's not from a small town or Ireland," said Gwen.

Iris led her to a reading room with large windows at the upper levels and shelf after shelf of tall bound volumes. There were several desks with large, flat, slanted tops, almost like easels, but solid.

"You take the *Times* index," said Iris, pointing to one section of the shelves. "I'm switching to the *Daily Express*. We'll grab a couple of plinths—"

"A couple of what?"

"Plinths. Those reading desks."

"They're called plinths? I always thought that was something vaguely architectural."

"A plinth is a thing upon which you can place another thing," said Iris. "Like one of those massive bound indices, or the massive bound volumes of newspapers they will bring us after we use the massive bound indices."

"Right," said Gwen, looking at them dubiously. "I do hope there are some muscular bearers to bring out the massive bound thingies. So I'm on Talbot patrol. Where do I start?"

"Begin at the ending," Iris said, very gravely, "and go on till you come to the beginning: then stop."

"Curiouser and curiouser," said Gwen, gazing along the dates until she found the most recent volume.

She pulled it out and rested it on a plinth, then began flipping through it until she got to the T's.

"Nothing," she said.

"You don't have to tell me that for every single one," said Iris, scanning the *Daily Express*.

"Sorry. Oh!"

"What?"

"This just covers part of the year. So I should continue with the other parts?"

"Yes," said Iris wearily.

This is going to be a very long afternoon at this rate, she thought irritably. What was I thinking, letting an amateur—

"Found him!" crowed Gwen. "That was easy."

Iris stared at her with a mix of astonishment and chagrin.

"Well?" she asked.

"I am now giving up any hope of interviewing the man," said Gwen.

"Why is that?"

"I've found his death notice. And his funeral. Both in April of last year."

"I was afraid that would be the case," said Iris, coming over to look at the spot where Gwen was pointing.

"Really? Why?"

"The anonymous letter. 'I know what he knew.' It put him in the past tense."

"Well, he's been put there on a permanent basis, it appears," said Gwen. "What do I do now?"

"Write down the dates on a call slip and take it to the desk. Someone will fetch that volume for you."

"A muscular bearer!"

"We can only hope."

Gwen trotted off, looking supremely pleased with herself.

Iris located the same information in the *Daily Express*, but elected to travel back into the past, searching for any other reference she could find. Somewhere in 1937, Gwen returned, staggering under the bulk of a thick, *Times*-sized book.

"I've joined the muscular bearers union," she gasped, lowering the book carefully onto the plinth. "It took ages for it to arrive from the mysterious bowels of the building. The woman who fetched it was eighty-seven and used a rolling cart, which I think is cheating."

"Let's take a look at our dead man, shall we?"

Gwen sat at the desk and flipped through the pages.

"Be gentle," urged Iris. "Newspaper is delicate."

"There's the notice," said Gwen. "Eighteenth of April 1945. 'Commander Sir Gerald Talbot, KCVO, CMG, OBE, RNVR (retired) died at Felixstowe yesterday.' Where's Felixstowe?"

"On the Channel, out past Ipswich. There's a port there."

"Sounds like a dreary place to die."

"Not if you were Royal Navy. I wonder if he was still doing his bit for the Crown then. What else does it say?"

"Um, born August 1881, so he was sixty-three. Youngest son of late Lieutenant-Colonel G. F. Talbot. Cheltenham, Caius College—"

"A Cambridge lad!" cheered Iris.

"RNVR in the last war, British Naval Attaché in Athens 1917 to 1920—Ah, here's a new item. Director of the London and North Eastern Railway Company. Didn't Sally say he had a locomotive tie pin?"

"He did. Anything else?"

"Married Hélène, widow of Captain C. Labouchere, French army, in 1920. He married a French war widow. *Trés gallant!* One daughter, not named here. And that's it."

"Fairly skeletal. Let's see who showed up at the memorial."

Gwen flipped through to the twenty-seventh of April.

"Here it is," she said. "Held at St. Martin-in-the-Fields. Nice choice. Reverend Loveday himself officiated."

"I've always liked St. M's," said Iris. "Nell Gwyn's buried there. Patron saint of mistresses."

"That last part isn't true," said Gwen.

"It should be," said Iris, resting her chin on Gwen's shoulder to get a better look at the article.

"My, look at all the knights and ladies who attended," said Gwen.

"And look at all the Greeks," pointed out Iris. "'The King of the Hellenes was represented . . . the Greek Chargé d'Affaires . . . Sir John Stavriki, Mr. Jean Romanos, Mr. P. Argenis, Mr. C. Torgos, Mr. D. Caclamenos, and other well-known members of the Greek Colony in London.'"

"But he hadn't been stationed in Greece since 1920," said Gwen. "And he was only a naval attaché when he was. Why was he still so popular with the Greeks twenty-five years later?"

"Why, indeed? It does sound like he's our man."

"Bad luck about his current lack of existence," said Gwen.

"Are you saying we've reached a dead end?"

"I was going to, but now I can't. What do we do now?"

"Keep looking," said Iris. "There may be more."

It was Iris who found it, nearly an hour later, poring through back issues of the *Daily Express* and sneezing profusely.

"Here it is," she said, her eyes streaming. "Blast the *Times* and their reticence. I should have looked in the *Daily Express* from the start."

"What did you find?"

"According to them, Talbot was in Paris when the Greek ministers and generals were arrested. He gets the word from Lord Curzon to go to Lausanne, then received instructions to head to Athens. Gets there too late to stop the first batch of executions, but in time to save Prince Andrea. He even arranged for the Minister of War himself to accompany them to the port in case there was anyone thinking of taking a potshot at the prince."

"We have our Talbot," said Gwen. "That doesn't sound very covert, landing himself in the papers like that."

"His cover wasn't blown until after he completed the mission," said Iris. "This story came out in late December, after he had already received the knighthood. Maybe that was his reward—being allowed to leave the Service, covered in glory."

"He traveled with the family from Greece?"

"Apparently."

"Then he would have been at Corfu when they picked up the children," said Gwen. "I wonder what he found there. I wonder if he kept it."

"Something someone thinks they can use for blackmail," said Iris. "Let's get back outside. I need some air."

They returned their volumes to the front desk and walked outside. Without saying anything, they wandered over to the charred wreckage of the bomb site.

"Paper burns," observed Iris gloomily. "When it survives, it holds information. Secrets. The questions are, what are we looking for, and where is it?"

"That doesn't narrow things down much," said Gwen.

"On the contrary—we've narrowed them down from everything in the world to one man's life."

"Which ended more than a year ago."

"But there are others who knew him. A widow. A daughter. Friends."

"Titled friends."

"Greek friends."

"'The King of the Hellenes was represented,'" quoted Gwen. "Talbot hadn't been involved in Greek affairs since he was exposed and knighted, yet over two decades later, the 'King of the Hellenes,' who fled like a Greek king does when there's trouble, cares enough to send a representative to his funeral. Gratitude for saving his uncle?"

"Perhaps," said Iris. "What else would you suggest?"

"The king in exile lives in London," said Gwen. "My mother-in-law came home from a party sniffing about seeing him with his current mistress."

"She disapproves of mistresses?"

"She disapproves of Greeks," said Gwen. "Along with Italians, Turks— Well, the list is very long. But what I am wondering is if this has something to do with the Greek throne. Aren't they considering restoring him?"

"There is supposed to be some sort of vote in September," said Iris.

"And how far down the line of succession is Prince Philip, again? Fourth? Or was it fifth?"

"Let me count," said Iris, flipping open her notebook. "King George the Second is his first cousin. George has a younger brother who has a son—that's three—then there's an uncle with a son, making five, except he married a divorcée, so he's out of the running, which means Philip is fifth."

"No women in line?"

"Plenty of women. The Greeks don't count women."

"And they claim to be civilised," sniffed Gwen. "Well, it's a long shot, but what if this ties into the Greek royal family? Marrying one of theirs to our heir apparent gives the monarchists legitimacy for this referendum."

"Then disgracing Philip could be a motive for the opposition," continued Iris. "Possible. So the opposition in this case would be the Leftists."

"Have we stumbled upon an international Communist plot of some kind? That would be beyond our abilities to fight. Well, mine, at least. You, no doubt, could take Stalin on single-handed."

"Not my type," said Iris. "I don't like his mustache. So, people close to Talbot and close to Prince Andrea."

"There's a widow apiece."

"We can't talk to Princess Alice," said Iris. "Those are toes we would not be authorised to step upon. The Widow Talbot, on the other hand, might be promising."

"Unless she's gone back to France. What about people who were in Corfu? The prince traveled with a small retinue of servants. And what was the name of that ship, again?"

"The HMS *Calypso*," said Iris. "Maybe the captain's still around. Know anyone with nautical clout?"

"I have a cousin who is some form of admiral," said Gwen. "Rear or vice, I forget which. They both sound horrid, when you think about it. I'll give him a ring."

"We have a plan, then," said Iris. "I call this a good day's work. Shall we—"

She stopped when she turned and saw Gwen looking at her sternly.

"What?" she asked.

"You're leaving out the most obvious avenue," said Gwen. "Titled friends. Greek friends. And—"

"No," said Iris.

"Spy friends," finished Gwen.

"I told you—"

"We have a job to do, and not much time in which to complete it," said Gwen. "If he was still in the spy game, then there should be other players who knew about it. You have access to them."

"Not as much as you think," said Iris.

"Still more than me," persisted Gwen. "They would have the most interesting scuttlebutt. If Talbot did turn up something in Corfu, don't you think he would report it back to his masters?"

"Unless he kept it for himself. A little side benefit to go with the knighthood."

"Ah," said Gwen thoughtfully. "Maybe that's been the source of his business success all these years. Funded through the sale of his silence. And now he's as silent as the grave."

"Only his secrets didn't die with him," said Iris.

"We still don't have proof of any of this," said Gwen.

"It's out there. Somewhere. I'm sure of it."

"Then let's go find it. Who was Calypso again?"

"A nymph. She fell in love with Odysseus and kept him on her island for seven years."

"Another woman in love with a married man," said Gwen. "I take it he left her in the end."

"He did," said Iris. "The gods intervened, and she had to let him go. She made him a raft, and off he went."

"What happened to her?"

"Homer didn't say. Maybe she's still on that island, hoping he'll come back. But I think she must have moved on by now."

"Good for her," said Gwen. "We should send her a flyer. We should be able to find a good husband for a raft-building nymph."

CHAPTER 5

By the time Iris reached her flat, the sniffles she had obtained in Colindale had escalated into a full-blown cold. She closed the door and put the kettle on, then hauled out a hankie and blew her nose loudly enough to summon the dead.

As the echoes faded and her ears returned to a partially clogged state, she became aware of a ringing that wasn't from an internal source. She staggered over to her telephone and picked up the handset.

"Hello," she said.

"'Allo, Mary Elizabeth McTague," came a man's voice.

She grinned in spite of her misery.

"'Allo, Archie," she replied, slipping into an East End accent.

"Now, no need to put on the act with me," he said.

"You called me Mary Elizabeth McTague," she said. "That's 'ow she talks, innit?"

"Yeah, let me talk to Sparks, then."

"Sparks here, Archie," said Iris, switching to her own voice. "How are you?"

"I find myself free for the evening," he said. "I was wondering if you'd be interested in stepping out."

"I'd love to," said Iris, "but my sinuses are under siege. I wouldn't be much for company, and I suspect I look all red and blotchy."

"Oh dear, oh dear," he said. "'Ave you eaten yet?"

"I have not. I just came back from the library."

"Sounds exhausting. But I'm a slow reader."

"Now who's putting on an act? How is it that you're free to-night, an established gang-leader like yourself? Shouldn't you be out leading the gang? Pilfering and pillaging and the like?"

"The benefit of leading the gang is I get to delegate the larcenies to my 'umble employees," said Archie. "So if I feel like taking the night off, 'oos to say otherwise?"

"Far be it from me to criticise," said Iris. "Unfortunately, I must confine myself to quarters and inhale steam. Thanks for thinking of me."

"You know I'm a sucker for damsels in distress," said Archie. "You 'old tight, old girl. Our planes are in the air."

"Planes? What planes?" asked Iris, but the connection had been severed.

She removed her makeup, then put a fresh kettle on. She picked up her copy of *The Fifth Man*, the latest Manning Coles book, kicked her shoes off, and curled up on the couch. She knew Cyril Coles, who was half the writing team behind the books, from his work for British Intelligence during the war. The books were nonsensical espionage adventures, but light reading with enough genuine pieces of spycraft scattered throughout to keep her from dismissing them out of hand. She had just got to a minor revelation when there was a knock on her door.

"Planes," she said to herself.

She got up and padded over to peer through the peephole. A grinning Archie stood in the hallway.

"What on earth?" she exclaimed as she opened the door.

"'Ome remedies," he said, holding up a pair of paper bags. "May I come in?"

"You may," she said, stepping aside.

Archie Spelling had a prizefighter's build and a heartbreaker's face, marred only by a nose that had been broken by both left-and right-handed punches, if its topography was anything to go by. Iris never asked what happened to the providers of the punches. Knowing Archie, he either bought them a drink after or left them in bloody piles in some alleyway. Possibly both.

There was something odd about him, she thought. Wait—

"You're wearing a suit!" she said.

"I always wear a suit," he said.

"No, a normal suit. You're not spivved up."

Indeed, he was clad in a light gray three-piece, with a narrow tie and a proper fedora. She was used to seeing him in something loud, with chalk stripes and a kipper tie. But now he could pass for a banker, albeit one with a history of getting his nose broken.

"Are you disappointed?" he asked, spinning like a model.

"I don't know," she said, looking at him critically. "You've shrunk to life size all of a sudden."

"I'm undercover," he said, putting his bags down on the tea table. "Can't stroll into Marylebone looking like I do in Shadwell. Every copper in the vicinity would be dogging me 'eels. So, remedy number one: Chicken curry, still 'ot, direct from Brick Lane."

"Which place?"

"The 'industani one on the corner."

"Ah. They're decent."

"This should clear those sinuses in no time," he said, pulling out a pair of cardboard containers.

"And remedy number two?" she asked, fetching a pair of soup bowls, spoons, and a ladle from her cupboard.

"The old reliable," he said, producing a bottle of whisky from the second bag with a magician's flourish.

"My goodness, did you raid your personal supplies for little old me?" she asked.

"My supplies 'ave been previously raided from elsewhere, so no loss," he said, pouring some into her tea. "It's for a good cause. Feed a cold, intoxicate a fever, I always say."

"You're a regular Florence Nightingale," she said, sitting on her sofa and ladling the curry into the bowls. "Will you be having a hot toddy as well, or will you take yours neat?"

"Neat."

She found a clean tumbler, took the bottle, and poured him a healthy dose.

"You're a generous bartender," he observed.

"For medicinal purposes," she said, raising her now loaded teacup. "I don't want to infect my guardian angel."

He clinked his tumbler against her cup. She gulped the tea down gratefully, the combination soothing the back of her throat.

"Let me administer the one-two punch," she said, digging into the curry.

The aromatics attacked her sinuses on two fronts, and she felt the drainage begin.

"Lovely," she sighed when they were done. "Thank you, Archie."

"You're very welcome. 'Ow goes matchmaking with the nephew?"

"Bernie is a quiet, well-behaved young man," said Iris. "It's hard to believe he's related to you."

"'E takes after me sister's 'usband," he said. "She married up. It's the quiet that does 'im in. 'E needs a noisy woman to rouse 'im."

"And you've just given me an idea," said Iris. "We've recently acquired a very noisy woman. Maybe opposites will attract."

"'Ow noisy?"

"On a scale of one to *BOOM!*, she breaks the scale," said Iris.

"Worth doing just to 'ear 'im tell the story after. Funny, I thought you'd be setting 'im up with one of them bookish types. You know, one of them smart girls what never gave me the time of day."

"What do you think I am?" she said, holding up her book.

"You are a puzzle," he said. "University girl like you, and 'ere I am, a proud graduate of the School of 'Ard Knocks. It's a wonder that we found each other."

"How did you know where to find me, by the way?" she asked, looking at him sternly. "I've never given you my address, and the flat and telephone are not under my name. Did you follow me?"

"I 'ave the feeling that if I 'ad, you would 'ave made me in no time," Archie laughed. "No, I did it the old-fashioned way. After our last night out, I got you a cab."

"Ah, the light dawns. He was no ordinary cabdriver."

"'E was a very ordinary cabdriver and, as such, eminently susceptible to noting your address in exchange for a small remuneration."

"And you did this to check me out?"

"After you played me so neatly, I wanted to make sure you weren't in no long game," admitted Archie.

"And what did you find out?"

"You've lived behind doors I can't open," said Archie, sipping his whisky. "I take it you 'ad an interesting war." He tapped the Coles book on the table. "You like spies, eh?" he said.

"I was a file clerk, nothing more," she said.

"Right," he replied. "A file clerk what infiltrates criminal enterprises and solves murders in 'er spare time."

"A girl needs a hobby," she said. "Anyhow, that was a one-time thing for a client."

"Well, you did right by me in the end," he said. "Now, what's the story with the bloke who 'as the lease for this place?"

"An ex," said Iris. "Let's call him by his rightful name. We were lovers."

"Married fellow."

"Yes."

"Makes no difference to me," said Archie, shrugging.

"It did enough for you to check me out. As well as my ex."

"Now, 'e's a puzzle and an 'alf," said Archie. "Flat's not under 'is real name, and I can't find out nothing about 'im."

"I recommend you don't try," said Iris. "The search will draw unnecessary attention."

"Yeah, I thought that might be the case," said Archie. "But 'e's definitely an ex?"

"The bridges are burned, the earth salted."

"Good," said Archie.

"Are you intending to make advances?" asked Iris, giving him a sidelong glance.

"What? To a woman in your condition? I don't want to catch your bloody cold."

Iris burst into laughter.

"Oh dear, I've got toddy up my nose," she gasped, grabbing her handkerchief.

"That should 'elp clear it," said Archie.

"So, now that you've vetted me, what are you going to do?" she asked.

"It's an interesting situation," said Archie, suddenly serious. "I like you, Sparks. I'm used to East End climbers and the odd upper-class girl out on a lark, but you're different. The problem is my profession. It's not one that lends itself to stability, if you know what I mean."

"I do, Archie," said Iris. "Stability has never been one of my strengths, either."

"So, the 'ouse in the country and the quiet life aren't likely to be in the cards for either of us, are they?"

"What if you got out of the game?"

"Still 'ave to eat, dun' I? And I'm surprisingly unqualified to make an honest living."

"I'm sure a man of your talents could figure something out."

"Not as easy as you think, once you get a few marks on your chit," said Archie. "Any'ow, this is all supposing you'd be along for the ride. We've 'ad two dates, far from the madding crowd."

"Three, now," said Iris, holding up her cup in salute.

"You count this as a date?"

"I do. One of the better ones I've had, to tell the truth."

"Is that a fact?" asked Archie, pleased. "Well, in any case, it's too early to be talking like this. But I like talking like this, and I ain't never talked like this to anyone before. So, what I wanted to know was if the road is clear."

"The road is clear, Archie. Where it goes—"

"Nobody knows," he concluded. "But we could drive along for a while and see what's around the next bend."

"Yes," said Iris. "I think we could."

"Well, then my work 'ere is done," said Archie, rising to his feet and putting on his fedora. "I'd kiss you good night, but you're all red and blotchy."

She got to her feet, pulled his head down to her level, and kissed his cheek.

"I'm not wearing lipstick," she said, "so you don't need to wipe anything off. Unless it's germs."

"I wash me face with carbolic soap at least every other week," he said. "Feel better, Sparks. I'll ring you up when larceny season 'its another lull."

"Good night, Archie."

She closed the door after him, then listened to his footsteps recede down the hallway.

I'm dating a gangster, she thought. That can only go well.

Gwen was on the telephone when Iris arrived at the office the next morning.

"And after that?" she was saying, jotting something down on

her notepad. "I see. No, I know where that is. I've taken Little Ronnie to the museum. That was Greenwich eight-three-nine-nine? Got it. You've been a tremendous help, Squiffy. Thanks so much, and we'll see you at Melissa's wedding. Goodbye."

"'Squiffy'?" asked Iris as she sat behind her desk.

Her cold was improving, thanks to Archie's prescriptions. She had taken another dose of the bottled one before coming to work.

"That's Rear Admiral Squiffy to you," said Gwen. "People started calling him Squiffy because he spent so much time at sea that he'd walk like a drunk man for the first few days back until he got his land legs again."

"And what did Rear Admiral Squiffy tell you?"

"That the captain of the *Calypso* when they rescued Prince Andrea was one Herbert Buchanan-Wollaston."

"I can almost hear you pronouncing the hyphen. And is Captain Buchanan-Wollaston still alive?"

"Alive, a vice admiral since thirty-two, retired and living in Greenwich near the National Maritime Museum. He should be in his late sixties by now."

"How long did he command the *Calypso*?"

"That's an interesting thing. He took command in September of twenty-one, and was replaced in December of twenty-two."

"December of twenty-two? Right after delivering the prince and family to Brindisi?"

"Apparently so."

"What ship did he go to next?"

"No ship at all for four years. A series of cushy desk jobs and training courses."

"That is interesting," said Iris.

"Yes," said Gwen. "The two principal actors involved in spiriting the family away from danger were both rewarded with safer lives."

"Almost as if they were bought off," said Iris. "That's speculation, of course. Very good. How do you want to play this?"

"'Play'?"

"Well, we can't just barge in on a naval officer and ask about an operation from twenty-four years in the past. Let's see." She rummaged through her bag. "Aha!" she said, pulling out a card and holding it up. "My press pass. We could pretend to be reporters—"

"Is that real?" asked Gwen.

"Real enough," said Iris. "Jimmy made it for me."

"Jimmy the Scribe? I thought he had gone straight."

"This was from during the war. I can't—"

"Don't bother," said Gwen. "But it's the sort of thing a suspicious man might check on. We would do better sticking closer to our actual selves."

"Fine," said Iris. "You pretend to be you, only more so. Give me that number, please."

She dialed it, then waited. A muffled male voice answered.

"Hello," she said in a crisp, efficient tone. "Vice Admiral Buchanan-Wollaston, please. It is? Please hold for Mrs. Bainbridge." She paused for a moment, then handed the receiver to Gwen.

"Hello, Vice Admiral," said Gwen. "This is Mrs. Gwendolyn Bainbridge, Lord Bainbridge's daughter-in-law. Yes, that Lord Bainbridge. Perhaps you've fired a few of his shells during your career. You have? And they exploded properly? I'll be very sure to tell him. He'll be so pleased. Now, Vice Admiral, to the purpose. My ladies club is putting together a series of lectures on the subject of naval warfare during the Great War. Yes, we still call it that. Yes, they are quite the bloodthirsty bunch, especially around teatime. I was wondering if you wouldn't mind my dropping by to speak to you about the possibility. How is this afternoon? Say, three thirty? Or should I say seven bells? Splendid. My secretary will accompany me, if that would be suitable. Very good. We shall see you then. Good day."

She hung up.

"You realise you've doomed us to a detailed recounting of every naval battle he was in," complained Iris.

"We can't just jump into the royal rescue," said Gwen.

"We could try," said Iris. "Fine, I'll pretend to look interested. Feigning interest in men is the best way to get them to talk. Is he married?"

"I believe so."

"Then it will be safe for you to flirt with him. That's the other best way of getting men to talk."

"You're better at flirting."

"I am but a mere secretary," said Iris meekly. "It would not be my place to do so, Mum."

"Oh, for heaven's sake," sighed Gwen. "Fine. I'll flirt, you feign, and together we'll find out what we can. Shall we get some work done until then?"

"Let's. So, I have a proposal for Miss Ack-Ack."

"We must not give our clients nicknames, remember? Although I do like that one. Who is your candidate?"

"Bernie Alderton."

"Archie's nephew," said Gwen, considering. "Interesting. A quiet egg and a noisy bird. She'd consider him a challenge. I like it. Well done."

"Thank you."

"How are things with Archie?"

"Fine," said Iris noncommittally.

"Only fine? You haven't added 'dandy' to the mix yet?"

"Fine and dandy, sugar candy," said Iris, picking up her pile of letters and opening them.

"And that's all you are going to say?"

"All right, you've bullied it out of me!" said Iris, slamming her correspondence down on the desk. "We have secretly married. I am going to run half the gang. And I am with child."

"My God, Iris!" exclaimed Gwen in horror.

"Triplets, in fact," continued Iris. "The middle one seems to be the brute, but it's difficult to sort out. They do keep moving about in there. It's like a shell game."

"Beast."

"Busybody."

"I'm concerned. Can't you see that?"

"It's only been three dates."

"Three? It was two as of yesterday."

"He came over last night," said Iris. "I was sneezing and blue. He brought curry for the one and whisky for the other."

"And after?"

"And after, he left. In between, he was the perfect gentleman."

"You've had the most well-behaved courtship of your life with a gangster," said Gwen.

"I know," said Iris. "I've gone through the mirror into Looking-Glass Land. But it's still early. Plenty of time for it to go horribly wrong."

They took the train to Greenwich in the afternoon. Gwen consulted her directions when they emerged from the station.

"It should be north, towards the river," she said. "We're early."

"We should have come at noon," said Iris. "We could have swung by the Royal Observatory and set our watches on the meridian."

The architecture evolved from Georgian to Victorian as they walked from the station. They emerged from the curved rows of houses and passed the Royal Observatory. Iris carried a small brown leather camera case at her side.

"Where are we going?" she asked.

"He lives near the Royal Naval College. He lectures there."

"War stories and he's a lecturer," grumbled Iris. "There had better be tea. There's the maritime museum. Have you taken Little Ronnie there yet?"

"Of course. It's part of every child's adventures. I really must take him again soon. Maybe Saturday—no, that won't do."

"Why not?"

"He will be attending a birthday party."

"That should be jolly for you."

"I was not invited."

"Really? Snubbed by a six-year-old?"

"By his mother. My psychiatric situation is known in our circles. She doesn't want me around her children."

"Why? Is she afraid you'll suddenly strip to your knickers and howl at the moon?"

"That would be educational for the children, wouldn't it? Yes, something like that. So I've decided not to press the issue with my mother-in-law. Not while things are on the mend."

"I'd go," said Iris.

"I know," said Gwen. "But I'm not you. And you're not Ronnie's mother. I'll choose my own battles, and a child's birthday party is not one of them, thank you. Here's the address. Oh, how pretty!"

Unlike in the center of Greenwich, the homes here were separated. The Buchanan-Wollastons owned a two-storey wooden house that possessed both a front porch and a small balcony, both overlooking the Thames. It was painted sea-green, with light blue-green shutters and railings. There was a pair of telescopes mounted on the balcony, one pointed out, the other up.

"He must be both a stargazer and a ship spotter," said Gwen.

"Or a connoisseur of bathing beauties," said Iris, glancing towards the Thames.

Indeed, a number of people were crowded onto a narrow strip of open shore, mostly mothers with small children, but with a scattering of young women taking in the sun. Gwen watched wistfully as a pack of small boys, younger even than her own, splashed about the edges of the water with their trousers rolled up as high as they could get them. Off to the right, a training ship from the Royal Naval College, covered with young cadets swarming about under the barked orders of their instructors, was carefully leaving its dock.

"I can see why he picked this spot to retire," said Gwen.

"Retire?" boomed a voice from behind them. "Not a bit of it!"

They turned to see a man in full dress naval regalia standing at the top of the steps leading to the porch. His beard was brown with streaks of gray, and so precisely trimmed that a sounding taken at any given point would have revealed a uniform depth to a thousandth of an inch. His bearing was straight as a mainmast, and as they approached, he removed his cap with a practiced flourish that had an old-fashioned gallantry to it.

"How do you do, Admiral Buchanan-Wollaston," said Mrs. Bainbridge. "I am Mrs. Gwendolyn Bainbridge. This is Miss Sparks, my secretary. Request permission to come aboard, sir."

"Permission granted," said Buchanan-Wollaston.

"One moment, if you please, sir," said Sparks, removing her Leica from her camera bag. "Could you put your cap back on for a moment? Perfect! Thank you, sir."

"My pleasure." Buchanan-Wollaston beamed. "May I invite you into my humble abode, ladies?"

He held the door as they entered, then followed them inside.

The two women glanced around the parlour, where a decorative civil war had taken place. Model sailing vessels fought for surface space with some amateurish attempts at pottery. The walls were covered with framed photographs of ships from the Royal Navy bumping up against needlepoint samplers with religious and nautical texts for their subjects. "HOME IS THE SAILOR, HOME FROM THE SEA," proclaimed one, while from across the room "THEY THAT GO DOWN TO THE SEA IN SHIPS, THAT DO BUSINESS IN GREAT WATERS; THESE SEE THE

WORKS OF THE LORD, AND HIS WONDERS IN THE DEEP" met their eye.

"'For he commandeth, and raiseth the stormy wind, which lifteth up the waves thereof,'" said Mrs. Bainbridge, finishing the quote. "That's from Psalms, isn't it?"

"It is indeed, Mrs. Bainbridge," said Buchanan-Wollaston. "Sounds like you could give my wife a run for her money."

"Alas, my needlepoint is inadequate for the task," said Mrs. Bainbridge. "Else I would be doing nothing more than creating such nautical inspirations. Ah, what lovely model ships! Am I correct in guessing that they are your work?"

"They are," said Buchanan-Wollaston, puffing up with pride as Mrs. Bainbridge examined a group of miniature brigs and schooners, some defended with arrays of tiny cannon. "Each was a vessel with the British navy two centuries ago. I copied the designs from paintings at the museum. Have you been there yet?"

"Not today," said Mrs. Bainbridge. "But it is a frequent stop for my son and me. I do believe the navy is in his future."

"How old is the lad?"

"Six. Too young as yet."

"Under the current regulations, certainly," he said. "Back in the days of the sailing ships, he could have begun as a cabin boy."

"How sad that these opportunities are no longer provided to today's youths," said Mrs. Bainbridge.

"So true, Mrs. Bainbridge," agreed Buchanan-Wollaston. "I myself signed up with the navy when I was fourteen, and I've never left it."

"Fourteen!" exclaimed Mrs. Bainbridge. "My goodness! And you have risen so far! I understand that you were made captain in 1917."

"Yes, of the *Fox*. I was the exec of the *Cornwall* before that. I was mentioned in dispatches for my conduct during the Battle of the Falklands, so naturally, I was on the list for promotion."

"The ladies will certainly want to hear about that," said Mrs. Bainbridge.

"Is that the *Fox* there?" asked Sparks, looking at one of the framed photographs.

"It is, young lady," he said. "Spent my command with her in the Red Sea. Not much of a war there at the time."

"Then came the *Caesar*," continued Mrs. Bainbridge, looking at her notebook.

"Depot ship," said Buchanan-Wollaston. "A relic. Couldn't manage nine knots if a typhoon was blowing up her . . . stern. Couldn't tell you how happy I was when they told me to bring her in to be scrapped."

"And then the *Calypso*," said Mrs. Bainbridge. "This was after the war, if I'm not mistaken."

"Well after," said Buchanan-Wollaston. "I took her over in twenty-one."

"Wait, did you say the *Calypso*?" asked Sparks, suddenly breathless with excitement.

"Yes."

"And you were her captain in 1921?"

"I was."

"Were you, by any chance, still her captain in 1922?"

"Yes, until the end of the year. Why?"

"Oh, Mrs. Bainbridge," exclaimed Sparks. "This is too wonderful!"

"What is it, Miss Sparks?"

"Why, he was the captain who rescued Prince Philip!"

"Were you?" asked Mrs. Bainbridge, rounding on the man.

"You mean Prince Andrea?" he asked. "The Greek chappie?"

"Yes, but his son as well!" said Sparks. "The baby prince!"

"But this is so exciting," burbled Mrs. Bainbridge. "Oh, we must hear that story at once!"

"But don't you want to know about the Battle of the Falklands?" he protested weakly.

"Oh, that too, of course," said Mrs. Bainbridge. "But the ladies are all atwitter about Prince Philip. Rumour has it that he may be the one to capture our own sweet Princess Elizabeth. And she has you to thank!"

"She does?" he said, bewildered. "I had no idea."

"Come, let's sit and hear all about it," said Mrs. Bainbridge, slipping her arm into his. "It's all so terribly romantic and heroic. I want to know simply everything."

"There's not all that much to say," he said.

"Then we won't be taking up much of your time hearing it," said Mrs. Bainbridge. "Where shall we sit?"

"I took the liberty of setting tea out on the deck," he said, recovering his manners. "Shall we go up top?"

"Let's. But first, could we get a picture of you by your models? You don't smoke a pipe by any chance, do you? You do! I adore a man with a pipe. Now, stand there—lovely! Did you get that, Miss Sparks?"

"I did, Mrs. Bainbridge."

"Then let's go have that tea, shall we?"

"This way, ladies," he said, indicating the stairs.

Hot tea out of doors in July, Mrs. Bainbridge thought in dismay when they got there, but the china was charming and the biscuits were yummy.

"Did you bring these back from your travels?" she asked, holding up a cup with a delicate floral pattern.

"Oh no." He laughed. "The missus bought them in a shop in Chelsea. Come on, lads! Put your backs into it!"

They turned to see the objects of his attention, a team of cadets wrestling a mock-up of an antiaircraft gun into position on the training ship. Mrs. Bainbridge wouldn't have thought they could hear him from that distance, but one of them looked up and waved, then nudged his fellows, who saw the two women with the vice admiral and commenced waving en masse. The two women waved back and blew kisses, which encouraged further waving by the young men until their instructors railed at them to get back to their task.

"What handsome young men!" said Mrs. Bainbridge.

"They are indeed, Mrs. Bainbridge," said Sparks. "A credit to the navy."

"Now, tell us about the thrilling rescue of the Greek royals," said Mrs. Bainbridge.

"There wasn't all that much to it," said Buchanan-Wollaston. "We were patrolling in the eastern Mediterranean when I received orders to make all speed to Phaleron Bay, no reasons given, no questions asked. We did. Next thing I know, a Greek launch motors up by us. A fellow with an enormous bald head comes up the ladder. I recognised him immediately. His name was Talbot. Gerald Talbot. He had been the naval attaché in Greece, but his term there was over, so I had no idea what he was doing in Athens. Turns out, he had made some kind of a deal for the prince's life. He handed me my orders, and suddenly a light cruiser in the British navy became a private yacht for a pair of royal Greeks."

"Were they with this Talbot fellow?" asked Mrs. Bainbridge.

"They were. Prince Andrea came up the ladder like a proper sailor, but she was terrified. Had to send down some men to help her up. When she came on board—well, she was beautiful. Ever seen her?"

"Only photographs," said Mrs. Bainbridge.

"She looked like something out of a painting from another century. Gainsborough or one of those fellows. Lit from within, like a great lady ought to be. She greeted me quite graciously once we finally got her on deck. She had a way of staring at you quite intensely when you talked. Found out after she was deaf, but could read lips in four languages. Then up comes a valet and a lady's maid—with luggage!"

"One would expect to be well attended, even under circumstances as trying as those," said Mrs. Bainbridge. "But where were the children?"

"That was the damnable thing, pardon my language," said Buchanan-Wollaston. "There we were, supposedly defending British interests at sea, and Talbot's telling us that we have to go to Corfu to pick up the children and the rest of their retinue and take them across to Italy. Like we were a bloody pleasure cruise, pardon my language again."

"Oh, a bit of salty language from an old salt is only to be expected." Mrs. Bainbridge laughed. "It will scandalise the ladies, and they will love it. Please, continue."

Buchanan-Wollaston stared out across the Thames, watching the boats go by.

"We didn't know if the Greeks would change their minds, so time was of the essence," he said. "One cable from Athens to Corfu, and we would have the local revolutionary garrison waiting for us. The *Calypso* had a top speed of twenty-nine knots, but only for the utmost necessities. We ran her at twenty-two knots and reached the island in the early morning."

He sipped his tea.

"Of course, there wasn't a dock there built for the likes of a C class cruiser, so we had to take a landing party in. We took two boatloads of sailors, issued with rifles and a pair of Lewis guns. The prince, the princess and Talbot came as well."

"Lewis guns!" exclaimed Sparks. "You were ready to go to war."

"You're familiar with Lewis guns? You surprise me, young lady."

"Military family," said Sparks quickly. "Learned all I know about guns from my uncles. The Lewis was a light machine gun."

"Quite so," said Buchanan-Wollaston. "I was ready to defend my men and my ship. The situation was iffy, to say the least. We docked at a marina about a mile and a half north of the villa. Talbot somehow commandeered a truck, and half of us piled in while the rest secured the dock. We pulled up at this rather pretty two-storey villa on a rise overlooking the straits. We woke the butler, and straightaway there was a quartet of young lovelies swarming the prince, crying their eyes out."

"His daughters," said Mrs. Bainbridge. "It must have been a terrifying experience, not knowing the fate of one's father."

"I suppose it was," said Buchanan-Wollaston. "After that, it was pure chaos. The prince ran around grabbing everything valuable he could carry. The girls had to pack, but only what they could fit into one trunk apiece. The nanny had the baby—I remember they fashioned a crib of sorts by putting his bedding into an orange crate, and he slept right through it all."

"And Princess Alice?" asked Mrs. Bainbridge.

"She saw to the children at first, but then she and Talbot started collecting papers from the offices and burning them."

"Did they?" asked Sparks. "What sort of papers, do you know?"

"Correspondence, I expect," said Buchanan-Wollaston. "Anything official that the revolutionary government might use against them in the future. Who knows? Didn't read them, didn't need to. We loaded what we could onto the truck. The butler and another servant took the family and servants to the dock in a pair of autos, and we loaded the entire lot, along with the nurse, a governess, and another lady's maid for the girls, back onto the *Calypso*. We left for Brindisi that same night."

"How were they? What were they like on ship?"

"Oh, no better place for a pack of young girls than a naval vessel," he snorted. "The two oldest flirted with every sailor they saw, while the younger two ran full speed along the decks like it was their own personal playground. More disruptive than a barrage from six-inch guns, to have young girls aboard."

"We girls do cause havoc, don't we?" commented Mrs. Bainbridge. "What about the prince and princess?"

"He stayed up on the bridge throughout and peppered us with questions. He was a military fellow himself, you know. Once he was on the ship, he never looked back."

"Did Princess Alice?"

"She was distraught. In tears, much of the time."

"Naturally."

"Yes. She stayed at the stern, watching Corfu and Greece disappear. I remember that Talbot fellow stayed with her."

"Did he?" asked Mrs. Bainbridge as Sparks shot her a look.

"Yes. Couldn't hear what they were saying, of course, but he seemed to be comforting her."

"Her husband should have been doing that," said Sparks.

"Not every husband is the comforting sort," said Buchanan-Wollaston. "Not every wife needs comforting. My Dora handled my absences without bursting into tears about it every other minute."

"No doubt," said Sparks. "Did you happen to know why the princess was crying?"

"Oh, there was something," he said. "Something she left behind at the villa, don't know what. 'We have to go back,' I heard her say to her husband at one point, but he dismissed her out of hand, and I can't blame him."

"No, of course you can't," said Mrs. Bainbridge.

"And Talbot was quite the stalwart. Whatever it was she left behind, he said, 'Don't worry. I'll get them back. When things are safe.'"

"Any idea what it was?" asked Sparks.

"None. We got into Brindisi the following day, sent them on

their merry way, and went back to acting like a proper naval ship. I am quite astonished to hear that the baby boy we carried over in an orange crate is now a suitor to our princess."

"He also ended up in our Royal Navy, you'll be glad to know," said Mrs. Bainbridge.

"Did he?" said Buchanan-Wollaston, looking pleased.

"Yes," said Sparks. "He served quite valiantly during the war, no doubt due to his early exposure to you and your crew."

"I doubt that highly." Buchanan-Wollaston laughed. "But I'm glad one of our boys may be joining the royal family. Puts us one up over the army, what?"

"Yes, it does," said Mrs. Bainbridge, giving him a tight smile. "Now, you left the *Calypso* shortly after that?"

"Yes. They sent me here for senior officer war training. I ended up as an instructor after that. I had one last command—the *Carysfort* in twenty-seven, then they kept me land-bound with the Reserve Fleet in Devonport. After that, it's all been lecturing and making up lost time with the missus."

"Who has the *Calypso* now?" asked Sparks.

"The crabs and the little fishies," said Buchanan-Wollaston. "She took an Italian torpedo amidships in 1940. The captain and thirty-eight men went down with her. The rest of the crew were picked up at sea."

"I'm sorry," said Mrs. Bainbridge.

"It's the risk one takes in joining the navy," said Buchanan-Wollaston. "I should have been out there this time, too. They didn't want me. Did what I could with training and bureaucracy and all that, but it's a younger man's navy now."

"Well, this has been fascinating," said Mrs. Bainbridge as she and Sparks rose to their feet. "We shall be in touch . . ."

"But you haven't heard about the Battle of the Falklands. I was the exec on the *Cornwall*. Captain was Walter Ellerton, good man, but without much imagination. Now, we were chasing the Jerries south along with the *Kent* and the *Glasgow* . . ."

Slowly, Mrs. Bainbridge sank back into her seat. Sparks gave her a rueful smile, then turned her gaze towards the handsome young cadets in the distance.

"It was a good story," admitted Gwen as they walked back to the station. "I never knew how complicated the mathematics were in launching shells from one moving ship to another. It almost made me want to learn to use a slide rule. Thankfully, that feeling has passed."

"If he told us how he was mentioned in the dispatches one more time, I was going to dispatch him," said Iris. "But we are getting somewhere. There was something left behind in Corfu, and that upset Princess Alice."

"And our Mr. Talbot knew about it," added Gwen. "Do you know if she ever went back to Mon Repos?"

"Nothing in my research so far says she did," said Iris. "She was in Athens when Greece was occupied."

"I wonder if Talbot went back on her behalf."

"I wonder why he would. What could be so important that a British Intelligence operative would turn errand boy for an impoverished princess?"

"She inspired chivalry in his buttoned-down soul," proposed Gwen. "We know what a gallant he must have been, coming to the rescue of that French war widow. How could he resist the plight of a beautiful, distraught mother with an uncaring husband?"

"If he did go back," said Iris.

"You know, I feel badly about giving the admiral false hope about preening before a group of upper-class biddies for an afternoon. Perhaps I should start a ladies club just for the occasion."

"Think your mother-in-law will join?"

"No. Oh well. We should at least send him copies of those photos that you took."

"What a nice idea," said Iris. "Too bad there wasn't any film in the camera."

CHAPTER 6

"Two lady's maids," said Gwen on the return train. "One nanny, one governess, one valet. A small group to take along."

"You consider that small?" asked Iris.

"For a royal family of that size, yes. They left the butler behind. And the chauffeur."

"They left the cars and the villa behind, too," pointed out Iris. "If they could have loaded them on the ship, I'm sure they would have."

"So they only took who they needed," said Gwen. "One lady's maid for the princess, one to manage all of those girls . . ."

"How I managed to dress myself without one growing up, I'll never know," Iris said. "Do you button your own buttons now?"

"I do. Did you find out the names of any of their servants in your research?"

"Not yet," said Iris. "That's not the sort of information that makes it into a news story."

"We'd have to find people who knew them then," said Gwen. "I wonder if the butler stayed with the villa while they were in exile."

"They settled in Paris after they fled Greece," said Iris. "If Talbot's widow is there, we could kill two birds. Maybe Lady M would approve that particular trip. Which reminds me, we should call her in the morning and let her know what we've found so far."

"I can do that," said Gwen. "Which one am I again?"

"Catherine Prescott."

"Right, you're Oona. And while we're speaking of clandestine contacts, there is a call you should make in the morning as well."

Iris looked out the train window as they descended into a tunnel, biting her lower lip in chagrin.

"I will call him," she said. "I'm not happy about it, but I'll do it. It could speed things up, and we've already been at it for three days."

"Two full ones, to be fair," said Gwen. "Thank you, Iris. I know how much this pains you."

"I'll be late coming in tomorrow, then," said Iris. "You can run the shop without me?"

"Of course."

She had bad dreams that night. The one where her parachute didn't open. The one where she trudged through a muddy fen and dead women's hands reached up to pull her inexorably down as she flailed and screamed. The one about Carlos . . .

Iris woke in a cold sweat, her chest heaving, arms thrashing about the bed, checking for dead men.

He's not here, she thought as she regained control of herself. He can't do anything to you.

You bloody well made sure of that.

Her eyes came to rest on a comforting sight. The bottle of whisky Archie had thoughtfully left for future colds. Or future visits.

Or future visitations.

It wouldn't be the first time she had taken a small dram of courage to get her through the morning. And she might need it to face Him again. And then it would be back to the office, and it would be just another Thursday—

Thursday. She was meeting that psychiatrist this afternoon. If she admitted that she had started her morning with the help of a whisky bottle, it would not make for a promising beginning.

She decided she'd save Archie's gift for special occasions. Like visits from him. Or her next cold.

Or Friday.

She got up, put the kettle on, washed her face, then dressed and applied her makeup, except for her lipstick. She poured herself a cup of tea and had it with a single piece of toast. Then came time for her most important decision. She pulled out her small collection of lipsticks and considered.

She normally wore a bright red to face the world with confidence, but this was an older man and prone to take umbrage at any attempts to flirt. She settled on a darker red, one that gave her a more subdued look.

When approaching the gods, one must do so with humility.

She popped the bright red one into her bag for afterwards.

She walked down the stairs from her flat to the end of the street where there was an available telephone box. She stepped in, popped a coin into the slot, took a deep breath, and dialed.

"Hello," said a woman's voice at the other end.

"Mr. Petheridge, please," said Iris.

"I'm sorry, you have the wrong number."

"Isn't this Welbeck four-five-three-eight?" she asked.

"I'm afraid not."

"I'm terribly sorry," said Iris.

She hung up, then walked briskly down the block.

Five minutes, she thought, looking at her watch.

She turned right at the next corner, then walked towards the intersection. There was another telephone box at the corner. She stepped inside and checked her watch. It was four minutes and thirty-six seconds after her previous call. She pulled the door shut and waited. Twenty-four seconds later, the telephone rang. She picked up the receiver.

"Hello, Sparks," said a man.

"Hello, Brigadier," she replied.

Gwen reviewed her notes, then dialed Patience's number.

"Lady Matheson's office. Mrs. Fisher speaking," came a sharp, no-nonsense voice on the other end.

"Catherine—"

Gwen blanked for a moment.

"Prescott, Catherine Prescott here," she finished hurriedly. "I would like to speak to Lady Matheson, if she's available."

"One moment, Miss Prescott."

She was connected immediately.

"Miss Prescott, good of you to call," said Patience.

"Is this a convenient time?" asked Gwen. "Are we able to speak freely?"

"We are. It's been four days. I was hoping to hear from you earlier."

"Three days, actually. We've been time-traveling," said Gwen. "Twenty-four years."

"Oh?"

"We know who Talbot is. Or was. He was a member of the British Secret Service, or some equivalent post. He was involved in spiriting Prince Andrea and his family out of Greece in twenty-two. I'm assuming you knew that already."

"As I said, I could not reveal any information directly to you."

"Well, it might have saved some time. In any case, we also spoke with the captain of the HMS *Calypso*, which transported the family, including Prince Philip as a baby. He told us that Princess

Alice was distraught over leaving something behind at Mon Repos. And that Talbot knew about it, whatever it was."

"Whatever it was," repeated Patience. "So, there could have been something. And Talbot could have recovered it."

"Could have been and could have done," said Gwen. "It's still all very speculative. We're following up a lead on Talbot, and we're going to try and track down the members of Prince Andrea's staff to see if they knew anything. We don't have any of their names, unfortunately. Do you?"

"I can barely keep track of my own servants," said Patience. "I have no idea who the prince and his family employed."

"I didn't think so, but it was worth asking. I know some people who know some people. I'll see if any of them know the right people. Have there been any other developments at your end?"

"None," said Patience. "Is there any way of speeding up this process?"

"Grant us clairvoyance and a team of researchers," said Gwen. "But that would create a higher risk of leaks. You're trading speed for confidentiality. We're working as fast as we can, but there are only two of us."

"True, very true," Patience sighed. "All right. Do keep me posted. Call the moment you learn anything new."

"How shall we reach you over the weekend?"

"Weekends do not exist for us until we sort this affair out," said Patience. "Mrs. Fisher will be at this number and will know how to reach me. And I have your number in Kensington if there is any emergency. Do you have Miss Travis's number?"

"I do," said Gwen, feeling pleased that she recognised Iris's cover name without hesitation. "She doesn't like me to give it out. Call me rather than her."

"Very well," said Patience. "Keep in touch. Goodbye."

"Goodbye."

She hung up.

Paris in the early twenties, thought Gwen. Someone well-connected in society, now in her mid to late forties, with children of the same age so they might remember an expatriate set of royals.

She thought of three possibilities. She pulled out her address book and began making calls.

Sparks sat on a bench in Paddington Street Gardens, reading the *Guardian*. It was hot, but a leafy chestnut tree gave her protection from the sun. After some time, an older man walked by. He stopped to watch a group of children playing in the distance, then noted the empty space next to her on the bench.

"May I?" he asked.

"Suit yourself," said Sparks, not looking up from her paper.

He sat with a sigh of contentment, but his back never touched the back of the bench.

"Nice to have all this shade," he commented.

"We live in the shadows," said Sparks. "Speaking of which, where's your bodyguard?"

"Shame on you, Sparks," he said. "You're slipping."

"Right," said Sparks, pulling her compact out of her bag and re-applying her powder while shifting the mirror about. "Ah. There's the Bentley, and there he is."

"So, what are we doing here, Sparks?" asked the Brigadier. "Have you reconsidered my offer?"

"No, sir. Sorry. I wanted to ask about an old colleague of yours."

"Why?"

"We're vetting a prospective bachelor, and this man's name came up."

The Brigadier was not known for showing reaction to situations, so the twitching of one eyebrow spoke volumes.

"Do you mean to say that you went through security protocols and dragged me away from fighting the secret wars so you could arrange a marriage?" he said.

"We don't arrange marriages," said Sparks. "We arrange introductions. The marriages happen or they don't."

"You were infuriating when you were young, Sparks, but this is another level."

"I still think of myself as young," said Sparks.

"You're making me feel older by the second. Well, I'm already here. Speak your piece, but make it quick."

"Gerald Talbot," said Sparks. "Old Greek hand."

"Died a year ago," said the Brigadier. "Therefore, not good marriage material. Anything else?"

"You weren't at the funeral."

"We sent flowers. Anonymously."

"Even though he'd been out of the Service since the early twenties?"

"Once in the Service, always in the Service. We'll send flowers to your funeral someday."

"Cheerful thought," said Sparks. "What intrigued me about Talbot's last guest list was the large number of Greeks on it. Unusual for a director of the London and North Eastern Railway Company, unless there is a national enthusiasm for trains in Greece of which I was previously unaware."

"He had worked in Greece."

"For us. For the Crown's interests, presumably. And not for decades. What had he done for Greece lately that so many of them showed up?"

"What does this have to do with some poor blighter's marriage prospects?"

"When was the last time Talbot went to Greece on behalf of the Service? His cover was blown after he rescued Prince Andrea and family. After that, his life was mostly tied to choo-choo trains. You brought him in for training the new boys and girls, but that was as a guest lecturer, not as an operative."

"It was all hands on deck then, Sparks. You know that. You still haven't given me any reason why I should divulge anything to you. You're an outsider now."

"Once in the Service, always in the Service. You said so yourself. Just now. I was listening."

"No," said the Brigadier. "Information does not travel on two-way streets. Not unless you tell me what this is all about."

"I've been sworn to secrecy," said Sparks.

"You were sworn to loyalty as well," said the Brigadier. "I assume that still means something to you."

"It does. But this involves the prospective happiness of someone."

"Yes, yes, some petulant young bride needs to know if her fiancé has a dark past as an agent, and the happiness of their marriage depends on her knowing the truth. What of it? I have the Crown to worry about."

"Well, this petulant young bride will be wearing that crown someday," said Sparks.

This prompted the twitching of both eyebrows. He may as well have shouted obscenities in front of the children's playground.

"Prince Philip," he said. "That's the man you're vetting."

"We may have to vet the whole damn family," said Sparks. "There may have been a secret, something Talbot found out about, but kept to himself."

"Then he took it to the grave with him, Sparks. Let it rest."

"That's the problem, sir. He may not have taken it with him."

"Who has it now?"

"By all rights, it should be you. And if it isn't, I'm wondering why not."

"Be careful of what you're accusing us, Sparks."

"I'm not accusing, I'm wondering. Did Talbot tell you of any secrets involving Prince Andrea, Princess Alice, or any of that family?"

"He did not," said the Brigadier.

"Where were you back then?"

"I was stationed in Rome. When Talbot succeeded in getting Prince Andrea out of custody, I received a cable to arrange for their transportation once they arrived in Brindisi. There was also the matter of obtaining a diplomatic passport for the prince, as the Greeks had seized his when they arrested him. I met the family when they debarked from the *Calypso* and traveled as extra security with them up to Rome, where they had an audience with the pope, and that was the end of my involvement."

"Remember any of their servants' names, by any chance? Or would there be a report about them I could get at?"

"No, and absolutely not."

"Did Talbot mention anything to you about anything anyone had left behind?"

"He did not."

"Did he ever go back to Corfu after that?"

"He did, come to think of it," said the Brigadier, thinking for a moment. "Several years later. Twenty-six, or thereabouts."

"Why?"

"The villa was still in the family's possession, although Andrea was persona non grata in Greece, unsurprisingly. They leased it to Mountbatten."

"Which Mountbatten?"

"Dickie."

"Princess Alice's brother," said Sparks. "He's been a champion of Prince Philip, hasn't he?"

"He has," said the Brigadier. "He arranged for his introduction to the young princess."

"Did he spend much time at Mon Repos?"

"I should doubt it very much. Mountbatten has been an active member of the Royal Navy since the Great War. I don't know when he would have had the chance to relax anywhere."

"Then it seems strange that he should want to lease the place, doesn't it?" asked Sparks.

"Maybe. I've never been the villa-leasing type myself, so I don't know why anyone else would go to the trouble. It might have been his way of funneling money to the family when they were hard up while still maintaining appearances."

"And what did that have to do with Talbot going back to Corfu?"

"Talbot went back on Mountbatten's behalf to make sure the place was still worth leasing."

"Talbot went on Mountbatten's behalf? Not for the Crown?"

"Talbot was out of the Service by then," said the Brigadier.

"But why would he be the one to go back for Mountbatten?"

"No idea."

"Were you still in Rome then?"

"I was."

"Were you aware of Talbot's journey to Mon Repos?"

"He came through Rome on his way there. We dined together."

"And he said nothing about why he was going to Corfu?"

"Just that he needed to make sure the place was livable before Mountbatten leased it."

"He went all that way for that trivial purpose, and you never thought it peculiar?"

"Let me think—was there anything else happening in Italy in twenty-six that might have been taking up more of my attentions? Oh yes. I vaguely recall a fellow named Mussolini and the rise of the Fascists. So, yes, Talbot's housekeeping expedition didn't raise any significant alarms amidst the constant clanging already around me."

"Did he pass through Rome on his return?"

"He did not. The next time I saw him, he was a stalwart man of railways and electric companies."

"Yet you brought him back to train the lads."

"He was a clever chap. I thought he'd be useful."

Sparks paused for a second, collecting her thoughts.

"Constantine Torgos was at his funeral," she said.

"What of it?"

"Torgos was our link to the Greek Resistance during the recent war. He worked with us. Not with me personally, but I knew who he was. What was his connection to Talbot?"

"I have given you everything you need, Sparks," said the Brigadier, rising to his feet. "More than you are entitled to. I won't be wasting any more time with this."

"Sir? May I say one more thing?"

He stopped.

"Go on, Sparks," he said wearily.

"I fully expect to outlive you by several decades," she said.

"Impudent woman. Is that all?"

"No, sir. What I wanted to say was that despite that, I am glad that you still consider me worthy of flowers at my funeral."

"More than worthy, Sparks," he said. "I hope you stay in touch. We may yet find a mission you'd consider taking."

"How is Andrew?" she blurted out.

"Can't tell you, Sparks. Good luck with the investigation."

He walked away. She read the paper until she heard the Bentley start up behind her.

Well, hardly likely he'd tell her about Andrew, she thought. An ex is an ex is an ex, especially the spying sort. It would be nice to know that he was safe, though.

She folded up the *Guardian* and walked to the office.

Gwen waved a piece of paper at her triumphantly when Iris walked through the door.

"I've located one of the lady's maids!" she crowed.

"How on earth did you manage that?"

"Well, the family settled in Paris after they left Corfu. I have a friend who has an aunt who was married to a French automobile tycoon during the twenties, and she is an invaluable gossip when it comes to *la société Parisienne*. It turns out that her lady's maid was a second cousin or something—"

"All right, I accept the bona fides of your investigation," interrupted Iris.

"This involved a great deal of work," said Gwen indignantly. "And we have to justify our information if we are going to act upon it."

"You're right, I'm sorry. Go on. Second cousin of the tycoon's wife's lady's maid or something, you were saying."

"Yes, I think—" Gwen glanced at her notes. "Lost my place for a moment. Right, there it is. So, her lady's maid was a second cousin to the young princesses' maid, whose name was Cécile Berteuil. She left their employ when they all got married, which happened within a relatively short space of time. She married a French chauffeur named Armand Bousquet."

"Where are they now?"

"In England! They are employed by Harold Cockerell and his wife, Felicity. Cockerell's in steel manufacturing or something and has a house in Sudbury."

"I wonder if she knows what Princess Alice left behind in Corfu."

"She might, she might not. But even if she doesn't, she might know the whereabouts of Princess Alice's personal lady's maid."

"Well, that's progress. Certainly more than I've made today."

"Did he see you?"

"He did. He wasn't happy about the purpose of my call, but that was to be expected. Here's the important bit: Talbot went back to Mon Repos."

"He did!" breathed Gwen. "That's stupendous. When?"

"In 1926, on behalf of Dickie Mountbatten, who was intending to lease the villa from Prince Andrea."

"Dickie Mountbatten? Princess Alice's brother?"

"And Philip's uncle. Now, in 1926, Philip is only five, and our Lilibet is a babe in arms, so I don't think there was any long-term intrigue in place for matching them at that point."

"No, of course not. But how did Talbot end up being Mountbatten's representative? How did they even know each other, unless—It had to have been Alice who made the connection."

"Or Andrea. So, let's put this together. The prince cannot return to Greek soil, which means neither can Alice. They need money, so brother Dickie steps in with a way to subsidise them while letting them save face. Alice sees an opportunity to regain the missing whatsit, and gets Talbot to undertake the mission for her."

"Then why wouldn't he have simply returned the whatsit to her?" asked Gwen. "Mission accomplished, end of story."

"Maybe he decided to blackmail her instead," said Iris.

"That's terribly unchivalrous for a Knight Commander of the Royal Victorian Order, I must say."

"Spies are not always chivalrous," said Iris. "I know that from firsthand experience."

"Could it have been something other than blackmail?" asked Gwen. "What if he kept it for sentimental value once he secured it? Or kept it safe for the princess?"

"Many things are still possible. But we have now made the possible . . . well, not real, but less impossible. Now, let's check the train schedule to Sudbury."

"No," said Gwen.

"No? Why not?"

"Because we have appointments this afternoon, as you very well know."

"We'll break them," said Iris blithely. "Duty beckons, one must put the country's interests—nay, the Queen's interests, before one's own."

"No," repeated Gwen. "First, one does not break an appointment with one's psychiatrist. Second, one does not break a promise made to one's friend to go to said psychiatrist."

"One doesn't?" whined Iris. "What if one is having second thoughts about the whole idea?"

"It's perfectly natural to be frightened the first time," said Gwen.

"How long before you got over your fear of him?"

"Oh, he still terrifies me," said Gwen. "When he stops, I will be cured. Or completely bonkers. I doubt that I will be able to tell the difference."

"It's good to have goals," said Iris. "Could we at least call this Cécile Berteuil Bousquet and see if she's available to speak to us?"

"I was waiting for you to return before making the call," said Gwen. "I thought you might want to handle this one, given that I've been making calls under my own name."

Iris held out her hand. Gwen passed her the number. Iris dialed it.

"Hello," she said. "Is this the Cockerell residence? Is there a Mrs. Bousquet there? Oh, Madame Bousquet, forgive me. Might I have a word with her? Yes, I'll wait."

Gwen watched as her partner subtly shifted character. It was evident in the body language. Iris was seated on the edge of her chair, leaning forwards, her eyes focused on some unknown point—well, more likely the dart board opposite her.

"Hello, Madame Bousquet? This is Mary McTague from the *Telegraph*. No, the newspaper. Yes, that one. Do you read it? Ah, pity. In any event, I'm with the Society section, and we've just learned that you were with Prince Andrea's family when they made their exciting getaway from Greece back in the twenties, is that right? It is! I am so glad I've found you. Would you be available for a brief interview, say, tomorrow morning? No, we don't pay for our in-

terviews. Not officially, anyway. I'm not saying I might not be able
to give you a little something for your time, but remember that
I'm just a lady journalist trying to get a story—they don't pay us
very much. I'll bet you make more than I do . . . Really? Well, then
we're both vastly underpaid. Yes, I agree, the class system is unjust.
When? You're available when Mrs. Cockerell goes on her missions
of mercy? Ten thirty will be fine. I will see you then."

She hung up.

"How much do lady journalists make?" asked Gwen.

"No idea," said Iris.

The waiting room at Dr. Milford's office could have been a waiting room for anyone or anything, thought Iris. A stockbroker. A
solicitor. A torturer. She envisioned the psychiatrist seated at a
desk inside a dungeon, or whatever one would call a dungeon on
a well-lit ground floor of a Harley Street office, replete with coiled
leather whips and arcane iron flensing instruments hanging from
the walls. The waiting room gave no indication of such infernal
purpose, however. She sat on a straight-backed wooden chair, the
two comfy couches being occupied by several young men, all but
one of whom were in uniform. The exception, who nevertheless
was of their age and bearing, was wearing a gray two-piece demob
suit. One of the sleeves was flat and pinned to his waist to keep it
from flapping around.

She filled out a questionnaire on a clipboard provided to her
by the receptionist who guarded the thick door that separated
them from the inner sanctum sanctorum, into which Gwen had
disappeared twenty minutes earlier, shoulders thrown back, deep
breath taken. She never talked to Iris about her visits, other than
that she was making them, and this was the first time that Iris
would be seeing her directly after having her psyche fumigated.
She wondered what Gwen would be like. She imagined her friend
as being temporarily softened, like moulded plastic fresh out of the

oven, still pliable until the hard outer shell re-formed in the harsh cold air of the world.

She wondered if that softening would take place with her. If she could be reshaped into something more—

More what?

She wasn't sure what she wanted to be.

She supposed that was what she had come to find out.

There were stacks of old magazines piled about. She searched for one Gwen assured her was always there, the centenary issue of the *Illustrated London News* with Princess Elizabeth on the cover. Their client, even if the princess would never know The Right Sort Marriage Bureau was on the case. She thought about what it might have been like had the princess actually walked through their doors, looking for a real husband, rather than being paired with some minor impoverished royal who fit all the external parameters for a princely consort. Who would she match with the heir presumptive from amongst their ninety-six single men? Maybe Mr. MacLaren. He looked like a prince, even though he was a banker and a banker's son. He was tall, with a courtly bearing, and had served with distinction in the Black Watch, First Battalion. He had shown up in their office for his first interview in dress uniform, complete with kilt and tam. And a very dashing eye patch, courtesy of the Battle of the Bulge.

Let's see if the Royal Navy can match that, she thought.

Yet it was churlish of her to belittle the young princess. Elizabeth could have escaped to safety in the country, but she had remained in London. They all did, living through the Blitz with their subjects. Royalty imposed its duties during wartime, and they accepted them without qualm, even taking, what was it, nine bombs to the Palace? The Queen said she was glad they had been bombed. Something about being able to look the East End in the face.

Although Iris doubted they'd let Elizabeth marry an East Ender. Maybe Margaret?

No.

She got up and returned her paperwork to the receptionist who began making up a file. Iris retook her seat.

"Would you prefer the couch, Miss?" asked the one-armed civilian. "That chair looks uncomfortable."

"I'm fine, thank you," she said, giving him a warm smile. "And thank you for your service. Thank all of you."

There was a group of muttered responses from several of the lads. None from two, who stared blankly across the room, seeing things the others didn't.

The door opened, and Gwen emerged, dabbing at her eyes with her handkerchief. She saw Iris looking at her with concern and smiled weakly.

"It's all right," she whispered as she sat next to her.

"But—"

"I'm fine."

The receptionist went into the inner office with Iris's file, then returned.

"Miss Sparks?" she called.

Iris sat unmoving, looking at her friend's tears. Gwen reached over and patted her hand.

"Be brave," she said. "Drinks and cake, remember?"

"Right," said Iris, getting to her feet. "Here goes nothing."

She strode to the door and knocked.

"Just go in," said the receptionist.

Iris opened the door. It was heavy, and the other side was covered in maroon leather padding.

There were no implements of torture in the room. At least, none visible. On the right was an examining table, with a scale on one side and a sphygmomanometer on a stand on the other. On the other side of the room was a long couch.

Dr. Milford sat at a desk, reading Iris's paperwork. He motioned to a chair in front of the desk without looking up.

"Be with you in a moment," he said. "Please take a seat."

"You made my friend cry," said Iris. "Don't even think about trying anything like that with me."

"Trying what, Miss Sparks?" asked Dr. Milford, looking at her for the first time.

"Whatever it is you do that makes people cry."

"You never cry, Miss Sparks?" he asked.

"Do you?"

"Yes. Please take a seat, and we'll start properly."

"What if I want to be improper?"

"You're taking an aggressive approach for our first meeting, I see."

"And that bothers you."

"Merely observing," he said, getting up from his desk. "Take your jacket off and sit on the examining table. I want to take your vitals."

"You cannot, sir, take from me anything that I will more willingly part withal," she said, removing her jacket and draping it over the back of her chair. "Except my life, except my life, except my life."

"We'll talk about suicidal tendencies later, Lady Hamlet," he said, removing a stethoscope from a case on the desk. "Up on the table, unbutton your blouse, and roll up your sleeve, please."

She complied. He listened to her chest and back, had her breathe deeply, then put the sphygmomanometer cuff on her upper arm and inflated it with a rubber bulb, making the mercury rise in the cylinder next to her while holding a pocket watch in his other hand. They watched the mercury drop together when he released the pressure.

"On the high side," he said. "How long has that been going on?"

"Since the war ended," she said.

"You may dress," he said, sitting down and jotting the information in her file. "Oh, step on that scale first."

She stepped on the scale, concealing her dismay as he slid the last weight further to the right than she had hoped.

I was wrong about the instruments of torture, she thought.

"Have a seat, please," he said. "Now, for the basics. Age?"

"Twenty-nine."

"Education?"

"Bachelor of Arts Title, Cambridge."

"Parents both alive?"

"Yes."

"Together?"

"No."

"Separated or divorced?"

"Formally divorced in thirty-two. Separated—well, it was a slippery slope. He came home less and less, then not at all. By that point, it was hard to notice that he had moved out."

"I doubt that very much, but we'll explore that in time. Married?"

"No. A couple of close calls."

"Interesting remark from someone in your line of work."

"Yes, isn't it?" said Iris smiling brightly. "I bet you think you're the first ever to say that."

"Sexually active?"

"Yes. One might even say overactive, but we'll explore that in time, too. Won't we?"

"If you like. Longest relationship?"

That caught her up short. She had never considered that question. Andrew. It was Andrew, damn him.

"I suppose my previous one," she said. "On and off for a while, then very much on for a longish time, and then off. Maybe two years and a month, overall."

"When did it end?"

"Last month."

"Why?"

"He was married. It wasn't going anywhere. It wasn't—it probably wasn't a good idea."

"I see."

"I'm dating a gangster now," she said cheerfully, watching his reaction closely.

"A gangster?"

"He's the head of a gang, therefore a gangster. A spiv from the East End."

"Have you become involved in crime yourself?"

"Not specifically. Some things that were crime-ish, but for a good cause. We met during the course of a murder case that Gwen and I were investigating. Do I shock you?"

"If you want to shock me," said Dr. Milford, "then you should be less obvious about your desire to shock me."

All right, she liked him, she decided.

"Fine," he said, putting down his pen. "Why are you here, Miss Sparks?"

"Fear of flying," she said promptly.

"And when did that start?"

She was taken aback. She had thrown it out as a flippant answer. She hadn't expected him to treat it seriously.

"Well," she began.

Falling through the night sky, the cold air whipping about her, the rip cord useless in her hands, not knowing how many seconds she had left—

"Well, Miss Sparks?" he asked gently.

"How much did Gwen tell you about me?" she asked.

"I can't discuss what transpired between any other patient and myself," he said.

"Confidentiality."

"Of course."

"How far does that go?" she asked.

"As long as you don't intend to commit any crimes, or things that are crime-ish, our conversations never leave this room."

"How about things clandestine?"

"Are we speaking of matters from deep within your psyche, or wartime activities?"

"The latter," she said. "Although there are vast territories where they intersect."

"You would not be the first person from Intelligence or Special Operations I have treated," he said, opening a drawer and removing a manila folder.

He opened it and slid it across the desk. Inside was a sheaf of typed papers.

"My copy of the Official Secrets Act," he said. "I became a signatory precisely for this reason. You'll find my endorsement on the bottom of the last page."

"Right," said Iris, flipping through it. "Have one of these myself." She closed the folder and slid it back.

"Satisfied?" he asked.

"Never," she said. "But let's proceed."

Gwen finally managed to get the tears under control. She looked up to find all the young men looking at her with concern. All but two.

"Are you all right, ma'am?" asked the one-armed man.

"I'm fine," she assured them.

"Well, if that was true, you wouldn't be here, would you?" he said, and his mates broke into laughter.

"Truer words," she said, laughing with them.

"You and your friend look familiar," said one of the soldiers. "Weren't the two of you in the papers last month?"

"Yes, I'm afraid so," she said.

"Were they?" asked one from the other couch. "What for?"

"Solved a murder, didn't you?" said the first. "The Yard had the wrong man practically dancing on the gallows."

"It wasn't quite that dramatic," said Gwen.

"You're a detective, then?" asked the one-armed man.

"Not at all," said Gwen. "We run a marriage bureau."

"And you're not going to solicit anyone for business in here," said the receptionist sternly. "Now please hush. Have some consideration for your fellow patients."

The room fell quiet, but the one-armed man winked at her before going back to turning the pages of a magazine on his lap.

She looked, as she always did, for the magazine with the princess on the cover, but it must have been buried in a different pile. She found the April issue of *Woman's Own*, which had an amusing cover illustration of a young man with a shock of unruly hair sitting in a chair, looking down with an expression of appalling dismay at a beautiful baby girl in his arms. Whether the dismay was caused by her wetting herself or his contemplation of life as a father, it was difficult to say. The two causes produced identical expressions, in her experience.

Except for Ronnie, she remembered. He embraced fatherhood, including its messier aspects, with joy and frequent glee. Even with their nanny hovering at his elbow, he insisted on making a ritual of changing Little Ronnie's nappies, nuzzling the baby's belly, making him squeal with delight.

He would have loved to see what his son had become now, she thought sadly. They would be out in the park, playing cricket—

Good Lord, she thought. Who will teach him cricket? She must get on that straightaway.

Prince Philip must play. He went to an English boarding school for a while. He never had much time with his father, as far as she could tell, and now his father was dead. She wondered how that had affected him.

Let's see, she thought. He was born in Corfu in June 1921, so . . .

June 1921. Seven years after the last daughter.

She thought about that, then pulled her notebook from her bag and started to write.

She became so enmeshed that she didn't even notice Iris had come back out of the office until Iris was standing directly in front of her. Gwen looked up at her friend's face. She saw no discernible change in expression, but there was something behind her eyes that made Gwen want to reach out and clutch her hand in sympathy.

She didn't, however. Not in front of the lads.

"Done?" she asked.

"For now," said Iris.

"Drinks and cake?"

"Just cake, I think," said Iris.

Gwen looked at her in shock.

Iris grinned, then turned and walked out the door, Gwen scrambling after.

CHAPTER 7

G wen held back her questions until the waiter was out of hearing range. Between the two women rested a pair of plates, each holding a rectangular piece of sponge cake, its cross-section a four-square checkerboard of pink and yellow, bordered with apricot jam, encased in marzipan.

Battenberg cake. They had both wanted it as soon as they saw it on the menu.

"I've often wondered why they didn't change the name to Mountbatten cake," commented Gwen when it arrived. "If the Battenbergs were so sensitive about sounding German during the Great War that they took a new name, then the cake should have followed suit."

"I had a birthday where they took sixteen Battenberg slices and arranged them into a chessboard, with dark and white chocolate chess pieces to play with," said Iris.

"That sounds too wonderful to eat," said Gwen.

"Oh, it was," agreed Iris. "At first. Then my aunt Prunella challenged me to a game, the winner of which would get to eat the other's king."

"Did you win?"

"Of course," said Iris. "It was my birthday. I figured out later that Prunella let me win quickly to break the spell and let us get to dessert."

They dug in blissfully, then had tea.

"I'm not going to ask what you talked about, of course," said Gwen. "But did you like him? Did you think it was worthwhile?"

"I liked him," said Iris. "He knows when to challenge and when simply to listen. As to whether it's worthwhile, time will tell. I hope he saves me from the asylum."

"If he doesn't, you can have my old room," said Gwen.

"Nice view?"

"I don't remember there being any view. Or any windows at all, for that matter. I think they were worried about me escaping. Or jumping."

"Ah."

"I was doing some thinking while you were at your appointment."

"What about?"

"The timing of all this. We've been so focused on tracking down Talbot and the Greek royals that we haven't stopped to consider why this is happening and, more important, why it's happening now."

"I'm listening."

"This thing, this information in whatever form it's in, has been around since 1926, assuming Talbot did bring it back from Corfu then."

"Talbot only died last year. He kept it safe and secret."

"But he died over a year ago, and nothing happened then. It's not the sort of thing one leaves to an heir. I doubt his daughter got a package with a note saying, 'Darling, use this for blackmail if you ever feel the need. All my love, Dad.'"

"No, he wouldn't have done that," agreed Iris. "I'll bite. Why now?"

"Because of who our mysterious correspondent sent it to,"

said Gwen. "Why, if it involves an old scandal of Princess Alice's, wouldn't he send it to her? And for that matter, who would care if she was involved in something back then? Where is she right now?"

"Athens, when she's not visiting her family. In a small apartment. She was there all through the occupation."

"That's another thing," said Gwen. "She was put into one sanatorium after another for years. Years! Even with all my troubles, I was in for half a year at most. You don't go in for that length of time unless there's something seriously wrong. Yet she was released, and has never gone back."

"The reports were that the death of her daughter and family in that plane crash jolted her back into—I don't know whether to call it reality or sanity," said Iris. "I don't necessarily agree that they are one and the same. Where are you going with this?"

"My point is that there is no profit in trying to blackmail Princess Alice because she doesn't have the wherewithal to pay to keep things quiet. Someone gets hold of Talbot's secret treasure trove, sits on it for over a year, and then something happens that makes it valuable: Prince Philip and Princess Elizabeth are photographed at the Brabourne wedding, and the world now knows they're in love. The exiled Greeks may not have two drachmas to rub together, but our own royal family can afford some hush money."

"Makes sense," said Iris. "What do you think the scandal is?"

"If it's being sent to Princess Elizabeth, then it must be something that would scuttle any possibility of marriage to the prince," said Gwen. "Something more than just the reputation of his mother. If insanity on his maternal side, adultery and abandonment on his paternal side, and Nazi brothers-in-law aren't enough to stop an engagement, then it has to be something massive."

"Go on," urged Iris.

"For the first part of Andrea and Alice's marriage, princesses are coming like clockwork," said Gwen. "Then after the fourth, no new children for seven years."

"There was a war going on," Iris pointed out.

"But Greece was neutral, wasn't it? So given that Andrea's wife clearly was capable of producing children, and assuming his male ego required a son no matter how long it might take, why did it take him so long? Yet Philip doesn't show up until 1921."

"These things happen."

"Yes, of course they do. Right, so prior to Philip, the family had been in exile, correct?"

"Correct."

"They are welcomed back to Greece and reestablish themselves in Corfu, and a bouncing baby boy is born. Where did they live before Corfu?"

"Switzerland," said Iris, pulling out her notebook and opening it to her research. "The Greek king in exile—"

"Pre–monkey bite?"

"Not that king. This was his father, Constantine the First, who had abdicated. He was Andrea's older brother. They were living it up at the Grand Hotel in Lucerne. Andrea and family were there, with the obligatory side trips to St. Moritz and Lugano."

"When did Andrea leave Switzerland to return to Greece?"

"Erm, ah, here it is. He goes to Rome in September 1920, then back to Greece in November."

"And Philip is born the following June tenth."

Iris counted back on her fingers.

"Nine months earlier is September tenth," she said. "Cutting it close. A nice farewell present to the wife, then off to the intrigues. The monkey strikes in October, the royal nephew dies, big brother retakes the throne a month later."

"Cutting it very close," said Gwen. "Philip must have been quite the surprise after so many years."

"Are you saying what I think you're saying?"

"Look at how Andrea behaves towards his wife and son after," said Gwen. "He shoves her into a sanatorium, sends the boy away, first to live with other relatives, then to one brutal boarding school after another. Barely visits him, never once visits his wife—his *wife*, Iris—in all the years that she's confined. Is that how a man treats his first and only son and the woman who bore him?"

"Yes, he was a nasty piece of work, I'll grant you. But are you suggesting—"

"That he was punishing her for having an affair that led to the illegitimate birth of her only son?" finished Gwen. "Obviously, I have no evidence to suggest that whatsoever."

"No."

"But what if someone else does? What happens to Philip's prospects?"

"They vanish like smoke," said Iris. "Bastards don't get to marry princesses. Officially, anyway. So the thing left behind in Corfu—love letters?"

"That would fit the theory, wouldn't it? Too precious to destroy, too risky to leave lying around. Hidden in the villa, or buried in an oilskin packet at the foot of a favourite tree, and forgotten in the haste of packing and fleeing until Princess Alice is safely on a British destroyer and it's too late to go back."

"It could be," agreed Iris. "Too bad we have nothing to back it up."

"Alice herself—"

"Is off-limits," said Iris. "Because if you're wrong about this, the mere asking would be disastrous for the royal romance. Her lady's maid, however, might have been a confidante. And the lover himself, if we could figure out who he was. Here's a question: why would Alice tell any of this to Talbot?"

"Could she have known him before?"

"He's in Athens in 1917, same year they flee the first time. There

may have been some overlap. He could have traveled to Switzerland to sound out the exiles on behalf of Britain."

"What about after he left Athens?"

"Let's see. He's naval attaché through 1920, then marries the
French widow that June."

"Where was the wedding?"

"London. Holy Trinity Church on Sloane Street."

"So, it's not likely he was bored with the widow by September.
She was French, after all."

"Good Lord!"

"Just thinking about other possible men in Alice's life. What
else did you find out about her?"

"She got heavily into spiritualism in Switzerland. Andrea's
younger brother, Christo, was obsessed with it. The sort of fad that
people with money and time on their hands will indulge in."

"Interesting. A younger brother with a sympathetic ear. Or
perhaps there came a dashing visiting lecturer on arcane matters, a
charlatan with a charismatic bearing and a hypnotic stare."

"Rasputin was elsewhere at the time. You have a marvelous
imagination, Gwen. You should sit in psychiatrists' waiting rooms
more often."

"Shake my brain sufficiently, things will come loose."

The bill arrived. Iris reached for her bag. Gwen shook her head.

"My treat," she said. "We are celebrating your courage."

"Courage? For facing an older gentleman in an office with you
guarding me just outside?"

"For facing yourself, darling," said Gwen. "There's nothing
more terrifying than that."

They walked out of the café.

"Are you all right with me handling the interview tomorrow
with Madame Bousquet without you?" asked Iris.

"It would make sense, given your choice of cover, unless I could
be the photographer this time. But that might scare her off, and we

do need to have someone in the office. So, go. You have my blessings."

"Thank you, Gwen," said Iris. "I should be back late morning."

"Good hunting."

They went their separate ways home.

Little Ronnie bounded down the grand staircase the moment Gwen came through the door.

"Mummy!" he cried, jumping into her arms. "You're home early!"

"The better to see you in daylight," she said, swinging him up into the air and catching him. "Goodness, you're getting heavy! I may not be able to do this for much longer."

"Someday I'll be big, and I'll pick you up like this!"

"I bet you will," she said, lowering him gently to the floor. "Is Grandmother in?"

"She's in the library. She said you're not coming to Tommy's birthday party."

"I'm afraid not, but you go ahead and wish him a happy birthday for me."

"Will there be cake, do you suppose?"

"Perhaps."

"One that doesn't have toothpowder frosting?"

"It all depends on how many coupons they've saved up. Maybe you'll get real icing this year."

"I hope so. See you at dinner!"

He dashed off. She thought about her post-session Battenberg indulgence with Iris and felt guilty. Wonderful, she thought. Grist for the psychiatric mill.

She walked to the library and knocked respectfully on the door.

"Come in," said Lady Carolyne.

Her mother-in-law no longer terrified her, but Gwen could not say they were on cordial terms. More of a tentative treaty, any of whose provisos could be violated by a single word muttered under a breath. Even the most casual of conversation topics required the utmost vigilance on Gwen's part, and anything involving Little Ronnie could provoke territorial disputes bordering on full-blown war.

"Good evening, Gwendolyn," said Lady Carolyne, putting down a letter she had been reading. "Any successes on the marital front?"

She was wearing a rose-coloured silk dressing gown with delicate silver filigree woven through it. It was what she wore before changing into evening dress, which meant that she would be going out shortly. Gwen anticipated the coming quiet in the household with relief.

"We're making progress," she replied. "Some money has come in this week, I'm happy to report."

"I find this approach to marriage most unsettling," said Lady Carolyne. "It would never have been heard of when Lord Bainbridge and I were courting."

"You and Lord Bainbridge had the advantage of seasons and balls," said Gwendolyn. "So did Ronnie and I. Those aren't available to the vast majority of Englishmen and Englishwomen. We're the next best thing."

"Parliament should fund seasons for the masses," said Lady Carolyne. "It would be much more efficient."

"When Lord Bainbridge returns, he can propose it," said Gwen. "Until then, we'll go on matchmaking. I wanted to speak to you about Saturday."

"Yes?"

"Will you be going to Tommy Hibbert's birthday party with Little Ronnie?"

"Of course. The Hibberts and we are old friends."

"Have you picked out a present yet?"

"I have not. I was going to send Percival to Hamleys tomorrow. He's good at picking out toys for children."

"Let me do it instead," said Gwen. "I know they don't want me there, but I would like to do that much, at least."

Lady Carolyne looked at her, considering.

"This is your attempt to worm your way back into their good graces," she said.

"I wouldn't call it worming, exactly," said Gwen. "But yes, I'd like them to know that I'm well enough to be around children at birthday parties. I never was a threat to anyone."

"Other than yourself," said Lady Carolyne.

"Other than myself," agreed Gwen. "And now I like myself again. I've grown quite fond of me, in fact. I've decided that I'm going to stick with me for the long haul."

"You're making light of a serious situation," said Lady Carolyne.

"Dr. Milford thinks that's a good sign," said Gwen.

"Does he? Sometimes I wonder about him."

"He was your choice," Gwen reminded her. "Yet I've continued to work with him, knowing that. Worked very hard, in fact."

"We shall see if that bears fruit," said Lady Carolyne. "Very well. You may purchase the gift."

"Thank you," said Gwen. "It should be fun. I haven't been to Hamleys in ages."

"I wonder if they've repaired all the damage," said Lady Carolyne.

"I'll report back and let you know," promised Gwen. "Thank you, Carolyne."

She located the Hibberts' number in her address book, then picked up the telephone and dialed. After several rings, a housemaid answered.

"Mrs. Bainbridge calling for Mrs. Hibbert," said Gwen.

"One moment, Mrs. Bainbridge."

A minute passed, then a woman's voice filled the receiver.

"Lady Carolyne!" cried Mrs. Hibbert. "So sweet of you to call."

"Actually, it's Gwen, Isabelle," said Gwen. "How are you?"

There was a pause.

"Gwen," said Mrs. Hibbert, not even bothering to hide the caution in her tone. "This is a surprise."

"Not at all, Isabelle. I'm sorry to be interrupting anything. I wanted to apologise in advance for not being able to come with Little Ronnie on Saturday."

"Oh, that's quite all right," said Mrs. Hibbert in relief. "You'll be saving yourself from the raucousness of six- and seven-year-olds."

"No, I'm sure it will be great fun," said Gwen. "I wanted to know if there was anything in particular that Tommy wanted in the way of a present. Children's desires are so changeable. Ronnie currently is mad about narwhals."

"What on earth are they?"

"A type of aquatic mammal with a long tusk on its nose," said Gwen.

"My goodness!"

"How about Tommy? I remember him loving fire engines when he was two."

"Yes, my little Blitz boy. No, that's several phases ago. He's obsessed with cowboys and Indians now."

"Perfect," said Gwen. "I shall find him something along those lines. I hope you have a wonderful time, Isabelle. Give your darling boy a kiss for me, won't you?"

"I will," said Isabelle. "Gwen?"

"Yes?"

Isabelle hesitated.

"Thanks for the call," she said. "It's good to hear your voice again."

"Yours as well, Isabelle. Goodbye."

She hung up, then sat by the telephone for a while until the tears stopped. Then she wiped her face and went in to dinner.

* * *

Sudbury was a good sixty miles from London, so Iris had set her alarm for the crack of dawn. The jangling sent her reaching for anything at hand to throw at the clock before she was fully conscious, but she stopped short of letting fly as her brain delivered the morning agenda in time.

She dressed quickly, looked longingly at the whisky bottle, then grabbed her handbag and left for the station.

She breakfasted from a tea trolley on the train, and was sufficiently revived by the time she reached the town to marshal her persona into Mary McTague, cub reporter for the *Telegraph*.

She didn't know Sudbury. She vaguely recalled waking up there once, in the bed of an American Army Air Force navigator whose name she could not remember and whom she never saw again. She sneaked out and caught the first train back to London, reporting for duty only a few minutes late, trying not to think what she must have smelled like. She wondered if the American ever thought of her. She wondered if he made it through alive. She wondered how she'd got to Sudbury in the first place. Navigators certainly knew their way around, she thought, smiling to herself.

Nothing about the town appeared familiar when she emerged from the station. It didn't help that the station itself was removed from the center, situated near a bend in the river Stour, which sidestepped the town on its way to more pressing business elsewhere. It had been prettier once, she supposed. Pretty enough for Gainsborough and Constable to paint their way around. She doubted they would be as inspired by the ugly concrete pillboxes now dotting the landscape, ready for the invasion that never came, their guns now removed. Sparrows flew in and out of their narrow window slots.

She consulted her directions and walked through the eastern part of the town, skirting the center.

The Cockerells lived in a large brick house, not what anyone would think of as a mansion, but certainly more sprawling than necessary to accommodate the needs of a single family. One wing was mostly glass, and she could see a veritable jungle inside—tropical trees and vines, a riot of flowers unlike anything she had ever seen in England. She thought she even glimpsed some brightly coloured birds flying through it all—parrots, maybe. The other wing held a small ballroom. She could see a grand piano covered with a muslin drape, and a small collection of carved wooden music stands huddling forlornly in a corner.

She walked up the driveway to the servants' entrance and rang the bell.

A young woman opened the door. A housemaid, Iris guessed from the uniform.

"May I help you?" she asked.

"I'm here to see Madame Bousquet," said Iris. "We have an appointment."

"Your name, please?"

"Mary McTague."

"One moment."

She closed the door. A minute later, it was opened by a woman in her mid-forties, also in a maid's uniform. Her hair was brown with wisps of gray scattered through it. Her makeup and eyebrows were impeccable, yet there was something about her eyes that seemed off. The expression—she was on edge, thought Iris. As if she expected to see someone over Iris's shoulder, watching. It was all Iris could do not to turn around and see for herself.

"Miss McTague," said Madame Bousquet, with only a trace of an accent. "I am sorry that you came all this way. I am afraid that I cannot talk to you."

"Madame Bousquet, I don't understand," said Iris. "When we spoke on the telephone, you seemed willing, even eager. Is it a question of money? Because I might be able to—"

"It is not the money," said Madame Bousquet. "It is the propriety."

"I don't intend to pry into anything confidential," said Iris. "Our readers merely would like to have the eyewitness account of—"

"I am sorry to have wasted your time," said Madame Bousquet, shutting the door.

Iris turned to see if there was anyone, but the street leading up to the house was empty.

Someone got to her, she thought dispiritedly. Damn. There goes half a day's work.

She looked at her watch. It was only ten thirty-five. She could make the next train back to London if she walked briskly.

Or she could stake out the house to see if Madame Bousquet had any errands to run in town.

She walked down the street, turned the corner so that she was out of sight of the house, and waited.

Hamleys didn't open until ten, which meant Gwen wouldn't be able to shop for Tommy's present until her lunch break, unless Iris returned earlier. She wished she could have gone with her. Iris had a habit of acting impulsively and jumping to conclusions quickly. They were usually correct, but not always. Without Gwen there to—

To what, exactly? Gwen herself had plunged into the rabbit hole of someone else's past with nothing more than some old newspaper articles and an old man's memory of a moment that could have meant any number of things. Yet it had felt right to her. Prince Andrea's behaviour towards his wife and son had been shameful. If she had been in Princess Alice's position, who knows what she would have reached out for to find solace? Not that Ronnie had ever given her any cause to. She doubted that he ever would have.

And yet she had had less time with him, counting their actual days together—

They married in June '39. He joined the Fusiliers at the end of August, and after that, she only saw him when he was on leave. Then came the Battle of Monte Cassino, and she was a widow.

She added up all the time they'd actually spent together as a married couple.

Somewhere between five and six months. Out of five years.

Barely any time at all, when you get right down to it. She had mentioned that to Dr. Milford, and he had shaken his head in sympathy.

"The pity of it is, you weren't together long enough to have a normal human experience," he pointed out. "He died before you learned all of his flaws, so he's a paragon forever. That may be what's holding you back from starting over again."

"The bar's set too high?"

"Perhaps."

The telephone jangled, startling her out of her misery.

"The Right Sort Marriage Bureau," she said. "Mrs. Bainbridge speaking."

"I'm calling for Oona Travis or Catherine Prescott," said a man's voice.

Her alarms went off. Patience hadn't said anything about anyone else knowing those names.

"I am afraid you have the wrong number," she said. "I'm sorry."

She hung up. A moment later, it rang again. She answered after the first ring.

"Sorry, Gwen," said Lady Matheson. "A tiny little test. You passed."

"Really, Patience, I should think we're beyond these games by now."

"Is Iris with you?"

"No. She's pursuing a lead. She should be back by lunch."

"A lead? That sounds interesting. Look, I hate to put you on the spot, but have you come up with anything by now?"

"A theory," said Gwen reluctantly. "A plausible possibility for what your letter-writer may be trying to do."

"Tell me," said Lady Matheson.

Gwen laid out the essentials. When she was done, there was silence on the other end of the line that lasted for a while.

"I may have to put you in my book under 'Prophetess' after this," said Lady Matheson finally.

"What happened?" asked Gwen. "Has there been another letter?"

"This morning," said Lady Matheson. "It contains demands and instructions. And there was a second letter with it. An older one, dated from 1919. Addressed to Princess Alice."

"My God," said Gwen, her heart racing. "Is it authentic?"

"Impossible to say. It was signed with only a single initial, and we have no others to which to compare it."

"And the demands? The instructions?"

"Have you any appointments this afternoon?"

"None."

"No one looks for wedded bliss on a Friday afternoon," Lady Matheson said, sighing. "Good. Clear your decks from two thirty on. We're coming over."

She hung up.

Gwen sat frozen, the handset still in her hand, then slowly took a pen and crossed out the afternoon slots in their appointment book. Then, before she could forget, she wrote "HAMLEYS" in her lunch break.

Iris glanced at her watch. She had been maintaining her vigil for nearly an hour. Whenever an auto approached, she walked down the street until it passed, then returned to the chestnut tree that shielded her from view of the house. A woman walking an Airedale terrier looked at her curiously, the dog even more so, but Iris squatted down and made cooing noises as she rubbed his head, and they parted without aroused suspicions.

She thought she would give Madame Bousquet until noon, then give up. A few minutes short of her deadline, she was rewarded by the sight of the Frenchwoman walking briskly towards the intersection. Iris slid behind the tree and waited until she walked by her. Then she followed, waiting until they were close to the town center before increasing her stride and coming up beside her.

"Hello again," Iris said.

Madame Bousquet glanced at her, then her eyes grew wide in surprise. Or was it fear? "Go away," she said.

Fear. Definitely fear, thought Iris. Why?

"I wouldn't be the crack reporter that I am if I did that," she said with what she hoped was a reassuring smile. "Look, this can be off the record, but once I have a lead on a story, I am very hard to get rid of."

"Please, I cannot. They told me—"

She stopped.

"Who told you?" asked Iris. "Who are they? How did they know about me?"

Madame Bousquet merely shook her head despondently.

"Come on! This happened twenty-five years ago. Nobody cares about it but me. If it's a question of money—"

"It is not money!" blurted out Madame Bousquet. "They—No, I cannot. Please go away."

"They? Who?" asked Iris. "Are you being threatened? I can help you. I have friends who can protect you."

"I lose my position," said Madame Bousquet. "My husband loses his position. We are not young anymore. New positions for a couple are difficult. I cannot talk to you."

"Then point me to someone who can," said Iris. "You were the lady's maid to the daughters. Give me the name of Alice's maid and where I can find her, and I'll leave you alone. No one will know that we spoke."

Madame Bousquet hesitated, looking around.

"There is no one here to see us," said Iris. "If you're still unsure, whisper the name, then walk away from me like you're angry. I don't reveal my sources. It's the code of the journalist."

Though not of the spy, she thought.

"Vivienne," whispered Madame Bousquet. "Vivienne Ducognon. She is on staff of Mrs. Calvert in London."

"Which Mrs. Calvert?"

"That is all I know. Now leave me alone!"

This last was spoken loudly enough to be heard to the end of the block. Madame Bousquet abruptly turned and stormed away, leaving Iris standing there openmouthed in what she hoped would present a suitable picture of shock and frustration. Then she closed it and trudged dispiritedly back to the station. She wasn't followed, as far as she could tell.

But she was much more mindful of the possibility that she might be.

Who got to Madame Bousquet? she wondered. Their mystery correspondent? He had to suspect that his letter would set off alarms. Was he covering his tracks by reaching out to threaten witnesses? After all, if one has the temerity to blackmail royalty, one would hardly pause at blackmailing a servant.

She had better find Vivienne Ducognon before he did.

It wasn't until she was safely aboard the London-bound train that she opened her notebook and jotted down "Vivienne Ducognon. Mrs. Calvert." She didn't know any Calverts, but the number of women in London employing experienced French lady's maids was finite.

And there was always Gwen. Gwen was bound to know her. At that level of society, she knew everyone.

Damn her.

Gwen looked at her watch. Twelve thirty and no Iris. She didn't want to have this meeting with Patience alone. She lacked the expertise that Iris had in matters . . . well, criminal, if one were to call them by their right name. Not that she suspected Iris of ever doing anything illegal unrelated to her wartime duties, or for a good cause, as she had demonstrated in their recent investigation.

Not that she thought Iris would do anything risky for the mere fun of it.

Yet she was dating a gangster, and still carried her lock-picks and a knife and God knows what other apparatus in her handbag. A grenade, perhaps? A sawed-off shotgun? Dynamite?

I need a bigger handbag, thought Gwen.

She glanced at the appointment book for the umpteenth time that morning. The word *HAMLEYS* seemed to float up from the page and dance accusatorially in front of her eyes.

Right. Promise made to a child's mother. Deadline looming.

She dashed off a note to Iris, stuck it in the keys of her typewriter, then left the office, the clock placard hung on the outer door knob guaranteeing her return.

Hamleys was on Regents Street, only a few blocks away. The largest toy store in London—in the entire world, proclaimed their sign. Five storeys of merchandise backed up this boast. Children clustered in front, pointing, begging and yelling, yanking their protesting mothers and nannies along as they succumbed to the mesmerising pull of the window displays. Bursting into uncontrollable sobs as they, in turn, were yanked away from the treasures that were so close yet just out of reach.

Gwen couldn't remember the last time she had been there. Little Ronnie and she had spent the war in the country, safely away from the Blitz. And then she went away for a while herself. She had never been to Hamleys with her own son, she thought with a shock. She would have to rectify that omission now that she was—

Well, she needed to regain custody first, didn't she? She hated that she had to ask her in-laws for permission to take her son shopping for toys. Maybe Lady Carolyne would relent while Lord Bainbridge was still in East Africa.

"BOMBED FIVE TIMES! EVEN THE JERRIES CAN'T DEFEAT A CHILD'S DREAMS!" shouted the sign over the entrance, illustrated with a photograph of staff members handing out toys while wearing tin air raid hats.

Gwen speculated for a moment about the efficacy of a tin hat in warding off bombs. She decided she'd rather be in the country.

A doorman held open the door and nodded encouragingly to her. She rallied her nerves and went in.

In the central atrium she was immediately overwhelmed by the bright colours flooding her view from every angle. The noise level rose exponentially, amplified by the towering space. A crying baby seemed to have been stationed at every intersection, and a shop girl to her left was frantically replacing an avalanche of stuffed animals cascading from a mountain of them on a display table, while a pair of twin girls wrestled for a bear dressed as Churchill that each wanted, not caring that there were dozens more exactly like it right by them.

The stuffed animals were thinner than she remembered, she observed. Even they had suffered from rationing. They bore up under the deprivation of their cotton innards quite bravely, under the circumstances.

She climbed the stairs to the Boys' Department and was rewarded by the sight of an entire Western section. Mannequins dressed as cowboys and Indians stood ready to go to war on top of the shelves and giant posters of Tom Mix, Roy Rogers, and other American actors smiled benevolently down from the walls, hands resting on the butts of their guns.

The aisles were filled with boys, many of whom were waging some kind of range war, galloping about while screaming and shooting at each other with their index fingers while the mothers and nannies minding them might as well have been bound and gagged and tied to railroad tracks, for all the good they were doing.

Whoopee ti yi yo, Gwen thought, and she plunged into the aisles, sidestepping ersatz Indians in short pants shooting invisible arrows with invisible bows while their counterparts clutched their chests dramatically and fell to the ground.

"May I help you, madam?" said a young sales clerk. "Or should I say, howdy, ma'am? What kin ah do fer ye?"

"Oh, you poor thing," Gwen laughed. "Is that required here?"

"Ah reckon," said the clerk. "What might you be prospectin' fer?"

"A birthday present for a young boy," said Gwen.

"Cap pistol, perhaps? We've got some mighty fine replicas. Gen-you-wine six-shooters, pearl-handled like General Patton's. Or these here Colt revolvers, the same what used to be carried by Pony Express riders through the Badlands."

"I'm trying to win my way back into his mother's good graces," said Gwen. "I don't think a cap gun will do that, although they do look quite authentic. What about a play set?"

"They went thisaway, ma'am," he said, leading her to another aisle. "This here's a popular choice."

He showed her a boxed set of die-cast metal figures—a bright red stagecoach pulled by a pair of brown galloping horses, plus four cowboys and three Indians in various combative poses, three of them mounted.

"You can vary the scenarios, which is what I like about them," he explained, momentarily dropping the accent. "The cowboys could save the stagecoach from an Indian attack, or they could be highwaymen and the Indians could come to the rescue, or whatever the young lad wants it to be. The young feller, I should say."

"I like it. American-made, I assume?"

"Ah'm afraid so, ma'am. Our factories ain't back up to speed, and there ain't enough metal available for toys just yet, so we're getting much of our stock from the States. Which you'd expect, given that's where the cowboys and Indians all live. Although we're starting to get the Japanese toys in now."

"Really? Already?"

"They weren't bombed as badly as we were," he said. "Cheap, inferior products, but they're out there. A lot of us don't take kindly to selling them, but the war's over, so what's a feller to do?"

"I'll buy the American set," said Gwen firmly.

"Thank you, ma'am," he said, plucking it from the shelf. "Ah'll ring that up for you. Will there be anything else?"

"Actually," said Gwen, considering. "One more item, if I may."

"Sure thing, ma'am."

CHAPTER 8

Iris was back at her desk when Gwen returned, shoving a sandwich into her mouth. She waved Gwen's note with her other hand and motioned her to her desk.

"Any luck with Madame Bousquet?" asked Gwen.

Iris shook her head, then pointed an imaginary gun at her temple and let her eyes grow wide in fear.

"She was threatened?" exclaimed Gwen. "By whom? And how did they know?"

Iris shrugged, still chewing.

"Could you please swallow that so we could skip the Marx Brothers routine?" asked Gwen. "My Italian accent is wretched, anyway."

Iris swallowed, then followed the sandwich with a glass of water.

"I left you high and dry too long," she said. "Had to dash once I got back. No time for a proper lunch. Apologies. So we're being paid a visit in a few minutes?"

"We are," said Gwen, putting her shopping bag under her desk. "They received a letter with instructions. More important, it contained a letter written to Alice. I assume it was of an intimate nature, given how careful Patience was not to say anything about its contents."

"Score one for you," said Iris. "Any clue as to who wrote it?"

"She said it was signed with one initial."

"Oh, I hope it was a Z!" said Iris.

"Tell me about Madame Bousquet. Use actual words in sentences this time."

"Someone must have threatened her since yesterday. She wouldn't give me much. But I did get the name of Alice's maid. Vivienne Ducognon. She works for a woman named Calvert. Know any?"

"Lorraine Simpson married a Daniel Calvert, but I have no idea if she has a lady's maid, much less a French one. I could give her a call, see if any of her husband's family employs one. But how could anyone have learned about Madame Bousquet since we did?"

"Either our blackmailer was following leads independently and found her, or—" She hesitated.

"Or what?" asked Gwen.

"Or there's a leak somewhere in our communications," said Iris. "And it wasn't us."

"You can't mean Patience," said Gwen.

"Lady Matheson is the Queen's solver of uncomfortable problems. She knew the truth about Talbot all along. She would have had a head start on all of this. She hired us to dig it up independently so she could pretend it came from an outside source."

"Then why shut down Bousquet?"

"Maybe Lady Matheson only needs part of the truth to come out for her purposes, and Bousquet has the wrong part."

"What purposes? Does she want this to be true or not?"

"I suppose it depends on whether she wants Philip to become Elizabeth's husband or not. And that depends, in turn, on to whom she owes her loyalties."

"The Queen, surely."

"One would hope," said Iris. "But employment doesn't always equal loyalty."

"So what do we do?"

"Until we know more, we do what we were hired to do."

"Then to whom does our loyalty belong?" asked Gwen.

"Good question," said Iris. "You're the one with the moral compass. You tell me."

"That's not fair."

"Have you recently become immoral without letting me know?"

"Of course not. It's just that—" She stopped.

"It's just that what?" prompted Iris.

"I don't exactly know what our choices are right now," said Gwen. "I would say our loyalty is to the King."

"But we're working for the Queen. Or, rather, the Queen's woman, who we assume is working for the Queen's interests, which we in turn assume are also the King's interests, which we also assume are the country's interests."

"The lines of accountability are stretched rather thin by the time they reach down to us," said Gwen.

"And we still have no direct evidence of anything," Iris pointed out. "Just a decent working theory, and now our correspondent is forcing the issue before we have any certainty."

"What do we do?"

"As I said, what we are being paid to do," said Iris. "Until and unless we come across some reason to do otherwise."

"Sounds manageable."

"But we are going to keep a sharp watch for that reason," said Iris.

"All right," said Gwen. "That's them coming up the steps, if I'm not mistaken."

Lady Matheson swept in, followed by a younger woman carrying a brown leather courier bag slung from her shoulder. The latter wore a tan linen suit, unadorned by any ornamentation, and had a terrier-like alertness, seeming ready to pounce on any small mouse of a detail before it could scurry away. She looked around the office with barely concealed disdain, her lip curling slightly as she saw *The Forsyte Saga* at work, bravely supporting Gwen's desk.

Behind them, they glimpsed the bodyguard standing in the hall. He reached in after the women entered the office and pulled the door shut. His silhouette filled the frosted glass, facing the stairs.

Lady Matheson looked at the guest chair, which seemed to shrink under her gaze, then looked back at Iris.

"Right," said Iris, getting up. "Please take my seat at my desk, Lady Matheson. And you are?"

"Mrs. Penelope Fisher," said the younger woman. "I believe we've spoken on the telephone, if the two of you are Miss Travis and Miss Prescott."

"Only to you," said Iris, moving over to sit on the windowsill. "I'm Iris Sparks. This is my partner, Mrs. Gwendolyn Bainbridge. How do you do? Please take that seat there, and then we'll begin."

"Thank you," said Mrs. Fisher, pulling the guest chair up to the desks.

"Isn't this cozy?" said Lady Matheson acerbically. "One would think with what we've paid you, you might have invested in another chair."

"It's on the list," said Gwen. "Now that we're all here, perhaps you should fill us in on the letters."

Lady Matheson nodded to Mrs. Fisher, who opened the courier bag and pulled out a manila folder. Gwen put on her gloves and took it from her, then opened it so that Iris could see its contents over her shoulder.

The first sheet was covered with the same scrawl as the previous letter, its top similarly torn off. Gwen held it up to the light.

"No watermark this time," she observed. "He's not continuing with the same stationery. Looks like the same handwriting."

"Looks like someone deliberately using the wrong hand to disguise his handwriting," added Iris. "But it's the same person as the first letter, if I'm any judge. Have you had them analysed by an expert?"

"Not yet," said Lady Matheson. "We're keeping the number of people who know about this to the bare minimum. Once we catch the man, we'll do more."

"Is that the plan now?" asked Iris. "To catch him?"

"The plan is to avert embarrassment to the Crown," said Lady Matheson. "There are alternative ways of accomplishing that goal. Read the letter."

"'Here's a taste,'" read Gwen. "'If you don't want the rest on the front page of the *Tatler*, put a personal advertisement in the Saturday *Times* to Violet from Lily with a telephone number. I will call at two in the afternoon with further instructions. The price is five thousand pounds. No bargaining, no excuses.'"

"Five thousand," said Iris. "Clearly, we're all in the wrong professions, although it's probably just mad money for the Queen. What about the other letter?"

The second sheet in the folder was of light blue onionskin, slightly faded. Its creases divided it into thirds, and the folds were loose and supple.

"It's been read many times," said Gwen softly. "Opened, then refolded and replaced. I have letters from Ronnie that—Well, speaking as a woman, this letter appears to have been kept by someone who valued it."

"There should be fingerprints," said Iris.

"We'll have that done," said Lady Matheson. "Read it."

"It's in German," said Gwen. "Shall I translate?"

"If you feel up to the task," said Lady Matheson.

"Finishing school in Geneva, thank you very much," said Gwen. "I'll manage."

It was strange, she thought, reading someone's letters from another era. Intruding on the past, where all those who lived there were now old. Or dead. She cleared her throat and read.

"'My dearest A.,'" she began. "'I will be in Lugano on the seventeenth, my usual rooms. Leave a note with Franz at the front desk. My heart will not be denied. C.' And that's all."

"That's it?" exclaimed Iris. "He expects to be paid for that? It doesn't name names. It could be from anyone to anyone."

"I imagine he's keeping the juicier ones in reserve," said Lady Matheson. "Princess Alice was in Lugano, wasn't she?"

"While they were in exile," said Iris. "Before Andrea came back to Greece."

"And he came back without her," said Lady Matheson. "He left her behind out of concern for her safety. You say the dates work out for Philip's birth?"

"They do," said Gwen. "Or at least, they don't not work out."

"Any 'C's in her life, assuming this purported lover was clumsy enough to use his actual initial?"

"Christo," said Iris. "Andrea's younger brother. He and Alice were close. How close, I wouldn't venture to guess."

"But every tabloid journalist in London would," said Lady Matheson. "We cannot discount it. That's the damnable thing about this entire business."

"Then are you going to place the advertisement in the *Times*?" asked Gwen.

"We already have," said Lady Matheson. "We will all meet back here tomorrow at one thirty."

"Here?" exclaimed Iris. "Why here?"

"Because we used your number in the ad," explained Lady Matheson, an amused glint in her eyes as she saw the gathering outrage before her.

"Who the hell said we would agree to that?" sputtered Iris in fury. "That was never part of the bargain!"

"I could hardly be publishing a private palace number in the *Times*'s personals, could I?"

"Really, Patience," said Gwen. "This is beyond the pale. Next thing you know, you'll be expecting us to make the purchase for you."

Lady Matheson and Mrs. Fisher exchanged glances.

"Now that you've mentioned it," began Lady Matheson.

"No," said Iris firmly. "Go to the police. You have the clout to keep this quiet, but what you're talking about is illegal."

"It is," said Lady Matheson. "Sometimes one has to ignore that, as I'm sure the two of you know, given your recent experiences."

"Why us?" asked Iris. "A man will be waiting in a deserted rendezvous for a woman to walk in with five thousand pounds. How do we know this won't result in a dead woman, no money, and no letters?"

"It's potentially dangerous," acknowledged Lady Matheson.

"Potentially, my foot," said Gwen. "It's nothing but dangerous."

"Which is why Miss Sparks is best suited for undertaking the task," said Lady Matheson.

"What makes you think that?" asked Iris.

"Your training during the war," said Lady Matheson. "You can handle yourself in a tight spot, even when unarmed. Don't ask me how I know about that, by the way."

"You are very well informed," said Iris. "But even with my so-called skills, why me? There are people—there are women working for the Crown in various capacities who are just as qualified. I'm a civilian."

"Which is the major part of why I'd rather you be the one," said Lady Matheson. "I want no connection between this transaction and anyone working for His Majesty's government."

"You had that in mind all along, didn't you?" asked Gwen. "You knew when you hired us to look into Philip's background that you might be using us for the exchange."

"Using Miss Sparks, Gwen," said Lady Matheson. "I wouldn't dream of putting you through this."

"That's unfortunate," said Gwen. "Because there is no possible chance of her going in without me."

"Wait a second," said Iris. "There's no reason for one of us to go in, much less both of us."

"There is every reason," said Gwen. "First, he's less likely to try something if there are two of us. Second, even though there will be two of us, it's still two women, so he won't feel as threatened. Third, as a practical matter, you need an extra person with an extra pair of hands. There are too many objects being passed around— money, letters, possibly torches to be held if it's a dark place, as one imagines it would be. We want Iris to have her hands free in case she needs to bring those special skills into play. Really, when you come right down to it, I should be the one making the exchange, with her as my protector."

"This is utter nonsense," said Iris. "We're not doing this, Gwen."

"I think we should," said Gwen.

"You do?" asked Iris, looking at her in surprise. "Why?"

"Because the Queen needs us," said Gwen simply. "You had an entire war to serve Crown and country, while I and my wealthy, married, maternal status fled to the safety of a country estate. I've contributed nothing, Iris, but now I have a chance to do something."

"You lost a husband to the war," said Iris. "The country cannot ask you to do more."

"If Ronnie was alive, he'd want me to do this," said Gwen. "We'll make the exchange, Patience. Both of us."

"Then it's decided," said Lady Matheson. "Thank you, Gwen. We'll meet back—"

"Of course, there will be an extra fee," said Gwen.

"What?"

"Well, you can hardly expect us to be putting our lives at risk without compensation," said Gwen. "We run a marriage bureau. Making secret payments to blackmailers does not fall within the purview of our business or our prior arrangement with you. If you can manage five thousand pounds to a criminal, then an additional fifty pounds each for the delivery girl and her muscle—"

"Oh, I say!" said Iris, flexing her biceps. "I like that!"

"As I was saying, that shouldn't stretch the black budget overmuch," finished Gwen. "Don't you agree?"

Lady Matheson began to laugh.

"Why, you conniving little—"

"Ma'am?" cautioned Mrs. Fisher.

"You're in the connivance game, Patience," said Gwen. "Don't get upset if we want to play, too. May I ask you a question?"

"Go ahead."

"What do you intend to do with the letters?"

"It depends on their contents," said Lady Matheson. "Burning them would be the best course of action, don't you think?"

"I do," said Gwen, smiling at her. "I am relieved to hear you say that."

"Well, this has been a most surprising day," said Lady Matheson, getting up from the chair. "Not the least of which has been discovering this hitherto unknown mercenary aspect of my cousin. I must remember to make further use of that in the future."

"Come to us for all your clandestine needs," said Iris. "You know our rates."

Lady Matheson walked towards the door, which the bodyguard opened before she even reached it.

"I'll need those back," said Mrs. Fisher, indicating the letters.

"Lady Matheson," called Iris.

The woman stopped and turned.

"Do you have any letters that you know to be written by Princess Alice?" asked Iris. "We should have them for comparison."

"We've already thought of that," said Lady Matheson. "Fortunately, she kept up correspondence with her family here after marrying. We retrieved a set from the archives. We'll bring them with us."

"Until tomorrow, then," said Iris.

"Goodbye," said Mrs. Fisher.

Iris and Gwen waited until the footsteps receded down the stairwell and the front door opened and closed. Then Iris went out to the landing and peered out the window in time to see the bodyguard holding open the door of a black Bentley.

"They're gone," Iris reported as she came back into the office. "Now, tell me what that was all about."

"I realised that I don't trust my cousin," said Gwen.

"Neither do I," said Iris. "Not from the first. What changed?"

"You asked where our loyalties should lie," said Gwen. "Well, I thought about that while we were all in here. What is it that we are doing at The Right Sort, Iris?"

"We run a marriage bureau," said Iris.

"Exactly. We bring people together. We each came to this enterprise from a different direction but with the same goals—part altruism, part fun, part profit, part whatever. Part friendship, I would hope."

"That, for me, is the largest part."

"For me as well," said Gwen. "But what we do here is in the service of love. It sounds corny, I know, but it's the truth. Don't you agree?"

"I suppose I do," said Iris. "I've never put it so bluntly. And it has been pointed out that I am working towards that goal having never experienced it myself."

"That was pointed out by your ex-fiancé under circumstances that were rather heated, as I recall," said Gwen. "I would not accept that as an accurate description of the Iris Sparks that I know. I think that you are entirely capable of love, and that you did love him, at least for a time."

"Then I destroyed that love in the service of King and country." Iris sighed. *"C'est la guerre, n'est-ce pas?"*

"But the war is over," said Gwen. "Now we are being asked to possibly thwart a relationship, one that could happily continue if the ignorance of the parties is maintained. Patience was lying about burning the letters. I could see it in her eyes. I don't believe for a moment that she would hesitate to destroy the royal romance if she saw fit, whether it suited the Crown's purposes or not."

"And you object to that."

"I do. Strenuously. And there's another thing."

"What?"

"These letters don't belong to her," said Gwen. "They didn't belong to Gerald Talbot, they don't belong to the blackmailer, and they don't belong to the Crown. The only person with proper rights to them is Princess Alice. That is why I said the two of us should handle the exchange. Once we retrieve the letters, we should return them to her and no one else."

"Oh my," said Iris, looking at her partner in admiration. "You want to steal them from the thief and the Queen's woman. Now, that sounds like fun!"

"Do you agree?"

"I do. I am now Love's Champion!"

"Good. Because we need to plan this now. And there is one more thing. Before Patience got here, we were talking about possible leaks."

"Yes?"

"How much did you tell your old boss when you went to him for information?"

"A fair amount," said Iris. "I had to convince him of the importance of the task before he would relent."

"You didn't consider him as a risk?"

"Of course I did."

"You didn't mention it during that portion of our discussion. Why not?"

Iris looked at her partner, who was staring at her with that unearthly focus that always seemed to penetrate Iris's innermost thoughts.

"Because I didn't want to think that of him," she said. "Because I want to trust him."

"When you made your list of those you trust the other night, there were only two people on it," said Gwen. "He wasn't one of them."

"I want him to be," said Iris. "I need to know that the things I did during the war at his behest were all for the good. Because some of them were quite terrible."

"And now?" asked Gwen.

"What are you asking?"

"You told me that you didn't want to work for him anymore. Yet I sense a yearning within you for that life, as duplicitous and dangerous as it was."

"I thought Dr. Milford was in charge of winnowing out my dark secrets."

"This isn't therapy, Iris. This is you and me. I'm not asking you to spill every sordid detail of your past, but if we are working together on something this risky, then I need to know that you won't have any blind spots about anyone involved."

"All right," said Iris.

"So, is it possible that your boss is the one who got to Madame Bousquet?"

"Yes. In fact, it would be exactly the sort of thing he would do."

"Which means he knew about her beforehand but lied to you about it."

"Also possible. And he might already have reached out to Vivienne Ducognon by now. He has more resources than we do."

"And more time. Well, that can't be helped. I'll make some calls to see if I can find her, but our priority is getting hold of those letters."

"And then keeping them, which might be the more difficult task," said Iris.

"Iris, why don't you trust Patience? I'm going on instinct, as I always do, but you usually have some concrete reason."

"She didn't have the letter fingerprinted," said Iris. "If they have old letters from Alice, then they would have fingerprints for comparison. Lady Matheson doesn't want the whole truth, just a truth that she can use, and that can't be good."

"How do we keep them away from her? She might have us followed."

"I have an idea. Pass me the telephone, if you please."

That evening, Gwen located some tissue paper and ribbons, then sat down in Little Ronnie's playroom and wrapped the present for Tommy. Another normal thing that normal mothers do, she thought. Maybe I am becoming normal again.

Then she thought about the next day's activities and rescinded that thought.

In the morning, she kissed Little Ronnie goodbye. He was in a little blue suit, with short pants. A blue-and-yellow-striped cap sat on his head. He could not have looked more darling, she thought, trying not to cry in front of him.

"You make sure you take your jacket and cap off before you play," she instructed him.

"Yes, Mummy," he said.

"And no roughhousing!"

"Yes, Mummy."

She handed the wrapped gift to Albert, the chauffeur. Lady Carolyne strode in, dressed to kill, an ermine wrap around her shoulders.

"This is a children's party, you know," said Gwen.

"A party at a fine house deserves one's best," said Lady Carolyne. "We must set a good example for the children."

"Of course," said Gwen. "Give them my love. I'll be at the office today."

"On a Saturday?" asked Lady Carolyne. "That's unusual."

"Not everyone can meet us during the workweek," said Gwen. "And sometimes we get more done when the block is less active. The noise levels are lower."

"Very well," said Lady Carolyne. "May you have a productive day."

"Thank you."

She watched them drive away, then pinned her hat on and left for the office.

It was eleven when she arrived. Mayfair was bustling with shoppers, searching for whatever was available with limited supplies on the one hand and limited coupons on the other.

The block on which their building was situated was comparatively quiet. The work crews who had been clearing the bombing debris on either side were off. Gwen realised that she had become oblivious to the noise since they had taken possession of their office on the fourth storey. She let herself in the front door, then climbed the steps to The Right Sort. She found Iris already there, leaning out their window with her hands gripping the sill.

"What on earth are you doing?" asked Gwen.

"Figuring something out," said Iris, pulling herself back in. "No trouble getting away?"

"I impressed my mother-in-law with the lengths of my dedication to playing Cupid."

"How are things going with her?"

"Peaceful. We're both waiting for Lord Bainbridge to come home before we resolve anything with Little Ronnie."

"Honestly, I don't know how you do it," said Iris. "You're like a prisoner of war in that house."

"A prisoner of war in a Kensington house with a full staff," said Gwen. "Let's not overstate the horrors of my life."

"But to live full-time biting your tongue," said Iris. "I think it would drive me mad."

"I do it for my son," said Gwen simply. "Every time I want to grab my mother-in-law by the throat and shake her until all of her jewelry goes flying in different directions, I think about Ronnie, count slowly to ten, and go about my business. And I have my job to escape to."

"With its absence of stress." Iris laughed. "Apart from the occasional murder investigation or rendezvous with blackmailers."

"Well, a touch of variety provides the spice, doesn't it?" said Gwen.

"I'm impressed that all it takes is a count of ten."

"There have been times when it took twenty," admitted Gwen. "Forty-seven, on one memorable occasion."

"You'll have to tell about that one someday. Now, let's go over the plan again."

At 1:25, Iris descended the stairs to the front door. The Bentley pulled up a minute after she took her post. The bodyguard got out and held the door for Lady Matheson and Mrs. Fisher, the latter once again carrying the courier bag. This time, it was bulging noticeably.

Iris opened the front door for the arrivals. The two women passed her wordlessly and began the climb. Iris started to follow them, then turned to face the bodyguard as he brought up the rear. He stopped to look at her.

"Are you going with us to the exchange?" she asked.

He shook his head.

"Pity," said Iris. "I could use some backup."

"I thought you didn't need any help in that regard," he said as they followed the others.

"Everyone could use someone," said Iris. "Speaking of which, are you single?"

"Looking for new business in the middle of all this?" he asked, laughing softly. "You've got some cheek, Miss Sparks."

"Emphasis on the 'Miss,'" said Iris. "Sometimes I ask for business. Sometimes I ask for pleasure. You're good-looking, you're single, and you're dangerous, which means you meet all my prime requirements, except for one."

"I'll bite," he said. "Which one?"

"I prefer men with names," whispered Iris. "It gives me something to say when things get going."

"And you'd like to get them going with me?"

"If you're free after the felonious transaction, Nameless Man. I am anticipating that we'll be losing our connection after today, so I'm not going to waste any more time. Interested? I only ask once."

"I've never gone out with a truly dangerous woman," he said, grinning. "Montgomery Stallings is the name. The girls call me Monty. Especially when things get going."

"Call me when this is over," said Iris. "Maybe you'll get me to call you Monty, too."

They reached the office. Lady Matheson had already taken Iris's chair. Iris grabbed her pad and pencil from the desktop and curled up on her perch on the windowsill.

Stallings closed the door after them and stood in the hallway, his back to the office.

"Even with no one in the building but us, he does that," commented Gwen.

"That's his job," said Lady Matheson. "Now, I will handle the call, but I'll try and angle the receiver so that you can hear the other end of the conversation. Any advice?"

"Make sure that you give us enough time to reach the rendezvous point," said Iris. "He thinks he's calling the Palace. Travel time from Mayfair might be longer, depending. I don't suppose you'd care to lend us the Bentley? And the driver, while you're at it?"

"We need the Bentley to be safely inside the Palace grounds when the exchange is made," said Lady Matheson. "It can be traced to us."

"You'll be somewhere in the Palace in full view of people who can later confirm you were there, I imagine," said Gwen.

"Of course. Some ceremonial function. I'm not even sure what it is."

"Her Majesty is meeting with a delegation from the Land Girls," said Mrs. Fisher promptly. "The press will be there."

"How tedious," said Lady Matheson. "But perfect. Let's give you the money. Mrs. Fisher?"

Mrs. Fisher opened the courier bag and began piling stacks of twenty-pound notes on Gwen's desk.

"I think this time, we had better count it and give you a receipt," said Gwen.

"I have already counted it," said Mrs. Fisher huffily.

"Nevertheless," said Gwen, riffling through each stack quickly.

"Think how awkward it would be if we were on the verge of securing the letters and we were short," said Iris, joining her. "Right, that's a hundred."

"And that's a hundred fifty," said Gwen. "Two hundred fifty times twenty is five thousand, received by The Right Sort for services rendered."

She scribbled it down on a piece of paper, signed it, then handed it to Mrs. Fisher, who folded the receipt and put it in the courier bag. She then took out five more twenty-pound notes and handed them to Gwen.

"In case you thought we had forgotten," said Lady Matheson.

"Not at all," said Iris, resuming her window seat. "Not with the fearsome musculature of Iris Sparks looming over you."

"Yes, I feel absolutely threatened right now," said Lady Matheson.

She reached into her bag and pulled out a plain white envelope. She handed it to Iris, who opened it. Inside were several sheets of light blue onionskin, a lighter shade of blue than the one purportedly sent by "C."

"Princess Alice's letters?" asked Iris as she gently opened the first one.

"Yes."

"'My dear Great-Grandmother,'" began Iris. Then she looked up at Lady Matheson. "These were to Queen Victoria."

"Yes. Take good care of them." She glanced at her watch. "Not long now. Let's see if our man is punctual. I do detest tardiness in a blackmailer."

The four of them stared at the telephone on Iris's desk, sneaking glances at their watches. The telephone ultimately gave in to the pressure and rang. Lady Matheson snatched up the handset.

"Lily here," she said, holding the earpiece outwards. "To whom am I speaking?"

"I want to talk to the princess," said a man's voice, tinny and soft. The other three women leaned forwards and strained to follow it.

"I speak for her," said Lady Matheson.

"You have the money."

"I have the money, but you will see none of it unless you tell me what we are getting for it."

"Love letters," he said. "From and to Princess Alice, and her husband ain't the other correspondent. They get awful steamy in places. You'd think a high-bred bird like her wouldn't know those words."

"How did you get them?"

"From a chap named Talbot. Used to be a spy for your side. I ran some errands for him once upon a time."

"Why did he give these letters to you?"

"Who said he gave 'em?" said the man, laughing. "I got 'em, and that's all you need to know about that. Hung on to 'em for a laugh, but now they're worth something. I get a yes from you right now, lady, or the deal's off."

"All right. My answer is yes. Where do we meet?"

"You know where Blackwall Yard is?"

Lady Matheson glanced over at Iris, who nodded.

"Yes," said Lady Matheson.

"Western side, next to Poplar Dock, there are a bunch of bombed-out warehouses. The one closest to the water, end of Brunswick Street."

"Last warehouse by Poplar Dock, end of Brunswick Street," repeated Lady Matheson as the others scribbled down the address.

"You come alone—"

"No, I come with my secretary," said Lady Matheson. "I am not venturing alone into a bombed-out warehouse on your say-so."

"All right, then," said the man. "But only her."

He was expecting something like that, thought Iris.

"You get there at three thirty."

"Four o'clock," said Lady Matheson. "It will take us some time from where we are."

"You're not at the Palace?"

"We're at a secure location, away from prying eyes. Don't question how we handle this business. Four o'clock if you want your money."

"Four, then. The two of you walk in. I'll have eyes on the place. If I see anything I don't like, I'm smoke in the wind. Understand?"

"I understand."

"Tell me what you look like."

"I'm tall, blond, thirtyish," said Lady Matheson, perusing Gwen as she spoke. "I'm wearing a light blue suit. My secretary is short, brunette, and wearing a cream-coloured linen suit. I doubt you'll find any other ladies of that description down that way."

"Oh, there's ladies enough wandering about the docks," said the man. "Only they don't dress so nice. Like I said, you go in and wait. Once I know the coast is clear, I come in after you. We make the swap, then I leave and you wait ten minutes. Four o'clock."

"But what if—" began Lady Matheson.

The line went dead.

Iris tore the address from her pad and folded it up.

"You can still say no," said Lady Matheson. "I don't like the sound of it."

"No," said Iris immediately.

"Yes," said Gwen, gathering up the money and putting it in a Hamleys shopping bag that she had saved from her recent expedition. "Go hide in the Palace, Patience. We'll call Mrs. Fisher when we're done."

"Good luck," said Lady Matheson.

Gwen waited until she heard them leave through the building's front entrance, then closed the office door and turned to face Iris, a look of rage on her face.

"Thirtyish!" she said indignantly. "She said I look thirtyish!"

"That's the part that upsets you?" Iris laughed.

"I look nothing of the sort!"

"You are twenty-eight. It's close enough to be in the -ish range."

"But I don't look it! I take a great deal of care not to look that old. You wouldn't describe me as thirtyish, would you?"

"Oh, twenty-fourish, no question," said Iris, smirking.

Gwen gave her the Stare.

"No, I meant nineteen, certainly," Iris amended hastily. "Fresh out of boarding school, strawberries and cream. Any man who sought you would be robbing the cradle."

"Stop," said Gwen. "The damage has been done. There will be no repairing my ego today."

She picked up the Hamleys bag and stared at the money inside.

"We could go on a massive shopping spree," she said. "I would feel so much better after."

"Moral compass," said Iris. "Remember?"

"Right," sighed Gwen. "Come, Muscle."

"Call me that again, and I may hit you."

"That's why I bring you along. Damn!"

"What?"

"I should have demanded cab fare while I was being so mercenary. I guess that will come out of our fee. I have so much to learn as a bagman. Shall we?"

"Ours not to make reply," said Iris, grabbing her bag. "Ours not to reason why. Ours but to do and die."

"Do," said Gwen firmly. "Only do."

It took over an hour for the cab to get from Mayfair to the head of Brunswick Street. The cabbie took one look at the wreckage littering the street and pulled over.

"This is as close as I get," he said. "Can't risk damaging the tyres. Are you sure this is where you want to go?"

"It is," said Gwen, paying him. "Thank you for your time."

"How are you getting back?" he asked. "Should I wait?"

"We may be a while. We'll find our way."

They got out and stood at the intersection, looking down towards the Thames. There were graving docks and warehouses still in working order off to their left, but the view directly in front of them was a war zone, untouched by repairs. Ruined warehouses lined the road, caved-in roofs surrounded by scorched walls. The road itself was lined with twisted rails, their jagged ends bent up towards the heavens in a final rictus of agonised steel. At the end of the street, a large crater marked where one of the heavy bombs had hit, bricks and cobblestones strewn carelessly about its edges.

"Cheerful sight," said Iris. "I don't suppose there will be tea available."

"We're early," said Gwen. "Do you think he's here yet?"

"I think he's here and watching us already," said Iris.

"Do you think he knows it's us?"

"Unless there have been other pairs of similarly dressed ladies wandering about, I should think we're obviously us. Let's go. And mind your footing."

"I never wear the right shoes for our more criminal endeavours," complained Gwen, looking at the broken surface dubiously.

They walked carefully down the street, stepping around the shards of broken glass and metal littering their path.

"I'm glad it's the last warehouse," said Iris. "It would be difficult to tell which of these ruins to count otherwise. You brought your torch, I hope?"

"Yes. A Girl Guide is always at the ready when things are at their darkest."

Iris scanned the ruins on both sides of the street.

"I don't see him," she said. "But there are more than a dozen places he could be hiding."

"There isn't a watchman on guard," Gwen noted.

"No need. There's nothing to steal except scrap metal. It's a smart choice of location."

"I'll remember that the next time I do this," said Gwen. "I'm frightened, I admit it."

"Now you're frightened," said Iris. "Where was this sensible reaction when we needed it? Shall we turn back?"

"No," said Gwen. "We've come this far. We have to see it through."

The last warehouse was mostly intact. A metal awning projected over the water, but the roof was heavily damaged. The brickwork, despite the utilitarian nature of the building, had bits of ornamental design riddling the surface, many of the bricks gouged and chipped from the debris of the blasts. An old sign dangled vertically from one rusting iron hook, the words "Midland Rai—" still legible under the soot.

They advanced towards the front door. Gwen consulted her wristwatch.

"Five of four," she said. "Do we care about making an entrance at the exact hour?"

"I'd rather not be standing about," said Iris. "Look! There's a padlock."

She pointed to where it lay to the side of the entrance, a chain lying next to it, still threaded through its loop. The plates to which the lock and chain had been secured were beyond them, separated from the door.

"Someone has prepared the way," said Iris. "With a crowbar. I don't like that he has a crowbar. Crowbars can do a lot of damage to thirtyish-looking women."

"In other words, you want me to go in first," said Gwen.

"Curse you," said Iris.

She pushed the door open and waited for a moment. The interior was dark.

"Ready?" she asked, pulling her torch from her bag and holding it in her left hand.

"Ready," said Gwen, holding hers. Both voice and hand were unsteady.

"Come on, Girl Guide," said Iris. "Be prepared."

She stepped inside, Gwen following.

The far corner on the left had crumbled, letting in some light, but the late afternoon sun was behind them, so much of the space beyond the doorway was dark. They stood side by side, letting the beams from their torches play across the cavernous space.

His eyes still glistened. He had been crying, thought Iris, as she went over to where he lay. He didn't die right away, so there were tears, whether from the pain or because he knew it was over and there was nothing he could do about it. The streaks marked his cheeks on both sides, falling towards his temples.

"Iris?" Gwen's voice quavered. "Is he—?"

Iris squatted down by him and felt for a pulse, just in case she was wrong. But she wasn't.

"Dead," she said.

CHAPTER 9

Iris stood, whipping her torch around.

"Gwen, get that door closed," she said.

"What?"

"Close the front door. And be a dear and wipe the outer handle for me first? I don't want to leave any prints behind."

"But—"

"No arguments with me right now," said Iris, and Gwen saw the knife in her hand, then heard a soft snicking sound reverberating through the space as she flipped it open.

"Iris?"

"Gwen. Door. Now!" said Iris, sweeping her torch in every direction, then striding through the debris. "And thank you for not screaming."

"I'm not screaming? I thought I was screaming," said Gwen as she moved numbly to the front door. "Why am I not screaming?"

She took her handkerchief out and wiped the outer handle, then shut the door. Then she realised she had her bare hand on the inner handle. She let it go like a hot poker, then wiped it over and over again.

She turned back to face the darkness. Iris was off to the left somewhere, her torch beaming its rays across the space, momentarily illuminating small portions of the interior—piles of rubble, old coal hoppers lying on their sides, a wheelbarrow split in jagged halves. There was a sudden flapping noise, and a group of rooks took flight through the hole in the corner, making rasping squawks as they were roused from their nests.

What was the collective noun for rooks? thought Gwen. Parliament? No, that was owls. A clamour. That was it. Too appropriate. A clamour of rooks fleeing Iris, a clamour fleeing the glamour and the glimmer of Iris, who was off to the left in the darkness with a knife in one hand, a torch in the other, seeking a killer.

Who, for all they knew, was to the right instead. Moving towards Gwen.

Gwen swung her torch in that direction, rewarding herself with a fleeting glimpse of the dead man, still staring up at the roof. Past him, the room was empty. There was another set of wide doors in that direction. Must be for loading whatever it once was from ships to hoppers, or hoppers to ships. So much she didn't know about what went on in warehouses, far from her Kensington life.

So much she didn't know about anything anymore.

Iris prowled through the expanse of the warehouse, flashing the torch down at the floor every other step to make sure she wasn't about to plunge through a hole into the Thames or whatever rat-infested sewer lay underneath.

"Come out, come out, wherever you are," she sang softly, her knife held before her, reflecting the torchlight.

She saw no one. Satisfied that the killer had fled, she picked her way back to where Gwen held her post, waving her torch around wildly.

"He's gone," reported Iris, taking a pair of black leather gloves from her bag and pulling them on. "Whoever he was, he chose not to hang around. Now, keep an ear out for anyone coming, and do me a favour and shine your torch at this poor chap."

"All right," said Gwen, complying. "But why—my God, Iris! You're—you're touching him! It! Him!"

"Can't leave without seeing if he has what we're looking for," said Iris, running her hands through his coat. "Blast. Nothing that feels like a packet of letters. Here's his billfold. Money still in it. And there's his ident card. Nikolas Magoulias."

"He's Greek?"

"Well, it's a Greek name," said Iris. "British ident card, though. I wonder if it's real."

She lit up the man's face again. Olive-complexioned, dark hair and mustache. Glistening eyes . . .

She reached down and closed them gently.

"I should leave pennies for the ferryman," she whispered to him. "I'm sorry that I won't be."

She replaced his billfold in his coat pocket. Something glinted a few feet to her right. She turned her torch towards it.

"Look," she said. "A dagger."

"He was stabbed?"

"He was stabbed, certainly," said Iris, shining her torch at the man's stomach, which was covered with blood. "Several times. But not with that."

"How can you tell?" asked Gwen.

"Look at the blade," said Iris. "Whoever stabbed this fellow plunged his knife in to the hilt, and did it more than once. That dagger's blade is only bloodied at the tip. Let me see—"

She slid her hands up his sleeves, then felt behind his neck.

"Yes," she said. "There's a sheath at his collar. The dagger must have been his. He was able to do some damage to his killer before he succumbed."

"Should we be glad for that?" asked Gwen.

Iris stood and shone her light at the ground around the man. Something red and wet caught her eye.

"There," she said, pointing to it. "A splash of blood. And another beyond it. The killer went that way, through that door."

"Then I think we should go out this way," said Gwen, reaching for the front door. Then she froze. "Iris. There's a siren. And I think it's getting closer."

"Let's take our chances with the killer, then," said Iris. "Come on."

Gwen stood anchored in place.

"We can't just leave him," she said. "It wouldn't be right. There will be vermin."

"Sirens, Gwen," said Iris, coming forwards to grab her by the arm. "The police will find him."

"What if they don't?"

"I promise you that we will make an anonymous call at the first telephone box we find once we're safely away," said Iris. "Now, come on!"

She hauled Gwen to a small door by the large ones facing the Thames.

"Step to the side," she instructed Gwen. "We don't want to get any blood on your shoes."

"We've disturbed a crime scene," said Gwen.

"We have," said Iris. "We've done many illegal things in a short space of time, and now we are going to run from the police like good criminals should."

She opened the door and peered out, knife at the ready.

"The coast is clear," she reported. "Follow me."

They emerged onto a strip of dock, half of which had fallen into the water. Iris took a quick look. The blood trail went towards their right.

"He doubled back to Brunswick Street," she said. "Maybe while we were in there. I'm not going to chance going after him and winding up in the arms of the police."

A sharp whistle hailed them from the middle of the river.

"There's our ride," she said, waving to a small boat with an outboard motor heading in their direction. The skipper waved back.

"Ladder," said Iris, pointing to one nearby.

"Wrong shoes for that as well," muttered Gwen.

Iris swung herself over the ladder and climbed down. Gwen gulped, then followed her.

Sally sat in the stern of the boat, smiling broadly, the engine idling behind him.

"Ahoy, ladies!" he called. "May I offer you a lift?"

Then he saw Gwen's face, and his expression changed immediately to one of concern.

"What happened?" he said, getting up to help them aboard. "Did you get what you came for?"

"Quite a bit, and no," said Iris. "But before I fill you in, have you any whisky handy?"

"Always," he said, producing a small pewter flask from his hip.

Iris took it, removed the cap, and held it out to her partner. Gwen didn't move, staring into space. Iris placed the mouth of the flask in Gwen's and tilted it up. Gwen came to life, spluttering, then burst into tears.

"That's a start," said Iris. "Get us out of here, Sally. Stay close to this side so the wall gives us some cover."

"Aye, aye, Captain," said Sally.

He took a small paddle and pushed the boat away from the dock, then throttled the motor up a notch.

"May I?" asked Iris, holding up the flask.

"By all means," said Sally. "If I had known we'd be imbibing on the high seas, I would have brought grog."

They passed by the Blackwall Stairs, then angled to the south as the Thames snaked between Greenwich and the Isle of Dogs.

"We should give Buchanan-Wollaston a wave," said Iris. "He's probably watching us right now."

"Who on earth is he?" asked Sally. "And when are you going to tell me what happened? Did you make the exchange?"

"No."

"Fellow got cold feet?"

"Fellow got cold everything," said Iris. "Fellow got killed. Stabbed to death, not long before we came on the scene."

"Oh dear," said Sally. "Inconvenient, that. Is that what was drawing the attention of the police as we made our getaway?"

"Very likely, and I'm wondering who alerted them. Did you see anyone going in or out from your vantage point?"

"I couldn't see the entrance," said Sally. "It was all I could do to get here on time. I caught the note you threw out the window with the address, hopped on my motorcycle, and drove like a madman to where I had the boat ready. Good guess that he'd be using a riverside location."

"It seemed likely," said Iris. "In any case, if it had been inland, you would have taken the car instead. What about the dockside door? Did you see anyone go in or out?"

"I was getting to that. About ten minutes before the two of you came out, a chap comes through that door, throws something into the Thames, and limps off to the west. I lost sight of him."

"Probably tossed the knife. He had a limp?"

"He had. Something wrong with his right leg, but I couldn't see what. I was focusing on his face."

"Did you get a good look?" asked Iris.

"Good enough," said Sally, holding up a pair of opera glasses. "Should I go to the Yard and volunteer to pore over mug books?"

"How would you explain your presence in a boat at that location?" asked Iris.

"Innocent fishing expedition?"

"Dressed in a suit? With neither pole nor tackle box?"

"Incompetent neophyte fisherman? No, I don't think I could sell that easily. What's your plan?"

"I don't have one yet," said Iris. "The original plan didn't allow for the blackmailer getting killed and relieved of the letters before we got there. We're back to—well, I was going to say square one, but there's a new game being played now. There's still the other part of the original plan, but I won't know the results of that until Monday."

"So, if you didn't get the letters, what happened to the money?"

Iris nodded towards the Hamleys bag sitting on Gwen's lap.

"Really?" said Sally, his eyebrows arching. "There's five thousand pounds in there?"

"Yes. Don't tell me you're thinking of tipping us into the Thames and sailing off into the sunset."

"No," said Sally. "But you could tell them the blackmailer grabbed the money and ran, then we could split it three ways."

"No," croaked Gwen. "Moral compass. Still functioning."

"And she's back," said Iris. "How are you feeling, darling?"

Gwen held out her hand. Iris placed the flask in it.

"I say," said Sally as she tilted it back. "Go easy. That's hard to get."

"It's terrible," said Gwen, replacing the cap. "What is it?"

"Canadian."

"We never should have colonised the place," she said. She was still trembling.

Iris put an arm around her and pulled her close. "You've had a shock," she said. "You'll be all right."

"Like hell I will," said Gwen. "How could the two of you be so calm? Rational? You were making jokes, for God's sake!"

"Not my first body," said Iris.

"And I've completely lost count," said Sally. "Not that I've gotten used to the sight. Still remember the first quite vividly. I plan to work it into a play some day, if I can stop screaming long enough to write the scene. But I didn't even get to see this one."

"Why did he go in first?" asked Gwen, her voice still on the edge of hysteria. "He was supposed to come in after us. What was he doing there?"

"Maybe he was checking out the location early to make sure it was clear," suggested Iris. "Only it wasn't."

"Could the killer have been someone there just randomly?" asked Gwen. "A tramp?"

"I don't believe that, and neither do you," said Iris. "Someone has raised the stakes considerably."

"But why? Because of money?"

"There are people who will kill for much less than five thousand pounds," offered Sally. "I can't give you the going rate, but one hears things."

"But it is more likely something to do with the princess," said Iris. "Either someone else is attempting to blackmail her—or someone's trying to protect her."

"He's doing a thorough job, if that's the case," said Gwen. "I wonder how far he'll go."

"Meaning?"

"What if he decides to eliminate everyone who knows about this?"

"He doesn't know about us, if that's what you're worried about."

"But what about Princess Alice's people? Vivienne Ducognon, for example? If she knew anything, she might be in danger."

"Then we'd better find her and warn her," said Iris. "Another item for the list. But I think we'd better find out more about Mr. Magoulias first."

"Magoulias?" asked Sally. "Who is that?"

"Our new dead friend," said Iris. "Nikolas Magoulias. Anything about that name?"

"Nothing," said Sally. "Greek, obviously, which means we're back to the Thrilling Adventures of Sir Gerald Talbot. Going to talk to your boss again?"

"Emphatically not," said Iris. "But if we trace the history of Mr. Magoulias, that might provide more for the provenance of these mythical letters."

"What about the murder, Iris?" asked Gwen.

"Let the police figure it out."

"But we have information. And there's a killer on the loose."

Iris and Sally looked at her. She was no longer trembling. Instead, she was staring over Sally's shoulder at the warehouse as it disappeared from view as the boat turned past the isle.

"The last time I saw that look in your eyes was when you plunged us into investigating Tillie La Salle's murder," said Iris. "That nearly got you killed, remember?"

"It was only a month ago," said Gwen. "Do you think I'd forget something like that? What is your point?"

"This time, we should let the police do their job. If we get involved—"

"We're already involved."

"Not in a murder investigation."

"It's part and parcel of what we've been working on," said Gwen. "If we still intend to intercept those letters, then we have to find the man who has them."

"I think we've missed our chance," said Iris.

"We've missed one chance," said Gwen. "We don't know that it's the only one. And what if the police get to those letters first? What happens?"

"They leak them to the press," said Sally.

"Whose side are you on?" asked Iris, turning on him angrily.

"Yours. Meaning both of you, of course."

"And when we disagree?"

"Then I will wait patiently for you to agree again," he said. "And then do your bidding, for I am your humble servant."

"You're being theatrical again," said Iris.

"Thank you, Sally," said Gwen. "For that, and for everything."

They rounded the Isle of Dogs without further discussion. When the stairs to Wapping High Street came into sight, Sally eased up on the throttle and guided the boat to the bank below them.

"I'm letting you off here," he said, helping Gwen onto the shore. "I have to return the boat before the owner notices it's gone missing."

"I thought you borrowed it," said Iris as she stepped out, unassisted.

"It's a loose concept," he said. "I also have to return the motorcycle I borrowed. And the auto I borrowed. What wonderful, oblivious friends have I! I'll call you if I need bail."

"We have it," said Gwen, holding up the Hamleys bag.

"That should be enough for a much larger crime spree," said Sally as he shoved off. "Here I go. Good night, ladies."

He waved and vanished around the bend.

"There's a pub at the top of the stairs," offered Iris.

"I know," said Gwen. "Not tonight. Let's get back to The Right Sort and figure things out."

They climbed the steps, then turned onto Wapping High Street.

"Call boxes," said Gwen, pointing out a pair on the corner.

"Yes, I see them," said Iris.

She stepped inside, inserted a coin, and dialed.

"'Allo, please?" she said in a high-pitched voice. "Ees police, please? Ees dead man in varehouse. Brunsveek Street, Blackvall Yard. No, no geev name. Bye!"

She hung up.

"What accent was that supposed to be?" asked Gwen.

"No idea," said Iris. "And they won't know what it was, either."

"Appalling," said Gwen. "We've become appalling people, Iris. When did that happen?"

*   *   *

It was past six when they finally got back to their building. Gwen unlocked the front door, and they trudged up the steps to their office. Gwen collapsed into her chair.

"Pass me the telephone," she said. "I should let them know I'm going to be home late."

"Here you are," said Iris. "And you had better give me the money. I'll put it in the strongbox until we need it again. When you're done calling home, we should have Oona and Catherine check in with Mrs. Fisher."

"What should we tell her?"

"That the mission was unsuccessful, and that the money is safe," said Iris. "And that someone was murdered, but we didn't do it."

She bent down and slid open the panel concealing the strongbox, then unlocked it.

"Poor empty sod," she said to it. "Mummy's about to feed you like you've never been fed before."

She transferred the money from the bag to the strongbox.

"Hello, Percival?" said Gwen as the butler answered. "It's Mrs. Bainbridge. I'm dining out with Miss Sparks tonight. Is your young lord and cowpoke home from the range?"

"He is, Mrs. Bainbridge," said Percival. "Unless I am mistaken, that is him stampeding towards the telephone now. Shall I put him on?"

"Yes, thank you," said Gwen.

She held back the receiver from her ear.

"Hello, Mummy," said Little Ronnie.

"You're not shouting," said Gwen proudly. "Well done. How was Tommy's birthday party?"

"It was wonderful! We played Pin the Tail on the Donkey and cowboys and Indians and there was cake with real frosting and lemonade."

"Did he like the present you gave him?"

"He loved it and he said I could come over and play with him tomorrow afternoon so may I please, Mummy?"

"Well," began Gwen.

Then she saw the man at the door pointing a gun at her. He put a finger to his lips, then motioned for her to hang up the telephone.

"Yes, that would be fine," said Gwen. "Mummy has to go now, darling. There's someone here."

"Someone here?" asked Iris, popping up from behind her desk as Gwen hung up the telephone. "Oh! Someone here with a gun. Hello, how may we help you? Are you looking for a wife? We have several gun-lovers amongst our female clientele."

"Shut it," said the man, coming into the office and closing the door behind him. "I came for the money."

He was tall and thin, wearing a brown raincoat over a brown three-piece suit despite the fact that it was a hot, sunny day. He was gray at the temples, and had a thin mustache that did little to improve a sallow, weaselly face.

"Money?" repeated Iris, a puzzled look on her face. "This is a marriage bureau. We don't keep cash on the premises. Why, whatever we have, we deposit on Fridays, which was yesterday. If you'd like to have better luck, may I suggest you come back next Thursday afternoon? I believe we have an open time slot for robbery available."

"Five thousand pounds," said the man. "A little kiss from Lily to Violet."

"That was given in exchange for a packet of letters," said Gwen. "I'm afraid you're too late."

"I don't think so," said the man.

He transferred the gun to his left hand, then reached inside his raincoat and pulled out a thick manila envelope.

"I've still got the letters," he said. "So you must still got the money."

"So you're the one who killed the chap in the warehouse?" asked Iris.

The man rapidly blinked twice.

"He's dead, then? The little Greek fellow?" he asked.

"You shouldn't be surprised after how you left him," said Iris.

"I didn't know he bought it," said the man. "I never was in there. I was watching for you from the other side. I saw him go in. Then a couple of minutes later, I see another fellow come out the dockside door, limping past my hidey-hole."

"Limping?" asked Gwen.

"I didn't know what was going on, but I didn't like it. Then I see the two of you go in, and I decided to sit tight and see what was going on. Then I hear sirens, and that was enough for me."

"And yet you came here," said Gwen.

"You've got the money here, don't you?"

"My point is, how did you know where we were? You didn't follow us here."

"I recognised you," said the man, smirking slightly. "You two were all over the papers last month. Even saw you on the newsreel. So, it didn't take much to figure out you'd come here."

"Enterprising fellow," commented Iris. "Well, if you're here to make a deal, put the gun away and we'll talk business."

"I don't think so," said the man. "The coppers are involved now. I feel a distinct lack of trust from your side."

"And yet you're here," said Gwen. "How do we know those letters are the genuine article?"

"That's your problem," said the man.

"We aren't paying for an envelope," said Gwen. "You let us examine the letters, and we'll decide whether they're worth paying for."

He hesitated.

"Nope, not convinced," said Iris. "Take your counterfeit correspondence and scurry back to your burrow."

He stepped up to Gwen's desk and put the muzzle of the gun to her forehead. She looked him in the eyes unflinchingly.

"Where's the money?" he asked.

"In a strongbox," Iris said immediately.

"In here?"

"Yes," said Iris. "Under my desk. Put that gun away, please."

"Open it," he said. "Nothing funny or your partner gets it."

"Iris, don't," said Gwen.

"It's only money, Gwen," said Iris. "You're worth far more than five thousand pounds to me."

She bent down to open the strongbox. The man watched her closely.

"Wait," he said when he heard it open. "Hands up slowly so I can see them. Now move away from the desk."

Iris obeyed, keeping her hands in the air.

"Turn around," he ordered when she was in the clear. "Put your hands on the blotter."

She did. He stepped behind her, pressing the gun to her back, then patted her down thoroughly. Too thoroughly.

"You can't do that!" protested Gwen.

"Let me know if you find anything interesting," said Iris.

"You're safe," he said, grabbing her by the shoulder and shoving her into the corner of the room. "Now stay there. Keep those hands up."

"I thought you wanted me to get you your money," Iris said.

"You're the dangerous one," he said, moving behind her desk and squatting down to reach into the strongbox. "I don't want you pulling anything on me. You're the one with the knife."

"And I'm the one with the gun," said Gwen. "Please don't move. I'm rather a good shot, not that I need to be from this close."

He glanced over at her. She was still sitting behind her desk, but now held a silver-plated revolver in her right hand.

"Your turn for hands in the air," she ordered. "Good. Now place your gun on the desk and sit on that chair."

He placed the gun on Iris's desk, then sat. Then his eyes widened.

"That's a toy!" he said, lunging for his weapon.

"This isn't," said Iris, moving quickly.

She plunged her hand down on top of his, grabbing the gun with her left. He screamed in pain.

A dart pinned his hand to the desk.

"Well, I suppose it is a toy," she said, stepping back and covering him. "But it's a dangerous one, all the same."

"You bloody stupid—"

"Not another word!" she snapped, raising the gun. "You've broken into our office, threatened us with a weapon, and manhandled us. I would be entirely within my rights to shoot you on the spot. Now sit."

"I can't," he whined. "My hand's too far—"

She reached forwards and yanked the dart out. He howled in pain, then heaved himself at her. She stepped back and swung the butt of the gun into his temple. He dropped like a stone, sprawling across the desk.

"And that was a little kiss from Lily to Violet," she said, breathing rapidly.

"Oh God. Is he dead?" asked Gwen.

Iris felt for his pulse.

"No, worse luck," she said. "Are you all right?"

"Me?"

"Second shock of the day," said Iris. "I'm concerned for the state of your nerves."

"I have something powdery at home that Dr. Milford gave me for this sort of thing," said Gwen faintly. "Well, not this exact sort of thing. I doubt that they make powders specifically for the finding of bloody bodies and the repelling of armed attackers."

"Can you squeeze by him?" asked Iris.

"I don't know that I want to," said Gwen, looking at the space between the desks.

The man's body overhung the edge of Iris's desk. His arms dangled over the front, one hand dripping blood from the puncture she had put through it.

"I probably should climb over the top," said Gwen.

"I don't know if the desk can take that weight," said Iris.

"Now you're being mean!" protested Gwen. "I'm not that heavy."

"All I'm saying is that the legs that are not *The Forsyte Saga* may not be prepared for you. Come out between the desks. I'll cover him in case he wakes."

Gwen stood and sidled carefully out, holding her breath as she arched her body away from the man. She finally exhaled when she reached Iris, then frowned.

"What?" asked Iris.

"I left my bag under the desk," said Gwen. "Would you be so kind as to cover me again?"

"Unbelievable," muttered Iris.

"Well, I can't just leave it there, can I?" complained Gwen as she edged her way back.

She picked up her bag, then looked at Iris.

"Do you want yours while I'm here?" she asked.

"Might as well," said Iris.

"See, this is me being helpful," said Gwen, reaching around the man's legs to grab it. "Who knows what useful weaponry you have in here?"

She began the return journey. Halfway across, the man groaned. Gwen made a quick sideways leap to the front of the office.

"Much better," she said, handing Iris her handbag. "What do we do with him now?"

"I'm trying to come up with a plan," said Iris. "We need to secure him first."

"I'm afraid I have no handcuffs on me," said Gwen.

"Not even toy ones? Never mind. Go down to Mr. MacPherson's office and see what you can find. Rope, cord, electrical wire—anything of that nature. And see if there's a first-aid kit. This man is bleeding all over our nice, clean office."

"How can I get into his office? It's Saturday. It will be locked."

Iris reached into her bag and pulled out a keyring. She sorted through it.

"This one," she said, handing it to Gwen.

"You're not supposed to have that," said Gwen.

"I know. Now, go!"

Gwen practically fled the office. Iris felt the pulse of their attacker one more time, then sat down heavily on the guest chair, resting the gun on her lap.

"We're going to find out who you are," she said to him. "After that—we'll see."

Gwen was back in minutes, her arms laden.

"Rope," she said, tossing a length of it onto her desk. "First-aid kit. Cleaning supplies. And the keys to the office of Cooper and Lyons, Chartered Public Accountants. We might need a place to stash him temporarily."

"Good thinking," said Iris.

"What's the best order? Treat his wound, then tie him up, or the reverse?"

"Bandage, then bondage," declared Iris, getting back to her feet. "You be the nurse. I'll keep the gun to his head."

Gwen took the first-aid kit, then circled around Iris to stay out of the line of fire. Iris stepped forwards, gun at the ready.

"I do hope he had his tetanus vaccination," said Iris. "I can't vouch for the cleanliness of that dart."

"We should call the police," said Gwen as she dabbed both sides of his hand with Merthiolate.

"Not yet," said Iris.

"But we have the letters," said Gwen. "And maybe he could help them catch the killer."

"You don't think he's the killer?"

"Not in the least," said Gwen, pressing cotton to the wounds and applying pressure. "There, that's stemmed the bleeding. No, he was taken aback to hear 'the little Greek fellow' was dead. I was watching him very closely, and I think that was a genuine reaction."

"Well, I trust your ability to read people," said Iris.

"And he wasn't limping," added Gwen. "Nor were there any telltale slashes on his pants leg."

"Even better," said Iris. "But I don't want to go to the police yet. Things are still out of control. There are too many sides involved now. Including ours."

"Yes, that makes three different mysterious men at the scene of the proposed exchange," said Gwen, wrapping the man's hand in gauze. "At least three. We don't know for certain that the limping man killed Magoulias."

"True," agreed Iris. "Look, we have still some leads to follow. We haven't even looked at the letters yet, or compared them with the exemplars. Remember that the happiness of the future queen of England is at stake. We have to guarantee that first. We will bring in the police when we can wrap everything up with a nice, big, red bow."

"All right," said Gwen.

She looked at the results of her handiwork.

"That should hold for now," she said. "Sir, just because I've been holding your hand, do not think that you can take further advantage of me."

She let it go. It swung limply against the front of the desk.

"What shall we do with him?" she asked.

"I have an idea," said Iris, picking up the telephone.

She dialed a number and waited. A man's voice answered after the first ring.

"It's Sparks," she said. "I need a largish favour."

CHAPTER 10

Gwen approached Cecil with a dust rag.

"Hello, darling," she said to the desk. "I'm going to clean you up. Be brave. I'll be as gentle as I can."

She wiped the dust off thoroughly, then patted the desk affectionately.

"You'll hold me without making any rude comments, won't you?" she cooed.

Then she sat on the newly cleaned surface, crossed her legs decorously, and sighed with content.

"You're insane," said their captive from the floor, where he lay trussed up.

"It's been said before," agreed Gwen, "and by people with more professional experience in that area than you have. And frankly, I've had a very long and trying day, the kind that would drive anyone to distraction, much less someone with such a tenuous grip on sanity as myself. So, here we are—you, the mystery assailant, tied up, lying on the floor, and me, the crazy lady, sitting on a desk. With your Mauser. Which is loaded. I checked."

She picked it up from the desk where she had placed it.

"So perhaps," she said, her voice rising to a shout, "given our relative positions, you might want to reconsider calling me names!"

She squeezed her eyes shut and took deep breaths until the pounding of her heart slowed to a normal pace. Then she opened her eyes, looked down at the man, placed the gun on her lap, and smiled.

He struggled for a moment against the ropes securing his hands and feet, then gave up. Gwen watched with interest.

"I wouldn't do that anymore," she advised him. "It might re-open the wounds on your hand. You made such a mess in our office, and we don't want you bleeding all over this one, as it isn't technically ours yet."

She patted the desk again.

"But it will be soon, won't it, Cecil?" she whispered.

"You demented—"

She grabbed the gun from her lap and pointed it at him, her grip rock steady.

"I'm glad that you're in such a talkative mood," she said. "Let's have a little chat, shall we?"

"Hello, Archie," said Iris as she opened the rear door to the building. "Thanks for coming."

"Oh, I wouldn't've missed this for the world," said Archie as he came in.

He was back to full-on Archie apparel, wearing a charcoal gray suit with broad chalky stripes and a wide, garish purple tie. Behind him came two other members of the spiv fraternity.

"You know the lads?" asked Archie, jerking his thumb at them.

"I do."

"Then forget 'em," said Archie. "We don't need anyone knowing anyone tonight. Where's the guest of honour?"

"Upstairs. Follow me."

She took them through the basement to the stairs, lighting their way with her torch. She turned it off when they reached the hallway by the front entrance.

"I'm afraid we're on the top storey," she said as she began the ascent.

"Bloody 'ell," said one of the lads, looking up. "We 'ave to drag 'im down all these stairs?"

"He's conscious," said Iris. "He can walk down on his own."

"Any reason we can't just toss 'im from the landing?"

"I need him alive," said Iris.

"For 'ow long?" asked Archie.

"For the rest of his natural life, I hope," said Iris. "But at least through Tuesday, if that isn't too inconvenient."

"There's nothing convenient about any of this," said Archie. "You know this is going to cost you."

"What's the price for holding a prisoner?" asked Iris.

"Depends on 'ow well we feed 'im," said Archie.

"Bread and water would be fine," said Iris.

"You know 'ow much bread is going for right now?"

"Tell me the rate."

Archie glanced at the others, then back at Iris.

"Since you're a friend of Archie, you get a discount," he said. "Twenty-five quid."

"Twenty-five?"

"Per diem," continued Archie. "Covers guards and food."

"Oh, and he'll need some medical attention," said Iris.

"For what?"

"I may have stabbed him a little."

"Did you now?"

"Only a little," she said. "Look, what if I throw in his gun? It's a Mauser automatic, in excellent condition."

"Guns we got," said Archie. "A Mauser, eh? This bloke's a Jerry?"

"He sounded English, but I didn't find any identification on him."

"Frisked him good, did you?" said one of the lads with a smirk. "Wouldn't mind getting caught by you meself."

Archie stopped and turned to face him.

"I expect you to show some manners in the presence of a lady," he said quietly.

"I was only—" began the spiv. Then he saw Archie's eyes and thought better of it. "My apologies, Miss Sparks," he said, raising his trilby.

"Accepted," Iris said quickly. "Here we are."

"'Cooper and Lyons,'" read Archie. "And 'oo are they?"

"Accountants, long gone to their final accounting, or so I've heard. Ready?"

"Masks, lads," said Archie.

They removed their hats and pulled on black woolen ski masks. Iris tapped on the door. A second later, Gwen opened it, starting as she saw the menacing-looking trio behind her partner.

"Nothing but scary things today," she said brightly. "Forgive me, gentlemen. I wasn't expecting you to be like this, but quite right. Won't you come in?"

She had the Mauser in her hand. Archie pointed to it, and she immediately handed it to him.

"The safety is on," she said. "I didn't tell him that, of course."

The man she referred to now had a handkerchief stuffed into his mouth. He looked up at the masked gang, but didn't flinch.

"Oh, 'e's a tough one, all right," said Archie. "Nice job with the knots, Sparks."

"That was me," said Gwen. "Between the first aid and the ropes, my Girl Guide training has proved exceptionally invaluable to-night."

"Did he tell you anything useful?" asked Iris.

"He said quite a few things," replied Gwen. "But nothing I can repeat in front of company."

"We could work 'im over, if you like," offered Archie.

"Is that extra?" asked Iris.

"No, we throw that in for free."

"Have you discussed rates already?" asked Gwen.

"Twenty-five pounds a day," said Iris.

"That sounds quite reasonable," said Gwen, opening her bag. "This will cover four days in advance. Probably more than we'll require, but let's do that to be safe." She handed them the notes she and Iris had received in payment from Lady Matheson. Easy come, easy go, she thought, casting a quick, regretful glance at Cecil.

"You carry that much with you all the time?" asked Archie.

"Today was a most unusual day," said Iris. "We were prepared for any number of contingencies."

"Right," said Archie. "Get 'im to 'is feet, then take the ropes off 'is ankles."

The other two hauled the man upright and freed his legs.

"Wait a mo," said Archie.

He took another ski mask from his coat, then pulled it over the man's face.

"Oh dear," he said. "I've put it on backwards. You won't be able to see a bloody thing, will you?"

The man didn't move. Archie placed his palm under the man's chin. "Will you?" he repeated, moving the man's head back and forth.

The man finally shook his head on his own.

"Good," said Archie, removing his mask and putting his hat back on. "Well, this 'as been entertaining, but we'd better escort our new friend away from the premises. We'll be in touch when we get where we're going."

"We don't want to know where that is," said Iris.

"No, you don't," said Archie. "Even if you did, I wouldn't tell you."

The two spivs walked the prisoner out of the office.

"Oh, and we'll need the rope back when you're done with it," Gwen called after them. "It's borrowed!"

Archie turned to Iris.

"Thank you," she said.

"It's not 'ow I 'oped to be spending a Saturday night with you," he said. "But it'll do."

"I believe I owe you a kiss," said Iris, stepping towards him.

He held up a hand to stop her. "Not when we've just done business together," he said. "It cheapens it. Do it when the circumstances are proper romantic, all right?"

"As soon as possible," said Iris.

He put two fingers to his hat brim, nodded at Gwen, then left.

"I think I'm beginning to warm up to your gangster," said Gwen.

"He's an acquired taste, to be sure," said Iris. "I guess we had better start scrubbing the scene of our latest crime."

"Goodbye, sweet Cecil," said Gwen, giving the desk a wave as they exited the office.

"You won't be talking to that desk like that all the time when we take possession, will you?" asked Iris. "It's unnerving."

"I shall maintain a businesslike sense of decorum," said Gwen.

"Good."

"But only during business hours. Come five o'clock, our passion will know no bounds."

"Then I shall make a point of leaving at five minutes of five every day. You really should let me fix you up, by the way. With an actual human being."

They went into The Right Sort, then stopped. There was a small puddle of blood on the floor in front of Iris's desk, and more on top where she had first skewered her quarry like a butterfly for her collection.

Gwen picked up the bucket. "I'll fetch some water," she said, grabbing the key for the lavatory.

Iris approached her desk and scanned it, thinking. Then she took the blotter and bent it in half, the bloody side in.

Gwen came back, water sloshing in the bucket, to see Iris inspecting the hole the dart had made in the desk.

"Not too much seeped through," she reported. "I never knew what a good blotter this was. I'll have to find another one like it in case of future bloodletting. I'll drop this one in a dustbin somewhere far away from here after we leave."

"We should call Mrs. Fisher," said Gwen. "It's getting late. She'll be wondering."

"She's probably typing up the list of Land Girl alibi witnesses as we speak," said Iris.

She picked up the telephone and dialed. Mrs. Fisher answered immediately.

"Mrs. Fisher, Oona Travis reporting," said Iris.

"Good evening, Miss Travis," replied Mrs. Fisher. "I have been awaiting your call. On tenterhooks, I should add. I'm dying to know what happened."

Someone beat you to it, thought Iris.

"I'm afraid our rendezvous didn't go as planned," she began.

"Difficulty locating it?"

"No, we found the place. Someone was already there. And someone else had killed him."

Gwen could hear a tinny shriek of dismay as Iris yanked the handset away from her ear, wincing in pain.

"I'm sorry, that cannot have been what you were expecting," Iris said. "Imagine how we felt."

"But, but," stammered Mrs. Fisher. "Oh my God. I thought—" She took a breath. "Are the two of you all right?"

"We are, thank you."

"And are the police involved?" Mrs. Fisher continued, her voice quavering. "Do they know about you? About—about us?"

"The police are involved, but we were long gone by the time they got there. Nobody saw us leave. Nobody knows about your involvement."

"What about—was there a cabbie?"

"We went to a cab stand several streets from here, and he left after dropping us off. He won't know our names, and it's doubtful that he could connect us to the murder."

"Murder," whispered Mrs. Fisher. "So it was murder."

"Yes, it was murder, Mrs. Fisher. There's no other word for it."

"And the letters?"

"We didn't find any."

"You searched him? You searched the, uh, body?"

"Thoroughly."

"That can't have been—my God, I can't even imagine what that was like."

"It wasn't pleasant, but it's what we were hired to do, wasn't it?"

"Not that."

"All right, not corpse-searching specifically, but that was well within the requirements of the job."

"What do we do now? This wasn't how things were supposed to go at all."

"What you and Lady M do now is nothing. We intend to lie low and not risk drawing any further attention."

"And the money?"

"It's safe. We'll return it, less some expenses, when it can be done without fear of . . . well, without fear."

"It all seemed so simple," said Mrs. Fisher, still in shock. "I'll tell Lady Matheson immediately."

"Yes, please tell her everything. I'm sorry it didn't work out. Goodbye." She hung up.

"That was handled nicely," said Gwen from the floor, where she was mopping up the blood. "You didn't quite lie to her. You simply didn't tell her the aftermath. What now?"

"We have the letters," said Iris. She yawned abruptly. "Long day," she said. "Look at me, completely played out on a Saturday night, and it's barely eight thirty."

"Understandable," said Gwen. "Being held at gunpoint is momentarily stimulating, but it never lasts, does it?"

"Speaking of which, may I see that six-shooter of yours?"

Gwen fished it out of her handbag and tossed it to her. Iris caught it and looked at it closely, then pointed it at Gwen.

"Stick 'em up!" she snarled.

"I think playtime is over," said Gwen wearily.

"I want to talk to you about that," said Iris. "The closest we came to getting killed tonight was when you pulled this on him. What were you thinking?"

"I was thinking that he was going to take the money and keep the letters for himself," said Gwen. "I saw an opportunity to stop him. I seized it."

"You gambled on him not noticing that this was a replica," said Iris. "And you gambled even more that his reaction would be something other than shooting you."

"I didn't think he wanted to kill us," said Gwen. "It wasn't in his eyes."

"Your intuition is excellent," said Iris. "But is it one hundred percent foolproof?"

"No," said Gwen. "But I figured my little charade would provide enough time for you to come up with something brilliant and heroic. Which you did."

"And if I hadn't, then he would have shot you dead right in front of me," said Iris. "And I would be forever wondering what I could have done differently. You can't put me through that, Gwen. I have enough—There's blood enough already on my hands. I don't want any more."

"I'm sorry," said Gwen. "I wasn't thinking it through properly. I wasn't thinking at all. It just seemed right, somehow."

"Well, it worked," said Iris, twirling the gun on her index finger. "This is rather a good replica, I must say. Hamleys?"

"Yes."

"What did you get for the birthday boy?"

"A cowboys and Indians set. With a stagecoach."

"Sounds delightful. I hope that he appreciated it."

"By all reports, which is to say reports from Ronnie, it was a huge success. He's invited to play with Tommy again tomorrow."

"A great honour, I'm sure," said Iris, grabbing a sponge to scrub her desk. "Did the invitation extend to his mother?"

"Not yet," said Gwen.

"Then maybe you could devote your quiet time to reading through these letters," said Iris.

"I shall sham headache from my night out cavorting with you," said Gwen. "Our staff knows all about Sunday-morning headaches, thanks to my mother-in-law. I shall rest abed, pampered and isolated. The perfect setting to read someone else's love letters."

"Sounds divine," said Iris.

"And you? Will you be observing the Lord's day, or continuing the investigation?"

"Both," said Iris. "I'm going to church."

"Really? I was under the impression that you were an atheist."

"I am. Atheist—a good Greek word."

"We're back to the Greeks, I see."

"Which is why I will be attending services at the cathedral of Hagia Sophia."

"The what?"

"The Cathedral of the Divine Wisdom. St. Sophia. The Greek Orthodox one in Bayswater."

"Oh, I've been by it, but I've never been inside. What's it like?"

"Lovely place. Good spot to pick up the local gossip, if one speaks Greek."

"Which you do."

"Not fluently, unfortunately. I'd be better off having a conversation with Erasmus than someone current, but I do have a smattering of Demotiki. The hometown Greeks, the diplomatic community, and the factions in exile will all show up. Even the Communists, hedging their bets with God. I'll try and find out if anyone has heard anything about our late friend Magoulias."

"You should take Sally."

"Sally would be noticed," said Iris. "I am a small, unobtrusive creature."

"Small, yes, but hardly unobtrusive."

"Oh, but I can be," said Iris. "Look, I'm not comfortable leaving the money here now, and I don't have anywhere secure enough in my flat. Take it with you and put it somewhere safe in that sprawling mansion you call home."

"It's not a mansion, it's a townhouse," said Gwen. "The mansion's in the country."

"Pardon me. Can you keep the money and the letters away from prying eyes?"

"I know a few good spots. I have an idea. Bayswater is just around the corner from Kensington. Why don't you come by after and visit me during my convalescence?"

"Could I? Won't I scandalise Lady Carolyne by bringing my sordid self onto the sacred Bainbridge premises?"

"That would be a bonus, as far as I'm concerned."

"Very well, so long as I don't end up chasing any leads after services. What excuse shall we make for me to be there?"

"We're business partners, Iris. We don't need an excuse to see each other."

"You mean we'll actually be using the truth," said Iris. "What a strange idea!"

Gwen wrung out her sponge and examined the floor.

"Blood-free," she pronounced. "I might be ready for that second career as a charlady."

"Let's clear out, then," said Iris, giving her desk one last swipe. "I've had more than enough of this day."

* * *

It was after ten when Gwen came home.

"Good evening, Percival," she said, making sure her face was close enough for him to catch the traces of whisky still on her breath. "I'm not feeling altogether chipper. Could you send Millicent up with some bicarbonate of soda? And I don't think that I shall be up to church in the morning, so please give everyone my regrets."

"Very good, Mrs. Bainbridge," said Percival.

She walked up the steps, wobbling slightly, which she realised was not just for effect. The eyes of Mr. Magoulias appeared before her, shining up at the ceiling, then lowering to stare accusingly in her direction, She clutched the banister for support.

"Mrs. Bainbridge?" Percival called after her, concern in his voice. "Do you require assistance?"

"No, thank you," she said, steadying herself. "Send Millicent as soon as you can."

She made it to the top of the stairs unassisted, then stopped, panting, willing herself not to be sick.

She failed. She dashed down the hall to the nearest lav, barely making it in time.

Thank heaven for small favours, she thought when she was done. She rinsed her mouth out thoroughly, ran a cold washcloth over her face, and staggered into the hallway.

Millie, the upstairs maid, was standing there, a robe over her nightgown, holding a tumbler on a silver salver. It fizzed comfortingly.

"Rough night, ma'am?" she said sympathetically.

"Rougher than I thought it would be," Gwen replied, accepting the tumbler gratefully.

"Still, good to see you out having some fun, if you don't mind my saying so," said Millie as they walked down the hall to Gwen's room. "It's been a long time. I suppose there's some getting used to it again."

"There are some things I will never get used to," said Gwen, drinking the bicarbonate. "Could you ask Prudence to send my breakfast up in the morning? I think I will be lying in tomorrow."

"Of course, ma'am," said Millie, taking the empty tumbler from her. "Shall I ask Agnes to keep Master Ronnie quiet and away?"

"Oh no," said Gwen. "No matter how I am feeling, I will always make time for my darling boy."

"Yes, ma'am."

"Thank you, Millie. That will be all. Get yourself some rest."

"Yes, ma'am. Good night, ma'am. I hope you feel better in the morning."

Gwen stopped by Ronnie's room and opened the door quietly. He slept, completely unaware of Mummy's mad adventures. And she would never tell him, of course.

She stepped inside and sat on the edge of his bed, resisting an impulse to throw herself on him and hold him tight. She restricted herself to stroking his hair, then kissing his cheek softly. He slept on, undisturbed.

She slipped out, closing the door behind her, then went into her room.

She knew of several places in the townhouse where she could secrete the letters and money, but it was late, and she didn't want to be heard prowling around the premises. Her husband had once shown her where he had loosened a panel in the closet for his secret stashes of whatever things he collected as a child. *I tried to hide a frog I had caught in there*, he had told her. *Didn't work out so well for the frog. I cried for days, and no one knew why.*

She walked into the closet and felt for the loose panel, then removed it and lit it with her torch, the action summoning up the memory of the dead man once again. No glistening eyes stared at her this time, thankfully. No remains of deceased amphibians, either. The space was empty. She put the Hamleys bag containing the letters and the money inside, then replaced the panel and lined up her shoes in front of it.

She undressed, put on her nightgown, then turned off the lamp and lay in bed.

It was her turn to stare up at the ceiling, but eventually the exhaustion overcame her. Her eyes closed, and she slept like a dead woman.

Sparks woke up early and sober, surprisingly undisturbed by any nightmares. She went through her limited wardrobe, selecting a dark brown jacket and skirt that were better suited to cooler weather. She didn't want to wear black. Someone might think she was a widow, and that would lead to conversations she'd rather not fake. Brown was a good colour for church. Men didn't flirt with women wearing brown, in her experience. At least, not in church. Not as much, anyway.

The cathedral was on Moscow Road in Bayswater, about two miles from her flat in Marylebone. It was a pleasant morning—she decided to walk.

There was no point in getting there early. The *orthros*, the early morning service, would be going through ten. Her friends who first invited her to join them for services when she was younger told her that nobody worth knowing came for the *orthros*, only old women dressed in black. Ten o'clock marked the transition from the early morning service to the Divine Liturgy, when the truly observant were joined by the merely devout, while the main body of the congregation would wander in on time for Communion, then socialising and gossip.

The walk took her half an hour. She paused when she reached her destination to admire the building. The cathedral was neither old nor immense by London standards—a nineteenth-century brick structure that occupied less than a third of the block on the eastern corner—but it was well designed and had largely missed being damaged during the war. The light brown brick walls were broken up by broad horizontal stripes of red, and the broad stone front steps brought one to a set of homey, human-sized doors on either side. The arches over the doors were made of alternating blocks of red and white, giving the whole facade a festive, almost candylike appearance. In all, it presented a welcoming face to those who wished to gain access to the Lord, unlike the judgmental and intimidating gray stones of the other Christian alternatives in town.

There was a young couple with a pram and a small boy in tow at the base of the steps. The boy, who could not have been more than two and a half, was acting well within the expected parameters of behavior for one of his years, which is to say, he was digging in his heels and refusing to go inside. The father was attempting to placate his son, with limited success, while the mother was trying to pull the pram up the steps on her own. Sparks hurried forwards.

"May I?" she offered, gesturing to the pram.

"Oh, please, thanks," said the woman, sounding harried.

The two of them carried the pram up the steps, Sparks taking the opportunity to coo at the baby within, who looked back at her suspiciously. When they reached the top, Sparks held the door open. The father by this time had given up negotiations and slung the boy over his shoulder, which did nothing to quiet him.

"Look, he's having one of his little moods," he called up to them. "Go in without me. I'll catch up when he's ready to meet God properly."

"Fine. I'll save you a pair of seats," replied his wife.

"I can help you with that as well," said Sparks as the woman wheeled the pram inside.

"Oh, that would be lovely," said the woman. "I'm Eleni. That's Athanasios in the pram—he's the quiet one."

"I'm Iris. Shall we grab some seats over on the side in case Athanasios needs any attention?"

"There's four on the right," said Eleni.

And now I'm one of the family to any casual observer, thought Sparks as they walked together down the side aisle.

Sparks took the seat by the right aisle while Eleni picked up Athanasios and carried him to the fourth seat in. She dandled him in her lap, wrinkling her nose and making faces to make the baby giggle. Sparks watched, smiling, her eyes scanning the seats beyond them to see who had shown up.

She didn't recognise anyone, but congregants were trickling in, filling the empty seats like pieces in a jigsaw puzzle. Or rather, tiles in a mosaic, she thought, glancing at the decorations of saints and holy scenes on the wall. Mosaics were favoured here, she had once read, because London weather was too damp to sustain frescoes.

The priest was reading some psalm or other.

"In your steadfast love, cut off my enemies," he intoned, "and destroy all my adversaries, for I am your servant."

Bloodthirsty enough, thought Sparks. You can always count on David for an appeal to God's warlike side.

"In peace, let us pray to the Lord."

Peace. They prayed for peace seven years ago, using the very words she was hearing now. And the other denominations prayed for peace in their own languages, in their own way. No doubt they prayed for peace on Sundays in Germany back then.

When she had declared herself an atheist at Cambridge, she had been following some ostentatious intellectual fad. Look how adorably rebellious I was, she thought with disgust.

Yet there was a basis for it. Every church she had been to, and she had explored many out of curiosity and—and what? Was she looking for something to soothe her soul? To match her spiritual longings?

The Right Sort of God?

Whatever the quest was, it was unfulfilled, and atheism made as much sense as anything. Then came the war. The horrors, the bombings, the betrayals, the deaths, the revelations of atrocities at the end. She may have gone into it mouthing her disbelief in a watchful, just, and merciful deity, but she came out of it absolutely convinced of His nonexistence. Or at least His nonparticipation.

So, on the many occasions where she found herself at a place of worship—and God only knew how many memorial services there had been—she bit her tongue and focused on the aesthetics of the architecture or the decorations, or listened to the music and criticised the performances, or summoned up her Latin and Greek to translate as the service went along so those mental skills wouldn't rust through dormancy.

And she never prayed. Not once. Not really.

She appreciated the Greek Orthodox service for its theatricality. The entrance of the priest, the opening of the doors, the vesting, the reenactment of the Crucifixion with a loaf of bread, all accompanied by a polyphonic choir "Under the direction of Ernest Moss," as a placard on an easel proclaimed when she came in. She had heard them often on BBC Radio. They were quite good today, especially with the echoing acoustics of the cathedral supporting them, and she allowed herself to take pleasure in the ancient beauty of the Byzantine chant.

The priest, now fully vested, took the censer and carried it up and down the aisles. Athanasios watched this portion of the ceremony with awe, his eyes swinging back and forth with the golden container as the smoke rose from it and the bells dangling from its chains tinkled sweetly.

Maybe religion is just a big rattle, thought Sparks. Something to distract us and keep us quiet.

She took advantage of the censing to scan the congregation again.

There. On the other side, settling into a seat. Constantine Torgos. The Greek Intelligence operative who had come to Talbot's funeral.

She recognised him immediately, though it had been three years since she had last encountered him. He was in his late fifties, balding, with a thick black mustache under a long, thin nose. He was draping his arm around the shoulders of a younger man, giving the impression of avuncularity, but his expression was anything but affectionate as he poured a stream of urgent whispers into his companion's ear. The other man began nodding in response, then shook his head in the negative twice.

That isn't prayer, thought Sparks.

A woman sat in the seat behind Sparks, then leaned forwards, tapped her on the shoulder, and whispered, "Slumming, Sparks? Or are you on the prowl for unmarried Greeks? We have our own matchmakers, you know."

"Kat! I was hoping I'd find you here," Sparks said in delight, turning to face her.

There were shushing noises from nearby. Sparks quieted immediately, but got up and sat in the seat next to the newcomer.

Katina Kitsiou had worked with Sparks during one of her assignments with the Brigadier before going on to coordinate joint efforts with the Allies and the various factions of the Greek Resistance. Known to her English friends and colleagues as Katty Kit, she was a lively, sharply observant, and witty woman who knew everyone worth knowing and several worth avoiding. She was one of the contacts Sparks had hoped to make in coming, but the Great Litany was starting, so all they could do was clasp hands in greeting, then join in with the "Lord, have mercy" responses when they came up.

Sparks kept watching Torgos and the other man out of the corner of her eye, but they had succumbed to the formality of the doxology. Katina noticed her attention and glanced across the center aisle.

"Who have you got your sights set on this time?" she murmured. "Have you finally smartened up and got yourself a Greek boyfriend?"

"Are there any good ones left?"

"More than you'd expect. There hasn't exactly been a rush to return to the homeland since the war ended. Many of them decided they prefer it here, despite the weather and the food."

"Oh—it's the Trisagion hymn," said Sparks. "Let's listen. I've always liked that one."

The choir sang, then the priest turned to the congregation, his arms out to entreat them.

"*Dinamis!*" he cried.

Once more with feeling, thought Sparks, but she dutifully sang along with the rest of the devout. The Thrice-Holy Hymn. Holy God, Holy Mighty, Holy Immortal—have mercy on us.

Well. Too late for that, isn't it? Better luck next time.

There was a buzz of excited whispers behind her, and she and Kat turned to see a man walking down the center aisle, a small coterie of people behind him. He had the look of someone who had been handsome when he was younger, but his face was wan, the portions below his cheekbones sunken and waxy, his lips compressed into a thin line. Yet he projected authority in the face of God and His servants, and most of the congregation nodded deferentially as he went by. Others continued to stare straight ahead, either markedly indifferent or outright defiant.

"Is that the king?" whispered Sparks.

"The twice-exiled George the Second in the declining flesh," replied Kat. "Ridiculous to call him a king now. He's not even king of Claridge's. Nice of him to leave the mistress behind while coming to worship, though."

"I like a church where the mistresses get to pray," said Sparks.

"She needs Sunday morning to recover from Saturday night," said Kat. "And the rest of the day to primp for tomorrow."

"What's tomorrow?"

"There's a reception in support of the monarchist referendum."

"Would he really bring his mistress to that?"

"No, of course not," said Kat. "But he'll want to celebrate before and after. I'm being harsh—I hear they quite adore each other. They have for years, but he can't marry her."

"Why not?"

"She's British. Joyce Brittain-Jones. Lives out in the suburbs, did her bit in an arms factory during the war after they fled the Nazis. On good terms with the inner circles both here and there, but she wouldn't help the cause if she showed up with a ring and a license right now."

"Poor thing."

Sparks turned her attention briefly back to the service and realised with dismay that they had come to the Credo. The very center of her disbelief, about to be chanted in unison by everyone there.

Say the words, woman. They're only words, not magic. Saying them won't make you believe. They'll make others believe that you believe. You've said far worse things that you didn't believe in the service of King and country.

She said the words.

She glanced up at the dome where Jesus watched over them, arms raised in exaltation. No lightning emanated from him to strike her down.

Missed me again, she thought.

The service continued through admonitions and prayers, hymns and appeals. They were collecting for a war memorial, which she donated to with a willing heart, but when it came time to receive Communion, she held back.

"Would you like me to hold Athanasios while you go up?" she offered Eleni.

"Oh, no," said Eleni. "I like him to see this. Come with us!"

"I can't, thanks," said Sparks. "I'm a stranger here myself."

The congregation queued up for the divine gifts. She was one of the few to remain in her seat, but there were enough similarly disinclined that she didn't draw any undue attention. She kept her face down, pretending to read the hymnal, glancing up from under her hat.

The king didn't assert any priority, she noted with approval. Torgos was also on the queue, behind his companion, still murmuring in his ear.

The service concluded, and the congregation was dismissed. Kat came back to where Sparks was sitting.

"Shall we go outside and listen to the gossip?" she asked.

"What's the latest?" asked Sparks as they headed out.

"Mostly politics," said Kat. "Does that sort of thing interest you?"

"I'm curious about everything."

"Why are you here? Seriously?"

"I'm vetting a prospective groom for a client," said Sparks. "Someone was going to meet me here so I could pump him for information, but it looks like he stood me up."

"You go through all that for matchmaking?"

"Of course."

"Sounds like Intelligence work."

"It's similar, but there's much more at stake."

"Well, at least nobody gets killed," said Kat.

You have no idea, thought Sparks.

They emerged from the cathedral and stood on the top step, surveying the newly absolved crowd, which had split into several small groups.

"One could re-create the entire civil war in miniature with this lot," said Kat. "That small noisy band on the left are the Communists, mostly ex-ELAS. There's three or four Trotskyists—they're the ones gesticulating a lot, but no one pays them much attention anymore. The Democratic Army supporters are that group in the front—they're on the rise. The Royalists are the ones surrounding the king, of course, and the Anti-Royalists are over there, casting stern looks at the Royalists. And that—that's just a group of young men flirting with young women while their mothers keep an eye on them."

"That's the group I should be handing cards to," said Sparks.

She spotted Torgos and his companion, continuing their conversation near the Royalist group.

"Would you mind if I get a closer look at His Majesty?" she asked.

"What on earth for?"

"I've never seen a live king up close before. Come with me."

"I've seen him."

"Come on. Even a Kat may look at a king."

"Oh dear." Kat sighed. "Do you think you're the first one ever to say that to me?"

Sparks slipped her hand through the other woman's arm and nudged her towards them, taking care to keep Kat between her and Torgos. They took up position on the outside of the group circling the king, just in front of her target.

Sparks feigned interest in the sight of King George graciously interacting with his admirers with a politician's skill while she tried to listen to the conversation behind her. It was in Greek, and she strained to pick up the words.

"Shall I translate for you?" said Kat sweetly.

"I'm sure I don't know what you're talking about, and shush, please," muttered Sparks.

Pou einai i allilografía? Where is the—the what? she thought. Correspondence! The letters? *Den gnorizo.* I don't know. That was a phrase she had used many times back in her school days, and Torgos's companion was repeating it over and over. Torgos mentioned something—

"Tell me more about this reception," asked Sparks. "Anything I could crash? Cadge a few shots of ouzo from some handsome olive-skinned men? They need some experienced party girls, don't they?"

"Come with me right now," ordered Kat. "Don't make a scene, or I'll make one for you and you won't be happy about it."

Her tone was soft but her expression was anything but. She took Sparks firmly by the arm and guided her away.

"I was under the impression that you left the Service when the war ended," she said when they were on the sidewalk, safely out of earshot.

"Officially, I have," said Sparks, arching one eyebrow.

"Oh, stop being mysterious," said Kat. "I'm not one of your impressionable young men. What are you doing here? Why the interest in Torgos?"

"Why are *you* interested in him?" responded Sparks. "And what makes you think he was the one I'm looking for?"

"Only your entire course of conduct from the moment I saw you," said Kat.

"Who was the good-looking chap he was dressing down?"

"No," said Kat. "You don't get anything from me until I know what you're up to. Who were you planning on meeting here?"

"He appears to have stood me up. Tell me about the party."

"You're not invited."

"That rarely stops me from attending. You know that."

"This one is by invitation only, and they will be checking."

"So get me an invitation. I'll wear a nice frock and everything."

"No. I don't know what you're up to, and I'm not about to jeopardise—"

She stopped abruptly.

"Jeopardise what?" asked Sparks. "What are you working on, Kat?"

"Nothing that concerns you. Stay away. Stay away from the reception, and stay away from me. And Sparks?"

"Yes?"

"Stay away from Torgos, in particular. He's in with a bad lot, funneling support to the White Terror groups. They say he's not above continuing the war on British soil."

"Was that what was going on with the other chap?"

"We're done. It was good to see you, Sparks. We'll have to catch up again sometime. Someplace less holy, I should think."

She turned and walked away. Sparks peeked back at the gatherings in front of the cathedral, but both Torgos and the other man were gone.

But they would be at that reception the next evening. She had heard that much.

And Torgos had said Magoulias's name.

Vres ton. Magoulias. Férte ton se ména.

Find him. Bring him to me.

Í tha se skotóso.

Or I will kill you.

CHAPTER 11

It was odd to be wearing gloves in bed, thought Gwen. As if one had suddenly transformed into a leper overnight, and was forbidden human touch for the rest of one's wretched existence. Only this leper had arms that were prepared to go to the opera, sheathed in white satin nearly to her shoulders.

The packet of letters sat on the night table next to her bed. She had had a boiled egg and toast for her breakfast, brought to her on a tray by Prudence herself, along with another glass of bicarbonate. Ronnie, forewarned by Agnes, had tiptoed in with such a serious face and exaggerated attention to quiet that she had almost started giggling. She gave him a hug and reassured him about the state of her health, then sent him off, first to church and then to playtime with Tommy in the Wild West.

She felt guilty, both for missing services and for shamming illness, or hangover, if that was what the staff truly believed, but she could not deny the pleasure of wallowing in bed for a late morning. The greater guilt was for missing church. Even in the sanatorium, she would be wheeled to the chapel, and she would duly read the responses and sing along with the raucous chorus of the disturbed.

She knelt by the side of her bed and prayed, hoping that God would find that sufficient. She had much for Him to forgive over the past few days. And it wasn't as if she were without purpose—she had letters to read.

She glanced first at the ones young Alice had penned to her great-grandmother. Ordinary accounts of ordinary events—parties, horses ridden, puppies embraced. The girlish scrawl was in English, complete with some misspellings. Well, one wouldn't expect perfection of a woman kept in aristocratic isolation. Even Gwen herself had more freedom growing up in the twenties and thirties than Alice had had in the waning years of the last century. And Gwen had more access to schooling, albeit in a primarily female environment, than Alice had had.

On the other hand, Alice had lived in a palace with Queen Victoria for a while, and that wasn't a bad deal at all.

The final letter was to her mother, written while on her honeymoon. She was eighteen, thought Gwen. In love with her handsome prince, discovering the unknown. One could sense the rush of the pen as she wrote of sights seen by day while trying to conceal the other sights seen at night that her mother must have known were hidden below the surface of her tale. There was a joy in this that Gwen remembered only too well.

She looked closely at the letter, examining the swoop and curl of each letter as it flowed into the next, how Alice had crossed her t's, how she made her capitals.

Then she picked up the first letter from the packet obtained at such a perilous cost. She should get cards made up: Mrs. Gwendolyn Bainbridge, Kidnapper, Conspirator, and Confederate of Spivs. No, that was too long. Mrs. Gwendolyn Bainbridge, Spivette.

She was beginning to consider the consequences of failure. What if their prisoner turned on them? Or tried to blackmail them, which was his likely bent? Calling upon Archie for help seemed like a good idea at the moment, but she couldn't help but think that rational thought was not what was taking place when the moment involved an unconscious man bleeding on Iris's desk.

Nothing to be done about that now. It was the blighter's own fault, wasn't it? It was entirely self-defense. Except for the subsequent kidnapping and imprisoning of their attacker.

Maybe Patience could wangle them a pardon from the king.

To the task at hand, Gwen.

She examined the first letter, a folded piece of blue onionskin like the one previously sent to the princess. She held it to her nose. It smelled faintly of must and old wax and linseed oil. She opened it. It was in German, from a different hand. A man's, she guessed.

> *My dearest A.,*
>
> *You have looked so sad upon your arrival here that my heart breaks every time I see you. Be happy! We are all alive, we are all together, and our sojourn will not be forever. The family is everything, but if you find that there are empty spaces in your existence that cannot be ignored, please accept the enclosed gift as a beginning to a remedy. It is a work that I find provides remarkable insight into our lives in this world—and the next. Read it, and come talk to me any time you are feeling lost.*
>
> > *Your loving C.*

C for Christo, the younger brother of her husband? There seemed to be a familiarity there that was consistent with the history. She turned to the next letter, written on cream-coloured stationery.

> *My dear C.,*
>
> *I cannot thank you enough for the book. I have been so busy managing the girls while putting on a cheerful face for my husband, not to mention the King and his family, that I have spared no time for myself. M. Schuré's work has opened my eyes—dare I say my soul? There is so much more to our*

existence than this world. I begin to see that now. If you can
spare the time, I would dearly love to speak of this with you.
My discussions with Andrea primarily consist of listening
to him plot their return to power, and I find that sitting and
nodding are all that he requires of me. My mind is starved
for real conversation.

Your friend, A.

Poor thing, thought Gwen. Another woman trapped in a velvet cage. It's so easy to withhold pity for someone living her exile at a first-rate hotel with a gorgeous view, but the lack of freedom was still oppressive.

The opportunity to escape, even if only through intellectual or spiritual means, must have been a heady temptation. If this was the beginning of a love affair, Gwen could well understand being toppled by the gift of a book.

My dearest A.,
Your beauty at dinner tonight made a startling contrast
to the melancholy that I know you to be feeling. My brother's
behaviour was appalling—as was Constantine's. If I only
knew some way to give you comfort. Perhaps we could take
a stroll along the lakeside tomorrow? I have yet to see the
paintings inside the Kapellbrücke—will you accompany me?
I am sure the girls will be amply cared for by their nanny.
Say yes, I beg of you!

Your loving C.

The old "let's take a walk and see the historic paintings" gambit. How many young men approached Gwen during her time in Geneva with some similar line? Yet Alice seemed to have taken the bait quite readily.

My dear C.,

The paintings were quite ordinary, the bridge was old and plain, yet the two of them in your company became something magical. My heart feels lighter than it has since we fled Greece, and I have you to thank for it. Let us make these walks a regular part of our existence!

Your friend, A.

Still friends, are we? When do we get to the good parts?

There were not many letters, which was not surprising when she thought about it. They lived in the same place, attended the same functions, ate at the same tables. There were lapses of time between the letters as a result, but when each appeared, the intimacy of the tone progressed by leaps and bounds.

My dearest A. . . .
My darling C. . . .

Your most loving A.
Your devoted C.

Yes, get on with it, Gwen thought impatiently. Then she came to one dated May 1918.

My darling,

It was wrong of you to kiss me. It was wrong of me to let you. I cannot, cannot believe that I followed you to the roof while the others were dancing, but Andrea was so oblivious, and you were so kind. The touch of your hand on my waist as we danced was agony—that that, and mine on your shoulder and our other hands clasped were all the contact that we were allowed was a cruel jest. But then we slipped away and found ourselves high above the world, dancing on the roof, our

*bodies drawing ever closer, the strains of the music drifting
up from the ballroom so far below. I could no more have
withstood you in that moment than I could a hurricane.*

Oh, my, thought Gwen. I don't know if I could have held out
under those circumstances, either. The trick is to not follow him
to the roof in the first place, but Alice had gone, knowing full well
what was coming. Knowing it was what she wanted.

She would have been, what, thirty-three then? Only a few years
older than Gwen was now. Married at eighteen, so fifteen years
into it, and with a husband who no longer cared for her.

Gwen would never have done that. Well, easy enough to say
that now. She wasn't much older than Alice had been when she
got married. What if Ronnie had lived? Would she be living her
life or his now? Would he have supported her desire to go to university? What would they have been like fifteen years later?

Would he have let her work with Iris at The Right Sort?

*Nonsense, darling. Our life is perfect. I shall provide everything
you could possibly want. Have some more children.*

"He died before you learned all of his flaws . . . a paragon forever."

Alice was married to Andrea long enough to see his flaws.

The letters rushed headlong into passion.

I cannot bear to be without you . . .
I must see you or I will lose my mind . . .
He will be away for three days . . .
*There's an inn on the Ruopigenstrasse. I have taken a
room there under the name Schmidt . . .*
*This is madness! We cannot continue, but I cannot
stop . . .*
No one can find out.

No one will find out.
How you made me feel last night—I did not even know
such things were possible . . .

She reread that one a few times. One could always count on German for exquisite detail.

You have asked about Nancy . . .

Nancy?

Yes, I still intend to marry her. I must, for the sake of the
family. She has money. She can help us.

He had a fiancée! She didn't know Christo's story. She would have to ask Iris. Not a Greek or German, with that name. English? American? Rich, in any case, and an extended royal family in exile is not inexpensive to maintain.

She read on.

But that cannot stop us. Our love is a True Love, a
Higher Love than exists on this mortal plane.

Oh please, scoffed Gwen. The mortal plane is the one where you're both horizontal. Spare us the spiritual blather.

The affair continued—stolen moments, private outings, those long, long "walks." Alice's legs must have been in superb condition. Then came the wedding.

My darling,
How hard it was to see the two of you together, holding
hands as everyone applauded, knowing that you now belong
to this woman. They intend to give her a title: Princess

*Anastasia. Princess! When all she did was marry a fortune,
then bury the man who made it.*

*Know that I am yours any time you want me. I don't
care anymore if we are found out.*

Forever, A.

My heart,

*We must be more cautious than ever, but I will find a
way . . .*

And apparently, he did. Well, if he didn't care about her marriage, or his brother's, why should he care about his own?

But all good things must come to an end, and so must the bad.

They had gone to Lugano for the summer months of 1920.
Events in Greece were mentioned. Martial law was abolished, with
the pendulum of national sympathy swinging back to the royal
family. Alexander, the nephew, just months away from his fatal
simian encounter, was on the throne, his own marriage a scandal.
The brothers began to plot their next move, including Christo.

My own darling C.,

*Andrea tells me that he intends to travel to Rome, with
the intention of going to Athens once he determines that he
will be welcome there. My heart leaps in anticipation! Our
world will open up with him away for so long . . .*

My love,

*I am going with him. Family and national affairs
demand it . . .*

Then came one terse note from her, devoid of salutation:

I must see you. Tonight. A.

It was dated the second of September 1920.

There was a small gap of time after that. A hastily scrawled note from him, apparently from Rome, describing their journey and safe arrival, with the postscript:

> *I cannot stop thinking about you, the loveliness of your nude, white form under the moonlight, like an alabaster statue of a goddess . . .*

All right, never heard that from my husband, thought Gwen, grinning to herself. But we never ran naked in the moonlight.

And never will, more's the pity.

She grabbed for a handkerchief as the tears caught her, couldn't find one, and ended up running one gloved arm across her eyes, leaving two jagged wet streaks across the satin.

Damn you, Ronnie. Why did you have to be so heroic?

The next letter abandoned all pretense to poetry.

> *C.,*
>   *Our last encounter has had unintended consequences. I am with child. I had suspected as much before you left, and took the precaution of bedding my husband under the pretext of wanting one last time with him before he went on his dangerous journey. His ego overcame his long coldness towards me, and I feigned—well, he will be satisfied that it is his. But it is not, I am certain of it. The timing will be satisfactory to any prying eyes, but I had to tell you. It will be our secret, a symbol of our Love, binding us forever . . .*

> *A.,*
>   *Speak no further of this. Write nothing of it. I am returning all of your letters—I wanted to burn them on the*

spot, but I couldn't. The child belongs to my brother. I take
no further responsibility for it, or for you . . .

C.,
    This cannot be! We are destined to be lovers, on this and
all higher planes . . .

C.,
    Why do you no longer correspond?

C.,
    I shall go mad . . .

That was the last one. Gwen folded it with a sigh and glanced at
the clock. It was one thirty.

I shall go mad.

And she did, according to all reports. This could have been
a plausible explanation for it, as well as for Andrea's subsequent
abandonment.

The letters would certainly destroy any hope of marriage between Elizabeth and Philip, should they come to the public's attention. Or even the private attention of the Crown.

And they were fakes.

Archie walked casually up to a maintenance building on the
grounds of the East Ham Jewish Cemetery and knocked on the
door. The lid of the peephole slid aside. A second later, the door
opened, and the caretaker looked at him.

"'Allo, Reg," said Archie. "I've come to pay me respects."

"You would pick a Sunday," said Reg, letting him in. "The place
is swarming."

"Which is why I brought 'im in on a Saturday night," said Archie as he came in. "Didn't think you'd be busy."

"I've got a life, too," said Reg. "What if I 'ad a date?"

"Then you'd break it," said Archie. "Because when I call the tune, you dance. 'Ow's 'e doing?"

"Ask 'im yourself," said Reg, opening a door to the stairs to the basement.

Archie went down to a dank room where another man sat at a table, playing solitaire.

"Afternoon, Owen," said Archie. "I brought you the *Telegraph*." He tossed the paper onto the table.

"Ta," said Owen, without looking up. "Doc told me to change 'is dressing every four hours. Like I'm a bleedin' nurse now."

"If you wanter take a break, get something to eat, I'll watch 'im for a while. 'As 'e said anything?"

"Said thanks to the doc, nothin' else," said Owen, picking up the paper. "I'll be back."

Archie waited until Owen had left, then took a key from a hook on the wall and unlocked a door next to it. He pulled a ski mask from his coat, put it on, then went in.

The captured man lay on a cot, his hand bandaged more professionally than the Bainbridge woman had done. The other hand was secured by a length of chain to a bolt in the wall.

The man was awake, and sat up as Archie entered. "You again," he said.

"You know who I am?" asked Archie.

"The boss man from last night."

"That's right," said Archie. "You got a sharp eye."

The man shrugged.

"You got a name?" asked Archie.

"Do you?"

"Yeah, but I already know mine. 'Ow about giving me yours, then we can get on with the conversation."

"Stuff it."

"In that case, 'ow about the names of your next of kin?" said Archie.

"Mr. and Mrs. Stuff It."

Archie grinned, then took a stool from the far corner of the room and placed it next to the cot. "Don't get any cute ideas about trying for me," he warned the man as he sat down.

"You don't think I could take you?"

"No point. I don't 'ave the keys to the cuffs. And no, I don't think you could take me, not that I'm looking to show off or nothing. A couple of women took you down last night, so I don't think I need to worry."

"Are you trying to scare me?"

"You strike me as someone 'oo don't scare easy," said Archie. "You should be scared. I would be, in your situation."

"Miss Sparks wants me alive," said the man.

"Miss Sparks doesn't call the shots 'ere."

"That's not what I saw last night. She the real boss?"

"I'm the real boss. She is paying me for your temporary quarters."

"Yeah, twenty-five quid a day through Tuesday. And then you let me go."

"Maybe," said Archie. "My inclination is to dump you in the river."

"But Sparks wants me alive. She your girl?"

"She's her own girl."

"Because I got the idea you fancied her."

"I don't give a rat's balls what ideas you 'ave."

"Then why are we talking?"

"We 'aven't talked yet. I'm 'ere out of, let's call it professional interest. I gather you were part of some blackmail scheme. Nice racket, pays well when it works, but what interests me is I don't know you, and I make a point of knowing people 'oo travel the shady side of the street. None of me lads know you, either. Your accent is London, no doubt about it, so if this was regular work for you, we would 'ave crossed paths at some point or another. So, what are you?"

"Just a chap trying to get two bob to rub against each other," said the man.

"Aren't we all?"

"Did Miss Sparks tell you everything about our little transaction?"

"She did."

"So you know about the five thousand pounds."

"I do."

"No, you don't," said the man. "A top spiv like you wouldn't have walked away from a payday that large and that easy. Three of you, two of them, me on the floor. I saw you. You were surprised the blonde had ready money on her to pay for these lovely accommodations."

"Say, for the sake of argument, that I didn't know about the five thousand," said Archie. "What's your point?"

"You let me loose, I'll tell you where to find the money."

"'Ow do I know you're telling the truth? That this money even exists?"

"That was the payoff for me turning over the letters. They got the letters, I never got the payoff, but I know they have it, because I got a glimpse before things went haywire. Cut me loose, and I'll tell you more."

"Maybe you just told me all I need to know," said Archie.

"You need to know about who you're dealing with."

"Tell me your name, then."

"Oh, I'm not talking about me," said the man. "I'm talking about your girl. I know all about Iris Sparks. You know she worked for Intelligence during the war? Special Operations, amongst others."

"So I gathered," said Archie.

"Did she tell you herself?" scoffed the man. "You must be a special one for her to let that slip. Yeah, I know Iris Sparks. I used to work that territory, too. Very popular with the lads, was our Iris, but there wasn't a one she fancied that she didn't turn on in the end. Sometimes she breaks their hearts, sometimes she leaves them bleeding in warehouses. Ask her what really happened at Poplar Dock yesterday if you don't believe me."

"And the five thousand?"

"That information comes with a price. That's what I traffic in. You see, that's why you don't know me, but I know you, Archie Spelling. I play in a much higher league than you and your boys do, and my associates eat spivs for breakfast."

"If what you're telling me is true, then I can find the money easy enough without you," said Archie, getting to his feet and moving the stool back to the corner.

"Probably," agreed the man.

"And you telling me my name only makes it more likely that you go for a one-way vertical swim."

"Very likely. But if I'm telling the truth about Sparks and the money, then I'm also telling the truth about who I work with. So no, I'm not scared. Maybe you should be. I would be, in your situation."

"I'll give it some thought," said Archie.

"You do that, Archie Spelling. Remember—no woman is worth five thousand pounds."

Archie walked out and locked the door, leaving the man alone in the unlit, windowless room.

There in the dark, he smiled.

Iris rang the bell at the Bainbridge residence. A minute later, a butler opened the door.

"Oh, you must be Percival!" she exclaimed. "I recognised you straightaway. Mrs. Bainbridge has described you to a T. 'In a world that aspires to be distinguished, he is the one man who truly is.'"

"She said that?" asked Percival, almost imperceptibly flustered. "About me?"

"Her very words, or near enough. Oh my goodness, I haven't introduced myself. Miss Iris Sparks, here to see Mrs. Bainbridge. Is she feeling better? She was not looking well after dinner last night. I thought she might have ingested a bad clam somewhere along the way. I wanted to look in on her and see how she is doing."

"I will see if she is up to receiving visitors, Miss Sparks," said Percival, holding the door open. "Please come and sit in the parlour whilst I enquire."

She went inside and looked around. The parlour could have contained her entire flat. A large painting depicting the current Lord and Lady Bainbridge, shortly after their marriage, dominated the near wall. In it, Lady Carolyne was sitting on a dark blue upholstered high-backed chair, strands of white pearls hanging from her neck, her brunette hair curled quite prettily in ringlets draped over each shoulder. She was slender then, the sort of woman people of the time would have described as handsome rather than beautiful. Lord Bainbridge stood behind her, both hands resting on the top of the chair, wearing a black tailcoat over a gray waistcoat, a red carnation the only spot of colour on him.

Neither of them was smiling. The expression caught on his face by the artist was one of stern judgment. Hers was—well, Iris may have been reading too much into it, but it seemed to be one of resignation.

Percival returned.

"Mrs. Bainbridge will receive you in her bedchamber," he said. "Millicent is waiting for you at the top of the staircase, and will take you from there."

"Thank you, Percival," said Iris.

She walked up the staircase, where a young maid curtsied and led her down a hallway. She stopped at a door and knocked respectfully.

"Miss Sparks is here to see you, ma'am," she said.

"Thank you, Millie," called Gwen from inside. "Send her in, then close the door, please."

Millie opened the door. Iris entered to see Gwen lying in melodramatic repose, the covers pulled up to her neck.

"Oh, my dear Miss Sparks," she gasped. "So good of you to visit me in my distress."

Iris waited until Millie had closed the door behind her, then grinned. "We're safe," she said.

Gwen immediately sat up, revealing her opera gloves.

"Hello, Gilda," said Iris. "Are we putting the blame on Mame now?"

Gwen looked at her quizzically.

"Gilda?" repeated Iris.

"Sorry, not getting it," said Gwen. "Who is Gilda?"

"The Rita Hayworth flicker? Where she does the glove-and-gown strip, only it's just the one glove?"

"Oh," said Gwen, getting out of bed and peeling off the gloves. "Let's see. I spent the latter half of forty-four in the sanatorium where they wouldn't let me watch the weekly films for fear they would upset me. Since then I've been living in this house doing my best to mother a small boy, which at times reaches a level of insanity greater than the one that had me institutionalised. Apart from cowboy movies and *Make Mine Music*, I haven't seen anything. Certainly nothing with a striptease number."

"What's *Make Mine Music*?"

"Disney cartoons."

"How was it?"

"Little Ronnie loved it. That's all that mattered."

"We should go out and see a movie. It would be nice to have a night out together that didn't involve either murder or psychotherapy."

"I'd like that very much."

"So, explain the gloves."

"I didn't want to leave fingerprints on the letters, and I left my wrist gloves at the office."

"How were the letters?"

"They paint a lurid picture of an affair between Alice and Andrea's youngest brother, Christo, while they were in exile in Switzerland, complete with the implication that he fathered Prince Philip."

"My, my. How lurid?"

"Downright explicit at times. Rather stimulating, if one goes for that sort of thing."

"Yet you kept the gloves on."

"I did, in case the forger left any prints."

"Forger? They don't match Alice's handwriting from the earlier letters?"

"Oh, the handwriting looks to be the same to my untutored eye, but the content gave it away. In this one, in particular." She held one up.

Iris plopped down on the bed next to her and read it. "Nope, not seeing it," she said when she had finished.

"Then I am one up on you," said Gwen. "It might be worthwhile getting an expert to look at them, in case my opinion isn't enough to satisfy the authorities."

"Which authorities?"

"Maybe the police, maybe whoever in your lot handles conspiracies," said Gwen. "If these letters are being forged, then the forger, or his employers, are trying to set someone up."

"Prince Philip, presumably."

"I'm not so sure anymore. Someone went to a lot of trouble to fake these, and I don't think they did it just to throw a scare into our young princess. Too many violent men are coming out of the woodwork for that. This smacks of being part of a larger plan. But you've already thought of that, haven't you? Here's what I've been thinking: what if Princess Elizabeth was never meant to be the intended recipient of the extortion request?"

"It was addressed to her."

"And intercepted by the woman in charge of screening her letters, who acted accordingly."

"Lady Matheson. She was their target?"

"If they knew how things worked at the Palace, then that would be logical."

"Then she's being drawn into a trap by someone. Maybe we'll know more when we get those photographs tomorrow. We should bring the letters to Jimmy the Scribe. I'd like his take on them. I wonder if we'll beat the police to the punch on this."

"They don't know what we know," said Gwen, picking up a pair of newspapers from her nightstand and handing them to Iris. "Guess who is the lead investigator?"

"'Man found stabbed to death in Poplar Dock warehouse,'" Iris read. "'Name being withheld by authorities pending notification . . . enquiries being made . . . anyone with information should contact Detective Superintendent Philip Parham.' Parham again! The Rota of Fortune has turned and landed on us twice. Well, we needn't worry about the competition if he's on the case."

"I wonder if your ex is assisting him on this one," said Gwen.

"Mike should be in the midst of his honeymoon at the moment," said Iris.

"Oh! That happened already? You never mentioned it."

"Needless to say, I wasn't invited to the wedding," said Iris. "*C'est la vie.* Or *c'est la guerre.* I'm not sure where we stood when we left it. I've moved on."

"Are you sure?"

"It's what I do best."

"Fine. How was Hagia Sophia?"

"Enlightening. I ran into one old friend, and saw a second."

"Tell me everything."

Archie sat at his kitchen table, making a list.

1. Office. Strongbox?
2. Office next door.
3. Somewhere else in the building.

Somewhere else would make things difficult, he thought. Plenty of places to hide it, but less safe. Custodian could find it. Workers renovating offices. Rats. There's always rats.

4. Her flat.
5. Bainbridge house.
6. Bank deposit box.
7. With a friend.

So. One and two were easy. One-man job. He knew a few yeggs he could trust with it. But it wasn't likely that Sparks would still be holding the bread on the premises at this point.

He crossed out the first three.

Her flat, then? Not a big place, but she'd been there long enough to find or make a hidey-hole. He hadn't exactly been scouting it when he paid his mercy visit the other day, and he hadn't seen the bedroom.

He was hoping to see it, he thought sadly. But five thousand pounds were five thousand pounds, and she was merely a girl he'd had two dates with.

Well, three, according to her. All he did was bring her whisky and curry, but women had their own funny ways of counting things. He had come away from there feeling pretty good, considering all he got out of it was a peck on the cheek.

Money, Arch, he admonished himself. Remember the money.

He wouldn't need a full-blown yegg for the flat. If Sparks had a hidey-hole there, it was more likely used for keeping weapons than money and jewelry. She was a practical girl. She'd know enough to keep valuables outside the flat.

But that would include the five grand, wouldn't it? Only it was Sunday, and the banks were closed, so it wouldn't be in a deposit box. He crossed that one out.

If she were going to put it in the bank, then he had a limited window to make a move. She'd be home at some point tonight, he guessed, which meant he'd have to have his boys go in armed and fast, and she wasn't the kind of girl who'd take kindly to that.

Someone would definitely get hurt in that scenario.

He crossed out item four.

The Bainbridge house.

Kensington. Ritzy part of town. Big place, lots of staff. On the other hand, not the sort of place where they had watchmen. Once everyone went to bed, the place would be ripe for the picking, if it was done silently.

He needed a creeper, he thought. Someone who could—

The telephone rang, jangling him out of his thoughts. He picked it up.

"'Allo?" he said irritably.

"Uncle Archie!" said a man excitedly. "It's Bernie! Is this a good time?"

"Just putting me thoughts in order," said Archie. "I always got time for you, lad. What's up?"

"I wanted to thank you, Uncle," burbled Bernie. "I never thought it would go like this, but it did! It's wonderful!"

"Well, good for you," said Archie. "What are you talking about?"

"I'm in love!" crowed Bernie. "Oh, she's wonderful! Not at all what I expected, not the type of woman I've dreamed about, but that's what happened! It's a miracle, Uncle Archie, and I owe it all to you for sending me to The Right Sort. Thank you, thank you, thank you!"

"All this after one date?"

"Two! And the second—well, it took us to—I really can't say any more, but we're in love, can you believe it? I wanted you to be the first to know. I'm calling Mum and Dad next to have her over for dinner. You should come, too. I want you to meet Tish. Will you?"

"Of course, lad. I'm delighted it worked out so well for you."

"Right, going to call them now. Good night, Uncle."

"Good night, lad."

He hung up, then looked at his list again.

No woman is worth five thousand pounds.

Except Iris Sparks was worth more.

He crumpled up the list, dropped it on an ashtray, and put a match to it.

"We need to get into that reception," concluded Iris.

"I wonder . . ." mused Gwen. "Come with me."

She had dressed while listening to Iris's summary of her morning and now led Iris downstairs in search of the butler. She found him polishing a set of candlesticks.

"Ah, Percival, good," she said. "Do you know if Lady Carolyne received an invitation to the reception at Claridge's for the Greek king tomorrow evening?"

"She did, Mrs. Bainbridge."

"Did she accept?"

"She did not, Mrs. Bainbridge."

"Do we still have that invitation, by any chance?"

"I believe so, ma'am."

"Could you fetch it for me, please?"

"Of course, ma'am."

He replaced the candlesticks in a cabinet, locked it, then went in search of the invitation. He returned a minute later carrying an envelope on a silver platter.

"Thank you, Percival," said Gwen, taking it.

They walked back to her room.

"Won't the lack of an RSVP be a problem?" asked Iris.

"Nothing I can't brazen my way through," said Gwen.

"Well, that gets you in the door. What about me? Shall I put on a fake mustache and trousers and try and pass as your escort?"

"I have a better idea," said Gwen, pressing a button on her nightstand.

Shortly thereafter, there was a soft knock on the door, and Millie entered.

"You rang, Mrs. Bainbridge?" she asked.

"Yes, Millie. Tomorrow is your night off, is that correct?"

"It is, Mrs. Bainbridge."

"Any plans?"

"I was going to visit my sister."

"Lovely. Would you mind standing next to Miss Sparks for a moment?"

"Ma'am?" said Millie in confusion.

"Ah," said Iris, stepping beside her. "I understand. Millie, would you like to make a little extra money?"

"What do I have to do, Miss?"

"Lend me your outfit. Mrs. Bainbridge and I are going to a party, and I need to go as a lady's maid. We look to be the same size. Shall we say ten shillings?"

"Oh! Well, if you promise to get it back right after. I'll need it in the morning."

"I will bring it back myself," Gwen assured her.

"Then I suppose it's all right. Shall I bring it to your office in the afternoon? It's on my way."

"That would be splendid, Millie," said Gwen. "Thank you."

Millie curtsied and left.

"Another odd item for the expense account," said Gwen.

"Easier to explain than the cost of holding a captive," said Iris. "Now, you need one more thing for this party."

"What?"

"An escort."

"Oh dear," sighed Gwen. "Maybe we should have stayed with you and the mustache. Wait. I have an idea."

They went downstairs and Gwen went to use the telephone. Iris waited patiently in the entrance hall. Suddenly, the doors burst open and a young boy flew in, skidding to a halt when he saw her.

"Hello," he said. "I'm Ronnie."

"Well, of course you are," said Iris, squatting so that she could shake his hand. "My name is Iris Sparks. I'm a friend of your mother. It is so very nice to meet you at last."

"Are you the lady she works with?" asked Ronnie.

"I am indeed."

"You find husbands for ladies?"

"We try. And wives for gentlemen."

"Are you going to find one for Mummy?"

"Only if she asks me to," said Iris, taken aback. "Do you think she should?"

"I don't know," said Ronnie very seriously. "She's sad a lot. It might make her happy."

"It might," agreed Iris. "But that's something she needs to decide for herself. I know that you make her very happy."

"But I can't marry her," said Ronnie.

"No," said Gwen, coming into the hallway. "And that is as it should be."

"Mummy!" cried Ronnie. "Are you feeling better?"

"I am, now that you're here," said Gwen as she lifted him up and hugged him tight. "I see you've met my friend Iris."

"She's very nice," said Ronnie.

"Thank you," said Iris. "And so are you."

"Maybe I'll marry her someday," said Ronnie.

"That's the best offer I've had in a long time," said Iris. "Let's wait until you're old enough, then we'll talk about it some more."

"All right."

Lady Carolyne came through the door, followed by Agnes. She looked askance at Iris, then at Gwen. "I see that you're feeling better," she said.

"Yes, I am, thank you," said Gwen.

"Agnes, take Ronnie upstairs and get him changed for dinner," said Lady Carolyne.

"I have to change again?" protested Ronnie.

"Your clothes are all dusty from having so much fun," whispered Agnes, taking his hand. "Come upstairs, Ronnie."

"Goodbye, Iris," said Ronnie, waving.

"Goodbye, dear," said Iris, waving back.

They watched until he was out of earshot, then turned back to each other.

"Was it a good visit?" asked Gwen.

"Of course," said Lady Carolyne. "What is she doing here?"

"Iris dropped by to see how I was feeling," said Gwen. "And to talk over some business."

"What sort of business?"

"Our business," said Gwen.

"I'm surprised that you are actually up at this time of day, Miss Sparks," said Lady Carolyne. "I would expect you to still be in someone's bed, trying to remember his name."

"As a matter of fact, I was in church this morning," said Iris humbly. "I'm seeking to mend my ways. Your daughter-in-law has been a very good influence, Lady Carolyne."

"Piffle," said Lady Carolyne.

"Look, while I have you here, I want to ask you a favour," said Gwen.

"What favour?"

"You have an invitation to the reception at Claridge's tomorrow for King George. May I take it, since you're not going?"

"For what reason, may I ask?"

"Business-related," said Gwen. "We're vetting a client who is Greek, and I could find out a few things in that crowd that I can't elsewhere."

"Very well," said Lady Carolyne. "If you wish to consort with Greeks, that is no concern of mine. I see the influence runs both ways. Good day, Miss Sparks. Gwendolyn, I shall expect you for dinner, now that you've fully recovered."

"Yes, Lady Carolyne."

"Good day, Miss Sparks," said Lady Carolyne. "Percival will see you out."

She walked away.

"I guess that means I'm leaving," said Iris. "I didn't hear an invitation to stay for dinner."

"I'm sorry," said Gwen.

"Well, that's progress, in any case," said Iris. "I have set foot inside chez Bainbridge, and met the young lord and master, who is delightful, by the way."

"Thank you," said Gwen. "I'm glad you like him."

"I'm glad he liked me. Let's see. He'll be old enough to marry me in twelve years."

"When you'll be—"

"Twenty-eight," said Iris firmly. "And I shall call you Mum after we're married."

"What a dreadful idea! Well, see you at The Right Sort in the morning. Oh, and I have an escort for the reception."

"Well done. Who?"

"I'll surprise you."

"I'm intrigued," said Iris. She paused. "How much of the conversation with Ronnie did you hear?"

"Do you mean did I hear when he asked if you were going to find me a husband?"

"Yes. Out of the mouths of babes—"

"Iris, I'm a professional husband-finder. When the time comes, I'll do it myself. And here is Percival. Goodbye, dear."

"Goodbye."

Iris's telephone was ringing as she entered her flat. She dashed to answer it before the connection was lost.

"Hello?"

"'Allo, Sparks," said Archie.

"Hello, Archie."

"So when were you gonna tell me about the five thousand pounds?"

CHAPTER 12

I gather he's talking," said Iris.

"'E's talking," said Archie. "'E's not saying much. Most of it is about you, so I'm applying grains of salt. But the five thousand was no porker, was it?"

"The five thousand is real, and it's alive and well."

"So you trust me enough to commit a major felony on your behalf, but not enough to tell me you were recently loaded."

"Oh, Archie." Iris sighed. "I trust you. I didn't tell you about the money for the same reason you didn't tell me where you were stashing the gent. I wanted to protect you and the lads."

"Protect me?" Archie exclaimed indignantly. "Just 'oo are you to be protecting me? I'm Archie Spelling! I don't need protecting."

"This situation comes from Very High Up," said Iris. "If it goes wrong, the powers that be will come down like a ton of bricks. I didn't want them to make a public example of you. I'm sorry, Archie, I didn't mean to hurt your feelings. Oh gosh, listen to us. Our first lovers' quarrel, and we aren't even lovers yet."

"I'm liking the 'yet' part. So where does the money go when all is said and done?"

"Back to its originator. Sorry again, Archie. Neither of us is getting rich off this one."

"'Ow do you resist the temptation? You can practically 'ear it breathing when there's that much of it lying about."

"By letting the Incorruptible One hold it. I don't entirely trust myself in this matter, either."

"Item five," muttered Archie.

"What?"

"Nothing. So this bloke talked like 'e knew you before."

"Clever boy, clever ploy. What did he say?"

"That you worked for British Intelligence. Special Operations. No surprise to me there."

"Old news, but very interesting that he claims to know about it," said Iris. "Anything else?"

"Suggested that you 'ad something to do with the feller who took a blade to the gut at the Poplar Dock yesterday."

"Did he say I was the one holding the other end?"

"Implied as much. Thing is, 'ad you done so, I wouldn't've found myself in a state of shock on that count, either."

"Sorry to disappoint you. I came in after the bloody deed was done."

"Ah, so that's 'ow it came about. That was where the money was going? To the deceased?"

"Not exactly. He seems to have been an uninvited guest. After we found him, we had to make a quick exit. Our new friend recognised us, showed up at the office waving his Mauser about, and things got complicated. And now he's trying to turn you against me. Thank you for not succumbing, Archie."

"It was a near thing," said Archie. "Shall I play along with 'im? Might get 'im talking some more."

"Actually, what he said is quite useful," said Iris thoughtfully. "We're treating the money as an expense account at the moment. How would you like to be an expense?"

"I'm listening," said Archie.

*　*　*

Iris came into the office Monday morning to find Gwen on the telephone, holding the earpiece several inches away from her ear.

"I am so pleased," she said. "No, you don't send us the marriage fee until after it takes place, but it all sounds like an auspicious beginning. No, auspicious, not suspicious. Yes, that means a good thing. I will. Thank you for letting us know."

She hung up.

"Miss Hardiman?" guessed Iris.

"How did you know?" asked Gwen.

"Because Little Ronnie uses his indoor voice on the telephone now."

"Sorry, couldn't hear what you were saying, I have this ringing in my left ear!" shouted Gwen.

"She called to say that things went spectacularly well with Bernie."

"She did. You already knew?"

"Heard it from his uncle Archie last night," said Iris.

"How is our guest?" asked Gwen. "Has he recovered from our tender ministrations?"

"Well enough to try and worm his way into Archie's confidences. Fortunately, Archie still likes me better, even after finding out about our having the payoff moola."

"Oh. Should we be moving that to a safer place?"

"No. We're going to be needing it for some not-so-petty expenses."

"You have a new plan," said Gwen.

"I have a new plan, but let's wait for the photos before we commit to it."

"And then?"

"We visit Jimmy, get his opinion on the letters. Then we get Cinderella ready for the ball."

* * *

There was a rap on the door an hour later, and a young man entered, a courier bag on his shoulder.

"Are you Miss Sparks and Mrs. Bainbridge?" he asked.

"We are," said Iris.

"I'm from Mr. Cornell," he said, pulling a folder from the bag.

"Good, we've been expecting you. He told you to await a reply?"

"Yes, Mum."

"Go get yourself a muffin and come right back," she said, tossing him a coin. He caught it, grinned, and vanished out the door.

Iris opened the folder, which contained a set of photographs. Gwen came over to her desk to look as Iris went through them one by one.

"That's our man," said Iris, pointing. "I'll bet anything."

"Too bad we don't have movie footage," said Gwen. "We could tell if he was limping."

"Well, he wouldn't be limping here. Wait, there's some more—oh!"

"That's him," whispered Gwen. "That's Magoulias. You were right."

"Right about him being there," said Iris. "I was wondering if he was in cahoots with the first fellow and they had a falling out. This actually makes more sense to me."

"We still don't know who Magoulias was working for."

"That's what tonight is for."

"Right," said Gwen, sitting down heavily.

"Are you all right?" asked Iris.

"Seeing his face again," said Gwen. "It makes me remember it from when we found him. I see his eyes whenever I close mine."

"Do you want to give Dr. Milford a ring? Maybe he could squeeze you in for a quick tune-up."

"It's not an emergency," said Gwen. "I have to learn how to get through these crises without running to him for help straight-away."

"If it's any consolation, you got through Saturday's events splendidly, in my opinion."

"Thanks. I guess I did, relatively speaking. Apart from going into catatonia on the boat."

"Luckily, Sally had the antidote on hand."

"I don't want whisky to be the answer to every problem."

"Of course not. Just the important ones. Why, we've gone almost two days without finding another dead body. I think that's progress, don't you?"

Gwen shuddered. Iris laughed, then took her notepad and scribbled something. She tore the page off and put it in an envelope, then sealed it.

The messenger returned, muffin crumbs still noticeable on his shirt. Iris handed him the envelope.

"Give this to Mr. Cornell," she instructed him. "Tell him that I will call when I know the time and place, and to bring a voucher."

"Yes, Mum." He saluted and left.

"One more piece of news," said Gwen. "I have a lead on Vivienne Ducognon. I spoke to Lorraine Calvert, and she thinks that her husband's cousin's wife has a French lady's maid. I could try calling on her on the way here tomorrow."

"Fine. Now, pass me the telephone. I'm going to call Jimmy. And then perhaps we should try and match a few people while we're here?"

"God, I'll be glad when this is over and done with," said Gwen. "Investigating murders does get in the way of one's actual work."

J. B. Smalley & Sons was an upscale shop selling prints and lithographs near the theatre district off Earlham Street. James B. Smalley, its proprietor, was a tall, elegant man, always impeccably dressed, with an encyclopedic knowledge of art and printmaking. He was also known in certain circles as Jimmy the Scribe, one of London's top forgers until the Metropolitan Police put an abrupt end to his career and his liberty in the mid-thirties. He was known in even smaller circles as the top maker of forged papers for British Intelligence during the war, which was why his liberty had been restored.

No one knew what the "B" stood for. Those who knew Smalley's past suspected that the "Sons" were nonexistent, added to confer further respectability on a newly forged life. He confined his lawless leanings to consulting for various British intelligence services and the police. Iris and Gwen had come to him on their previous investigation and had found him invaluable.

A smile lit up his face when he saw them enter the shop.

"My dear Miss Sparks! And Mrs. Bainbridge!" he said, coming forwards to shake their hands warmly. "You do my humble establishment honour. Mrs. Bainbridge, how is your young narwhal enthusiast doing? I pray that he continues to show interest in the subject."

"Oh yes," said Gwen, laughing. "Your reproduction of that print has been a great inspiration to him. His illustrations of Sir Oswald the Narwhal are much more accurate now, although putting him in a cowboy hat while riding a horse in the American West is biologically unsound, I suspect."

"Nonsense," said Jimmy. "A narwhal must go wherever his adventures take him. I would love to see these pictures sometime. Well, ladies, enough pleasantries. I was given to understand by Miss Sparks that you have need of my expertise."

"We do," said Iris. "May we go in back?"

"Certainly," he said, leading them into the storage room. One corner was reserved for a small office. He held their chairs as they sat, then went behind his desk.

"What's the scheme this time, Sparks?" he asked.

"We'd like your opinion on some letters," she said. "To see if they're genuine."

"Who wrote them?"

"I won't influence you by telling you," said Iris.

"How can I know if they're real if I don't know more about them?"

"We have others for comparison," said Gwen, pulling a folder from her bag. "Here are two of the originals."

Jimmy pulled on a pair of cotton gloves and took them from her. Then he picked up a magnifying glass from his desk and peered at them closely.

"These go back some fifty years," he said. "You can tell by the onionskin—it was much in vogue here then. Good handwriting, poor spelling. And—Ah! These are actually written to Queen Victoria! One of her granddaughters? No, a great-granddaughter. Where did you get these?"

"We can't tell you, of course," said Iris.

"And they have to go back," said Gwen.

"Pity. I know some collectors who would pay nicely for these."

"Now, here are the ones we need you to analyse."

She handed him two of the less incriminating missives from "A."

He took the first page by the corner, then held it up to the light. Then he sniffed it carefully. "Smells like it's been kept in oilskin," he said. "Forgive me, ladies, for the impropriety I am about to commit."

He brought the paper to his mouth, placed the tip of his tongue against the back, and licked it delicately.

"My goodness!" exclaimed Iris. "What can you glean from that?"

"Texture, chemical treatment," explained Jimmy. "Every country makes its own paper. Each process uses different proportions of chemicals, different sources of wood, rags, what have you. I haven't even looked at the writing yet, and I can tell you that this came from Switzerland."

"You can tell that already? I'm impressed."

"We faked a lot of Swiss documents during the war," he said, picking up the magnifying glass again. "Had to get the paper to match. The Nazis paid just as much attention to detail as we did. Let's take a look at the handwriting."

He pored over the newer letters, then went back and forth between them and the originals.

"There's a passage of time involved between the exemplars and the subjects, of course," he said. "But one's handwriting from one's adolescence will not change overmuch by the time one reaches one's thirties, barring injuries or other infirmities. She had none?"

"Nothing that would affect her handwriting, as far as we know," said Iris.

"There are enough capital letters in both sets to compare, as well as all the little connections between letter pairs, which is where the giveaways can occur."

"Have you found any?" asked Gwen.

"I have not," he pronounced. "These are dated from 1918 and 1919. The paper and ink are completely consistent with that period and location. The handwriting is the same. If I were called on to testify in a court of law—and God help the side that calls me, with my record—my expert opinion would be that these are the real article."

"They are?" exclaimed Gwen in dismay.

"Yes. That is not happy news, I take it?"

"We had a small wager on the outcome," said Iris, smiling in triumph. "Now, we have a second set. No exemplars this time, so just your conclusion on time and place again."

Gwen handed him two of the blue onionskin letters from "C." Jimmy repeated his taste and smell tests, then peeled off one glove and trailed the tips of his fingers lightly over the papers.

"Also Swiss, same period," he said. "And may I venture one psychological observation?"

"Certainly."

"This is the sort of stationery one buys when one doesn't wish to be connected to it. If, as I gather from the small sample you've provided me, your fellow 'C.' is not using his personal stationery, then I would suppose that the remainder of this correspondence is of an illicit nature."

"Which will remain confidential," said Iris.

"Of course," he said. "I am scandalised that you even feel the need to say that, Sparks."

"My apologies, Jimmy," she said, patting his hand. "I do hope that your sense of honour is not so offended as to refuse a small fee for your services?"

"Happily, it is not," he said. "Do you need an invoice?"

"Strangely enough, we do."

"How shall I make it out?"

"'For expert services,'" said Iris. "The client won't want to know more than that."

"They rarely do," he said, writing it out and handing it to her along with the letters. "Don't forget these. Unless you'd like to make a quick deal on them—as I said, there's a market for them."

"We know," said Gwen. "At the moment, it's booming."

Gwen was gloomy when they left the shop.

"Cheer up," said Iris, noticing.

"I was counting on him backing me up," said Gwen.

"If it's any consolation, I still think you're right," said Iris.

"And what was that about a wager?" asked Gwen. "We never said anything about it."

"I didn't want you to go any further on the topic," said Iris. "You were so surprised by his answer. I was worried you might let something slip."

"Well, the forger certainly knew his business if he could get these by Jimmy," said Gwen. "Do you think he's local?"

"I do. But we can't do anything more about that today. We have to get ready. What time do you expect your Miss Millie to arrive?"

"Soon," said Gwen, looking at her watch. "The reception is not until seven. We should have ample time."

Millie rapped on the office door right on time, two garment bags slung over her shoulder and a hatbox in her hand.

"Millie, please come in," said Gwen.

"So this is it," said Millie, looking around. "I was expecting it to be bigger."

"It is in our dreams," said Iris.

"Any trouble getting away?" asked Gwen.

"Oh no," said Millie. "I told them that I needed to bring you your dress, and Mr. Percival approved. Would you like me to help? I'm still on service until five. I wouldn't mind."

"Thank you, Millie. I would appreciate the assistance."

"We want you to look your best, don't we, ma'am? Everyone knows you're going to the reception. The staff is all atwitter about it."

"Goodness, I didn't mean to set things off like that," said Gwen.

"You going on a fancy date for the first time? We're all happy for you."

"I don't know if I would call it a date," said Gwen. "It's more business-related."

"You're putting on extra makeup?"

"Yes."

"You're wearing a fancy frock?"

"Well—"

"Jewelry?"

"One must consider—"

"And there's a gentleman going to take you?"

"Yes."

"It's a date," concluded Millie. "Let me get you made up. Where's the ladies'?"

"Down the hall," said Gwen, picking up her makeup case and following her to the door.

"And I'll just dress myself, then," said Iris, taking the other garment bag. "Because I'm a big girl and I know how."

She closed the door after Millie and Gwen, then took a small mirror from her desk and propped it against her typewriter. She started by pulling on a pair of black woolen stockings, then put on Millie's black dress. She coiled her hair into a neat, conservative bun, pinned it securely, then wiped off her lipstick and applied a softer, duller tone that wouldn't attract much attention. She added the uniform's white apron and tied it in back, then topped it with the frilly cap.

She inspected her handiwork in the mirror, frowned, then pulled a pair of spectacles with thick black frames from her bag and donned them.

Men seldom make passes at girls who wear glasses, she thought. The last thing she needed to be tonight was desirable to the male sex. The more eyes on Gwen, the easier it would be for Iris to accomplish her goals.

Then Gwen walked back into the office and Iris realised there would never be any danger of anyone looking at any other woman but her.

She was wearing an indigo silk chiffon gown with a scalloped hem that swirled about her ankles with every step. Every step was taken inside a pair of gleaming white ankle straps with heels just below the maximum two inches. She wore a matching sequined bolero jacket and the same white evening gloves that Iris had last seen holding racy letters in bed. A double strand of matched white pearls draped over her modest décolletage, and a diamond-studded tiara topped her chignon.

The whole ensemble drew one's eyes to her face, which had gone from merely beautiful to something Titian wished he could paint. She had gone with a classic English Rose look for her makeup, but with red lipstick bright enough to cut through a fog bank.

"Madeleine Carroll has just been relegated to second place on every man's list," said Iris. "Is that Hartnell?"

"The frock's a Hartnell," replied Gwen, placing a folded, dark blue cape on her desk. "I've had it since before the war, but we aren't showing our shoulders nowadays, more's the pity, so I found the jacket at Paquin and had them dye it to match."

"You are a walking *Vogue* cover."

"Please, don't be ridiculous," said Gwen. "This is all Millie's magic."

"Oh no, ma'am," protested Millie. "All I did was put a few finishing touches on what's always there."

"I need a Millie," said Iris. "Can I have Millie?"

"No," said Gwen.

"May I borrow her occasionally?"

"Tell you what," said Millie. "You make sure my lady goes out more, and I'll make up the two of you together when you do."

"Done and done," said Iris.

"I'm not going out more," insisted Gwen. "I told you, this is for business."

"And what business are you doing done up like this?" asked Millie.

"We're secretly vetting an aristocratic bachelor for a prospective bride," said Gwen.

"At an opulent ball," added Iris. "Which we are crashing."

"Is your job always like this?" Millie sighed. "It sounds wonderfully exciting and romantic. Take me next time, and you can both dress up."

"Next time, we will," said Iris. "How do I look?" She twirled in front of her desk.

"Hang on one second, Miss," said Millie, coming over and

retying the apron. "There. Now the bow's done properly. There's one more thing."

"What's that?"

"Your shoes," said Millie. "They're too nice for a lady's maid."

"Oh dear, so they are," said Iris, inspecting them. "Say, what size are yours?"

"Fours."

"Perfect. May we trade for the night?"

"Oh, I wouldn't mind wearing those for a night out," said Millie, eyeing Iris's peep-toe sling-backs.

"I thought you were visiting your sister," said Gwen.

"My sister who's got a boyfriend who's got a best friend who is dreamy," said Millie wistfully.

"Sounds like you'll be having a more romantic time than we will," said Iris as she traded her heels for Millie's sensible work shoes.

"Here's hoping," said Millie. "Good night, ma'am, Miss Sparks. Good hunting!"

"Thank you, Millie," said Gwen. "Good night."

Iris walked around the room, staring at her feet. "Could these be any clunkier?" she complained. "And I lose an inch. I was short enough before."

"The better to hide in dark corners," said Gwen, sitting behind her desk. "I wish I could disappear."

"What's wrong?" asked Iris, sitting across from her.

"I'm nervous, is what's wrong. I haven't been to one of these affairs—Well, there haven't been many lately, of course, but the last one I went to was with Ronnie, and that was years ago. Little Ronnie was still in nappies, and I was feeling bloated and unattractive and said so, and the next thing I knew, my husband had whisked me out shopping for a new frock and shoes and we ended up dancing at the Dorchester. I think I danced with every man in the room that night, possibly including a waiter."

"What time did you get home?"

"We didn't," said Gwen. "Ronnie had booked a room. I don't think we left it for two days after that night. And the first thing he did when we got to it was massage my feet for an hour."

"What a lovely man!"

"He was. And then he shipped out, and I barely saw him after that. And then—oh, I've got to stop talking, or I'll start crying and ruin the wonderful work Millie did on my face. I used to so love this life—the seasons, the dressing, the music, the champagne, the romance. It's over, isn't it?"

"It will come back," said Iris. "The war is a year behind us, and rationing can't go on forever."

"It may come back, it may not," said Gwen. "Even if it does, will I?"

"I would think Ronnie would want you to."

"He does, that's the thing," said Gwen miserably.

"Excuse me?" said Iris, startled. "How would—how do you know?"

"Don't worry, I'm not communing with his ghost, as much as I wish to." Gwen sighed. "I found a letter he had left for me, one of those 'In case I don't come back' missives."

"What did he say?" Iris asked.

"Quite a lot about Little Ronnie, which has provided some useful ammunition in my personal World War. But the part that relates to me—basically, he urged me to remarry. He gave me permission."

"Ah."

"The problem is that I haven't given myself permission," Gwen continued. "In fact, I'm more than a little peeved that he had given me up so easily."

"What did you expect?" asked Iris.

"That he'd want me to wait until he either figured out some way to claw his way back from death, or until I had joined him in the afterlife, preferably in some place with a dance floor and a decent band."

"The first won't happen," said Iris. "And postpone the second for as long as you possibly can. You are needed in this world."

"By a son whose custody I don't control."

"By him. But also by me, darling. I can't run this place alone. And how would I be able to sneak into this reception without you?"

"You'd find a way." She got up and paced the small room, executing the turns at each wall with dance steps, then stopped. "I haven't danced properly in years," she said. "I'm going to be terrible!"

"You've danced at weddings."

"Yes, but you know what those are like for a recent widow? One or two turns around the floor out of pity with married cousins who are woefully out of practice. I'm blanking, Iris! Every step I've ever learned has vanished!"

"Come on," said Iris, grabbing her by the hand and leading her out into the hallway.

"What are you doing?"

"Foxtrot, for a start," said Iris, turning to face her. "Give me your hand, other on my shoulder. Basics first. Slow, slow, quick quick!"

She danced Gwen down the length of the hall, then led her through an outside turn. "You remember twinkles?" she asked. "Good! Promenade. Turning box. See, it's all coming back."

"Muscle memory," said Gwen. "Where did you learn to lead so well?"

"All-girls boarding school," said Iris. "We took turns. They said I was the best boy there. All the girls wanted to dance with me. Let's try a spin. Excellent! Now, the hallway's too narrow for a full waltz, but we could do the basics. And one, two, three!"

They whirled down the hallway.

"Frame, darling," said Iris as they turned back in the other direction.

"Oh, that brings back memories," said Gwen, throwing her shoulders back. "Sorry, I was adjusting to your height."

"Think of me as a short Greek man with feelings of inadequacy," said Iris. "Dare we tango?" She struck a fierce pose, stamping her foot, throwing one arm up with the other bent across her chest. "Zee song eez 'Jalousie'!" she cried. "We weel forgo zee cadenza. Come, my lady—we dance!"

"Yes, you look exactly like Douglas Fairbanks," said Gwen.

"It's been said before," said Iris, swooping in. "Dahmp, da dahhh, dah dah dada dahmp, da dahhh!"

"Are those the actual words? Oh, hello, Mr. MacPherson!"

Their custodian was standing on the landing, gazing up at them openmouthed.

"Hello, Mr. MacPherson," echoed Iris, waving. "We're rehearsing a sketch for a party. What do you think?"

"It doesn't make any sense to me," said Mr. MacPherson. "What are the two of you supposed to be doing?"

"It's the one where the maid teaches her mistress the newest dance styles," explained Iris. "I saw something like it in a two-reeler and thought it would be fun to do ourselves. I don't suppose you could sing for us—it's hard for me to do both."

"Don't sing, don't dance, don't see the point to any of it," said Mr. MacPherson. "Don't you go clogging up my hallways with this nonsense."

"May we remind you that we are the only tenants on this storey," said Gwen. "There is nothing about not dancing in our lease."

"Get on with you," he said. "I'll be needing to mop that floor soon."

"Spoilsport," muttered Iris as they retreated to the safe confines of The Right Sort.

"Thank you for the refresher," said Gwen. "That was helpful.

Still need to try the rumba and the quickstep, but I think my memory has been sufficiently jogged. Oh, it's about time for us to depart. Hand me my cape, will you, Millie?"

"Yes, milady," said Iris. "I should put it on for you, shouldn't I?" She stood behind Gwen and fastened it around her neck, standing on tiptoe to reach. "Very good, milady," Iris said. "Your chariot awaits."

They walked down the steps. Iris held the front door for Gwen.

Captain Timothy Palfrey of the Grenadiers stood in full dress uniform in front of an idling cab. He removed his cap upon seeing Gwen.

"Mrs. Bainbridge, you are a vision," he said. "This humble soldier is honoured to be your escort tonight."

"Thank you, Captain," said Mrs. Bainbridge. "Millie, you may ride in front."

"Yes, ma'am," said Sparks, keeping her head down as Palfrey held the door open for her.

He did the same for Mrs. Bainbridge, then sat beside her.

"Claridge's," he told the cabbie. Then he turned back to Mrs. Bainbridge. "I must say that I was surprised to receive your invitation, after how we left things at Sally's."

"It was very kind of you to accept, especially upon such short notice."

"Not at all. Who was the unlucky lad who dropped out at the last second?"

"It was nothing like that," said Mrs. Bainbridge. "I am representing the family interests. My father-in-law sells ammunition to the current Greek government. He's in East Africa, and my mother-in-law wasn't feeling up to the task, so I've put on the old uniform and am going to support the troops."

"Clearly, I joined the wrong branch of the service," he said. "So, you need me to be what tonight?"

"My reason to fend off aggressors."

"And my reward?"

"As many dances as you can muster, Captain, with as much conversation as I can provide."

"And after? Will there be more evenings together? Preferably without any international arms dealing?"

"Let's see how tonight goes, Captain."

Claridge's was a short ride away, fortunately. Never taking his eyes off Mrs. Bainbridge, Palfrey paid the cabbie as the doorman held the doors for the two women.

There was a trio of photographers lolling about near the entrance. As Captain Palfrey came up to take Mrs. Bainbridge's arm, the photographers looked at each other, shrugged in puzzlement, then held up their cameras.

"A smile for us, madam," one of them called.

Sparks stood a respectful distance away as Mrs. Bainbridge radiated towards them.

I live in the shadows, she thought.

She followed them in as the photographers pestered the doorman, trying to find out who they had just captured for the morning tabloids.

They crossed through the lobby over the black-and-white-marble floor, past the mirrors with their Art Deco inlays. Mrs. Bainbridge paused as they reached the center of the Winter Garden, breathing deep as she stared up at the dome.

"You'll protect me, won't you, Captain?" she said softly, resting her free hand for a moment on Palfrey's forearm.

"Of course." He laughed. "I will be the Troy to your Helen. Let the Greek hordes fall beneath our walls."

Bad metaphor, thought Sparks. The Greeks won that one. Eventually. But it sounded gallant.

At the entrance to the ballroom, two young men sat at a table. Two others stood by the door, eyeing Mrs. Bainbridge with appreciation but no welcome.

"Let's see, where did I put it?" Mrs. Bainbridge said, fishing through her bag for the invitation. "Ah! Good evening, gentlemen. Mrs. Gwendolyn Bainbridge, on behalf of Lord Bainbridge. Captain Palfrey is my guest."

She handed the invitation to them with imperious grace.

"Good evening, Mrs. Bainbridge," said one of the young men, taking it, while the other ran his fingers down a list, then turned to a second page. A look of consternation crossed his face.

"I'm sorry, madam, but your name does not appear on the list," he said.

"Nonsense," said Mrs. Bainbridge. "I have the invitation."

"The invitation is in order, but there must not have been an RSVP."

"Don't be ridiculous."

"I am not, I assure you, madam."

"There must have been some kind of mistake."

"We don't make mistakes," he said huffily.

"You are about to make a very serious one," she said in a low tone. "Do you know who I am? Who the Bainbridges are and what we represent?"

"I am afraid—"

"You should be afraid. While you are bravely sitting at this table in your tuxedo, your countrymen are blasting away at the Reds in the mountains using Bainbridge shells and Bainbridge bullets. Do you truly wish to insult our family?"

"Please wait here a moment," the man stammered, before fleeing in search of someone with authority.

Go get him, Gwen! thought Sparks.

The man returned with an older gentleman wearing a tuxedo.

"Mrs. Bainbridge, do forgive us," said the older man. "May I have the name of your escort so that I may announce you?"

"Certainly. Captain Timothy Palfrey of His Majesty's Grenadier Guards, Second Armoured," she replied.

"This way, if you please," he said, leading them into the ball-room.

"Wait," commanded Mrs. Bainbridge.

She inhaled, gathered herself, then nodded to Palfrey. They stepped in, pausing at the entrance. She stood for a moment, allowing those present to take her in, then unclasped her cape and held it out. Sparks stared at it blankly for a moment, then Mrs. Bainbridge gave it a slight twitch. Sparks, recollecting her position, scurried forwards to collect it.

There was a small receiving line. The tuxedoed man murmured, "Mrs. Gwendolyn Bainbridge and Captain Palfrey," then beckoned them forwards to be greeted by King George II.

Mrs. Bainbridge walked up to him, hearing Miss Betty's endlessly repeating instructions. *Left foot behind! Back straight! Don't incline the head yet! Wait until you can sink no more. Back straight, I said! Bend the head now. NOW!*

Mrs. Bainbridge nodded, then rose and smiled, concealing the agony of her right leg, which was protesting furiously from not having done this for so long. Still, she finally got to use the Vacani Curtsy after all that practice.

"I am not your first king, I see," said King George, smiling back.

"I was presented, of course, Your Majesty," said Mrs. Bainbridge. "So many years ago, it seems more like a dream."

"It cannot have been that many," he said.

"You are most kind. May I present Captain Palfrey of His Majesty's Grenadiers?"

"How do you do?" said Palfrey, bowing.

"Captain," said the king, nodding back. "I would salute, but I am not in uniform, I'm afraid."

"Quite all right, Your Majesty," said Palfrey. "I've done more than enough saluting over the past few years."

"I'm sure you have, Captain. My thanks to you and your compatriots. The Grenadiers' reputation precedes you."

"Thank you, Your Majesty."

They moved down the line, greeting the ambassador and other dignitaries, then were directed to a table at the side by the windows, which were draped for the evening.

"Nice to see the old drapes back," commented Palfrey. "Last time I was here, it was all blackout curtains and sandbags at the entrance."

"Who was playing?"

"No band. They had commandeered the room for war planning. I prefer it like this. So tell me—have we just crashed this party?"

"I do have an invitation."

"Which was sent to Lord and Lady Bainbridge. We are crashing, aren't we?"

She shrugged.

"What fun. Ah, that's Bill Savill," said Palfrey as the bandleader strode to the front. "Nice choice."

"You know him?"

"He's on *Music While You Work*. We have it on at HQ. Strings and woodwinds, none of that blasting brass derailing one's train of thought. You can dance and have a decent conversation. Shall we?"

He stood and held out his hand. She took it and allowed him to lead her onto the dance floor. Only a few other couples were dancing. She had mixed feelings about that. On the one hand, it meant more people could see her dancing. On the other, there were fewer people in the way, and it was a foxtrot. She rested her hand on his shoulder and smiled.

He was a decent dancer, she was grateful to find out. He had a strong lead, and negotiated her through the turns and corners with gentle but firm signals on her waist and through their clasped hands. She found her body reacting before her mind could summon up what it was supposed to do.

"What song is that?" she asked.

"'I'm Stepping Out with a Memory Tonight,'" he said.

"Ah yes," she said. "Too appropriate for me. Ronnie and I danced to it at the Mayfair."

"He sounds like he was a splendid chap."

"I haven't said all that much about him."

"I may have made a few enquiries," he confessed. "Knew some men who knew him, as it turns out. Men who fought with him."

"Were you investigating him? Or me?" she asked.

"Both," he said. "Assessing the defenses, as you said at Sally's. I wanted to know more about you."

"What did you find out?" asked Mrs. Bainbridge.

"That you spent some time in—" He hesitated.

"Go on," she said.

"Deep mourning," he said softly.

"That's a delicate way of putting it."

"But now you're dancing," he said. "That has to be an improvement."

"My body is dancing," she said. "Honestly, I feel more like an automaton than a woman half the time."

"Keep dancing, then," he said. "Your soul will catch up to your body in time. It took me a while, too."

"How long?"

"I'm still working on it," he said. "We all are. Think you could manage a dip?"

"No idea. Let's give it a go. Don't forget to pick me up from the floor when it's done."

They partner well, thought Sparks enviously. Too bad I'm only a maid tonight, or I'd be out there, too.

She stood in a corner with other lady's maids and gentleman's valets, Mrs. Bainbridge's cape draped over her arm, watching as more couples filled the floor. None of the ladies present matched Gwen in beauty and elegance, in Iris's opinion.

"Who is she?" asked one of the maids. "She's gorgeous!"

"Mrs. Gwendolyn Bainbridge," said Sparks.

"How did you get her hair so perfect?" asked another.

"Oh, there was a team of us," said Sparks. "Millie did her hair. I did her makeup."

"Lovely work. Is that a Hartnell?"

"It is."

"So that's the Bainbridge widow," said a valet. "She must've got a day pass from the looney bin."

Sparks walked over to him, looked up at his face, and smiled.

"You have a choice to make," she said.

"What's that, love?" he asked, leering down at her.

"You can either shut your stupid face, or I can report your unpleasantness to your employer," she said.

"You have any idea who my employer is?"

"It doesn't matter. If it's someone with manners, then you're out on your ear," said Sparks. "Not another word against my lady, do you hear me?"

He smirked. Sparks beckoned to him. He bent his head down, and she put her lips to his ear.

"I will hunt you down and geld you," she whispered.

He snapped his head back. She smiled again, then returned to her post.

The guests were a mix of Greek and British dignitaries. She recognised a few of the latter—mostly Foreign Office, but one or two from Intelligence. She didn't see Kat.

Then the young man she had seen speaking to Torgos entered and paused in front of the doorway, looking around. He was wearing a tuxedo, and had his hair slicked back nicely.

He looked nervous. Sparks wondered if he had found out what happened to Magoulias. It would go better for him if he had. Otherwise, appearing without him in tow or stashed somewhere would have devastating consequences if Torgos was serious about his threat.

And Torgos had a reputation for being a very serious man.

The young man turned abruptly and headed out.

"If Mrs. Bainbridge requires me, please inform her that I will return momentarily," Sparks whispered to one of the other maids.

"Will do," the woman replied.

Sparks walked briskly out the door and looked around. She spotted the young man vanishing down a hallway and followed him. One advantage of Millie's shoes was that they allowed her to pad softly on the marble floors, compared with the clicking of her normal heels. And even if he was to look, who would think anything of a maid walking down a hotel corridor?

He stopped in front of a door, knocked twice, then went in. Sparks crept up and put her ear to it for a moment. Across the hall, another door opened.

"Miss Sparks, isn't it?" said Torgos, a small automatic in his hand. "Please. Come in."

CHAPTER 13

"Did you ring for maid service, sir?" asked Sparks.

Torgos gestured with the gun for her to approach. Behind her, the other door opened and the young man emerged, shoving her ahead of him.

"Gently, Tadeo," Torgos admonished him. "It is not yet time to use force."

"No, it isn't," said Sparks. "So put the gun away."

"I said not time to use force," said Torgos. "For threatening, however? Yes, it is time."

"Your clock works differently than mine," said Sparks, following him inside.

They were in a small, unused private dining room. There were cloths covering all the chairs and the large table, giving a ghostly aspect to it all.

"You thought I would not remember you," said Torgos.

"I hoped you wouldn't," said Sparks.

"Perhaps you expected me to believe that Iris Sparks is now working as a lady's maid."

"Times are hard. One takes the jobs that one can. What gave me away?"

"I always make a point of observing who your Miss Kitsiou

speaks to, Miss Sparks. When that person is one whose path crossed mine during the war, I take note. When that person shows up again the very next evening, I take action."

"Good," said Sparks. "This actually saves me a great deal of time. I was hoping for some clever seductive banter while we tangoed, but it wouldn't have worked in these shoes."

"Why are you pursuing me, Miss Sparks?" asked Torgos.

"I'm not pursuing you specifically," said Sparks. "I was pursuing something with a Greek aspect to it. And then I realised that I had the opportunity do something beneficial."

"Which is?"

"I came to save Tadeo's life."

"What?" exclaimed Tadeo.

"You were supposed to bring a particular person here to meet your boss," said Sparks, turning to him. "He threatened to kill you if you didn't."

The two men stared at her, then at each other.

"He threatens to kill me every day," said Tadeo, starting to laugh.

"I do," Torgos chuckled. "It is out of love."

"The truly terrifying one is my mother," said Tadeo. "Why you married that woman, I will never know."

"You should have seen her in her prime," said Torgos, shaking his head sadly.

"He's your son," said Sparks, looking back and forth at the two of them. "And there I was, worried for him."

"So, you eavesdropped on our conversation, and elected to come to his rescue through this elaborate disguise," said Torgos. "That does not explain why you came to services yesterday."

"How do you feel about direct questions?" asked Sparks.

"A novel approach. Why should I agree?"

"Because I have information that you want, and you have information that I want."

"Perhaps. But are we on the same side?"

"I think the situation may be polygonal, but even if we aren't on the same side, we aren't necessarily on opposing sides."

"Are you sure that you are not Greek?" asked Torgos.

"You want to find a man named Magoulias."

"Yes."

"Here is the first exchange: you tell me who he is and what side he's on, and I will tell you where to find him."

"How will I know that you are telling me the truth?"

"You won't. Nor will I. We talk, we go our separate ways and decide how to act on what we know."

"What do you think?" Torgos asked his son.

"I would like to know why she no longer works for the Brigadier," said Tadeo. "And who she is working for now."

"Good boy," said Torgos. "Will you answer those questions first?"

"As to the first—I lost many friends and was betrayed by others," said Sparks. "I was tired of it all. The current battle doesn't interest me."

"And the second?"

"No more. We have to agree before I continue."

"The problem, Miss Sparks, is that not knowing the answer to that question means I cannot trust anything you say. If you still worked for the Brigadier, I would be able to weigh your responses accordingly. But now that you've gone rogue—"

"I most certainly have not."

"And given that you are a superb liar—"

"Now you're making me blush."

"I cannot assess the value of what you provide," he concluded.

"May I propose a solution?"

"Certainly."

"As you are quite capable of evaluating someone who has not had our professional training, I suggest that you ask Mrs. Bainbridge to join us. She will answer your questions adequately, and she is a civilian and an amateur. I will remain in here as a token of good faith until you have retrieved her."

"Who is Mrs. Bainbridge?"

"My partner at The Right Sort Marriage Bureau, as well as in this investigation. She's at the reception as we speak."

"Do you know this woman?" Torgos asked his son.

"I have never heard of her," said Tadeo.

"Neither have I," said Torgos. "Which speaks well for her not being of our community. Very well. Describe her to me."

"Tall, blond, wearing a blue frock and a matching bolero," said Sparks.

"I will go find her," said Torgos to his son. "You stay with Miss Sparks."

"Yes, Father," said Tadeo.

"And if I am not back in ten minutes, strangle her."

"Yes, Father," said Tadeo, producing an automatic of his own.

Torgos made a slight bow to Sparks, then left the room. Sparks sat on the edge of the table and glanced at Tadeo.

"Tell me," she said. "Are you single?"

"Well, we barely survived that one," gasped Mrs. Bainbridge as they headed back to their table. "They should give a warning for the quickstep. Sound an air raid siren or something."

"You were splendid," said Palfrey.

"I was hanging on to you for dear life, Captain."

"I enjoyed that part of the experience the most."

"The next time I hear the introduction to 'Anything Goes,' I will run for the nearest bomb shelter. Oh, hello!"

An older Greek gentleman was standing in front of her, holding out his hand.

"Madam," he said. "May I have the pleasure?"

"Of course," she said, allowing him to lead her back to the

dance floor. "Let's see, what are they playing? Oh, 'La Cumparsita'! A tango. Yes, I think I could manage that."

"A tango," he said, shaking his head slightly. "Of course it would be a tango."

He slid his arm behind her back and pulled her to him.

"Mrs. Gwendolyn Bainbridge, by the way," she said.

"Constantine Torgos, Ministry of Defense, at your service."

She stiffened for a moment, remembering his name from somewhere.

He swept her around his hip, swiveling her back and forth before moving her towards the corner as she tried to pin it down.

The funeral. He had been at Talbot's funeral.

The other dancers filled the floor and Captain Palfrey disappeared from her view. Torgos bent her back into a corte, and smiled.

"Miss Sparks described you by your gown," he said. "She simply should have told me to find the most beautiful woman in the room."

"I'm sorry, Mr. Torgos," said Mrs. Bainbridge. "Who did you say told you that?"

"Miss Sparks. Your maid."

"I'm afraid you're mistaken, sir. I have no maid by that name."

"A pity," he said, bringing her back up to him. "Because if you deny her now, we will have to kill her. Will you come with me, Mrs. Bainbridge?"

She hesitated.

"There is little time to waste," he said. "Don't let your caution mean her death."

"Very well," she said. "Where is she?"

"This way," he said, leading her past the band and slipping behind a curtain to a side door.

She found herself accompanying him down a deserted hallway.

He stopped at a doorway halfway down and opened it, then beckoned to her.

They entered to see Sparks sitting on the front edge of the table, a gun in her hand. She pointed it at Torgos.

"You took your sweet time getting here," she complained. "Did I not describe her adequately?"

"Where is Tadeo?" he asked wearily.

"He's fine," she said. "Well, unconscious, but he should be fine eventually."

She nodded down to the floor under the table, where the younger Torgos lay in a crumpled heap, something blue wrapped around his head.

"Is that my cape?" exclaimed Mrs. Bainbridge indignantly.

"Sorry, darling," said Sparks. "It came time to use force. Oh, Constantine, be a dear and toss me your gun, would you?"

He looked at his son in chagrin, then pulled his gun out and threw it to her. She caught it with her free hand, then motioned him to the corner of the room.

"The good news is that in spite of all this, my original offer still stands," she said. "We can trade information. As far as it goes, anyway. We don't know everything, but we know a lot. More than you, I suspect. Shall we parley?"

"Do I have a choice?" he asked.

"We can all walk away from each other," she said. "But your curiosity must be aroused by now."

"Very well," he said. "What is your question?"

"Who is Magoulias, and why are you so keen on finding him?"

"He worked for me," said Torgos. "He had heard a rumour of letters for sale, letters that could have an impact on the Royalist cause. He telephoned to say that he had a lead on obtaining them. Then he vanished."

"Did he tell you the source of the rumour?"

"No. There are always rumours, always sources. This was one amongst many."

"What kind of an impact?"

"One that would embarrass our royal family and yours, if the letters were brought to light. The plebiscite is a little more than a month away. If we wish to restore the king, we cannot afford even the slightest hint of a scandal. Now it is my turn."

"One moment," said Sparks, turning to Mrs. Bainbridge, who had been studying Torgos carefully. "The arrangement is that he will ask the questions of you."

"Me? Why me?"

"Because you're not as good at hiding lies as I am."

"That's certainly true," said Mrs. Bainbridge. "This will be a different kind of dance, won't it?"

"Not as pleasurable," said Torgos. "Do you know where Magoulias is?"

"On a slab in the city mortuary," said Mrs. Bainbridge.

"Is he?" breathed Torgos. "When? And how is it that you know this when we do not?"

"He was murdered sometime on Saturday afternoon," said Mrs. Bainbridge. "We know it because we found his body. The police are keeping his identity secret."

"Where was he killed?"

"In a bombed-out warehouse at Blackwell Yard. He had been stabbed."

"Why were you there?"

"We were also after the letters."

"Who killed him?"

"We have a theory," said Mrs. Bainbridge.

"And we have a plan," added Sparks.

"A plan? To do what?"

"Catch the man who did it," replied Sparks.

"What if it was someone sympathetic to our cause?"

"He's still a murderer," said Mrs. Bainbridge firmly. "There is no cause worth that."

Torgos gave her a sad smile. "I wish you were right about that," he said. "Unfortunately, I have had to disagree with that principle on more than one occasion. You understand, don't you, Miss Sparks?"

"Back to our questions," said Sparks, ignoring him. "You knew Gerald Talbot."

"I did."

"You went to his funeral."

"I go to many funerals," said Torgos. "They amuse me."

"What did Talbot have to do with Greek politics lately that so many of you attended? He's been out of the game since twenty-two."

"He never left the 'game,' as you call it. He played it on a higher level. One involving banks and railroad construction and arms. To many of us, he was the greatest friend we had here in England."

"Do you know if he ever had those letters you mentioned?"

"He never said anything to me about them."

"Would he have told you if he did have them?"

"I would like to think so," said Torgos. "Gerald and I knew each other from the Great War. We wanted the same thing—for Greece to stay out of it. And we were successful on that account. It was an alliance that continued until his death."

"Were you friends?" asked Mrs. Bainbridge.

"As much as two men in our professions could be, Mrs. Bainbridge."

"Say he did have these letters," said Sparks. "He would have made some provision for either their disposal or their preservation upon his death. To whom would he have entrusted them?"

"It would have depended on the nature of the letters," said Torgos. "He sympathised with the Royalist cause, but he was a pragmatic man. He would have done whatever was best for England. If he felt that our king in exile could rally Greek forces from afar to help defeat the Axis, then he would have seen that any threat to him would be destroyed."

"The Axis has been defeated, Talbot is dead," said Sparks. "Yet the letters remain, if rumours are to be believed."

"Do you know who has them?"

"Another part of the plan," said Sparks. "Are you free tomorrow night?"

"We're inviting him now?" asked Mrs. Bainbridge.

"I think he needs to be satisfied as to the truth," said Sparks, pulling a small notebook from her apron and tossing it to him. "Give me your number. There's another party you need to attend. Not fancy dress this time."

He looked back and forth between the two women, then took a fountain pen from inside his jacket and jotted down a number.

"Right," said Sparks, taking the notebook back from him. "These are yours." She handed him the automatics. He held them, a speculative look in his eyes.

"Put them away," said Sparks. "The time for force has passed."

"And when it came, you were the one who used it," commented Torgos as he concealed the guns inside his jacket.

"Tadeo was getting antsy," said Sparks. "I don't like being strangled. We should go back to the reception."

"Fetch my cape, would you?" asked Mrs. Bainbridge.

"Yes, ma'am," said Sparks.

She lifted Tadeo's head from the floor and unwrapped the cape carefully. She placed him gently down, then stood and snapped the cape open by her hip.

"Olé!" she said.

"It's wrinkled now," sniffed Mrs. Bainbridge. "And is that blood? How horrid!"

"Just a speck," said Sparks, examining it critically. "Nothing a real maid couldn't get out."

"That's my favourite cape," said Mrs. Bainbridge desolately. "I'll never be able to look at it again without thinking about this."

"You have more than one cape?" asked Torgos curiously.

"Of course. This one goes with this outfit."

The door opened. They turned to see Captain Palfrey poking his head inside.

"Ah, there you are," he said to Mrs. Bainbridge. "I've been looking everywhere. I say, is that chap all right?"

"He overdid the drinking," said Mrs. Bainbridge. "Millie found him sleeping it off in here, and came to fetch this gentleman to help."

"Very decent of you," said Palfrey. "Need a hand with him?"

"Thank you, I will be fine," said Torgos. "I will see that he gets home to his mother."

"Excellent. So, Mrs. Bainbridge, to the reason for my seeking you out. The king wishes to dance with you."

"Oh," said Mrs. Bainbridge. "Then let us return at once. Good evening, Mr. Torgos. Thank you for the dance. You tango well, I must say."

"It was a pleasure, Mrs. Bainbridge," responded Torgos, bowing.

He watched as the door closed behind them, then looked down at his son, who was beginning to return to consciousness.

"Idiot," Torgos said, and sighed.

Sparks glanced over her shoulder as Palfrey escorted Mrs. Bainbridge back to the ballroom, but no one followed them. They re-entered through the main door, and she watched as Palfrey brought Mrs. Bainbridge over to the king's table. His Majesty stood and bowed, then took Mrs. Bainbridge by the hand and led her onto the dance floor. The orchestra struck up "You and the Night and the Music," and the guests applauded as the couple began to spin around the room.

A waltz. Good luck, Gwen, thought Sparks.

She needed a drink. Badly. She walked over to the bar.

"Whisky," she said. "Make it a double, if you don't mind."

"And who do you think you are, missy?" sneered the bartender.

She stared at him blankly, then remembered what she was wearing.

"A maid," she said. "I'm a maid, of course. I'll just go stand over there with the others."

King George II smiled at Mrs. Bainbridge.

"There were many women I have had to dance with tonight," he said as they whirled around the room. "There is only one I wanted to dance with."

"Then I'm sorry she couldn't be here, Your Majesty," replied Mrs. Bainbridge. "I hope that I prove an adequate substitute."

"You are very well informed," he said, laughing ruefully. "Still, it is a lovely thing to dance with a beautiful woman, no matter what the circumstances. One can forget that the world exists outside the dance floor. One can forget that one is no longer young, or healthy. Or king."

"There are things I should like to forget as well, Your Majesty," said Mrs. Bainbridge. "Let us be amnesiacs together."

Bill Savill must have received some cue to prolong the moment, for he signaled the orchestra to take the repeat. Mrs. Bainbridge closed her eyes for a moment, and it was Ronnie holding her, spinning her into a dream. Then she opened them and saw the king looking at her sympathetically.

"I think that you were not forgetting at all," he said softly.

"I can't dance with the one I want to dance with, either, Your Majesty," she said. "And I never will again."

"Close your eyes again and think of him," he urged. "It is all that I can offer."

"Thank you," she said.

And she closed her eyes and remembered it all. His arms became Ronnie's arms. Another orchestra played in another ballroom, and they were young and looking forward to everything.

When the music stopped, the king released her, and she went into her curtsy again. This time, her leg didn't complain at all. When she rose, he bowed and kissed her hand.

"Thank you for this respite," he said.

"Thank you for letting me remember," she replied.

She returned to her table, where Captain Palfrey stood and applauded.

"That was a sight to behold," he said. "You danced with a king."

"I danced with a king," she said. "And stepped out with a memory. I think I would like to go now, if you don't mind."

"Anything else would be anticlimactic," he agreed.

They paid their respects, then left, Sparks scampering to catch up.

"Your cape, ma'am?" she gasped.

"Hang on to it for now, would you, Millie?"

"Certainly, ma'am."

The doorman signaled for a cab, then held the doors for them.

"Where to?" asked Palfrey.

"Back to our office, please," said Mrs. Bainbridge.

He gave the address to the cabbie, then turned back to her. "And then? The night is still young."

"The night is still Monday, and the woman still has to get up and go to work on Tuesday. My regrets, Captain."

They traveled in silence. Sparks stared straight ahead, wanting very much to turn and watch the two in the passenger compartment.

"We shall have to have another date so you can explain to me exactly what was going on during this one," said Palfrey when they arrived at the office.

"I may not be able to do that to your satisfaction," she said. "But I am so grateful to you for accompanying me."

"It was my great pleasure," he said. "And I claim my reward."

Before she could react, he pulled her close and kissed her. She tried to shove him back, but he was stronger than she was. When he finally released her, she was trembling in anger.

"I would say ask next time," she said. "But there won't be a next time."

"There never was going to be a next time," he said. "We both knew that. Good night, Mrs. Bainbridge. Good night, Miss Sparks."

The cabbie opened their doors, shaking his head slightly. The two women got out and stood watching as the cab drove off.

"Are you all right?" asked Iris.

"I forgot how brutal these things could be," said Gwen, rubbing her mouth with her handkerchief. "Bastard. He didn't even have the courtesy to ask first."

"Men like him know the answer," said Iris. "That's why they don't ask."

"And he was doing fairly well up to that point," complained Gwen as they went inside. "How the hell did I not see that coming?"

"You're out of practice," said Iris.

"Did you know he would try that?"

"You yourself said he was NST. And there we were, in a taxi."

"So you're saying I should have seen it coming."

"It's been an action-packed evening. One can't keep track of everything. You were still flying from dancing with the king. How was that, by the way?"

"He was rather sweet, which surprised me," said Gwen as Iris unlocked the door to The Right Sort.

"I need to change," said Iris. "Close the door, would you?"

"I'm not going to bother changing again," said Gwen. "Just my shoes, I think. How are your feet after a night in Millie's?"

"I don't think I've walked a mile in her shoes yet," said Iris. "But they held up well. Don't forget to get mine back. My sling-backs probably had more fun than I did tonight."

"You had fun. You got to hit someone. You enjoy that."

Iris hung Millie's uniform on a hanger, then put on her own suit. "My disguise didn't fool anyone that mattered tonight," she said as she removed her glasses.

"Putting on glasses doesn't change you from the Scarlet Pimpernel into Sir Percy, you know."

"Alas. But we learned a few useful items. What did you think about Torgos?"

"A mixture of truth and lies," said Gwen.

"Which were which? You're the one who reads people."

"There were two moments in particular when I thought he was lying."

"Which were?"

"When he said Magoulias was working for him."

"That makes sense. He would have kept closer tabs on him for something like this. So, if Magoulias wasn't with the Royalists, he was with some other faction. Anti-Royalist, maybe one of the Leftist groups. He must have let slip something about the letters to someone loyal to Torgos. What was the other item?"

"When he said Talbot was his friend," said Gwen. "Torgos has never had a friend in his entire life."

"Yet I can't bring myself to feel sorry for him," said Iris. "That's it?"

"That's it."

"Which means he's not our man. He's looking for the letters, too."

"Which he heard about through rumours. Our rumourmonger was exceptionally busy, wasn't he?"

"He was. Now it's time for us to put an end to all of this. Tomorrow, we send out our invitations."

"I wonder what I should wear," mused Gwen as they left the office. "I've never been to this kind of party before. Have you?"

"This kind of party never existed before," said Iris. "Wear something comfortable. Something you don't mind getting dirty if we have to dive for cover."

"Are we expecting a shooting war?"

"Not if it all goes according to plan," said Iris as they headed out the front door.

Then she stopped.

"But when does it ever do that?" she said as Gwen came up beside her.

There was a black Bentley parked in front of the building. A large man in a black suit stood in front of it. Iris glanced to her right, then her left. Other similarly dressed men were positioned in both directions, blocking their escape. She knew even before she heard footsteps that another man was coming up behind them from inside the building.

"Excuse me," said the man by the car, opening the rear door. "The proctor would like a word with you."

"Right," said Iris, her shoulders slumping in resignation. "I'll see you in the morning, Gwen. At least, I hope I will."

"Nonsense," said Gwen, stepping up to the Bentley with Iris. "I'm coming, too."

"This doesn't involve you," said Iris.

"Actually, it does," said the man. "The 'you' was plural. As in, both of you, in case I wasn't being clear."

"Perfectly clear, thank you," said Gwen as they got into the car.

The man closed the door. There was a click as the driver engaged the locks.

"Iris, are we being kidnapped?" Gwen asked as they drove away.

"I'm not sure," said Iris.

They were separated from the driver by a thick glass panel. Iris leaned forwards and felt along the back of the bench seat until she found a small latch. She opened it and slid a panel to the left. The compartment it revealed held a whisky bottle and a pair of tumblers.

"Want some?" she asked.

"God, yes," replied Gwen.

"Hey, that's not yours," called the driver.

"If we're guests, then you should offer us a drink," said Iris as she poured herself and Gwen a generous amount.

"And if we're prisoners, then to hell with you," added Gwen.

She clinked her tumbler against Iris's, then paused. "What if it's drugged?" she asked. "Or poisoned?"

"He knows I know about it," said Iris. "He left it for us to find."

"You're certain that he doesn't wish us any harm?"

"Not yet," said Iris. "Cheers, darling. This will be the best whisky we'll have had in a while."

"Well, in that case, cheers," said Gwen.

CHAPTER 14

The whisky was excellent. They opted for a second drink when the first was done, as the car headed somewhere north. Mrs. Bainbridge gazed out the window.

"We're in Highgate," she said. "There's the cemetery. Oooh, spooky!"

"You're drunk!" said Sparks.

"I am not!" insisted Mrs. Bainbridge. "Well, maybe a little. I had a few at the reception." She started to giggle.

"What's so funny?"

"I just figured it out," said Mrs. Bainbridge. "He left the whisky because he knew we'd drink it and let our guard down."

"Fiendishly clever," said Sparks. "Little does he know a veteran deb's capacity for alcohol. We shall wear our most serious faces and frown at him severely when we see him. Let's see your best frown."

Mrs. Bainbridge furrowed her brow and made a disapproving expression.

"Oh, that's good," said Sparks. "Now let me try."

She glared at Mrs. Bainbridge, who immediately burst into laughter.

"That was not the intended effect at all," said Sparks.

"I'm sorry, I'm sorry," Mrs. Bainbridge gasped. "Let me compose myself. There. Now, try again."

Iris imagined a water buffalo facing down a hyena, and tried to duplicate the expression. Mrs. Bainbridge took one look and started up again.

"It's no good," she guffawed. "I can't help myself."

Sparks, no longer able to hold back herself, joined her.

The driver looked at them in the rearview mirror. "Unbelievable," he said, shaking his head.

"Oh, don't you start," called Sparks. "I've already sent one irritating bloke to the emergency department tonight. I'll be happy to have you join him."

"You wouldn't stand a chance in hell, Lollipop."

"Hell is my turf, Big Boy," Sparks retorted. "Name the time and place, and we'll have a proper do."

"Me too," growled Mrs. Bainbridge. "Marquess of Queensberry rules be damned!"

"You don't fight, remember?" said Sparks.

"You were going to teach me, remember? We'll start with him."

"Save it, ladies," said the driver. "We're here."

He turned into a drive and passed under a stone arch. They looked out the rear window and watched as a man closed and barred a large wooden gate behind them, then picked up a shotgun that was leaning against the wall.

"Not our best escape route," observed Mrs. Bainbridge.

There was a large stone mansion to their right, but the driver took them to the rear of the building, where a garage had been fashioned from what had once been a carriage house. They pulled in, and a door lowered behind them. A man stepped forwards and opened the car door.

"This way," he said.

"Do you mind if I leave the dress bags in the car?" asked Mrs. Bainbridge. "I'd rather not lug them around."

"Fine," he said.

"You keep an eye on them," said Mrs. Bainbridge to the driver. "And don't go trying anything on."

Sparks snickered.

The man led them to a rear door, which opened onto a stairwell going up.

"He's at the top," he said.

"Naturally," said Sparks, leading the way. "Ever been in a chauffeur's digs before?"

"I'm sure I haven't," said Mrs. Bainbridge. "You?"

"Mmm. Tell you all about it sometime. Ah, there's the old man now."

The Brigadier was sitting behind a small card table, leaning back in his chair, his hands steepled on his chest.

"Sit," he commanded, nodding to a pair of folding chairs in front of the table.

The two dutifully sat down, folding their hands on their laps.

"Do you have any idea what—" he began, then he stopped as the two women broke into laughter. "What on earth?"

"It's the face," Sparks giggled. "You're doing the face."

"Sorry," said Mrs. Bainbridge. "You're exactly how I expected you to be."

"This is not a laughing matter!" he shouted.

"No, it isn't," agreed Sparks, regaining control. "Apologies, sir. You know how it is when women stumble into a man's world, don't you? Everything looks so, so—"

"Pathetic and ridiculous?" suggested Mrs. Bainbridge.

"I was going for exaggerated and melodramatic, but those will do nicely. Well, sir, how may we be of assistance to you?"

"You can start by telling me about him," he said, tossing a photograph onto the table.

They leaned forwards to look. It was the man they had subdued at The Right Sort two nights previous. The photographer had captured him walking on some unidentifiable London street, wearing a tweed coat and a leather cap.

"Oh, look," said Mrs. Bainbridge. "Someone dressed up a weasel in men's clothing."

"Who is he?" asked Sparks.

"Don't play games with me, Sparks," said the Brigadier. "You know damned well who he is."

"Sorry, the face doesn't ring a bell," said Sparks. "What does he do?"

"We believe him to be a blackmailer," said the Brigadier. "We also believe that he's been in contact with you."

"Since when does your office concern itself with blackmailers?" asked Sparks.

"After our last meeting, we did some poking around," he said. "We heard some chatter about someone holding a set of letters that could prove an embarrassment to certain people in whom we have an interest, or a benefit to other people in whom we also have an interest."

"Who was doing the chattering?"

"Can't tell you that. But this fellow was supposed to be involved. By the time we knew who he was, he had disappeared."

"What does any of this have to do with us?" asked Sparks.

"We have ears inside the Palace, Sparks," said the Brigadier. "We know who hired you. We know there was to be a meeting. Then some unlucky fellow bought it at the rendezvous."

"Don't know anything about any of that," said Sparks.

"On the supposition that this man contacted you later, we decided to search your office yesterday."

"You did what?" exclaimed Mrs. Bainbridge, rising to her feet.

"Sit down," he directed her.

She sat, glaring at him with all her might.

"What did you find?" asked Sparks.

"That one desk had a blotter, and one did not."

"Heavens!" cried Sparks. "Someone stole one of our blotters! Call Scotland Yard!"

"There was a small hole in the surface of that desk. We recovered a trace amount of blood from within that hole. And more blood on one other item."

"Which other item?" asked Sparks.

"You neglected to clean the dart," said the Brigadier.

He took the photograph, came around the table, and thrust it in front of her face.

"Is he still alive, Sparks?" he asked.

"I have already told you, sir. I don't know the man."

"But the blood—"

"Mine, I expect. I've nicked myself playing with darts plenty of times. Bad habit, but just one out of so many."

"If only I had a shilling for every time I've had to bandage her up," added Mrs. Bainbridge.

"Where are the letters?" asked the Brigadier.

"I don't have them. Yes, we were supposed to make the exchange at the warehouse, but we found a dead man with no letters, so we got out before anyone could start blaming us. We never saw this man there. Is he the killer, do you think?"

"My chief suspect for that title is you, Sparks."

"Will you still send flowers to my funeral after they hang me, sir?"

"Not the large arrangement. You're certain you don't know where this fellow is?"

"Brigadier, you know me," said Sparks. "Trust me when I tell you that I haven't the slightest notion where he is."

"She's telling the truth," said Mrs. Bainbridge. "Neither of us knows where he is. You could inject me with truth serum, and I still wouldn't be able to tell you. Do you have truth serum? I've always wondered what it was like."

"I think that's what we were drinking in the Bentley," said Sparks.

"Oh really? It was rather good. Let's have some more on the trip home."

"Carruthers," called the Brigadier. The man who had met them in the garage appeared at the top of the stairs. "Put these women back in the Bentley and send them home."

"Yes, sir. This way, ladies."

"Carruthers?"

"Yes, sir?"

"Remove my whisky from the car before they leave. I've wasted enough of it tonight."

"Yes, sir."

Carruthers brought the two women back to the garage, where the driver was leaning against the car and smoking.

"Where do I dump the bodies?" he asked, looking directly at Sparks.

"My place is in Marylebone," she said. "Mrs. Bainbridge is—"

"We know where you live," he said, opening the rear door. "Get in."

"One moment," said the other man, reaching in and grabbing the whisky and tumblers. "Right. In you go. Good night, ladies."

They were silent on the ride home. When they reached Sparks's flat, she took off Millie's shoes and gave them to Mrs. Bainbridge.

"Tell her thanks, and make sure I get mine back," said Sparks. "Oi, you!"

"What?" asked the driver, who was opening the door for her.

"She doesn't call me the minute she gets home, I phone Scotland Yard. I know your face, and I know your plates. Understood?"

"Go to bed, Lollipop," he said. "She's safer with me than with you."

"That may actually be true," conceded Sparks as she got out. "Good night, Gwen. You danced with a king and a spy tonight."

"Just another Monday," said Gwen. "See you at the shop in the morning. The world must be peopled!"

"The word must be peopled," echoed Iris.

She went inside, climbing the stairs in her stocking feet, then stared at her telephone until it rang, fifteen minutes later. She grabbed it immediately.

"Safely home," said Gwen.

"Thank goodness," said Iris.

"Were you worried something might happen?"

"I didn't think it likely, but I didn't think it wholly impossible, either. One more thing before I let you go."

"Don't you want to talk about tonight?"

"I do, but we shouldn't speak on this line. It wasn't tapped as of last night, but it wouldn't surprise me if it was now. Yours may be as well."

"How exciting! If only I knew some obscenities, I could entertain our monitors."

"I'll teach you some after your fight training."

"Goody. Maybe we could go terrorise some sailors after. Iris?"

"Yes?"

"It was strangely fun tonight."

"It was, wasn't it? Best of luck with the hangover."

"You, too."

Gwen walked up the stairs to the servants' rooms and tapped lightly on Millie's door. Millie opened it, saw her, and smiled.

"How was your date?"

"Interesting," said Gwen. "Here are your uniform and shoes. Miss Sparks sends her thanks. How was your date?"

"Oh, he was wonderful," sighed Millie as she took them. "A real gentleman."

"I'm glad one of us went out with a gentleman tonight," said Gwen.

"Yours tried to get fresh?"

"He did. There won't be a second date."

"Oh dear. Did you get to dance with anyone special?"

"Two older gentlemen. One was very nice, the other less so, but he tangoed well."

"Sounds lovely."

"Not as nice an evening as yours," said Gwen. "Let me get Miss Sparks's shoes before I forget. There'll be hell to pay if I don't."

"Here they are," said Millie, fetching them. "Tell her they did the trick."

"I doubt you needed any help, Millie," said Gwen. "Oh, I need you to do something for me."

"Of course, Mrs. Bainbridge."

"There will be a parcel on my dressing table that someone will be picking up tomorrow afternoon. I would like you to keep it in your room until he gets here. I'll leave you written instructions. Could you do that for me, and not tell the others?"

"Certainly, Mrs. Bainbridge. Is this part of these mysterious doings that you've been up to?"

"It is. Thank you, Millie. Good night."

"Good night, Mrs. Bainbridge."

Gwen had a headache in the morning. It was not improved when Lady Carolyne strode into the dining room during breakfast and tossed the morning paper, opened to the Society section, onto the table.

"'Mystery woman dances with King,'" she said. "'London society abuzz.'"

Gwen looked. There she was, smiling as the cameras caught them in mid-twirl. "I told them who I was," she said. "They're trying to make it more lurid."

"They've succeeded," sniffed Lady Carolyne. "Is that why you begged me for that invitation? So that you could audition for the position of royal mistress?"

"He already has a mistress," said Gwen calmly. "This was only a dance. With a king."

"He's not a king at the moment," said Lady Carolyne. "Why, when I danced with a king, he was the actual king of Great Britain."

"Who is now a duke who married his mistress," Gwen pointed out. "Lady Carolyne, you should thank me. I represented the Bainbridge interests to one of their customers last night. Think of all the shells I'll sell."

By the seashore, she was tempted to add, but refrained.

Lady Carolyne shook her head and left the room, fuming.

The walk to work helped relieve both the headache and Gwen's irritation with her mother-in-law. She carried the Hamleys bag in one hand. She had a stop to make on the way.

Lorraine Calvert's cousin lived in a brick townhouse on Pont Street in Chelsea. It was the long way to the office, but not worth the expense of a cab.

Gwen passed St. Columba's church and made the slight turn to the left, then pulled up short and backtracked rapidly. There was a black Bentley parked opposite her intended destination, and the driver was one she had seen all too recently. She quickly walked the other way and turned onto Walton Street.

She had waited too long. They had got to Vivienne Ducognon first. There would be no information from that quarter.

The Tuesday-morning Mayfair commuters bustled about her, but petered out considerably when she turned onto the street on which The Right Sort was located. A boy of perhaps fourteen was bouncing a rubber ball against a wall. He tipped his cap as she passed, then suddenly took off past her, snatching the Hamleys bag from her grasp.

"Hey!" she shouted, but he had already turned the corner and vanished from sight.

* * *

Torgos sat in the passenger seat of a dark green Triumph Dolomite, waiting.

"There," said Tadeo, glancing in the rearview mirror as the boy came running up with the Hamleys bag.

"Any problems?" asked Torgos as he handed the boy a pound note.

"Nah," said the boy, handing him the bag. "Could've grabbed her purse if I felt like it. Might've been worth it. She looked posh."

"You do exactly what I tell you to do," said Torgos. "No more, no less. Now go home."

"Yes, Uncle," said the boy.

Tadeo put the car in gear while Torgos looked inside the bag.

It was filled with crumpled tissue paper, in which nestled a pair of women's shoes. There was a small envelope tucked into one of them. He grimaced, then opened it. Inside was a note in a woman's handwriting.

"'Nice try. Now bring the shoes back and go wait by your telephone,'" he read aloud.

"These ladies seem to know what they're doing," said Tadeo, absentmindedly rubbing the bruise Sparks had left on his jaw. "What now?"

"We will return the shoes and go wait by our telephone," said Torgos. "As instructed. No more, no less."

Iris was typing a letter on her Bar-Let when Gwen came in.

"How did it go?" she asked.

"I couldn't speak to Vivienne Ducognon. They were already there."

"Not surprising. Were you followed there?"

"I may have been. I didn't notice anyone in particular, but I wasn't trying to look behind me."

"I expect you were, which is fine. You didn't do anything other than what you would be likely to do, so they'll think we're still on the hunt. I was trailed from the moment I left my flat. We'll have to ditch them when we leave tonight. I'll let Archie know."

"Good. Also, my Hamleys bag was snatched outside a minute ago."

"It was?" exclaimed Iris. "Are you all right?"

"I'm fine," said Gwen.

"But the letters—"

"They're safe," said Gwen. "The bag was a decoy. Iris—I'm afraid your shoes were in it."

"Now it's war," said Iris grimly.

"Any word from Archie?"

"Everything will be ready tonight," said Iris. "I am going to hand-deliver this invitation, then come back. We'll make the rest of the calls after lunch. See you in a while."

The Brigadier was going over reports when his secretary knocked.

"What is it?" he asked.

"Miss Sparks," she replied, handing him a number on a piece of paper. "You have four minutes."

He looked at his watch, then went back to his reports for precisely three and a half minutes. Then he dialed the number.

"Good morning, sir," said Iris.

"Why are you calling me, Sparks?" he asked.

"It's me conscience, guvnor," she said. "Couldn't sleep a wink thinking about what I done."

"Cease the charade, if you don't mind," he said wearily.

"Fine, I'll get to the point. I may not, strictly speaking, have told you the entire truth last night."

"You astonish me."

"Ah, I've driven you to sarcasm. It concerns that man in the picture. I was telling the truth about not knowing where he was. But I might know someone who knows someone."

"Who?"

"Can't tell you, sir. However, give me until this afternoon, and I will make some enquiries."

"And then?"

"And then we shall see. There is something you must do in exchange."

"What?"

"Remove the wiretaps on our homes and office."

"What makes you think there are any?"

"Because I know how you work. Just as I know that you have a man following me even as we speak. I am about to lose him, by the way. Goodbye, sir."

"Sparks, I will not—"

There was a click as the connection was severed.

He sighed, then dialed another number.

"Remove the taps on Sparks and Bainbridge," he said. "For now."

His telephone rang again a few minutes later. He answered it.

"Sir, it's Williams," came a voice. "I'm afraid she's given me the slip. I have no idea how."

"Never mind, Williams," he said. "Go back and watch the building."

Iris was back at the office by noon, carrying a large, flat object.

"What's that?" asked Gwen.

"New blotter," said Iris, removing it. "Oh!"

Her sling-backs sat on top of her desk, next to a vase holding an arrangement of summer blooms. Gwen held up a small envelope.

"The note says, 'I await your call.'"

"Very good," said Iris. "Classy of him to send flowers."

"Everything go well?"

"The invitation has been delivered. Shall we treat our watchers to the riveting sight of us eating lunch?"

"Why not?"

* * *

Millie had just finished straightening Gwen's room when Prudence knocked on the doorway.

"I've been looking for you," Prudence said. "There's a . . . man at the back door."

"What kind of man?" asked Millie. "What's he want with me?"

"He said he was a delivery boy. He doesn't look like a delivery boy."

"Oh yes. I've been expecting him. I'll be right down."

She went up to her room and collected the parcel with which Mrs. Bainbridge had entrusted her. It had turned out to be three shoeboxes, tied securely with string. She brought them down from the servants' quarters to the kitchen, opened the door, then started.

"You're a tall one, then," she observed, looking up at Sally.

"Am I?" he replied. "I had no idea. I thought everyone else was short."

"I am that, no matter what the occasion," said Millie. "You're the gentleman I'm supposed to give the parcel to?"

"I am," he said. "I'm a friend of Mrs. Bainbridge."

"She said I was supposed to say something to you, and you were supposed to say something back," said Millie.

"Go ahead," said Sally.

Millie screwed up her face in concentration.

"He'll find us," she said dramatically. "There are no more hiding places."

"They've lit up Dreamland with carbon arc searchlights and surrounded it with barbed wire, and no dreams can escape it anymore," he replied, even more dramatically.

"She said you wrote that."

"I did."

"I like it," she said, turning over the parcel. "This is very exciting, exchanging secret passwords and handing over parcels holding I don't know what. Do you know what's in them?"

"Stacks of twenty-pound notes," he whispered, putting a finger to the side of his nose. "And things to blackmail people with."

"Well, I never!" she said in dismay. "Is she up to no good?"

"Mrs. Bainbridge is up to the greatest good," he reassured her. "Thank you for your assistance."

"Good luck, sir," she said.

He loaded the boxes onto the front of a delivery bike, which looked like a child's when he got on it. He looked back at Millie, touched his fingers to his cap, and pedaled off.

"What was that all about?" asked Prudence when Millie passed her.

"I can't tell you," said Millie.

Iris glanced out the restaurant window. Across the street, a man stood in a doorway, reading a newspaper.

"He's a very slow reader," she commented. "He hasn't turned the page the whole time we've been in here."

"Should we send him a cup of coffee or something?" asked Gwen. "I'm starting to feel sorry for him."

"Coffee would be cruel," said Iris. "He's been watching the entire day. His bladder wouldn't survive the extra pressure."

They paid their bill and left.

"Let's use those telephone boxes on the corner," suggested Iris.

They each stepped into a box, dropped their coins in their respective slots, and began to dial.

The Brigadier's secretary answered the call.

"Is Mr. Petheridge, blah, blah, blah," said Sparks. "I'm bored with protocol, Sylvia, and I don't feel like walking. Would you mind putting him on?"

"But—"

"Oh, never mind. Write this location down. Seven o'clock on the dot, just him and the driver, no one following."

"But—"

"Corner of Norbiton Road and Salmon Lane. That's in Limehouse. Have you got it?"

"I've got it, but—"

The line went dead.

Sylvia finished scribbling down the location, then tore the leaf from her pad. She walked to the Brigadier's door and knocked.

"Sir," she said hesitantly. "Miss Sparks called."

Mrs. Fisher answered when Gwen called.

"Catherine Prescott calling," said Gwen. "Is she there?"

"One moment," replied Mrs. Fisher.

After a brief interval, Lady Matheson's voice came on the line.

"What is it?" she asked.

"We've got hold of the letters," said Gwen.

"What? That's marvelous!" exclaimed Lady Matheson. "How on earth did you manage it?"

"No questions," said Gwen. "Now, we need to turn them over tonight, and we don't want to do it at the office. It isn't safe. Here's what you have to do . . ."

Torgos answered the call himself.

"Yes? One moment."

He took out his pen.

"Proceed. Seven o'clock. I understand."

He jotted down an address, then hung up.

"Yes?" asked Tadeo from across the office.

"You and me, no one else," said Torgos. "Unarmed."

"I don't like it," said Tadeo.

"Neither do I," said Torgos. "Which is why we'll be armed."

Iris and Gwen emerged from their building at five. A car pulled up immediately, and they clambered into the rear. By the time Williams had flagged down his partner, they had already made the turn at the end of the block.

"Step on it," urged Williams as he closed the door.

His partner hit the gas, but as they reached the intersection, a lorry crossed in front of them, then stopped with a squealing of brakes, blocking their path.

Williams's partner hit the horn several times. The lorry driver ignored them, sitting calmly in his seat, a smile slowly spreading across his face.

"Shall I back up and try the other way?" asked Williams's partner.

"Don't bother," said Williams. "They're gone."

The prisoner in the basement of the cemetery maintenance building was awake when the three men came in. They were larger than the men he had been dealing with, though similarly dressed and wearing ski masks. He sat up on the cot, the chain sliding through the loop on the wall.

"Now, 'ere's the situation," said the man in the middle. "We are taking you somewhere. The reason there are three of us, and us three in particular, is that we 'ave been told that you 'ave a tendency towards violence."

They fanned out across the room.

"We 'appen to share this tendency," he continued. "We suspect that you've 'ad some training in this regard. So 'ave we. There are three of us, and you only 'ave one good 'and at the moment, so attempts at any foolishness will be met with a stomping such as you've never dreamed about. Now, you 'ave our word that if you are cooperative, no 'arm will come to you. And when I say 'cooperative,' I mean if you so much as twitch the wrong way, the stomping will commence. Do we 'ave your word that no such twitching will occur?"

The prisoner looked at the three of them.

"You do," he said. "Where are we going?"

"Somewhere other than here," said the man, tossing him a key. "Unlock the cuff from your wrist. Get up nice and slow, put your 'ands behind your back, and face the wall."

The man complied, moving slowly. The three men converged on him, the outer two grabbing his arms while the one in the center handcuffed him. The man did not twitch.

"Well done," acknowledged the leader. "I'm afraid the ski mask 'as to come on again. We don't want you retracing your steps back 'ere."

"Why?" said the captive. "Do you think I've acquired a liking for these accommodations?"

"I should 'ave added, we also need you to shut up until further notice."

He grabbed the prisoner by the shoulders, turned him around, and pulled a ski cap over his face, reversed so the solid side covered his eyes.

"Right then," he said. "Time to go. Mind the doorway."

The Bentley pulled up to the corner of Norbiton and Salmon. It was a quiet, narrow residential street. The Brigadier and his driver looked around.

"Good choice," observed the driver. "She can see if we're being followed, and there's plenty of places to get to on foot in case of trouble."

"Sparks has a knack for escaping," agreed the Brigadier. He caught movement off to his right. "Bogey at three o'clock," he said.

"I see him," replied the driver, easing his gun from his holster.

A man dressed in a pinstripe suit with a hideously wide tie ambled up to the vehicle. He held his jacket open, then turned slowly. No weapons were visible. He tapped on the window. The driver rolled it down, keeping his free hand on his weapon.

"You'll be the gents Miss Sparks is meeting," said the man.

"Who are you?" asked the driver.

"Call me Petheridge," said the man. "Or better yet, call me Orpheus. I am your guide to the underworld."

"Tell us where to go," said the Brigadier wearily.

"I don't tell you, I show you," said the man. "I 'ave to go with you. Frisk me first, if you like. I would, if I were in your shoes."

"Frisk him," ordered the Brigadier.

The driver got out and patted the man down.

"He's clean," he said.

"Next to godly, I'm so clean," agreed the man. "I'll get in back with you, shall I?"

"Get in front," said the Brigadier.

"You and me, then," said the man to the driver as he sat next to him. "It's all about the separation of classes with these blokes. Oppression of the working man."

"This working man needs to know where we're going," said the driver.

"Of course. Take the next left."

Stallings stopped the Bentley at the location and looked around suspiciously.

"I don't see them anywhere," he said.

"Are you sure this is the right address?" asked Lady Matheson.

"It's the one she gave me," said Mrs. Fisher, checking her note. "I made her repeat it. This is the place."

"There's someone coming up," said Stallings, getting set to put the car in gear.

"Are you Lady Matheson?" asked a man at her window.

"I am. Who are you?"

"I'm to take you to Mrs. Bainbridge," he said. "I'll need to get into the car."

"Not bloody likely," said Stallings.

"I don't like this man," said Mrs. Fisher. "He frightens me."

"It's all right, folks," said the man. "You can trust me, or my name ain't Catherine Prescott."

Stallings glanced back at the two women.

"Let him in," said Lady Matheson.

"Oh dear," Mrs. Fisher said with a shudder.

"You're the Greek fellow?" said the spiv to Torgos as Tadeo drove.

"That depends on who is asking," he replied.

"I got to see Athens while I was in the navy. Best-looking girls in the whole war, except for Cairo. You been to Cairo?"

"Many times. Where are we going?"

"We're almost there. Take the next right."

The Brigadier's car pulled into a lot enclosed by a board fence next to a dark warehouse. There was another Bentley there already.

"Put these on," said their guide, handing them black ski masks and donning one himself.

"Why?" asked the Brigadier.

"Because it's a masked ball, innit? Now, do me the courtesy of leaving any weapons inside the car. It's my turn to do the frisking."

"Sir?" asked the driver.

"Do it," said the Brigadier, putting his Browning in the compartment where the whisky had sat. "I have the feeling we're outgunned tonight."

The driver left his gun in the glove compartment and stepped out of the vehicle.

"Who else is here?" asked the Brigadier.

"Other people in masks," replied their guide as he patted them down. "Should be a lark. Gentlemen, please follow me."

Torgos's car arrived shortly thereafter. He and Tadeo looked at the ski masks dubiously when they stepped out.

"Why?" he asked.

"Because that's how the ladies wanted it," said the spiv. "And leave your weapons in the car."

"And if we choose to keep them?"

The spiv whistled sharply through his teeth, and a dozen masked men appeared out of a dozen locations, guns out.

"I don't see as you have any choice on that," said the spiv, backing out of the line of fire. "Remove them 'olding the butts between your thumbs and forefingers. Toss them in the car. Lovely. Masks on, then follow me."

Torgos and Tadeo followed as the rest of the men took up positions around the warehouse.

It was almost pitch black inside once the doors were closed. Torgos sensed others nearby, but couldn't count how many.

"You stand 'ere," said the spiv, bringing Torgos and Tadeo forwards. "Team three in position. Take it away, ladies."

A pair of matches were struck in the middle of the space, revealing Sparks and Mrs. Bainbridge, standing ten feet apart. They dropped the lit matches into a pair of oil drums filled with scrap lumber. The wood must have been soaked in paraffin, for it immediately caught fire, shooting flames several feet up in the air, illuminating a small table holding a pair of shoeboxes and a bit of the area around it.

Others stood at the perimeters of the room, barely visible. All were masked. Most were men, but Torgos glimpsed a pair of women on the other edge of the light cast by the fires.

Sparks and Mrs. Bainbridge stepped between the fires, arms raised to the ceiling.

"Given the Greek aspects of this matter, we thought it would be appropriate to invoke the rituals of Delphi," said Sparks. "It was there, at the Omphalos, the navel of the world, that both the mighty and the small would come to seek the higher truth. It was recorded by Plato that carved into the temple walls were three phrases: *gnōthi seautón*, or 'Know thyself,' a worthy admonition that nevertheless scares the hell out of me; *mēdén ágan*, or 'Nothing in excess,' another useful piece of advice that I routinely ignore; and my personal favourite, *engýa pára d'atē*, which translates roughly as 'Make a pledge and mischief is nigh,' which anyone who has ever tried to marry me would know is certainly the case."

"Welcome, ladies and gentlemen," intoned Mrs. Bainbridge. "You are now in the Temple of Delphi, and we are your Oracles."

CHAPTER 15

The space was huge, with rusting beams crossing high overhead, unlit lamps dangling from them like jellyfish floating in the night seas. The corrugated metal roof met the irregular walls at odd angles, so sound was reflected strangely, sending footsteps from locations that were empty, while silence surrounded whoever lurked in the darkness pervading the room's outer reaches.

The light cast from the oil drums didn't illuminate much. Small clumps of shadowy figures could be glimpsed, scattered about like standing stones, the only brightness being the loud wide ties that marked the many spivs present.

There were guns in the darkness. They were hidden away, but of this, one could have no doubt. Mrs. Fisher, under her mask, certainly had none, her head swiveling around like an owl's, trying to detect hidden threats.

"Introductions first," said Mrs. Bainbridge. "I am Mrs. Gwendolyn Bainbridge. This is Miss Iris Sparks. We are the proprietors of The Right Sort Marriage Bureau in Mayfair.

"Not everyone here knows everyone else, but that's the basis for a good party, don't you think? I won't introduce you, because that ruins the point of the masks. Each of you has some information or connection relevant to this matter, and we want all of you to walk away at the end of our presentation sufficiently enlightened so that you can get on with your lives without further assistance from us. Miss Sparks?"

"Thank you, Mrs. Bainbridge," said Sparks. "On Monday last we were retained by representatives of the Queen. An anonymous letter had been sent to Princess Elizabeth, which they intercepted. It read, 'I have what Talbot found in Corfu. I know what he knew. Ask Alice if she wants them back. There will be a price.' We were asked to investigate if there was any potential scandal in the family of Prince Philip, Alice's son, who is a suitor of our princess.

"Talbot turned out to be a member of British Intelligence, stationed in Athens at the end of the Great War. We learned that in 1921, he had been instrumental in saving the life of Prince Andrea, Philip's father, and spiriting away the rest of his family, including Princess Alice, from their villa on Corfu. In a subsequent letter, our Mr. X stated that he had a trove of love letters between Princess Alice and another man, recovered by Talbot from the villa. Letters that could throw into question the legitimacy of Prince Philip."

"This past Saturday afternoon, still acting on behalf of the Queen, we went to a rendezvous with Mr. X to obtain the letters," continued Mrs. Bainbridge. "The Queen's representative received the address on our office telephone. It was a bombed-out building at Poplar Dock. Inside, we found a dead man. He had been stabbed repeatedly. He had a dagger of his own with blood on its tip. His name, or at least the name on his ident card, was Nikolas Magoulias. The letters were not on the body."

"We escaped from the scene with the assistance of a friend of ours who was waiting in a motorboat," said Sparks. "We thought that was the end of it—but then Mr. X decided to make a personal visit to our office after we got back. He tried to initiate hostilities. There was a bit of a fracas, and when all was said and done, we were in possession of both the letters and Mr. X himself."

"Which presented us with a number of choices," said Mrs. Bainbridge. "The first was to go straight to the police with everything we knew, of course, but the happiness of the royal family was at stake. There was no ensuring that the letters would stay secret, and without learning more, we might have been playing into the very hands of the man or men who had concocted this scheme in the first place."

"Scheme? What scheme?" called out Torgos.

"We're coming to that," said Mrs. Bainbridge. "I read the letters. They described a torrid affair between Princess Alice and another man. They made for a convincing narrative, and cast much doubt on Prince Philip's parentage."

She paused and glanced around the room.

"And they were fakes," she said vehemently, "as I am about to prove."

She went over to the table holding the shoeboxes, removed the lid from one, and plucked out a cream-coloured piece of paper.

"They were written in German," she said. "I am going to translate for the benefit of those who do not speak it."

She cleared her throat, held the letter up to the firelight, and read.

My darling,

It was wrong of you to kiss me. It was wrong of me to let you. I cannot, cannot believe that I followed you to the roof while the others were dancing, but Andrea was so oblivious, and you were so kind. The touch of your hand on my waist as we danced was agony—that that, and mine on your shoulder and our other hands clasped were all the contact that we were allowed was a cruel jest. But then we slipped away and found ourselves high above the world, dancing on the roof, our bodies drawing ever closer, the strains of the

music drifting up from the ballroom so far below. I could
no more have withstood you in that moment than I could a
hurricane.

She finished and looked around expectantly.

"Well?" she asked. "Don't you see how that proves they weren't written by Alice?"

"No," called one of the spivs. "But I wouldn't mind 'earing you read that one again!"

"Sir, you are a romantic underneath that mask," she said as the raucous laughter of the man and his mates echoed through the room. "Here's the thing: she claimed to have heard the music from inside the hotel several storeys below while she was being kissed on the rooftop. Neat trick—considering Princess Alice was deaf."

There was silence in the room as she looked around. Sparks grinned in approval.

"There were other references of that nature," said Mrs. Bainbridge. "Birds chirping in the trees, rushing cataracts, and the like. Either love made a miracle happen for a relatively short term, or these are forgeries."

"When Mrs. Bainbridge told me this, I wanted a second opinion," said Sparks. "As it happens, I know an excellent forger from my days with British Intelligence. I'm guessing many of you know him, too. We took some of the letters to him, and guess what? He said they were the genuine article!"

"I was gobsmacked," said Mrs. Bainbridge.

"But then something peculiar happened," said Sparks. "That same night, we were picked up by British Intelligence and questioned about the late Mr. Magoulias, the still living Mr. X, and the letters. This wouldn't have happened unless my friend the forger had called them up the moment we left to let them know that we did have the letters, despite the failure at the rendezvous."

"And the conclusion you drew from that?" prompted Mrs. Bainbridge.

"That we had brought the letters to be verified by the very man who had created them," said Sparks. She turned to look at the Brigadier, who stood impassively in his mask. "And that he was doing it on behalf of British Intelligence," she concluded.

"Why would British Intelligence go to all this trouble, Sparks?" the Brigadier asked.

"Why does British Intelligence do anything nowadays?" she asked. "To winnow out the spies in our midst. Which brings us back to the most important question: who killed Magoulias?"

"And the question you should be asking us first is, how did our friend get to the rendezvous point ahead of us?" asked Mrs. Bainbridge. "For that, we must call him as our next witness. Sally?"

The silent manifestation of Sally's massive physique out of the dark caused a stir in the room.

"Theatre in the round," he muttered to Mrs. Bainbridge. "I love it!"

He stepped between the fires and held out his arms, embracing the invisible audience.

"O for a Muse of fire, that would ascend the brightest heaven of invention!" he declaimed.

"Sally?" interrupted Mrs. Bainbridge.

"A kingdom for a stage—"

"Sally," said Sparks.

"Princes to act and monarchs to behold the swelling scene!"

"Sally!" cried the two women together.

"Sorry," said Sally. "I couldn't resist. That's from *Henry the Fifth*, Act One—"

"We know the bloody play," called one of the spivs. "Get on with the important bits. You can do the Saint Crispin's Day speech later."

"Yeah, after we're gone," added another.

"Critics everywhere," Sally sighed. "Call me Sally. I am a friend and odd-job boy to these two. On Saturday afternoon, at the request of Miss Sparks, I embarked on one of the odder jobs I've ever been given. I stood under the window of The Right Sort. A note came fluttering down, giving me the time and place of a rendezvous, though, alas, not one of a romantic nature. We had allowed for a number of contingencies. This one required escape by water. I jumped on a motorcycle, roared through the streets to where I had a boat stashed, and putt-putted my way to a location by Poplar Dock, where I maintained vigil with a pair of opera glasses.

"Shortly after my arrival, I observed a man emerge from the warehouse, toss something into the Thames, then limp off. Minutes later, Miss Sparks and Mrs. Bainbridge came through that same door, and I transported them away."

"As I stated, we have Mr. X," said Sparks. "Bring him forwards, lads."

The captive, now with his hands free and his face visible, was shoved towards them. Sally peered at him closely. The man smirked.

"No," said Sally. "That's not him at all."

"Right," said the man. "So I can go?"

"We're not done with you," said Sparks. "Thank you, Sally. Stand by for a moment."

She beckoned to someone behind the table.

"The main point of Sally's story was to show how we could get someone else to the rendezvous point ahead of us on short notice," she said. "Obviously, two other men also got there: Mr. Magoulias and his killer, the limping man. You also saw the limping man?"

"Yes," said the captive. "I don't know when he got there. He must have come up from the other side. But I saw him come out."

"So you would recognise him if you saw a photograph?"

"I would."

"Mr. Cornell, I believe that's your cue," said Sparks.

A man stood behind the table. He was small, with thinning

hair and a narrow nose on a narrow face. The sort of man who would be unnoticed in a crowd. Or standing alone.

"My name is Morris Cornell," he said. "I am a licensed private investigator. I was hired by The Right Sort Marriage Bureau to maintain surveillance on the front entrance to their building on Saturday afternoon, and to photograph everyone going in and out. I was situated in a car parked about eighty feet down the block, and was using a Zeiss fifty-millimeter lens."

He held up a manila folder, then removed a stack of photographs from it.

"These are the pictures I took. At one twenty-six, a Bentley pulled up in front of the building. Three people got out: the driver—a man—and two passengers, both women."

He removed three pictures, showing close-ups of Stallings, Lady Matheson, and Mrs. Fisher.

"This woman is our contact with the Queen," said Sparks, pointing out Lady Matheson. "With her are her secretary and bodyguard."

"So much for keeping our identities hidden," said Lady Matheson. "I'm taking this damned thing off. It's ruined my hair."

She peeled off her ski mask. Mrs. Fisher and Stallings followed her lead. Mrs. Fisher stood nervously, eyes shooting about, while Stallings stood expressionless, his body tensed and ready to leap into the fray.

"As you wish," said Sparks. "Please proceed, Mr. Cornell."

"Here you see them entering the building at one twenty-seven," he said, holding up another picture. "You can get a glimpse of Miss Sparks at the door. Now, one minute later, this fellow shows up."

The photograph showed a powerfully built man with blond hair, wearing a cheap brown suit that fit him tightly across his chest.

"The next picture shows him entering the building. There was a period of time when nothing happened. Then at eight minutes past two, he came out again. He moved quickly in my direction, then crossed the street. I got one more quick shot, which showed his face, then put my camera down so he wouldn't see what I was doing. He got into a car across the street from me and drove off."

Sparks picked up the close-up picture and held it up for all to see, then walked over to Sally, who looked at it.

"That's the man I saw come out of the warehouse," he said. "The one with the limp."

"Mr. Cornell, did he walk with a limp when you saw him?"

"No, Miss Sparks, he did not."

She turned to face their former captive, looking at him contemptuously.

"How about it?" she said, holding it up.

"That's him, you clever little witch," he said.

"Know him?"

"Never saw him before that afternoon."

She turned back to her audience.

"Three men found their way to that warehouse before we arrived," she said. "Sally has told you how he learned about the location. This man got that information as we did—from the conversation in the office."

"But he was never in the office," protested Lady Matheson. "He couldn't have been—my bodyguard was—Oh!"

Stallings made a break for the door, but Archie's men were waiting. There was a struggle in the dark, then a blow and a cry. Then two of them brought Stallings forwards into the light, holding his arms behind his back. A bruise was forming on his jaw.

"Five thousand pounds is a lot of money, isn't it, Mr. Stallings?" Sparks asked softly. "You were standing right outside our door, guarding—and listening. You passed the information to your confederate, who was waiting on the stairwell, and off he went."

"He wasn't supposed to kill no one," said Stallings. "He never knew the Greek fellow was going to be there."

"No, he was waiting with a knife for two young women to show up with a bag of money," she said. "What was he going to do to the two young women? Especially if they resisted? Who was he, Stallings?"

Stallings said nothing.

"We don't need you to answer that question," she said. "This morning, I brought copies of these photographs and the results of our investigation to Detective Superintendent Parham of the CID. Get any results yet?"

"As a matter of fact, we have," said a man, stepping forwards.

He removed his mask and nodded convivially at the room, smiling slightly as most of the spivs recoiled.

"At ease, gentlemen," said Parham. "I'm with the Homicide and Serious Crime Command. Your preferred activities don't interest me at the moment. Mr. Stallings, this afternoon we arrested Zacharias Stallings on suspicion of the murder of Nikolas Magoulias. A cousin of yours, I believe?"

Stallings said nothing, his body sagging between the two men holding him.

"Upon examination of the suspect, we found a recent knife wound on the back of his right calf," continued Parham. "It had become rather badly infected, I'm afraid, so he is currently in hospital, but we expect him to pull through well enough to face the gallows. When the ladies have finished their presentation, I shall be taking you into custody for conspiracy and other charges. Ladies?"

"Thank you, Detective Superintendent," said Mrs. Bainbridge. "Now, that accounts for the murderer's presence at the scene, but what about the late Mr. Magoulias? How did he get there? Was he also there for the money? We believe it was for something else. We suspected at first that there might have been a plot to destroy the budding romance between Prince Philip and Princess Elizabeth. The elevation of a member of the Greek royal family in exile to this status would be a tremendous boost to those supporting their restoration to the throne, while Prince Philip's disgrace would provide equal support to those opposing it. But we realised—"

"You realised," said Sparks. "Take credit where it is due."

"I realised that the sender of the letters must have known they'd be intercepted by Lady Matheson, which means they were intended for her, not the princess. And when we received the photographs from Mr. Cornell, we realised that the origin of this scheme, at its heart, was something even more tawdry. Mr. Cornell, if you would?"

"Certainly, ma'am," he said, holding up more photographs. "I continued to maintain my watch as instructed. At twelve minutes past two, the three people from the Bentley exited the building. The driver, as you see here, held the door for the ladies. The one who was in charge got in first, followed by the shorter one. The car then drove off. Now, look at the sidewalk here." He pointed at a small bit of white that was resting by the curb next to where the car had been parked.

"If you compare it with this photograph from before they came out, you'll notice that the sidewalk was clear," he said, holding up an earlier one. "Look again at the ladies entering the car. Look closely at the right hand of the shorter lady. There's a bit of white showing as she gets in. I was lucky enough to catch it as it fell from her now empty hand."

A woman began to weep in the darkness.

"Immediately after the Bentley departs, this gentleman walks up," continued Cornell. He had caught Magoulias mid-stride. The following sequence of photographs showed Magoulias stopping in front of the building, kneeling and reaching for the scrap of paper, reading it, then dashing back to a nearby car.

"We don't know for which faction Mr. Magoulias worked," said Mrs. Bainbridge. "We suspect one in league with the Soviets, given that this despicable plot had its genesis in British Intelligence. It was cooked up to draw out spies who had infiltrated the Palace, and whatever networks they were connected to. In this case, by throwing red meat into shark-infested waters. Only the plan didn't anticipate another plot, one based on simple, brutal greed, getting in the way. We don't know which man got there first, but they were both armed, and both ready to kill. Mr. Magoulias was sent to his doom by the woman who dropped that note. Mrs. Fisher, come into the light, please."

"No!" Mrs. Fisher shrieked, struggling in the grasp of two spivs who had come up behind her. "It wasn't like that! I'm loyal, Lady Matheson. You must believe me!"

"What is happening to me?" asked Lady Matheson faintly.

"To you, nothing," said Sparks. "You've done nothing other than hire one spy and one thief for your staff. Happens to the best of us. Well, not to Mrs. Bainbridge and me—we don't have a staff."

"Hey," objected Sally.

"You're not staff, darling, you're a freelance private contractor."

"Oh. That's all right, then."

"So now that we've caught these two, there is only one thing left to do," said Mrs. Bainbridge.

She picked up the shoebox containing the letters, walked over to one of the drums, and upended the box. Blue and cream-colored stationery cascaded into the fire, causing a momentary flare.

"No!" cried Lady Matheson.

"What's the matter?" asked Mrs. Bainbridge, turning to her. "'Burning them would be the best course of action.' Those were your exact words, weren't they?"

"Of course," stammered Lady Matheson. "But—"

"Anything else would suggest that you still had ulterior motives for these letters," continued Mrs. Bainbridge. "Such as using them to influence the selection of the princess's future consort. Perhaps steering her away from Prince Philip so that some favourite of yours, or of one for whom you are working, might benefit."

"I wouldn't—"

"Or just to hold as a threat over her husband after the marriage. You do play the long game, Patience. Your name was well chosen. But this is all idle speculation on our part, isn't it?" Mrs. Bainbridge walked over to her cousin, drawing herself up to her full height to look down at her.

"Isn't it?" she asked again.

"Burning them was the proper thing to do," said Lady Matheson, choking slightly on the words. "You saved me a match."

"Then I think we're done," said Sparks brightly. "Thank you all for coming. Leave your masks with the lads outside."

The Brigadier walked up to the edge of the firelight.

"Detective Superintendent," he said.

Parham turned towards him. The Brigadier pulled out his wallet, removed a card, and showed it to him.

"Right," said Parham. "She's yours. But Stallings is mine."

"That will be satisfactory," said the Brigadier. "Take her to my car."

His driver took Mrs. Fisher from the men holding her and led her away.

Parham turned to the spivs holding Stallings. "Now, would you two fellows mind taking my prisoner to my car?" asked Parham. "It's parked a block away. I'll meet you outside."

"Look at us, assisting Scotland Yard in their enquiries," muttered one of the spivs as they dragged Stallings towards the door. "I'll never be able to look anyone in the face again."

"Wait!" commanded Lady Matheson.

They stopped. She walked up and stood in front of them.

"Stallings?" she said.

"I'm sorry, Lady Matheson," he said. "I never meant for it to—"

"The keys, Stallings. I need the keys for the Bentley."

One of the spivs patted Stallings's pockets, then reached into his coat and pulled them out. "Here you are, lady," he said, handing them to her.

"Goodbye, Stallings," she said.

She turned and walked back to Sparks and Mrs. Bainbridge, without watching as the spivs dragged him away. "What about the money?" she asked. "I assume, since it wasn't exchanged for the letters, that you still have it."

"Most of it," said Mrs. Bainbridge, fetching the other shoebox from the table and opening it. It was filled with banknotes, with a neatly typed sheet of paper on top. "There were expenses," she said. "The rental on this building for one night was surprisingly affordable."

"So glad to hear it," said Lady Matheson. "I shall host my next party here."

"But the security costs were hefty," said Sparks. "Along with the fee for Mr. Cornell, the consultation with our forger, and some miscellaneous items. It's all there in the itemised inventory on top. We took the liberty of deducting those portions to save you the trouble of writing so many cheques."

"How thoughtful of you," said Lady Matheson. She looked down at the car keys in her hand. "I don't know how to drive," she said. "Is there anyone here who can bring me and the car back without depriving me of both car and money?"

"Sounds like a call for Odd-Job Boy," said Sally, holding out his hand for the keys.

"Do you trust this man?" Lady Matheson asked Mrs. Bainbridge, looking up at Sally dubiously.

"With my life," she replied.

"Very well," said Lady Matheson, tossing him the keys. "Come along."

"Oi, Big Man," said a spiv, coming forwards. "You do any fighting? You could make a nice bit of change. We could set something up."

A momentary spasm of self-loathing passed across Sally's face. Then he collected himself and stared down at the spiv.

"Sir, I am a man of the theatre," he declared haughtily. "I detest actual violence in all of its forms. Good evening to you, ladies and gentlemen. Oh, and one more thing. 'This day is call'd the feast of Crispian. He that outlives this day—'"

"Oh, bloody hell!" cried someone in dismay.

"'And comes safe home,'" continued Sally, "'will stand a tip-toe when this day is named, and rouse him at the name of Crispian!' There's more, but I have to drive this lady to the Palace."

He bowed with a flourish, then followed Lady Matheson out the door.

"Well, ladies, that's two murders solved in two months," observed Parham. "You're giving us quite a run for the money."

"You can have the next one," said Sparks wearily. "Did you ever find out who called the police to the scene?"

"It was Zacharias. He was hoping to have you keep them occupied while he made his escape. Now, as to the man who attacked you—"

"He's ours as well," said the Brigadier.

"Is that so?" asked Parham. "I must say, I don't like the game you've been playing in my city."

"You protect the city, we the Empire," said the Brigadier.

"I'm still of a mind to haul you ladies in for kidnapping and interfering with an official police investigation," continued Parham. "Not to mention destroying evidence right before my very eyes."

"As to the kidnapping, I don't believe there will be a complainant," said Sparks, looking at their former captive, who was standing next to the Brigadier. "Will there?"

He gave her a long look, then shook his head.

"Nor will we be pressing charges against him," said Mrs. Bainbridge. "As for destroying evidence, wait one second."

She walked off into the shadows, then returned, carrying another shoebox.

"We don't expect the Stallings cousins to go to trial," she said. "If they do, then of course you may use these. But once they've been sentenced, we expect you to consign these to the fires."

She handed him the box. He opened it and peered inside to find the complete set of fake correspondence.

"The ones you burned?" he asked.

"Blank stationery purchased for the purpose, of course."

"But you read one."

"I have an excellent memory, Detective Superintendent. Too good, sometimes."

"Right, that's two crimes swept away. As for interfering with a police investigation?"

"We apologise," said Mrs. Bainbridge, casting her eyes downward.

"And we promise never to do it again," added Sparks.

Parham looked back and forth at the two, then nodded.

"See that you don't," he said brusquely.

Then he walked out, the shoebox tucked under his arm.

A man began to applaud in the darkness. Torgos walked up, still masked.

"Satisfied?" asked Sparks.

"Very entertaining," he said. "You know that the Greeks invented theatre."

"Yes," she replied. "But the English perfected it."

Torgos turned to the Brigadier.

"You will let us know what you learn about their networks," he said.

"We'll talk."

"We always talk," said Torgos. "You never say anything. Good night, ladies. Perhaps we will tango again some evening."

He and his son walked out, handing their masks to the spiv at the door.

Sparks turned to the letter carrier.

"We still don't know your name," she said.

"And you're not going to."

"How's the hand?"

"Hurts."

"It's your own damn fault. You were stupid. You overplayed the situation. All you had to do was exchange the letters for the money, but you thought it would be fun to terrorise two defenseless women. Put a gun to one, run your hands over the other."

"Thought you enjoyed that," sneered the man.

"You picked the wrong women," said Sparks. "You got off light. If I ever see you again, it won't be a dart, and it won't be your hand. Take your boy home, Brigadier."

"Come along," said the Brigadier, walking towards the exit. The man followed him.

Around them, men were slipping out of different doors into the night. Two folded up the table and carried it out, waving to the women as they did.

"And that's that," said Gwen as she waved back.

"That's that," agreed Iris. "Excuse me."

She walked up to one of the remaining masked men, threw her arms around his neck and kissed him hard.

"'Ow did you know it was me?" said Archie, lifting his mask.

"What makes you think I did?" replied Iris.

"Oh, that's nice, that is. I thought we 'ad a rule about kissing while conducting business."

"You should know by now that I'm not good at following rules," she said. "Profitable night?"

"Profitable and entertaining," he said. "Think we'll get invited to the royal wedding?"

"Probably not," she said. "Maybe it will be on television. We'll have to buy a set."

"'Buy'?" replied Archie. "Not familiar with the concept."

"I'll explain it later. Gwen, are you ready?"

"I am," said Gwen, coming to join them. "You got kissed, I noticed."

"You got kissed yesterday."

"Not by anyone worth kissing."

"I've got a friend," offered Archie.

"So I've heard. Thanks, but no. Let's get out of here."

"Pubs are still open," commented Archie as they went into the lot. "We should celebrate."

"Sparks, a word with you," called the Brigadier, standing outside his car.

"He can see your face," Gwen said to Archie in alarm.

"It's all right," said Archie. "'E knows it already. I was the one who brought 'im 'ere."

"Yes, sir?" said Iris as the Brigadier came up to them.

"How did you know?" asked the Brigadier. "You had the photographer waiting. You knew something was up before the call came. What gave it away?"

"Why should I tell you? So you'll be better at deceiving the next one?"

"Yes," he said simply. "Which I do for the greater good."

"Where the hell were your men?" she snapped. "When the two of us walked into that warehouse with who knows what lying in wait? Well? Your messenger boy can't have been the only one watching."

"Men were in place," he said. "When Stallings came out, he was followed. We assumed he was our target. When it turned out he was merely a run-of-the-mill thief and murderer, we dropped the surveillance."

"You didn't turn him over to Parham, though."

"That would have compromised the operation. We didn't know Magoulias was dead until after the police rolled up. Finding out who he was was useful. Your connecting him with Mrs. Fisher was even more so."

"What if this scheme you set up put Mrs. Bainbridge and me in a dark spot with a murderer?"

"I was confident that you could handle it, Sparks."

"And if those letters ended up destroying a young couple's happiness?" asked Gwen.

"Any ruler worth his salt knows that sacrifices must be made for the good of his subjects."

"Did you ask her so she could make that determination?" asked Gwen.

"She's not a ruler," said the Brigadier. "Not yet. How did you know, Sparks?"

"Because you were too damn easy," said Iris. "Getting anything out of you normally is like chipping through a thousand-foot stone wall to get at one moldy apple, yet there you were, showing up in the park for your prodigal daughter, practically dripping with information. Laying out just enough to point me in a particular direction, cutting off the wrong forks along the way. Like I was a cow in the chute to the slaughterhouse. You were the one who recommended us to Lady Matheson, weren't you?"

"Is that what she told you?"

"I don't care what she told me. Those letters were meant for her, but they were also meant for me. You recommended us to her because you knew I would recognise Talbot's name and go chasing down the trail you laid. Was Buchanan-Wollaston part of it?"

"He knew where his duty lay," said the Brigadier. "I only wish you did as well."

"Then you should have told me up front what you were doing," said Sparks. "If you needed my help exposing a Leftist Greek spy network with tentacles inside the Palace, you should have asked me directly."

"You refused to join this fight when I asked you before," said the Brigadier.

"Yes, I did. Do you know why, sir?"

"Tell me, Sparks."

Iris glanced back at Gwen, who was watching, enraptured, then turned back to the Brigadier. "Because what I'm doing now is more important," she said. "Goodbye, sir. We're done, you and I, until it's time for flowers."

Archie held open the door to his car, and Gwen and Iris climbed in.

As they drove away, Gwen glanced back to see the Brigadier staring after them, his mouth pressed into a grim, angry line.

"He's going to ask again," said Gwen. "Not soon, maybe. But he will ask."

"I know," said Iris.

"What will you do?"

"Spit in his face. Or maybe say yes. We'll see. In the meantime, let's go have that drink."

CODA

Gwen stared glumly down at their bank statement.

"We should have charged Patience extra," she grumbled. "Hid it under some line item in the inventory. 'Miscellaneous nefarious activities,' or the like."

"Moral compass bothering you this morning?" asked Iris, her nose buried in a letter she was proofreading. "What does that feel like? Does it itch?"

"We are so close to getting that office," said Gwen. "So many clients getting attached, Iris, but no one wants to get married in July. Or August. We may not see another bounty until the autumn."

"We'll just have to keep recruiting new clients and try for that loan," said Iris. "Did you talk to the woman who typed up Sally's play?"

"We can't afford her," said Gwen. "She's too experienced."

"Any luck with the advert?"

"Someone's coming in to interview for the position. The trouble is where to put a secretary if we hire one when we don't have the space? If a client came in, we'd have to send her to the lavatory to type."

"She could sit in the stairwell."

"She might get vacuumed up by Mr. MacPherson."

"Does he vacuum? Do you know, I've never seen him do any actual work the entire time we've been here."

"Excuse me, is this a good time?" said a young woman at the door.

"Be right with you," said Iris, who had just caught an error. "If it's about the secretarial position, you're hired immediately. If it's for our regular business—"

"Iris, stand up," said Gwen softly while rising to her feet.

"What?"

"Stand up. Immediately."

Iris glanced over the top of her letter, then jumped to her feet, knocking her chair back into the wall.

She was just like her magazine covers, thought Iris distractedly. Lovely, fresh-faced. She must have the best Millie in the country working for her. A team of the best Millies, standing ever at the ready—if one faints, then another steps in immediately, powder puff in hand . . .

"I'm afraid my typing is arduously slow and my shorthand is nonexistent," she said as she came into the office. "I'm a good driver, though, and a dab hand with an engine, if that's of any use."

"Forgive me, Your Royal Highness," said Iris. "We weren't expecting you."

"Of course not," she said, smiling. "Do sit."

"Not until you do, ma'am," said Gwen.

"Don't be ridiculous. There's no one to see us. Let's be normal."

"I can't," said Gwen. "It's ingrained in every fibre of my being. Tendons would rupture in protest if I so much as tried."

She looked at the guest chair. "This will hold me?" she asked doubtfully.

"With honour, ma'am," said Iris.

"Very well," she said, sitting. "Now, the two of you. Please."

Gwen sat while Iris restored her chair to its proper position.

"Forgive the surprise call, but this is not meant for public knowledge," said their guest. "I received an unexpected visit yesterday from Lady Matheson. She was distraught. She had come to beg my forgiveness. I had no idea that there was anything to forgive, and told her as much. Then she confessed all."

"Did she?" asked Iris. "All of it?"

"When I say 'all,' I mean that she confessed some, and concealed a great deal more, or so I suspect," she continued. "Am I to gather that there had been some sort of plot to discredit Prince Philip?"

"Yes, ma'am," said Gwen. "Amongst other things."

"And that she hired the two of you to investigate it?"

"Yes, ma'am."

"And that you were successful in thwarting it?"

"We were, ma'am."

"So there will be no stain on his reputation as a result?"

"No, ma'am," said Gwen. "His reputation is safe."

"And well-deserved," added Iris.

"Thank goodness," she said in relief, suddenly looking like the twenty-year-old she was. "I don't know what I would have—I think he's going to propose, you see. I adore him, and he's going to propose, and there are difficulties enough. I can't let anything else get in the way."

"This will not hinder you, we promise," said Iris.

"Thank you," she said. "Thank you both."

"It must have been a shock when Lady Matheson told you," said Iris.

"Oh, one doesn't grow up in a palace without acquiring a taste for intrigue," she said. "I should have known she was screening my mail. I've put my foot down with Mother, so one of my ladies has taken over the task. It turns out that I've had several proposals already. None that I would ever accept, of course, but it's good to know one is considered to be marriageable. I suppose you two are the experts on that. Any advice?"

"Marry for love," said Gwen. "It sounds simple enough, but it isn't."

"No, it isn't," she agreed. "What do you think of Prince Philip?"

"Handsome, courageous, and intelligent," said Iris. "You're very lucky."

"Assuming he pops the question," she said.

"He would be a fool not to," said Gwen.

"You're very kind. He's coming with us to Balmoral. I'm hoping it will happen there. If he doesn't, maybe I'll come here for a recommendation."

"Let me give you one of our flyers," said Iris.

"Iris," warned Gwen.

"A joke. Although I do have a possibility in mind—"

"Iris! Stop!" protested Gwen.

"Still joking," said Iris. "We wish you the best of luck and all the happiness in the world, ma'am."

"Thank you," she said, digging into her handbag. "I wanted to express my gratitude for what you did in a more substantial way. Lady M mentioned that you were still struggling as a new business. I thought I could help." She pulled out an envelope.

"Ma'am, we couldn't possibly—" began Gwen. Then she caught Iris's look. "I mean to say, thank you, ma'am. It is quite generous of you."

"It's not as if I'm granting you a royal charter," she said as Iris came around to accept the proffered envelope. "Consider it an investment in a promising venture."

"Thank you, ma'am," said Iris.

"And I must go," she said, rising to shake hands with each of them. "Best of luck. I don't know if I want to hear the entire story, but what little I gleaned from Lady M was quite exciting. Someone was murdered, I take it."

"Yes, unfortunately," said Iris. "But the men responsible were apprehended."

"Thanks to you," she said. "It was lovely to meet the pair of you."

"Thank you, ma'am," said Gwen.

She walked out, then turned in the doorway.

"It's a pleasure to see women running things," she observed. "It gives one hope."

Then she left.

The two stared at the doorway for a good long while until the opening and closing of the front door echoed faintly up the stairwell.

"Did that actually happen?" asked Gwen dazedly.

"We have tangible evidence that it did," said Iris, holding the envelope. "Let's take a peek."

She opened it and looked inside. Then a smile spread across her face.

"Let me see!" urged Gwen.

Iris handed it to her, and she looked.

"Hello, Cecil!" she exclaimed, her eyes growing wide.

They collapsed into their respective chairs and stared at each other.

"We should call Mr. Maxwell straightaway and tell him we're taking the office," said Gwen, picking up the phone. "Tell me, who were you thinking of fixing her up with?"

"Mr. MacLaren," said Iris.

"Oh," said Gwen thoughtfully as she dialed. "Yes. He would have been good."